Hannah Hooton grew up in Zimbabwe
lifelong involvement with horses and the
added authenticity to her books. Her
published in 2012 as an ebook.

**Praise for Hannah Hooton**

'Whether you know anything or nothing about horse racing... there is
something for everyone here' *Amazon reviewer*

'A must-buy for those who love racing, horses and, of course,
romance!' *Amazon reviewer*

'A great first novel by a new young author. Easy reading – romance,
intrigue and the insight into the racing world makes a nice change'
*Amazon reviewer*

'Georgette Heyer updated to the 21st century' *Amazon reviewer*

'An incredible talent for making completely loveable and relatable
characters' *Amazon reviewer*

'It's not often that I find an author who can write about racing
without me wanting to pull my hair out, but Hannah Hooton gets it
right' *Amazon reviewer*

Also by Hannah Hooton

*At Long Odds*

# Keeping the Peace

HANNAH HOOTON

ISBN: 978-1-62050-424-6

Cover image by
Pro Book Covers

Published by Aspen Valley Books, 2012

# Acknowledgements

There are a fair few people who helped bring this book to fruition, directly and indirectly. First and foremost, my eternal thanks to the members of fictionpress.com. Without their encouragement and feedback *Keeping the Peace* would still be sat gathering dust in the bottom drawer, barely a third completed. This book is most definitely for them.

To the people who inspired this book, those whom I greatly admire for the often unrecognised hard work which they put into the racing industry: the racing secretaries. Jo Cody-Boutcher and Sarah West were instrumental in contributing material for my research.

Thanks are also due to Weatherbys for taking the time to explain to me the finer details of entering horses in races and race requirements, and to the various racecourses across Britain, most importantly Aintree, who supply technical and geographical information on their websites.

I owe a debt of gratitude to the readers of the Romantic Novelists' Association New Writers' Scheme who gave me some much needed self-belief with their critiques of *Keeping the Peace* and their constructive feedback has helped it to become a better book.

To Thure Etzold, who has again come to my rescue and taken on the hair-tearing task of turning my manuscript into an electronically readable format and saved me many hours of frustration.

Last but by no means least, my thanks to friends and family, who have sat through my moaning and supported me in the bad times as well as the good.

Although I've done my best to make *Keeping the Peace* as technically accurate as possible, there are doubtlessly going to be some errors which are in no way a reflection of the expert opinions mentioned above and are solely of my own doing.

# Chapter One

Map-reading was bad enough when it appeared all of the road signs for the narrow country lanes had been pinched for scrap metal. But add to the mix an unfamiliar car and less than a hundred miles driving experience on your licence and one would begin to understand how Pippa was feeling.

The small hire-car juddered as if in disgust at being made to travel at twenty through the potholed West Country. Pippa grinded the gears, frantic to change down and keep from stalling. Living in London, she hadn't needed to drive anywhere and had only ever used her driver's licence for ID when getting into clubs. Of course, when she did need to use a car, there was always Ollie.

She allowed herself a smug smile. She had been dating in-between-roles actor Ollie Buckingham for three years now. He had a gorgeous red sports car over which he was terribly protective. Also charming and creative, Pippa liked to think that had he not had an audition first thing tomorrow, he would have offered to be her chauffeur for the day. On the other hand, she wanted to sort this business out herself. Dave Taylor's posthumous involvement somehow made it more personal. Anyway, Ollie had never been too keen on Pippa's rather capricious uncle. Or the countryside for that matter.

'It wouldn't be so bad if any of the roads had signs on them,' she grumbled. She batted down the centre fold of the map onto the steering wheel. Squinting ahead into the darkening afternoon, she saw the outline of some life form approaching and it wasn't a cow or a sheep. Pippa sighed with relief. A human at last!

She stopped the car and wound down her window.

'Excuse me,' she called to the jogger.

The young man, his face shiny and his sandy blond hair damp with sweat, slowed to a halt beside her. He rested his hands on his thighs to catch his breath.

'Y'right there?' he said with a deep Irish brogue.

Pippa's eyes widened. She knew she was lost, but Ireland... was it possible? She shook her head, ridiculing herself. There was no way she could drive to Ireland on one tank of fuel.

'Not really.' She gave him an apologetic smile. 'I'm trying to find Aspen Valley Racing Stables. I think I must have taken a wrong turning somewhere.'

'Aye, but you're not far off course. Go back the way you came, take the first road on your right. That'll take you for a mile or so to the old oak. Aspen Valley is the next turning on your left after that.'

Relieved that she was still in England, Pippa closed her eyes, reopening them to find the man grinning at her. Could he tell what she was thinking?

'Thank you,' she said. 'God knows where I would have ended up if you hadn't stopped.'

'Helensvale more than likely or at worst, Bristol. But you're all right. You'll be there in ten minutes.'

'Thanks for your help.'

'Not a bother. Good luck.'


Pippa watched his disappearing figure in her rear-view mirror before moving again. This could be tricky. She hadn't done a three-point-turn since her test eight years ago and certainly never on this sort of road.

'Maybe three is a bit ambitious,' she muttered a few moments later as her fourth manoeuvre wedged her across the entire road.

A loud hoot from her left made her jump. Frantically, she rammed the car into First. The car shot forward into the hedge.

'Bugger, bugger, bugger. Shit, shit, shit.' She hauled the wheel anti-clockwise and the car groaned. It lurched backwards as she dragged it into Reverse. The silver Land Rover waiting flashed its headlights at her.

'I know you're there, you prat,' Pippa exclaimed. 'What do you expect me to do?'

It tooted its horn again.

Her blood already pumped with panic, Pippa experienced the cocooned safety of road rage for the first time.

'Oh, for fuck's sake!' she yelled, slamming her palm on her horn in response. 'Just have a little patience!'

She saw the driver's arm appear out of the window in a heavenward gesture. Pippa gritted her teeth.

'You are just going to have to wait.'

Two minutes later, she sank back into her seat. The Land Rover blasted past, rocking her car from side to side, and roared off round the next blind bend.

'Arsehole,' she muttered, drying her palms on her skirt.

At a more sedate pace, she followed in its wake. Before long, she found the road the jogger had referred to, almost hidden by the bordering hedges. With a triumphant smile, she identified the oak tree and a red and white sign heralding Aspen Valley Racing Stables. The bumpy driveway snaked up a rise, flanked by post and rail-fenced paddocks. Long distorted shadows seeped across the emerald-lush grass from several horses grazing with the setting sun warming their supple bodies. Up ahead she could see two barns. Beside them was a large block of brick stables and offices shaped into an EI block with the stables making up the E and the I consisting of offices and store rooms. Her blood chilled momentarily when she noticed a silver Land Rover parked at a haphazard angle in the gravelled car park up ahead.

'This should be interesting,' she said as she pulled up beside it. With a quick check of her reflection in the mirror, she tucked a tendril of her short dark auburn curls behind her ear and stepped out into the cool dusk. It really was a lovely end to a gorgeous day, and in spite of the trauma of driving the three-hour journey from London, she had rather enjoyed herself. Moreover, it was bound to get more interesting now, Pippa thought, tripping in her heels over the uneven surface towards the buildings.

Despite the Land Rover parked out front, the place appeared deserted. Only snorts and whickers from the stables' residents broke the silence. She was tempted to tiptoe amidst the calm. She stopped at the first stable and peeked inside. Suddenly, half a ton of horseflesh came hurtling towards the door, teeth bared, ears pinned back. Pippa gave a startled yelp and jumped out of harm's way. She yelped again as she collided with a neat cutlery set of pitchforks and spades leaning against the wall. They crashed to the ground around her in a crescendo of sound, the tinny intrusive noise echoing around the block. With her hands clutching her head, Pippa cringed and looked around to see if anyone would come to investigate. Several inquisitive equine heads appeared over their respective half-doors before a heel scraping against concrete behind her caught her attention.

'What are you doing?' the owner of the heel called out across the yard.

Pippa pushed her sunglasses onto the top of her head, revealing her blue eyes. She pasted a smile on her face and walked towards the man, appraising him as she approached. Her smile became more genuine as she got closer. He looked in his mid to late thirties but, Pippa thought, you can never really tell with these outdoorsy types. Tall with broad shoulders covered by a flying jacket, he had dark hair and stern brows. He made no attempt to return Pippa's smile; his tapered mouth instead set in a grim line above a jutting chin. He stood with his hands on his blue-jeaned hips.

'I'm looking for Jack Carmichael.'

'Well, you've found him,' he replied with a curt nod.

Really, Pippa thought indignantly. He could be a bit more polite, considering she might well be a customer. Which she was. For now, anyhow. She wondered if he recognised her from their previous meeting on the road.

'I'm Pippa Taylor. My uncle was Dave Taylor... he owned a couple of horses here,' she added when he didn't say anything.

'I know who Dave Taylor is,' he said. Sighing, he softened his tone, 'I'm sorry to hear about his death.'

'Thanks, it was a bit of a shock. But you know Uncle Dave – he always loved the element of surprise.' She attempted a cheery laugh without success.

Jack Carmichael shifted uncomfortably. He gestured to the office behind him.

'Would you like to come in and have a drink?'

The idea of a vodka and Coke suddenly became very appealing.

'Ooh, that would be nice.'


She followed his broad jacketed back into what was obviously a reception judging by the big professional office unit directly opposite the door. Standing in an expanse of slate-coloured carpet, Pippa was drawn to the two meagre framed photographs on the glaring white walls. The bright-patterned silks of the jockeys frozen in time injected the only real colour into the room. According to the captions, neither Virtuoso nor Black Russian belonged to her uncle. Jack strode over to an adjoining room on the left.

'Tea or coffee?'

'Oh – um – coffee please.' Damn, that vodka and Coke was looking even more attractive now that it wasn't on offer. She followed him as far as the doorway to a kitchenette and watched him briskly prepare their drinks. A kettle, imitating a jet engine, made it impossible for conversation. Pippa fiddled with her necklace as she stood against the doorframe. She wasn't used to someone else making the coffee, being a waitress by day, and by night Ollie always insisted she made better coffee than he did. Which was true, even if she did say so herself.

'Milk? Sugar?'

'Milk and two sugars please.' She watched him heap two Matterhorns of sugar into a Jockey Club coffee mug and half a pint of milk. He left the second mug a thick black, stirring it twice before tossing the teaspoon into the sink with a clatter. Pippa wondered how much sleep this man managed every night with that much caffeine raging through his system.

'Come through,' he instructed. He led the way back across the reception to the other side where another door led into a second office. He put her coffee down on the heavy wood desk before settling himself in the high-backed leather office chair round the other side. Pippa perched on the visitor's chair, her gaze drawn to a display cabinet along one wall featuring various trophies and salvers and bronze works.

'You're lucky you caught me. I'm only here because I left my wallet.'

Her attention recaptured, she smiled apologetically.

'Sorry, I should have rung ahead to make an appointment.'

He sat, impassive, not contradicting her. Pippa cleared her throat self-consciously.

'I wanted to speak to you about Uncle Dave's horses.'

'I suspected as much,' he replied, blowing on his drink.

Pippa primly chose to ignore him.

'Uncle Dave's left just about everything to me –'

'Well done,' he muttered into his coffee before taking a sip.

Pippa bristled.

'I haven't done anything *well*. It's not like I've been working on my inheritance for the past twenty years. I – oh, never mind. Anyway, he left me two racehorses. What would I want with a racehorse?'

'Nothing by the sounds of it.'

'I have no interest in horses,' Pippa continued. 'From what I've heard, they're just a drain on the bank balance.'

'Just about sums it up, yes. What are you trying to say? That you want to sell them?'

'Yes. Would you be interested in buying them?'

Jack's deep attractive laugh would have been much more appealing had it not been at her expense.

'Not even if I could afford them,' he chuckled. He put his mug back on the desk to avoid spilling it and smiled at Pippa, the crows' feet at his eyes deepening.

'Why not?'

'Because –' Pippa saw him quickly glance at her bare-fingered left hand holding her drink, '– Ms Taylor, I train racehorses. I don't own them. You might be able to get a late entry in the HIT sales next month.'

Pippa frowned. What the hell was a HIT sale - where hitmen were paid to shoot horses?

'*HIT* sales?'

'Horses In Training. I'll get my secretary to enter them.'

Okay, Pippa reasoned with herself. That made more sense.

'And what do I have to do?'

'Make sure the last bill is paid, and that's it.'

'Don't I need to meet the new owners, to make sure they won't mistreat them or something?'

Jack frowned in bemusement.

'Have you had *anything* to do with racing before now?'

'The most I've had to do with horses was through Uncle Dave and a pony ride on a seaside holiday in Brighton.'

'How old are you?'

'Twenty-six. Why? That seaside holiday was some years ago,' she said, her back stiffening in defence.

'No particular reason. Your uncle must have been well into his seventies when he died.'

'My parents are older than average if that's what you're getting at. I'm an only child.'

'One enough for them?'

'No, they knew perfection when they saw it. Why ask for more?' Pippa smiled into her coffee mug, feeling stangely triumphant when he gave a reluctant chuckle.

'And may I ask what you do for a living?'

'You may. I work at Vivace Restaurant in London.'

'Restaurant manager?'

'No. Waitress actually.' Her curt response made her blush in attrition. How she would like to be able to say yes, she was the manager at Vivace's. She'd been waiting four long years to say it. And it seemed just as likely to happen now as when she'd first joined the restaurant. She pushed it to the back of her mind. 'How much do you think you could sell them for?'

Jack shrugged.

'I wouldn't put a very high reserve on them.' He hesitated and looked at Pippa with narrowed blue eyes. 'You know what a reserve is, don't you?'

'Of course. I shop on eBay all the time.'

Jack snorted.

'I'll take you to meet them in a minute if you want.'

'Yes, please. It does feel rather grand owning two racehorses. What are their names?'

'Astolat and Peace Offering. They're not as grand as you might think. I don't know what kind of inheritance Dave has left you, but he certainly wasn't making a profit out of those two.'

'But he enjoyed having them though, didn't he?'

Jack paused to consider this for a moment.

'Yes, I suppose he did.' He looked at his watch. 'Have you finished your coffee? I'll take you to see them quickly.'

Pippa was only halfway through her drink. Nevertheless, she nodded.

'I'm sorry if I'm delaying you for anything.'

Jack grunted. She wasn't sure if it was an acknowledgement that she was or an assurance that she wasn't, although she suspected the former.

Hurrying in his wake, she struggled in her heels to keep up with his long strides. He paused as they passed the archway leading to the car park. His eyes narrowed at the hire-car sitting beside the Land Rover.

Pippa held her breath, feeling his eyes travel from the vehicles to her.

'How many horses do you train?' she blurted.

He regarded her for a moment longer, re-evaluating her now that recognition had set in. Waiting for him to comment on her driving skills, Pippa raised a challenging eyebrow. Jack dropped his gaze and carried on walking down the long line of stables.

'About sixty at the moment,' he said.

She breathed a quiet sigh of relief and trotted after him to catch up.

'At the moment?'

'Some still haven't come back from their summer holiday. When the National Hunt season starts proper, we should have about a hundred.'

'Wow,' Pippa said in awe. 'When is that?'

'A couple of weeks' time.'

'Poor Uncle Dave. He picked a bad time to pop his clogs when he was always so excited about racing.'

'Is there ever a good time?'

'I guess not.' Gazing around her, she almost walked straight into Jack as he stopped beside a walkway to some fields behind the stable block. He scowled at her pink slingbacks.

'You're going to need more suitable footwear than that.' He disappeared through a dimly-lit doorway to their right. A moment later he reappeared holding a dirty pair of Wellington boots aloft.

'Try these.'

Pippa looked in horror from the boots to Jack and might have argued had his eyes not clouded indigo with brimming temper. She went to take off her shoes, hopping around on one foot until an uneven paving slab sent her reeling. She grabbed the closest thing there was for support... which was Jack's shoulder. He stiffened at her touch and she mumbled a hurried apology. She took the Wellies and pulled them on, trying to ignore how ridiculous she must look in her short skirt and oversized boots. Looking up, she saw a faint glimmer of amusement in his eyes. She flashed him a warning look that forbade him from saying anything.

He turned away to lead them out to the fields, but wasn't quick enough to hide a suppressed smile.

'How far away are they?'

'Next paddock.'

'Do they always live outside? Even at night time?'

'In summer, yes. Your two should start coming in round about now, although since your circumstances have changed, you might prefer them to just stay out.'

'Why would I want that?'

'It's cheaper. And you're not intending to race them.'

'But the person who buys them will probably want to race them.'

'Your choice,' Jack shrugged.

He stopped alongside the fence to the second paddock. Pippa could see a small group of five grazing horses at the far end. He gave a loud piercing whistle, making her wince and want to cover her ears. The horses all threw their heads up and as one, came cantering over, play-biting and bucking.

'Don't you worry they'll hurt each other?' Pippa asked.

'They're only playing. The bully on the far left is Astolat,' Jack said, pointing at a big dark bay horse who was snapping his teeth at his companion. 'And that at the back is Peace Offering.'

Pippa detected the slight resignation in his voice as he identified the smaller, slighter-looking bay happily bringing up the rear. An odd sense of excitement stole over her as the stampede halted before the fence and she was introduced to her new horses. *Her* horses. It did feel terribly grand, especially as they were racehorses.

*And this year's Derby winner is Peace Offering, owned by Pippa Taylor.*

It had a certain ring to it, although she was a bit hazy about race names. Her uncle had been a fan of jump racing or National Hunt racing, and as far as she could recall, the Derby didn't have any jumps in it.

*And this year's Grand National winner is Peace Offering, owned by Pippa Taylor.*

That sounded better.

Jack frowned at her smug smile and reached forward to stroke Peace Offering's nose. Pippa hung back, pushing her hair behind her ear with a nervous hand. Jack's furrowed brow softened.

'Come pat Peace Offering. He won't bite.'

Pippa remembered those snapping yellow teeth as they'd galloped towards them and hesitated further.

'I can see them okay from here, thanks,' she said with a small anxious smile.

'He's an old softie. Come on.' Taking her hand, he guided her forward and placed her palm beneath his onto the horse's long bony nose. 'See?'

For a moment, Pippa was only aware of the heat radiating from his hand as it engulfed hers. Then her attention became engrossed by the horse. She looked in wonder at the big kind eyes fringed with sweeping lashes and the white blaze that spilled down from his forehead to his nostrils. It made him so pretty. As if he had been a plain-coloured horse who'd had his make-up done.

'He's beautiful,' she murmured.

'Maybe I shouldn't have shown them to you,' he said, releasing her hand. 'You don't want to get attached when you're about to sell them.'

Pippa let her fingers trace the delicate contours of the horse's nose, between his velveteen nostrils, smiling as his whiskers tickled her palm. She let her hand drop and nodded.

'I know,' she sighed. 'He's so pretty though, I'm sure he'll sell well.'

'I wouldn't be too sure about that.'

'Why? Isn't he very fast?'

'Quite simply, no. Astoalt is half-decent at least.'

'That's a pity. Never mind, I know someone will see that he's a sweetheart.'

Jack gave a snort of derision.

'I've got to get a move on. Are you travelling back up to London tonight?'

'No, I've got to go see a house – or a cottage, I'm not sure which yet, that used to be Uncle Dave's.'

'More inheritance?'

'Something like that. Although they told me not to expect too much. Apparently, it's a bit of a shambles. I'm sure it can't be as bad as all that though.'

'Good luck,' Jack said with more doubt than sincerity.

'Thank you,' Pippa replied sweetly. 'Nice to meet you Peace Offering. Nice to meet you Astolat.'

Jack rolled his eyes and began to walk away. Pippa skipped after him back onto the main path.

'Thank you for showing them to me.'

'My pleasure,' he said, sounding like it was anything but. 'I'll have Gemma send you the details of the sale next month.'

'Who's Gemma?'

'My secretary.'

Poor girl, Pippa thought, having to put up with his moodiness. She shot a rueful glance at the horses still milling by the fence behind them and sighed. 'It's such a pity.'

'What is?' Jack looked at her suspiciously.

'Having to sell them.'

His blue eyes narrowed.

'You having second thoughts?'

Pippa shrugged.

'Can't afford to have second thoughts. But wouldn't it have been fun?'

'You're better off without them.'

Half a stride behind, Pippa frowned at the negative attitude radiating from the unyielding set to his shoulders.

'Don't you train horses for a living?'

Jack looked at her sharply.

'Yes. Why?'

'Well, you don't sound like their biggest fan.'

'I'm just being realistic. You could never afford two racehorses on a waitress' salary.'

Despite having said much the same thing less than a minute before, Pippa raised her chin involuntarily in a stubborn stance.

Is that right sunshine, she challenged silently.

# Chapter Two

Within twenty minutes of following Jack's Land Rover out of Aspen Valley Stables and, surprisingly, not one single wrong turning later, Pippa found Hazyvale House. Gloriously secluded at the end of an avenue where the last rays of the sun filtered through the autumnal trees, what Pippa now realised was little more than a cottage stood not quite foursquare, like a sway-backed donkey resting a hindhoof while it dozed.

'Oh, Uncle Dave,' she breathed, stepping out of the car. 'This is heavenly.' Her eyes travelled over the old Cotswold stone and sagging moss-covered roof, conveniently overlooking the missing slate tiles and rotting window panes. She picked her way across the overgrown forecourt and along a short path to the front door over a soggy carpet of fallen leaves scattered from an overhanging oak tree. She butted the warped front door with her shoulder as it stuck, shovelling back a mountain of junk mail.

Once inside, she moved from musty room to room, girlish excitement rising inside her like a bubble. Downstairs, she discovered a lounge, dining room, a beautifully large but crumbling kitchen and downstairs loo, all in various stages of disrepair. Upstairs, there were two open-beamed and vaulted bedrooms and a shared bathroom. Each room overlooked the back of the house, which in the gathering darkness wasn't clearly visible, but what was certain was the garden that had once been there was a small jungle now, falling away into a scattering of trees down into a shallow valley. She could hear the last chorus of birdsong drifting on the mild autumn breeze.

Sighing with contentment, Pippa turned away from the view and focused on the night that lay ahead. She wasn't scared to be here alone, but she did feel just a tiny bit vulnerable knowing how isolated the cottage was from the rest of humanity. She flicked a light switch. Unsurprisingly it didn't work.

'I hope you've got candles hidden away somewhere, old man,' she said, heading back downstairs to the kitchen.

Pippa woke early, cold and with a stuffy headache. Despite her unfamiliar surroundings she had slept like the dead, the peace and quiet acting as a drug to her consciousness. The bedding, which last night she had unearthed from the linen cupboard by candlelight, smelt of damp and dust. Pippa wrinkled her nose and rubbed her head, acknowledging the benefits of a properly ventilated airing cupboard sadly lacking in her new house. Groggily, she pulled herself out of bed and stumbled across the room.

She gave a surprised gasp as she drew level with the window. She crept forward, as if too much noise would spoil it. She leant her hands on the low windowsill and gazed out at the view. She had never seen anything like it.

Someone had photoshopped Somerset. She could see right down the valley and for endless untouched and unscarred miles of countryside a smooth silken sheet of mist, rose pink from the young morning sun, draped across the land.

Pippa couldn't move. It was so very different from her second floor flat in London, which overlooked a convenience store and off-licence. Even the wilderness down below, which any canny estate agent would dub 'a gardener's dream', did nothing to hinder the heavenly dawn.

Pippa stayed where she was, only leaving the window once to retrieve a blanket from her bed before resuming her post. The mist turned from pink to gold to ivory before dissipating with the strength of the sun.

She turned away from the window and concentrated hard on remembering every detail so she could put it onto canvas later. Her fingers itched for her brushes and watercolours.

She busied herself preparing for her journey back to London, cursing that there wasn't any running water. But although she would have died for a bath, she could have killed for a cup of coffee.

With a last look around Hazyvale House, she locked the front door regretfully and returned to her car.

The nearest town she found was ten minutes away, which might not seem very much, but to Pippa, who had been brought up within thirty seconds of fellow humanity, it seemed a different country. Helensvale was quaint and tidy with a narrow High Street. Pippa easily found a parking space outside a small café. The jangle announcing her arrival as she opened the door brought a lady in from the back of the shop. She was small like Pippa, but plumper and more buxom, rather like a favourite aunt – if she'd had one.

'All right, love? What can I get you?'

The curiosity in her voice, Pippa knew wasn't just of her order, but of her presence in town. She returned the lady's smile.

'A cappuccino to go please.'

'Right y'are. RANDY!' she shouted over her shoulder.

Pippa jumped in terror, only fractionally calmed when a gawky ginger-haired teenage boy stuck his spotty face through the serving hatch.

'We got more of them Styrofoam cups back there?'

The boy frowned for a moment's thought then shook his head.

'Nah.'

The lady turned back to Pippa.

'You in a rush anywhere?'

'Well,' Pippa began awkwardly, 'I do need to get back to London...'

'Ah, London,' she said, nodding, as if that explained a lot. 'Sorry, love. The coffee's going nowhere but the tables today. Why not have a seat and I'll bring one over to you.'

Pippa thought about the long drive back to the city where she was bound to get stuck in gridlock traffic. Sticking around just made the journey seem longer. On the other hand, the smell of coffee and breakfast wafting around the warm and cosy café was hard to resist. Her stomach gave a thunderous rumble, reminding her she hadn't eaten since yesterday lunchtime.

'Okay. Could I have a blueberry muffin as well if you've got any?'

The lady chuckled and shook her head.

'You London folk. Blueberry muffin coming up.'

Pippa sat down at a table next to the window and looked out at the passers-by. She noticed most of the men wore tweed and flat caps. Wow, she thought, this really *is* the country. Across the street was a post office-cum-grocery shop where an elderly man was setting the newspaper sandwich-boards out on the pavement. He paused to greet a couple walking past with two black Labradors.

*CHILD'S BIKE STOLEN FROM DRIVEWAY* screamed the headline. Pippa couldn't help smiling. It made such a change from the latest stabbings and gun shootings.

'Here y'are, m'love.' The lady placed an obese muffin and cup of coffee on the plastic table before her.

'Thanks.' Pippa took a big unladylike slurp of the hot drink and sighed with satisfaction as she felt the warmth filter through her body. 'Oh, that's lovely.'

The woman, who hadn't moved away, chuckled.

'Mind if I ask what you're doing round these parts?' she asked.

'My uncle owns – or rather *did* own – I own it now – a cottage not far from here.'

'Oh, yes?'

The fact that Pippa had opened up a little appeared to be an invitation for the woman to sit down opposite her. Pippa didn't mind. In fact, she was quite enjoying this friendly, enquiring company. It was so far removed from the anonymity and severe self-privacy of London.

'Yes. Hazyvale House. Do you know it?'

'Ah, yes. Old Dave Taylor. Wily old man. Full of stories, he was. Sorry to hear of his passing.'

'He was full of stories, wasn't he?' She smiled at her childhood memories when Uncle Dave would come to visit and regale exciting and, she now realised, completely farfetched stories. 'He left me his house and his horses.'

'That right?' she said with raised eyebrows. 'And what do you intend to do with them?'

For a moment Pippa thought she was overstepping the line between being curious and being nosy. But then in such a small town, she probably had every right to know if she was going to sell the cottage or move in.

'Well, the plan is to sell everything eventually. The cottage is gorgeous, but needs so much done to it. So once that's all sorted then I'll probably put it on the market.'

Her plans while she had lain in bed last night had built a picture of selling the horses and using the money to hire some local tradesmen to fix the cottage up, after which she could sell it. It would probably do for some London couple who wanted a weekend pad in the country to escape the hustle and bustle of the city.

She noticed the lady wasn't too impressed by the news, but she was saved from any comment by the jangle of the door opening. A thin stooped man who looked about a hundred creaked in. A dog, looking equally ancient, pottered at his heels.

'All right, Norm, my love?' The lady jumped up and bustled around to the other side of the counter. The man grunted and made his way to a table next to Pippa's. 'RANDY! Norm's here for his breakfast!'

This time Pippa was a bit more prepared for this bellow at the poor teenager. She also liked the way the old man hadn't needed to tell her what he wanted. She'd do that too at Vivace's if she could ever remember what their regulars ordered.

He looked short-sightedly across at Pippa through milky cataracts, but turned away to the hostess as she came over with a cup of tea.

'New clientele you have here, Wendy?'

'Just passing through, she is. From London,' she added with extra emphasis.

'Ah, London. Needed a change of scenery, did you, love?'

'That too,' Pippa said hesitantly. She didn't want to go upsetting any more townsfolk with her news of selling up. 'I inherited a cottage near here. It's a beautiful part of the country.'

The old man smiled. His grey eyes softened and all of a sudden he didn't seem so grumpy.

'What's your name then?'

'Pippa Taylor.'

'Old Dave Taylor's niece,' Wendy inputted.

'Don't you go calling Dave Taylor old, Wendy Tarver. If he's old, what does that make me?'

*Prehistoric* sprang to Pippa's mind and she bit back a smile.

'You've been around too long to be in denial about your age,' Wendy said, batting a dishcloth in his direction. She moved over to the hatch to retrieve his cholesterol-pumped fry-up which Randy had just cooked. 'Now, put that down you and don't be bothering my customers, you hear?'

Pippa thought this was a bit rich, but didn't comment.

Norm took no notice of her warning and after giving his dog a hash brown, he turned once more to Pippa.

'Are you sorting out all Dave's affairs now he's kicked the bucket? Not something I'd envy.'

'I'm going to do up his cottage and sell it – hopefully. I was thinking of getting someone local to help,' Pippa replied, finishing off her muffin.

'Well, now. That might make it easier to swallow if you bring some work into this place. You'll be selling to some city folk no doubt?'

Pippa hesitated, feeling unnecessarily guilty.

'That is the plan, unless of course someone local wants to buy it.'

'No one will probably be able to afford it, but don't let that worry you. If it's city folk you must sell it to, then so be it.'

She gave him a grateful smile, faltering slightly when she became aware of Wendy regarding her from behind the counter.

'Well, I'll certainly advertise it locally to begin with,' she said, trying to appease her.

Norm grunted and scooped another forkful of beans and sausage into his mouth.

# Chapter Three

'Ow, fuck. That's hot,' Pippa muttered, trying to pick up a plate of Vivace Restaurant's homemade lasagne. Finally laden with three plates, she weaved through the tables to deliver the order. The lasagne-requestor looked suspiciously at his food.

'What is this?'

'Lasagne,' Pippa said slowly.

'Is that meat?'

Pippa peered at the plate then looked back at the man. Was this a trick question?

'It looks like it.'

'I ordered vegetarian lasagne. Not this.'

'No, you ordered regular lasagne,' Pippa frowned. She could have sworn he hadn't mentioned anything about being a vegetarian.

'I think I know what I ordered!'

'Okay. I'm sorry for the mix-up. I'll go order you a vegetarian dish.'

'So I can sit here watching my colleagues eating their food? I don't think so!'

'There's a complimentary bread basket,' Pippa suggested.

'Bloody ridiculous!'

'Excuse me, is there a problem?'

Pippa closed her eyes and counted to five as Jayne, the restaurant manageress appeared at her shoulder. As usual, her boss was dressed in a power pinstripes more suited to a lawyer's office or tycoon PA.

'Yes, my friends and I ordered a meal and *she* couldn't even get three orders right! I wanted vegetarian lasagne!'

'I do apologise. I can assure you this sort of mistake does not happen often. I'm sure Chef has some freshly-made vegetarian lasagne.'

'Oh, forget it. I'll just have a salad.'

Pippa slunk away, avoiding eye contact with Jayne. The manageress wasn't to be deterred that easily though.

'Pippa, where is your head tonight?' she demanded once they were out of earshot of the customers.

'I'm sure he didn't say veg lasagne. Honest.'

'Well, it's too late to try pinning the blame back on the customer. Remember *the customer is always right.*'

Pippa had difficulty not rolling her eyes.

'What were they drinking?' Jayne said.

'House white.'

'Fine. Go get them a complimentary bottle and *apologise*.'

Pippa dragged her aching feet up the last remaining stairs to the flat and let herself in quietly. She wasn't sure if Ollie was back yet from his bi-weekly Boys' Night Out at the pub although it was long past midnight.

Switching on the lights, she found her answer. The coffee table in the open-plan living room was strewn with empty beer bottles and crisp packets; crumbs ground into the rug. Either Ollie had stayed home and drunk himself into a stupor or he'd had his mates round.

Pippa resigned herself to clearing up the mess. Collecting up the bottles, she sympathised with her boyfriend. He had been under so much pressure lately. His agent hardly ever called nowadays and when she did, it so often ended up in disappointment. Just like that last audition almost a month ago when she'd gone down to Somerset. Ollie apparently hadn't fitted the role of Brave Cop #4.

She left the crumbs for the next morning's hoovering, but hesitated when she turned towards the closed bedroom door. She was tired, but she couldn't bear to be faced with alcohol-enforced snores that she could hear rattling through the door.

Instead, she opened the lounge window and lit a cigarette, watching the plume of smoke mingle with the night's damp air. She thought back to the beautiful dawn she had witnessed at Hazyvale House. With a sigh she looked out at the off-licence across the street. A cold drizzle fell, highlighted in the dirty yellow glow of a street lamp.

Glancing at the dresser next to her, she looked disinterestedly at the small corner of a recycled Amazon Rainforest that was Dave Taylor's personal paperwork. She'd brought everything back to London after her primary visit four weeks ago, but hadn't got very far through it all. Reaching out, she flicked through the uppermost paperwork, reading adverts for car boot sales and couple of dog-eared *Racing Post* newspapers. An industrial-sized diary slipped off the pile and landed on Pippa's already aching foot.

'Ow!' she cried, leaping precariously on one slim heel. She shushed herself, glancing across to the bedroom door as she tenderly massaged her toe. She picked up the offending book. As she did so, two sheets of paper slid out and, catching a draft, winged their way into the centre of the lounge. Pippa balanced her cigarette on the windowsill and went to pick them up. The names PEACE OFFERING and ASTOLAT boldly titled each page.

'Hello. What's this?' She picked them up and returned to her smoking post. At first, she couldn't quite understand Dave's writing, but she gathered from the dates and bulleting that it was a stats list.

PEACE OFFERING
1963 – Ayala – 66/1
1966 – Anglo – 50/1
1967 – Foinavon – 100/1
1971 – Specifiy – 28/1
1980 – Ben Nevis – 40/1
1985 – Last Suspect – 50/1
1987 – Maori Venture – 28/1
1989 – Little Polveir – 28/1
1995 – Royal Athlete – 50/1
2001 – Red Marauder – 33/1
2007 – Silver Birch – 33/1
2009 – Mon Mome – 100/1
1995 – Royal Athlete – last win 1993
2004 – Amberleigh House – last win 2002
2007 – Silver Birch – last win 2004
Almost half of winners in past 50 years have been 9-year-olds.
Only 5 favourites in past 50 years have won.

'Won what?' Pippa turned the sheet over to see if there was more, but the other side was blank. Looking at the page with Astolat's name on it, it was much the same except with different names and dates. It didn't give any clues either. 'Hmm. Oh, well.'

With a shrug she added the papers to the rest and set about tidying it. The two horses were going to be sold the next day anyway. What small compensation she could muster from not being able to afford to keep the horses, she could perhaps invest in getting a better job.

# Chapter Four

'Hey Tash,' Pippa greeted her best friend the next morning. Scooping her mobile phone between her ear and her shoulder, she wandered over to her smoking window in the lounge with a cup of coffee and fumbled for her cigarettes on the dresser. 'Here's your wake-up call.'

'Huh! Since when have you ever had to get me up? You all right?'

'Hmm, not bad, thanks. Just wanted to remind you that the sale at Harvey Nicks closes today if you still wanted to buy that pair of Jimmy Choos.'

'Already there. I'll nip in at lunchtime and pick them up. Thanks for reminding me. Even so, this is a bit early for you, isn't it?'

'Yeah, well, Ollie's agent rang at the crack of dawn wanting him to go for an audition. At last! And hopefully I'll be a whole lot richer by the end of today.'

'Really? Why?'

'Those horses that Dave gave to me. They're being sold today. Remember?'

'Ah, yes. Life with the jet-set short-lived then, eh?'

Pippa snorted.

'You could say that. Oh, shit.'

'What?'

'Oh, nothing. I've just knocked everything off the dresser. Hold on.' Pippa rounded up a mound of paperwork and hefted it back onto the dresser. The paper of stats she had been looking at the night before caught her eye on the top of the pile and she frowned at it. 'Tash, do you know anything about horses?'

'Course not, you know that. I grew up half a mile from you in central London. Remember? Why?'

'It's just these papers I've got here. They were amongst Uncle Dave's stuff and it's got a whole lot of statistics and the names of horses on them.'

'What sort of statistics?'

'I don't know. Listen to this...' Methodically, Pippa read through Peace Offering's piece of paper. 'Any idea what this race is?'

'You know what, sweets? I think I do! Only because I decided to have a flutter on the horses a couple of years ago. Mon Mome won the Grand

26

National at some huge price. Only put a pound on him, and bought a lovely coat with the return.'

'The Grand National?'

'Yes. I bet if you Google all those names you'll find they all won the Grand National. Ooh, how exciting! Dave's leaving you messages from the grave!'

'Messages? God, Tash, what are you on? They're being sold today anyway.'

'Dave obviously had plans to enter - who was it, Peace Offering - in the National and was trying to prove that even the outsiders have a chance.'

'That's really sad. Such big dreams for his horses and now they've all come to nothing.'

'It might have been his dying wish.'

'What are you talking about?'

'Don't you see? Dave has given you these horses. It's your - your *duty* to fulfil their destiny!'

'Did you mistake the cocaine for the sugar on your cornflakes this morning?'

'Pippa, you can't sell them!'

'It's too late. They're at the sales now.'

'Ring up that trainer guy -'

'Jack Carmichael.'

'Yeah, ring up Jack Carmichael and tell him to withdraw them.'

Pippa pulled a face.

'But Tash - I don't know. Is it worth the hassle? He's a right grump. He'll give me such a bollocking.'

'Who cares? They're your horses, aren't they?'

'Yes, I know, but -' Pippa thought back to Jack's scathing comments about Peace Offering and then had a sharp painful memory of Dave sitting with her as a child and describing a particular race with such passion and enthusiasm. Had it been the Grand National? Didn't the name Foinavon ring a bell? She couldn't remember. 'Ooh, what if it was his dying wish? Maybe he was the only one who believed in him...'

'Exactly. Peace Offering's future depends on you. The Grand National might be there just waiting for him to go and win it. But he might not be entered if you sell him,' urged Tash.

Pippa wavered, curling her toes in her slippers as Tash's influence swayed her. What would the new owners' plans be for the horse if she left

27

things be? Would they see him as a potential Grand National horse? Probably not, if the formbook was anything to go by.

She took a troubled drag of her cigarette, exhaling the smoke with force as if she was trying to dispel her indecision. This might be the one moment in Peace Offering's life for him to shine and she was about to throw it all away. She was about to ruin Peace Offering's life.

'Oh, Tash! I've got to stop them being sold!'

'Pippa, get off the phone and ring Jack Carmichael!'

'Okay, okay –'

'But ring me back!'


'His phone's turned off!' Pippa wailed two minutes later.

'Did you leave a message?'

'Yes, but will he get it in time, do you think?'

'I don't know. Where is the sale?'

'In Doncaster.'

'Right. Get up there!'

Pippa stubbed out her cigarette, but nearly upended the ashtray.

'It's about two hundred miles away! How am I supposed to get there?'

'By car, silly. Go find your nearest car hire shop and get one. Do you know what time they're being sold?'

'About lunchtime his secretary told me. But that could mean any time between twelve and two. She sent me a sales catalogue and they're Lots 281 and 282.'

'Well, get moving!'

'Oh, God.' She whirled round, unable to decide what to do first. 'Ohgodohgodohgod.'

'Don't panic! Now get yourself dressed and go get a car.'

Pippa pulled up short.

'How did you know I'm not dressed?'

'Pippa, I've known you for the past twenty years. You're wearing your pyjamas.'

'Oh. Okay.'

'GO!'

'All right! I'm going!'


Pippa slammed the front door behind her and clattered down the two flights of stairs in her heels. The car hire company she had used last time was at least twenty to thirty minutes away, if one considered journeying through the streets and Underground of London at peak time. She looked unenthusiastically down the road, the far end of which was blurred by a fine drizzle. Her gaze flickered closer, to Ollie's beloved red Alfa Romeo in its usual parking space ten feet away.

She rustled through her handbag for her mobile and checked the time. It was a quarter to nine. Even if she left now she wouldn't get to Doncaster until at least twelve o'clock. She chewed her lip. Would she be too late if she had to traipse across London to the car hire company? She looked at Ollie's pride and joy again. Ollie had left about seven-thirty, hung over but cheerful that he had an audition planned. Dare she risk phoning him in the middle of it?

'Who am I kidding? Of course he's not going to let me use it,' Pippa muttered before whirling round and hurtling back up the stairs to get the spare set of car keys.

After eventually mastering the gears and the Sat Nav, Pippa found the Alfa quite easy to drive. Its powerful acceleration let her zip clear at the traffic lights and merge two cars further up. She grimaced as angry hoots followed her and she silently apologised to all women drivers for giving them a bad name.

Once on the M1, Pippa put her foot down. The drizzle had now become fully-fledged rain and the car's windscreen wipers batted frantically to clear her view. As the weather worsened, Pippa found herself easing her foot off the accelerator. When she saw the illuminated clock hands on the dashboard reaching for eleven o'clock she hastily pushed on. Twice more, she tried Jack Carmichael's number. Both times she got his voicemail. Gripping the steering wheel and inadvertently shredding her lower lip with her teeth, she refused to let herself wonder what on earth she was doing. Common sense could feature later.

She groaned as the midday news jingle began on the radio. Thoughts of Peace Offering being led into the sales ring flashed through her mind, making her grit her teeth and tighten her hold on the steering wheel. She gave another howl as the petrol light on the dashboard flickered into life, the dial pointing ominously below E. She didn't have time to stop, but should she risk running out of fuel?

Her anxious gaze moved from the fuel gauge to the clock, now beginning its descent past noon. If she stopped she would surely miss the horses being sold, but if she ran out of petrol then there was no chance of getting there in time. A sign for a service station flashing by made up her mind and she swung into the left lane and took the exit. Keeping to the twenty mile-an-hour speed limit through the entrance, Pippa felt like she was moving in slow motion.

'Oh, God, no! What more?' she yelled in anguish.

There was a tailback of at least six cars waiting to refuel. She drummed her fingers on the wheel as she waited in the queue, her eyes forever being drawn to the clock whose hands seemed to be gathering momentum.

Gradually the queue shortened, but she was still three cars back. She would be sitting there for another quarter of an hour, Pippa predicted. It would be nearly one o'clock at least by the time she got to the sales. Taking a deep breath she took the initiative. It would be so much easier to push in front if you didn't have to stop immediately to put fuel in so she decided against that tactic.

'I'm just going to have to risk it.'

Spinning the wheel, she put her foot down and powered past the white van in front. She exhaled as she zoomed past the stationary cars towards the exit, relief at being on the move again. For how much longer was anyone's guess, but while there was heart, there was hope.

Pippa whooped with joy five minutes later when she saw the first signs for Doncaster Racecourse just as the sun came out. Trying hard to control her breathing and mounting excitement, she eased the Alfa Romeo off the M28 exit, praying the car would get her there. The light on the dashboard seemed to glow brighter and brighter. If she ran out of fuel there – well, she would tackle that hurdle when it arose.

'Come on. Don't let me down,' she said, patting the steering wheel.

The Alfa rose to the task. Pulling up in the racecourse car park, she tried Jack Carmichael one last time while reattaching her heels and scrambling out of the car. There was still no answer. Heart pounding, Pippa ran through the lines of parked Range Rovers and Jaguars. An icy hand of fear clutched her gut as she heard the echoing voice of the auctioneer from a nearby loudspeaker.

'Lot 282 from the Aspen Valley consignment. This is an eight-year-old gelding by Off The Record, out of Forgiven...'

'Oh, no! No, no, no!'

Ignoring the curious stares from bystanders, she sprinted towards the sales room.

'Next we have Lot 283, from Dunstanton Fields...'

Her spirits belly-flopped down to her arches and seeped out of her open-toed sandals.

'Oh, God. I'm too late.' She slowed to a walk, her ragged breaths shaking her narrow shoulders. With weary footsteps she skirted the main auction house to the rear. She sighed as she recognised the broad white blaze down the face of a bay horse being led away. An oval sticker on his rump read 282.

'Wait!' Pippa called, her voice laden with disappointment.

The blonde girl leading Peace Offering stopped short and looked up in surprise.

'Can I help you?'

'No - no, I don' think you can anymore.'

'Pardon?' The girl pushed up her red Aspen Valley baseball cap and looked at Pippa with curious hazel eyes.

'Sorry, don't mind me. I'm Pippa Taylor. I own - or did own - Peace Offering and Astolat.'

'Oh. A pity about Peace Offering, isn't it? At least Astolat got some attention.'

'They're sold?' Pippa's shoulders drooped as the reality hit home. There would be no Grand National for Peace Offering. After all her uncle had done for her and given to her, she couldn't even manage this one thing in return. 'Poor Dave. If only I could have got here just a few minutes sooner.'

'Are you okay?'

Pippa looked bleakly from Peace Offering, who was trying to eat his lead rope, to his lass.

'No. Not really.'

'There wasn't much you could have done about Peace Offering, I'm afraid. But like I said, at least Astolat did well. He went for more than we expected.'

'Oh, dear.'

The girl looked anguished.

'I'm sure Mr Carmichael can find a private buyer for Peace Offering.'

'What?' Pippa said, for the first time listening to what the girl was saying.

'I said I'm sure Mr Carmichael can find someone else who wants Peace Offering.'

Pippa's heart began to thump again.

'You mean he isn't sold?' She held her breath.

'Well, no,' the girl replied, puzzled. 'Weren't you watching?'

'No, I've only just arrived. He's still mine? How come?'

'He didn't reach his reserve.'

'Thank God!' Pippa wanted to hug the girl, but managed to restrain herself by squeezing her hands together.

Peace Offering's handler looked at her in bemusement.

'You're glad?'

'Yes! I didn't want to sell him! What about Astolat? Is he still mine?'

'No, he sold. Quite well actually.' As an afterthought she added, 'Sorry.'

'Oh, dear. Never mind, Peace Offering's the one I really wanted to keep.'

'Are you going to keep him in training at Aspen Valley?'

Pippa twisted her sales catalogue in her hands as she considered the question.

'Um, I think so. I haven't really thought that far ahead. Where is Jack Carmichael?'

'Mr Carmichael? He was in the ring, but he was going straight to see some client or other afterwards. You might catch him if you're quick.'

Imagining the trainer's inevitable response to her idea of keeping Peace Offering, Pippa stalled.

'Maybe not just yet.' It wasn't a response she was looking forward to getting.

She gazed up at the lanky horse. He looked so majestic with his Roman nose held high and his long ears pricked forward. The lead rope now hung limp between his lips, forgotten momentarily as he watched the activity around him.

Her heart softened. For a moment, she imagined the warm smile on Dave's face.

The girl grinned at Pippa.

'I'm glad you're keeping him. Peace Offering might not be Kauto Star, but he has just as big a heart.'

'Who?'


Pippa's initial excitement of keeping Peace Offering began to subside as she drove back to London. How on earth would she be able to afford him *and* do up Hazyvale House? If Jack Carmichael trained a hundred horses then he must be pretty good at his job, which usually meant he would be expensive. Her waitressing job and her art commissions, which came by

32

less frequently than Haley's Comet it seemed, would probably not cover training fees. But how much could it possibly be? Ollie's flat, which had been a present from his rather overbearing parents, was always a constant drain even without a mortgage to pay. Moreover, with him not earning anything, Pippa had already told him not to worry about the bills until his agent found something for him and the small rent she paid saved him having to go begging to his folks.

Maybe she had been a bit hasty in deciding to keep Peace Offering. But every time that thought crossed her mind, she reminded herself of his sweet nature and Dave Taylor's dream of running him in the Grand National. Was it so wrong to want to follow a dream?

By the time she had parked Ollie's Alfa Romeo she had convinced herself she had made the right decision. She couldn't wait to tell Ollie.

'You what!'

Pippa jumped in fright.

'I decided not to sell him. Coffee?' she said, trying to avoid the confrontation.

'What? Yes, okay. But Pippa, have you gone mad? First you drive off with my car without asking –'

'I would have rung, but I didn't want to disturb you in the middle of your audition. How did it go, by the way?'

Ollie's face, twisted in anger, softened into a smirk.

'Pretty well, actually. They want me to go back again – hey, stop changing the subject. You steal my car, drive four hundred miles across the country. Thank God you didn't have an accident.'

'I'm fine. Don't worry.'

'You're not insured to drive the Alfa! It would have cost me a fortune if you'd crashed. Pippa, really! What do you want with a racehorse? You don't even like horses.'

'I never said that,' Pippa said over her shoulder as she prepared some coffee cups in the kitchen.

Ollie followed her in.

'You've never shown *any* interest in horses. Why would you want to go throwing money away like that? If you'd sold them both then imagine how much easier things would be here.'

'Peace Offering didn't actually meet his reserve so technically I didn't stop him from not selling.'

'What does that mean? That he's so useless no one even wants him? Now you're going to waste money on paying for his upkeep. We could've gone on holiday. Or done some redecorating around here. God knows we could upgrade this kitchen.' Ollie threw a disdainful gesture to his surroundings.

Pippa tried to stem the defensive barrier which rose inside her by searching for a teaspoon. Why were there never any in the cutlery drawer?

'The original plan was to do up Hazyvale House, remember,' she said.

'More bloody expense. Jesus, for once, I have to agree with your parents. That Dave Taylor is more trouble than he's worth.'

Pippa held up a threatening teaspoon in his direction.

'Hey, only I am allowed to slag off my family. Okay?'

Ollie shook his head.

'I don't believe you did this. And my Alfa – God, if you'd crashed her...'

'Ollie, come on. It'll be fun! We could go to the races to watch *our* horse run. We could get all dressed up and have a really *exciting* day out.' Pippa handed him his coffee and beamed at him, trying to ignite some enthusiasm.

Ollie grimaced as he took his first sip.

'How much bloody sugar did you put in here?'

'Two.' Pippa took a sip of her own coffee only to find it without sugar. 'Oh, you've got mine as well, I think. Sorry.'

'Remind me what you do for a living?' Ollie tossed his coffee into the sink and slammed the mug onto the draining board.

'You were distracting me,' Pippa protested.

'I thought women were renowned for multi-tasking.'

Pippa pouted. Yes, she understood Ollie's mood swings were frequent because of his lack of work, but he was being unnecessarily cruel. Her mobile began to ring and with a sigh of relief at the escape it gave her, she pulled it out of her pocket. She groaned when the caller's name flashed on the screen.

*Aspen Valley*

No doubt, it was Jack Carmichael wanting to give her a bollocking as well. She couldn't face him right now. Besides, she wanted to see him face-to-face to discuss Peace Offering's future. She switched her phone off.

'Who was that?'

'Just someone I don't want to speak to right now.'

Ollie dragged his fingers through his short dark hair.

34

'Jesus, Pippa. I don't understand you. You've done some crazy things in the past, but this just takes the biscuit.' He shook his head and walked out of the kitchen.

Through the gap of the doorway she could see him unhooking his jacket from the coat stand on his way to the front door.

'Where are you going?' she called after him.

'To the pub. I'll be back in time for dinner.'

'I'm working the evening shift tonight.'

'Oh, for fuck's sake. Fine, I'll eat at the pub.'

Pippa took a thoughtful sip of her coffee in the wake of Ollie's departure. She grimaced before throwing her coffee down the plughole as well.

# Chapter Five

Pippa could feel the heat of Jack Carmichael's wrath before she'd even reached the door to Aspen Valley's racing office. His raised voice bounced out of the open doorway.

'What do you mean "a couple of weeks"? I need someone right now! How can you call yourself Rush-Hour Recruitment if you can't supply people at short notice?... Yes, I want someone qualified... No, I've already said there isn't accommodation provided. This isn't a hotel! He-hello? Fucking hell!'

Pippa knocked on the door. Jack halted in his pacing. Leaning up against the doorframe, she gave him a sympathetic smile.

'Bad day?'

'You could say that. Bloody Gemma has up and left on some delusional romantic quest after her boyfriend to Cuba.'

'Your devoted secretary?'

'Or so I thought. And you, Miss Taylor? The only thing you can say to improve my day is to tell me you've changed your mind again and want to sell Peace Offering.'

'Nope. Sorry, can't help you there.'

Jack shook his head.

'Great. Well, come in. Don't stand there in the doorway looking smug.'

'I'm not looking smug. I'm just looking cheerful.'

'Why?'

Pippa pushed herself off the doorframe and sauntered in.

'Because I am now the proud owner of a racehorse and this is a fresh new chapter of my life.'

'Why do you want to keep him?'

'Because Dave wanted to enter him in the Grand National.'

Jack's blue eyes widened.

'I don't believe I'm hearing this. Peace Offering? In the National? That's only the biggest steeplechase in the world. He'd have no hope!'

In her mind, Pippa saw the paper full of statistics.

'Neither did Mon Mome or Foinavon. But they won.'

'Foinavon only won because there was a pile-up at the Foinavon Fence.'

'Wow, that's creepy. Everybody crashes out at a fence with the same name as the eventual winner.'

36

Jack looked at her under heavy lids.

'It only became known as the Foinavon Fence *after* the race and for that precise reason.'

Pippa grinned.

'Did you know only five favourites have won it in the last fifty years?'

Jack regarded her with a wry smile.

'My, my. You *have* been doing your homework.'

Pippa's cheeks flushed.

'It's true though. It's not as unrealistic as you're making it out to be.'

Jack sighed and raked a hand through his thick dark hair.

'And presumably you want to keep him in training here?'

'Yes.'

'Miss Taylor –'

'Pippa, please.'

'*Pippa.* Please excuse me if I sound presumptuous, but how do you intend to afford his training fees on a waitress' salary?'

'With the money from Astolat's sale.'

'What about Dave's house? I thought that was the whole point of selling the horses.'

'How much do you charge?'

'More than you can afford, believe me.'

'Do you do discounts?'

'No. I –' Jack was interrupted by his mobile phone ringing. 'Bloody Lady Pennington. I don't have the strength to talk to her right now.' He viciously cut off the call, but almost immediately it rang again. Jack sighed. 'Hello, Melissa... Tonight? Do we have to? You know I can only take so much of your father...'

Realising she was eavesdropping on a personal call, Pippa tried to distract herself. Peering over the reception unit, she saw a chaotic jumble of papers covering the entire desk, the message alert on the telephone was flashing and the innards of a *Racing Post* had spilled onto the floor. Jack wasn't coping well without Gemma, it would appear. A smile touched her lips as an idea occurred to her.

'...Okay, see you later.' Jack snapped shut his phone and took a deep breath. 'Right, where were we?'

'You were about to offer me a discount on Peace Offering's training fees.'

Jack stared at Pippa's beaming face.

'What? I don't do discounts. I told you.'

'But you would if I were to work for you?'

'That's ridiculous! By your own admission, you don't know anything about horses.'

Pippa examined her nails, avoiding his eyes. Her fingers trembled and she put her hand away. She wouldn't allow him to see just how shaky the ground was beneath her.

'Maybe not, but I do know that whatever person being supplied by that agency you were talking to earlier isn't going to know much either,' she said coolly. 'And whereas they can't get you anyone for at least two weeks, I can start immediately. Almost.'

'Absolutely not. You're a waitress. I need a secretary. There's more to this job than making the boss coffee. Do you have office experience?'

'Yes, I worked in a lawyer's office before.' Did two weeks' work experience as receptionist at Hodder & Barrett, Inc. count?

Jack's phone rang again.

'For God's sake!' he roared. 'What is it with people today? I'm a racehorse trainer, not a fucking receptionist. Hello, Mr Cox. How are you?' His tone changed like a channel had been switched. 'Good, good. Yes, sorry about that, I haven't had a chance to check my messages yet. My secretary isn't in today... Tomorrow afternoon sounds just fine. Dexter and Lugarno will be getting fed about five o'clock... My pleasure.'

The reception phone began to ring as Jack patiently dealt with an owner and Pippa took the initiative. Walking round the desk, she went to pick up the phone as Jack ended his call.

'Aspen Valley Stables,' she carolled. 'Oh, hello, Lady Pennington.' She grinned as Jack's face fell in terror and he frantically waved the phone away from him. 'I'm afraid he's unavailable right now,' she continued, laughing silently at Jack. 'I'm very sorry you've been trying for so long – yes, I understand you must have a very busy schedule. As such, I'm sure you can appreciate Mr Carmichael has as well. I'll pass on the message as soon as I see him though. Okay, bye for now.'

Jack looked traumatised.

'God, what did she want?'

'Just that she wanted to discuss the four Lord Pennington bought at the sales. She sounds like a right toff.'

'She is. The worst kind. Thank you for lying to her.'

'Pleasure. Does that get me the job?'

'No, of course not. Besides, you live in London. Are you going to commute every day?'

'I also have a house less than half an hour away.'

'Which is barely habitable by the sounds of it –'

'Mr Carmichael?'

They turned at the sudden interruption. Pippa recognised the girl wringing her hands in the doorway as the one she had met at the sales.

'Yes, Emmie? What is it?'

'Um, the hay from France has arrived.'

'Wow, you really do treat your horses well here. Do you serve them white Alba truffles imported from Italy too?' Pippa said, impressed.

Jack didn't deign to answer.

'Okay, tell them I'll be there in a sec. You wait here, Miss Taylor. And don't answer the phone. *Please.*'

'Pippa,' she correctly faintly to his departing figure.


'This. Is. Only. Half. What. I. Ordered!'

Jack's deliberate words rang through the yard as Pippa ventured out of the office to investigate. In the car park, Jack stood facing a man in shabby jeans and a crumpled leather jacket. The trainer's broad shoulders were tensed and rose up and down with each controlled breath. The other man shrugged, relaxed in comparison. She turned her gaze from the men to a vast shaggy lorry bundled high with hay bales.

'How am I supposed to fee a hundred horses with this?' Jack said through clenched teeth. 'Bloody hell. Why am I even asking you this? They can't even send a driver who can speak fucking English!'

'*You English people are mad,*' the man replied in French.

'What?'

'Are you okay?' Pippa said with some concern. Jack was almost hyperventilating.

He turned and frowned at her.

'I thought I told you to stay in the office? But since you ask, no, I'm not. I've got a hundred horses to feed and only half the hay I ordered. What's more, they send a driver who can't speak English. Sometimes I think they do this on purpose. The French have a twisted sense of humour.'

'Better than none at all.' Pippa raised her eyebrows meaningfully at him and he glared back.

'Why don't you go back to the office like I asked and I'll be with you once I've cleared up this mess?'

'How do you intend to do that if you don't speak French?'

'We're in England! I'm allowed to not know French. He's not!'

The Frenchman might not have been able to understand them, but he understood Jack's aggression clearly. He muttered under his breath.

'Maybe I can help,' Pippa said.

'Do you speak French?'

'Well, I learnt a bit at school and –'

'Somehow I doubt whether your schoolgirl French lessons are up to this.'

'Suit yourself.' Pippa turned to the Frenchman. '*You're right, but it's only some English who are mad,*' she said to him fluently. The man grinned. 'I'll go wait in the office, shall I?'

Jack grabbed hold of her arm.

'Wait! You do speak French! Tell him he hasn't delivered the full order. What's on this order form isn't what's on that lorry.'

'Hmm. My schoolgirl French lessons might not be up to it,' Pippa said slyly. Her two years spent at an art college in Paris might have been though.

'Stop taking the piss!'

'That's no way to speak to an owner. Do you want my help?'

'Yes! Tell him –'

'I know, I know. *Are all racing trainers like this?*' she asked the Frenchman.

'*Some, but this one is particularly bad.*'

'What did he say?'

'He said you're a very good trainer.'

'What's that got to do with anything? Lose the chitchat. Ask –'

'*He seems to think you have delivered too little hay, but are charging him for the full price.*'

'*He thinks I am trying to cheat him, but I keep telling him that I'm not! He won't listen. He is being completely unreasonable.*'

'What?' Jack interjected.

'He says he can understand where the confusion has arisen. It's completely understandable.'

Both men regarded each other suspiciously.

'*I have travelled from France with another lorry which has broken down somewhere in this crazy country. Now I wish I had offered to stay behind with the broken down lorry than come up here. I could have let Francois deal with this bastard.*'

40

Pippa murmured her sympathy and asked herself equally why she was doing this.

'What?' Jack said impatiently.

She looked at him with an increasing lack of understanding. *It's for Dave and Peace Offering*, she told herself.

'He said the other half of your order has broken down somewhere on the way. He regrets you should be put in this situation.'

'Great. When am I going to get it?'

'*Do you know when the other lorry will be fixed?*'

'*They are working on it now. It should arrive tomorrow. The sooner the better I think. For me though, I'll make sure I don't have to do orders for Monsieur Carmichael in future.*'

'What did he say about me?'

'He said he admires you very much and it's a pity you have met under these circumstances.'

'A pity indeed. When is my hay going to arrive?'

'Tomorrow hopefully. They're doing their best to get the lorry going right now. What are you doing ordering hay from France anyway? What's wrong with British?'

'That bloody awful summer we've had this year ruined the crop. Instead, we've got to dish out a fortune to the French for theirs.' Jack turned back to the stables. 'BILLY! TOM!'

Two lads appeared from within the yard.

'Come help this guy unload the hay into the barn, will you? Billy, I don't want you climbing up top. You're better off on firm ground. And if you don't know any French, don't bother trying to make conversation. How can they send over someone who can't speak the bloody language?'

'You don't know French,' Pippa reasoned as the Frenchman and lads began unfastening the load.

'Yes, but I don't need to. Everyone speaks English. Or they *should*.'

'Well, since they don't, do you admit that I might have my uses? I might be a waitress, but I'm not stupid, Jack.'

Jack sighed and looked away.

'Okay, I'm sorry. I don't think you're stupid. I'm sorry if I implied that you were.'

'So do I get the job?'

Jack gave her a resigned look making Pippa brighten with hope.

'Do you know what you're letting yourself in for?'

'I love a challenge,' she grinned.

'Peace Offering might not be worth it. He hasn't won in two years.' Jack tried once more, but Pippa knew she had him beat.

'Neither had Silver Birch.'

For the first time, Jack smiled, flashing a row of even white teeth.

'Okay, fine. When can you start?'

# Chapter Six

Pippa pouted ruefully as she opened the flat's front door and heard the canned laughter from a comedy sitcom on the television. Ollie was home. That wasn't unusual in itself, but right now she could do without him. Just for a short time while she gathered her thoughts and prepared herself for the subject she knew she had to broach. She had tried to plan ahead, but driving on the motorways back to London was a deeply traumatic experience and Pippa had needed all her wits about her.

How would Ollie take it? Ollie, being the creative spirit that he was, also had a creative temper. Pippa never knew what she wase going to get dealt with. Despite reason, she found his extravert temperament very attractive. When guided the right way he could be a most passionate, and compassionate, man. She decided to dive straight in.

'A'right, m'lover?' she said in her best West Country accent.

Ollie raised an eyebrow at her from his horizontal position on the couch. But then his face split into a wide grin.

Pippa grinned back, glad that, for whatever reason, Ollie wasn't sulking anymore.

'I got it!' he said, sitting up and spreading his arms in triumph.

Pippa's smile clung to her face as she furiously tried to recall what Ollie had planned on getting.

'Got what?'

'The part. I had the second audition today. Remember?'

Oh, hell, Pippa inwardly grimaced. She had completely forgotten about Ollie's follow-up.

'Of course! Well done, Ollie!' She rushed over to hug him. 'What is it again?'

'A doctor in *Holby City*. Meet the new Doctor Fletcher! It's only a small part, but they want me to feature as background cast as well.'

'That's great! I'm so happy for you, Ollie. What a breakthrough! I knew you could do it.'

Ollie folded his arms behind his head and lay back again.

'So did I. Mind you, I can't afford to pay for this racehorse of yours. Are you going to go out every weekend and see him? He's going to cost you a fortune anyway, never mind your travel costs.'

'Well, there's the thing,' Pippa began. She wiped her damp palms on her skirt and paused as she chose carefully what to say next. 'He is going to cost me a lot of money, you're right. And Astolat's sale was meant to go towards renovating Dave's house. So I thought I might move down there for a while, do the house up myself and save some of the expense,' she concluded cheerfully.

Ollie looked horrified. He pulled himself up on the couch to get a better look at Pippa.

'What?'

'I thought I might move down there for a while –'

'I heard you, Pippa. What I meant was, are you crazy?'

This was the second time in as many days that Ollie had asked this and Pippa was beginning to think he might not be wrong.

'How are you going to live? What about your job? What about *me*?'

Pippa idly straightened the photo frames on the coffee table.

'I have a job. I'll be working for Jack Carmichael.'

'Who?'

'Peace Offering's trainer.'

'Doing what? Making his coffee?'

'No, as his secretary. His up and left yesterday without notice.'

'But Pippa, you're not a secretary! You're a waitress.'

Pippa twisted her toes in her shoes at his derisive tone.

'I know, but I can learn, can't I?'

'And this, here? You're going to leave me?'

Pippa swept down beside the sofa and took Ollie hands.

'No, no! I'm not leaving you, Ollie. Of course not. I thought maybe you'd like to come down and live there with me.' She looked at him uncertainly. 'That was, until I heard you got this part. You must go for that, of course...' Her voice trailed off as she watched Ollie's expression.

'Damn right I'm going for it!' he said. '*Me* in the country? Can you really see it? I'd be bored out of my mind!'

'Not if you helped fix up the house with me.'

'Oh, so you'd just want me to be your live-in handyman, right?'

'Of course not. I'd want sex as well.'

Ollie looked violated, making Pippa laugh.

'Don't be silly, Ollie. You know it wouldn't be like that. You'd love Hazyvale House. You would, honest.'

Ollie snatched his hands back.

'I did drama at school, Pippa. Not woodwork. Plus, I get hay fever.'

She thought back to the French hay incident and had to stop herself from smiling.

'There's no hay this year. They had a bad crop because of the wet weather.'

'Pippa, I don't know what's got into you lately. Ever since Dave Taylor kicked the bucket, you seem to have lost all of your senses. Why are you doing this?'

Pippa considered his question for a long moment. Why *was* she doing this?

'Ollie, I've been working as a waitress for four years now. The biggest promotion I've had was from Sid's Greasy Spoon to Vivace Restaurant. It's not going anywhere and I'm not going to be a waitress for the rest of my life. I needed a kick up the backside to do something and Dave's given it to me. I can't just throw it away.'

'A kick up the backside, maybe. But moving to the country on some *Grand Designs* venture and getting a job in something you know nothing about? Come on, Pippa, get real. And what about our life here? Together?'

'Like I said, I thought you might like to move to the country.'

'I don't know why we're still arguing about this. I'm not going anywhere. But did you really think I would agree to this? I'm a city guy, not a country yokel. And I hate tweed.'

Pippa sighed in surrender and stood up.

'Fine, Ollie. But I'm going.'

'So you *are* leaving me.'

'No! It's only three or four hours' drive away. And it won't be forever; a year maybe. By then the cottage will be redone and sold and I won't have to work for Jack Carmichael to afford Peace Offering's training fees. You can come and visit any time. We can still be together.'

'Thanks for the invite,' Ollie huffed.

'My pleasure. Now, shall I make us some dinner?'

As Pippa walked out of the room, she could hear Ollie mumbling about the ludicrousness of everything. He would come round to the idea once he'd got used to it. Once he saw Hazyvale House he'd see it as a challenge, just like she had.

Challenging was one word which could be used to describe Pippa's new adventure. Slightly uncomfortable was another. With her knees drawn up under her misshapen jumper, she sat huddled in the dark in her brand new second-hand VW Beetle at the end of Hazyvale's driveway the next evening. The full force of the heater tinged her cheeks. Still trembling with cold, she flicked the ash from her cigarette through the inch-open window. She held her mobile phone to her ear, wondering if there was some small corner of the house which she might have missed that had signal, instead of only at the end of the driveway.

Vaguely, she watched the shadows of the overhanging branches dance over the dashboard, dark against the silver base of moonlight. It was a clear frosty evening with more stars in the sky than Pippa had ever seen in her life. Neither had she been so cold, unless you counted that drunken night two Februarys ago when she and Tash had taken a dip in the Thames for a dare.

'I can't believe you've actually done this, Pip.' Tash's tone was admiring.

'You don't think I'm being crazy?'

'I always think you're crazy. But in a loveable way, not an unstable asylum-case way.'

'That's where Ollie thinks I should be. In an asylum.'

'Bugger Ollie, what does he know? You've done the right thing moving away. You needed a change.'

'You think so?' Pippa needed Tash's reassurance.

'Yes. You were getting yourself stuck in a rut, working at Vivace's and playing housekeeper to Ollie.'

'I wasn't –'

'And I Googled your Jack Carmichael and he isn't half fit. I wish I was going to be his secretary.'

Pippa laughed.

'Firstly, he is not *my* Jack Carmichael. Secondly, he's not my type.'

'Rubbish, he's everyone's type. Is he married?'

'I don't know. I didn't notice a wedding ring.'

'So he *is* your type.'

'Why, because he isn't married?'

'No. The fact that you noticed he wasn't wearing a wedding ring. That's proof you found him attractive. Him not being married is a bonus, of course. Could get messy otherwise.'

'Tash!' Pippa laughed. 'I'm not about to seduce Jack Carmichael, regardless of how good-looking he is. He's a right grump.' She took a drag from her cigarette and tapped its ash against the window crack. 'Anyway, I think he's got a girlfriend.'

'How do you know that?'

'He took a call from someone called Melissa when I was there and it just sounded like she was his girlfriend.'

'In what way?'

'He didn't want to have dinner with her folks.'

'You're probably right then.'

'Besides, you're forgetting that I already have a boyfriend as well. Just because I'm moving away doesn't mean Ollie and I have split up.'

'Hmm.' Tash didn't sound convinced. 'What is this house that you've moved into like?'

Pippa glanced in her rear-view mirror where she could see the security light at the front door lighting up the nearby oak tree. With its sagging roof the cottage looked like it was smiling.

'It's nice. A bit shabby at the moment, but it'll be fun getting it straightened out.'

'It'll also be a lot of hard work.'

'I know. Will you come down and help every now and then?'

'Of course I will. On one condition.'

'Which is?'

'I get to meet your boss.'

Pippa snorted.

'Tash! Really, you're incorrigible.'

'When do you start the new job?'

'Tomorrow,' Pippa said with a grimace.

'Looking forward to it?'

'Like a bullet in the head. I don't even know how to type, Tash. How am I going to cope with being a secretary?'

'You learn. Just like everyone else did. Nobody was born knowing exactly how to do their job. If you're worried about typing just remember "Pack my box with five dozen liquor jugs".'

'What?'

'Keep practising that sentence. It uses all the letters of the alphabet. Keep your forefingers on F and J, hit the spacebar with your thumb and you're away. You just need to practise.'

'And wages and accounts? I'm bound to have to do all that.'

'Well, that might take a bit more practise. I flunked GCSE Maths with flying colours so I won't give you any advice on how to do accounts. You're good at numbers though. What are you worrying about?'

'Messing up,' Pippa admitted. 'He's doing me a favour giving me this job. He knows I'm not qualified enough.'

'You're also doing him a favour, remember. If it wasn't for you, he wouldn't have a secretary at all.'

Pippa exhaled a long plume of smoke, abstractly watching it escape through the window slit.

'He might wish he didn't have one when I make a hash of everything.'

'Pippa! Snap out of it! Stop being a defeatist; it doesn't suit you. You walk in tomorrow and you sit down at your desk and you do what needs to be done. I'm sure he's not just going to dump everything on you and expect you to know how to do it. In every job you have to learn new things. Everything will be fine. Understood?'

Pippa swelled with renewed bravado.

'You're right, Tash. How bad can it be?'

'Good girl! And remember why you're doing all this.'

'Peace Offering?'

'Yes. To Peace Offering and his glorious future.'

'Are you toasting him, Tash?'

'Yes, of course. It's half six. Haven't you opened a bottle yet?'

'No, I'm sitting at the bottom of the driveway in my car.'

'Why?'

'Because this is the only place I can get signal.'

'Oh. Okay. Well, I'll drink for both of us. How does that sound?'

Pippa smiled and hugged her knees to her chest.

'Sounds good, Tash. Thanks.'

# Chapter Seven

A low-lying mist cloaked the countryside the next morning. Pippa shivered as she got out of her car in the Aspen Valley car park. The tangy aroma of newly tossed hay and straw wafted up her nose and she blinked as the brisk breeze stung her eyes. She wrapped her coat firmly around her and hurried towards the yard. A hive of activity greeted her as she turned the corner. Grooms were busy mucking out, tossing soiled straw into rickety wheelbarrows parked in the entrance of the stables. Others strode along the concourse, hefting saddles and bridles in their arms. The hollow clip-clop of shod hooves rang round the buildings as horses were led to and from their work.

Pippa gazed, wide-eyed, at this vibrant workplace. She hadn't realised so many people worked here. No one had noticed her presence yet and she took a moment more just to enjoy watching them. Eagerly, she tried to identify Peace Offering from the horses being led around, but couldn't see him. Her attention was captured by one familiar face though. Jack was bending down next to a steaming horse, feeling its foreleg whilst its rider stood to the side holding the reins. Rising to his full height, he gave the horse a distracted pat on the neck and spoke to its rider.

Pippa couldn't hear what was being said, but she saw the girl nod and smile at him before leading the horse to an adjoining stable. He caught sight of Pippa as he turned around. A small smile touched his mouth. He walked over, his long strides eating up the ground.

'Morning, Pippa. I was wondering if you would be joining us.'

'I said I would, didn't I?'

'And you always do what you say?'

'Most of the time,' Pippa replied loosely.

Jack gave a humourless chuckle and motioned her towards the office.

'Let me show you to your cell.'

'You'd suit being a prison guard, you know,' she said as they walked.

Jack gave her a sidelong glance, but said nothing.

'This is where you sit.' He gave her a patronising smile, making Pippa feel about five as she settled herself on the chair behind the reception unit.

He's just waiting for me to fail, she thought. I'll show him. He ain't seen nothing yet.

'First things first. Entries and declarations.'

Hmm, I ain't seen nothing yet either, Pippa thought again.

'Okay,' she replied uncertainly.

Jack sighed.

'Before a horse can race he will initially need to be entered in one, usually five or six days before it takes place. This is like letting them know that you intend to run. And you must make sure this is done by twelve o'clock. One minute past twelve and they won't accept it. Next stage is declarations, which is like a confirmation that you're running. This is done twenty-four hours before race-day and must be in by ten o'clock. Again, they cannot be late. I'll give you a list every morning of what horses need to be entered in which races and you can then go onto the Weatherbys website and fill in all the details.'

Pippa nodded fervently. It didn't sound that bad after all.

'Wages day is every second Wednesday. This must be done without fail once entries and declarations are completed. We've got fifty staff here, most of them seasonal and they cannot miss a payday.'

'Of course.'

Jack looked at his watch.

'I've got to get back for the next lot, but I'll be back later this morning. I've left a list of horses that need entering and declaring. The website is fairly straight forward; I'm sure you'll figure it out. Any complicated phone calls just take messages for now and we'll sort them out later. I need to call the vet out to take a look at Try That's leg, but I'll do that from my mobile. Have a look at the emails, but don't do anything until I get back. Most of them will be from people wanting photos and shoes and tail hairs from Virtuoso.'

'Who's Virtuoso?'

Jack shook his head helplessly.

'We won the Cheltenham Gold Cup with him earlier this year. Won eight Grade Ones on the bounce. He's a bit of a celebrity.'

'I know Cheltenham!' Pippa cried, excited that she knew something to do with horseracing.

'Good, that's reassuring. Think you can cope?'

'Piece of cake,' Pippa grinned.

Jack almost smiled, but ended up just looking grim. He seemed loathe to leave her on her own, but after a moment he kicked into action.

'Oh, and one more thing.' He paused by the door. 'If you get chilly, there's an electric heater in my office. The heating in here works, but it isn't up to scratch.'

She smiled her thanks and watched him walk out into the cold.

Taking a deep breath, Pippa turned to the computer on her desk and switched it on. It whirred into life and an icy dread clutched her throat as a box popped up.

*Username*

*Password*

Oh, God. He hadn't mentioned that bit. Thankfully the username was already filled in, but the password field gaped white. The cursor flashed, almost like it was daring Pippa to try. She darted a look towards the door. She was damned if she was going to fall at the first hurdle by running to Jack before he'd hardly walked out of the office.

'Right. Let's think.' She flexed her fingers over the keyboard then, taking a deep breath, tapped out *Aspenvalley*. She hit Return.

*Incorrect password. Please ensure CAPS lock is switched off before trying again.*

'Okay, so it's not that. How about... *password?*'

It was the oldest trick in the book. It was like the banks who advise you not to use 1234 as your PIN number, but it's the last thing any thief will think of since nobody is so stupid to use it.

*Incorrect password...*

'Oh, shit. Okay, maybe not so clever.' Pippa bit her lower lip. How many attempts would it give her before locking her out completely? Her laptop at home only ever gave her three tries before telling her to contact the system administrator. Who would the system administrator be here? She had an uneasy feeling it was meant to be her.

She flipped through a notebook on the desk, but it was just full of horses and race meetings, written in an almost illegible scrawl. The drawers under the desk didn't give her any clues either. Pippa frowned at the flashing cursor. It reminded her of someone tapping their fingers on a counter, waiting for you to make your decision. She looked around for more inspiration. The white walls were stark and bare apart from a couple of small framed photographs of horses winning races.

'Of course!' she cried. Eagerly, she punched in the letters.

*Virtuoso*

Pippa whooped as the box disappeared and Windows began to load.

*

With a triumphal jab to the Return key, Pippa leaned back and smiled at the screen then gave a curt nod at the door and towards Jack's general direction. It was five to ten and all the entries and declarations had been completed. She'd had three phone calls – one from the farrier who said that he was running about half an hour late, another from someone wanting a photograph of Virtuoso (and if at all possible, Jack Carmichael as well, the caller had asked shyly), and another from an owner who wouldn't leave a message, but would call back later.

This secretarial lark was easier than waitressing. What she been worrying about?

It didn't cross her mind that this was but the calm of an eight-month National Hunt storm season and only the tip of the iceberg.

'How's it gone this morning?' Jack said, making his reappearance a couple of hours later.

Pippa looked up and smiled, half an automatic gesture, half a genuine appreciation that she now had some company. With her limited tasks and the phone being unnervingly quiet, the only interaction she'd had was with some miserable man called Simon who had come in with a list of supplies to get for the yard.

'You still have a business. Can I get you some coffee?'

Jack hesitated on his way to his office.

'That'd be nice. Thank you.'

A couple of minutes later Pippa joined him in his office with a mug of steaming coffee. Jack lowered his *Racing Post* at her knock on the door. He still had his coat on and she noticed the tip of his nose was pink from the cold.

'Would you like your heater back? It's really quite toasty in Reception now.'

'No. Keep it. I'll warm up in a minute.'

After a moment she relaxed, reassured that he wasn't going to bite her head off for anything. He seemed in a much more agreeable mood today than on any of the other occasions they had met.

'Who's Simon?'

Jack paused from blowing on his drink.

'My head lad. You met?'

'He came in earlier. He didn't seem terribly keen.'

'Did you want him to be keen? I can't have you seducing all the male staff here, Pippa.'

Pippa felt oddly complimented that he thought her capable of this and was reminded of her conversation with Tash the night before.

'I'm not about to seduce anyone, don't worry. I've got a boyfriend in London still.'

'Do you? I didn't know that. How has he taken to you coming down here?'

'Ollie has his own way of dealing with things.'

'Not happy then?'

'Not really. But the good thing is his work is distracting him now.'

'What does he do?'

'He's an actor.'

'An actor? How very glamorous,' Jack drawled. 'What has he been in?'

'Well, he's just been given a small role in *Holby City* and he's had a few cameo parts in some other soaps, but –' Pippa hesitated. Her conscience battled with remaining loyal to Ollie and admitting his hopelessness. 'He prefers the theatre really,' she said finally.

'Can't say I blame him. Soaps are ridiculous.'

'No, they're not. They're entertaining.'

'All they ever do is argue, are closet gays or else sleep with people they shouldn't.'

'It wouldn't be entertaining if they didn't.'

Jack scoffed in derision then looked at his watch.

'Gemma usually took her lunch between one and two. Does that suit you?'

'Sounds fine. I might pop into the village and have a look around. How far away is it from here?'

'Helensvale? About ten minutes' drive. And it's a town by the way, not a village. I see you've got a different car.'

'The other ones were hired. This one's mine,' Pippa said proudly.

'Buy it yourself?'

'No, I stole it.'

Her solemn reply made Jack look at her sharply. Pippa couldn't contain her amusement when confronted by his expression.

'Oh, you're joking. Did you get it from a dealer?'

'Yes. I don't know why they've got such a reputation. The dealer who sold me mine was charming; a lovely old guy. He was very honest about it all, saying it isn't perfect – it has a rip in one of the backseats – and he let me have it really cheap.'

'Oh, God.' Jack closed his eyes. 'If that car lasts you 'til Christmas I'll be amazed.'

'That's only a few weeks away. Of course it'll last. It's a bit noisy, but it's a Beetle. They're supposed to be noisy.'

Jack looked at her under heavy eyelids.

Pippa licked her lips.

'Aren't they?' she ventured.

'I just hope you've got breakdown cover.'

Pippa was about to reply when the phone rang next door and she hurried out.


'PIPPA!'

Jack's bark from the adjoining office made her leap out of her seat. Frantically, she tried to think what she might have done wrong. That phone call five minutes earlier had been from an owner and she had put them through to Jack's extension. Was that so wrong?

'Yes?' Pippa popped her head round the door.

'We need to have a chat.'

Oh, God, was he firing her already? She gulped before straightening her shoulders and walking in.

Jack nodded to the visitor's chair.

'We need to chat about a few things. Your job here for starters, Peace Offering, and how we're going to sort out the financial side of everything.'

Pippa's thundering heart eased. She still had a job.

'Okay.'

'I've got a couple of runners at Wincanton this afternoon so I'm going to be out until about five or six. Your working hours are until five so you don't have to wait for me to get back.'

'Okay.'

'You'll be expected to work Saturdays as well.' Jack paused for reaction, but Pippa just nodded. She wasn't particularly bothered about work encroaching on her weekends. Waitressing had taught her this. 'Gemma was in the middle of organising Aspen Valley's Open Day before she went AWOL, so that will be one big thing you'll need to take over. We'll be having the public, the media, present and potential owners all milling around looking at the horses Tuesday after next. You'll need to organise some sort of catering. Given your background in waitressing, I'm sure you won't have too much of a problem with that.'

Pippa briefly flashbacked to the vegetarian lasagne man at Vivace's and concluded that was an incident best kept to herself.

Jack tapped his pen on his desk, frowning and Pippa could see him considering the forthcoming season, not as an exciting adventure like it was for her, but as serious business manoeuvres, battle plans almost.

'The closer we get to Christmas, the busier we are going to become,' he continued. 'It's the King George VI Chase at Kempton on Boxing Day where Virtuoso is due to run, so there is going to be huge pressure in the run-up. The media are going to be looking for comments and quotes so keep your mouth shut.'

Pippa pouted.

'Hey, that's a bit unfair.'

'Keep your mouth shut,' he repeated. 'Whether you know something or you don't, if the press get hold of it, it'll get whipped into a frenzy and rumours spread like wildfire. It's also the Christmas Hurdle and the name on everyone's lips will be Black Russian.'

'Black Russian? I entered him in a race this morning, didn't I?'

'No, you *declared* him in a race – or I hope you did, anyway. He's running tomorrow in the Fighting Fifth Hurdle.'

He closed his eyes for a moment and Pippa imagined him praying she had done the correct procedure.

'When you get phone calls for me when I'm in the office, tell them you'll see if I'm available first before putting them through. Some of their requests can be dealt with by you. Owners want to come see their horses. As long as it isn't in the morning or evening when they're being fed, they're welcome to come round. A lot of other calls will be from jockeys' agents wanting to know what we have running.' He paused and wagged his pen towards her to amplify the importance of what he was saying. 'First and foremost, we already have two stable jockeys. Rhys Bradford is number one, Finn O'Donaghue is number two. If we have horses running at three different venues or more than two horses in one race, we look for other jockeys. And, unless under the owner's insistence, these two jockeys will always get first pick. Understood?'

'I think I can handle it so far.' Pippa struggled to keep her voice polite in response to his patronising tone.

'Now...' Jack exhaled and placed his hands wide on the edge of his desk. 'About Peace Offering. What is this farcical you've got going about him running in the National?'

Pippa lifted her chin.

'I was going through Uncle Dave's stuff and I came across something which suggested he wanted to enter him.'

'Suggested? You mean you high-tailed it up to Doncaster to pull your horse out of the sale, quit your job in London to slave for his training fees whilst living in a dump, all on a *suggestion?*'

'You missed out that I had to steal a car to get to Doncaster.'

Jack's face fell and Pippa batted her hand at him.

'Long story. Anyway, it was more than a suggestion. It was a dream. Is that so wrong?'

'Some dreams are just pie in the sky.'

Pippa folded her arms and locked Jack in a stern gaze.

'How long have you wanted to train racehorses?'

Jack's eyes flickered away from her and he fiddled with his pen.

'Since I was a boy if you must know. I wanted to ride them first, but...'

'But?'

Jack looked up.

'I grew too heavy. So I got into training. I went from work rider to head lad to assistant trainer to having my own yard.'

'And now you're champion trainer. From what I've learnt only in the last few hours, you also have two champion racehorses in Virtuoso and Black Russian. I bet you dreamt of this when you were younger. Didn't you?'

Jack shifted in his seat and flicked at the pages of a notebook in front of him. When all he did was shrug, Pippa carried on.

'And I bet at the time some people probably considered that dream to be pie in the sky.'

'Yes, but –'

'But?'

'This is different. I was a boy, I was unproven! Peace Offering has been racing for five years now and he *is* proven. He's proven that he can't win a National!'

'How? Has he run in it before?'

'No, but –'

'So, how do you know then?'

'I just do!' Jack exclaimed, throwing up his hands. 'I train the bloody animal, I should know. He'll be ready to run in a couple of weeks' time. Then you can see for yourself!'

'Jack,' Pippa said firmly.

'What?'

'I'm not going to change my mind. I've done this whole thing in order for Peace Offering to have a crack at that race – everyone thinks I'm crazy for doing it – so I'm not going to let you talk me out of it.'

Jack glared at her, considering whether to challenge her obstinacy.

'Which leads us to the next thing. I'll give you a discount on training fees, but you'll still need to pay for his shoes, his transport and his entries and vets bills, if any.'

'Okay. The money which I got from Astolat's sale can go towards that.'

'It won't leave you with much to spare on Dave's house.'

'There isn't a mortgage to pay and I've got a loan approved so what I get paid from you will go towards that and repairs. I'm also intending to sell some paintings while I'm out here to bring in a bit more.'

'You're an artist?'

Pippa tipped her head from side to side, non-commitally.

'Some might say so. I kind of lost my inspiration these last couple of years living with Ollie – living in the city, I mean – but now I'm out in the country, I can feel it coming back.'

Jack gave her a lazy smile.

'Is there no end to your talents, Miss Taylor?'

'Not now that you mention it...' Pippa grinned.

'Not interrupting anything, am I?' a cool voice from the open doorway said. A tall willowy blonde woman tapped on the door twice for effect before breezing in. Jack stood up and came round the desk to give her a brisk peck on the cheek.

'Melissa. I wasn't expecting you.'

'We were going to have lunch before the races this afternoon. Remember?'

'Dammit, sorry. Completely slipped my mind.'

'You used to have everything in your diary – oh, Gemma kept that, didn't she?'

She gave Pippa a slow smile, reminding her of a cheetah, the smile always present, but the hunter wholly apparent.

'You must be the new girl.'

'Melissa, this is Pippa, my new secretary. Pippa, this is Melissa, my, er – my –'

'*Girlfriend* is the correct term, Jack. Although sometimes I wonder.' She winked at Pippa in false sisterhood. 'It seems I have to make an appointment to see him these days.'

Pippa didn't know what else to do except laugh obligingly. Jack looked even more uncomfortable.

'Are you ready to go?' Melissa asked him.

'Yes, I think so. Pippa, you'll be all right, won't you?'

'You don't have to worry about me. Good luck.'

Melissa laughed, a tinkling of ice cubes in a crystal glass, and she placed a slim manicured hand to her chest.

'Pippa, what would he need luck for? I don't intend to *eat* Jack, just eat *with* Jack.'

'Oh, no! I didn't mean that! I just meant for this afternoon – the racing this afternoon.'

Jack nodded and unhooked his jacket from the back of his chair.

'Thanks. I'll see you tomorrow.'

He guided Melissa out of the office with his hand in the small of her back. Pippa watched them leave, a curious frown on her brow. So that was Melissa. She looked like a right madam, and she was certain that handbag was an authentic Louis Vuitton.

Pippa was just slipping into her coat, looking forward to her lunchtime cigarette and exploration of Helensvale when the office door opened. A young man stepped in, a gust of icy wind accompanying him. His sandy blond hair and comic grin looked vaguely familiar.

Pippa's brain rushed to place him.

'Jaysus, that wind'd freeze the balls off a brass monkey. Howsa goin'?'

'You're the jogger!' Pippa cried, pointing at him in triumph as she recognised the broad Irish accent.

The young man studied Pippa for a long moment.

'Aye, I've been known to.'

Pippa stared back at him, still astonished how small the country must be compared to the city.

'Sorry, I'm Pippa. We met a few weeks back. I was trying to find this place and you stopped to give me directions.'

A grin of recognition split his face.

'That's right. I remember now. You found us a'right then? Couldn't find yer way back though?'

Pippa gestured to the office they stood in with outstretched arms.

'I work here now. As Jack's secretary. Today's my first day.'

He ran his hands through his hair and shook his head.

'Do you know what you're letting yourself in fer?'

'Oh, it can't be as bad as that.' She fobbed him off with a wave of her hand. 'I've survived the morning anyhow. I was just about to go into Helensvale for lunch. Can I help you with anything before I go?'

'That you can. Yer man, Billy, has cut himself on some fencing wire, so he has.'

'Is he okay?' she said uncertainly. She knew how to dress burns from hot plates, but fencing wire hadn't been in abundance in London kitchens so hadn't been included in her First Aid training.

'He's all cleaned up, the eejit, but it'll need to go in the Accident Report Book.'

Pippa gave an audible sigh.

'Thank God for that. I wonder where the Accident Report Book is kept...' she murmured to herself, opening and closing the desk drawers.

Her guest didn't comment, happy to rest his arms on the reception unit and watch her.

'A-ha!' she announced, brandishing a grubby hardback notebook from a tray. 'Here we are. Date... Nature of Incident... Persons Involved – God, this isn't the first time Billy's been in the wars,' she said, noticing his name listed in numerous other reports. 'Action Taken... Reported by...' She halted her pen. 'Sorry, I didn't catch your name.'

He gave her a mischievous grin.

'Finn O'Donaghue, at yer service.'

'Oh! Jack mentioned you. You're the jockey,' Pippa said, pleased to be able to put a face to the name she had been inputting during her entries and declarations earlier.

'More commonly known as The Jogger, but I answer to both.'

Pippa chuckled, shaking her head and wrote his name in the book. She closed it and glanced up to find Finn regarding her with laughing green eyes. Not knowing what to say next, she smiled again at him and fiddled with the top button of her coat.

'I'll not keep you from yer lunch,' he said after a pause. He tapped a quick beat of finality on the reception unit and turned to go. 'I'm glad we've met, Pippa. I'll be seein' you about.' He flashed her a grin and exited the office.

Pippa sunk back into her chair and gawped at the closed door.

'Oh, that *accent*,' she breathed. 'Tash would be in heaven if she was here.'

# Chapter Eight

A supercharged sneeze sent Pippa reeling backwards and she clutched the counter behind her to break her fall. Whimpering in its sniffling after-effects she tackled the kitchen cabinets once more. Only now was she realising the challenge she had set herself in clearing up Uncle Dave's house. This was just the kitchen and she was still scouring away at the dirt and grime on Sunday evening. Already, she'd scrubbed her way through a multi-pack of Brillo pads and her nails were as blunt as butter knives. The maple units were still a dull and dark shadow of their former self and the chipped and cracked worktops were the first thing Pippa realised would need replacing.

Her mobile phone buzzed on the windowsill and she sighed with relief at this interruption. Hoisting herself onto the counter she huddled in the corner of the window and pressed the phone against her ear.

'Tash. What's up, dude?'

'You answered! Was expecting to get your voicemail.'

'No, I've found signal in the house at last. In the kitchen sink of all places.'

'You're sitting in the sink?' Tash's tone was disbelieving.

'Well, on the draining board really.'

'May I ask how you discovered signal in the sink?'

'Through admiring the views. It's so beautiful out here, Tash. You've really got to come visit.'

'Oh, I intend to. You working hard?'

'I'm exhausted already. I've still only got as far as the kitchen.' Absent-mindedly, she reached out and scrubbed at some dirt ingrained in an earthquake crack along the counter. 'Tash, how do you break a granite worktop?'

'I don't know. Drop a piano on it? Why do you want to break a granite worktop?'

'Not me. It's already broken. I was just wondering how Uncle Dave managed to do it.'

'Like I said, he probably dropped a piano on it. It's the sort of thing he'd do just to find out. How is work going?'

'It's okay. Busy,' Pippa admitted. 'There's about a hundred horses at Aspen Valley and Jack says I'll know them all soon. Somehow I don't see that happening. The only ones I know are Peace Offering, Virtuoso and Black Russian.'

'Only ninety-seven more to go then.'

Pippa groaned. Cradling the phone between her ear and shoulder, she pulled off her luminous marigold gloves then grimaced as the smell of her sweaty, rubbery hands wafted up her nose.

'How are things with you?' she asked.

'Same ol', same ol'. Nothing much changes here. I made Liam, from Design, blush on Friday.'

'Oh?'

'Yeah, he came over to my desk while I was scratching a boob. Took me completely by surprise. Asked me which layout I liked breast.'

Pippa giggled. Tash might have a high-powered job in advertising, but that didn't stop her from being human.

'You're terrible, you know?'

'I am, I am. I know. I bought those lovely Jimmy Choos the other day, by the way. They go so well with my layered Indian skirt. When can I go racing to show them off?'

'Well, Jack says Peace Offering will be ready to race in a couple of weeks so I guess round about then.'

'Before Christmas then?'

'Yeah. What are you up to at Christmas? Going to stay with your mum and dad?'

'Yeah. Mum wouldn't forgive me if I skipped this year as well. I just so needed to have roast turkey outside in the sunshine for once last year. South Africa was like paradise. What about you?'

'No, my folks are off cruising. I don't think they're back until halfway through January.'

'My God. Excuse me for asking this, Pip, but how do your parents afford this? They spend half the year away.'

Pippa shrugged, looking at herself in the reflection of the kitchen window. There was a streak of grime across her forehead. She wiped it with a weary hand.

'Savings. They're both retired now. The house is paid off.'

'Couldn't they lend you some to get Dave's place sorted out?'

'No,' she replied firmly. 'This is something I'm going to do on my own. Besides, Dave wasn't hugely popular in my household. He was a gambler and a risk-taker, and well, you know what my parents are like.'

61

'God, yes. Buying Crunchy Nut instead of corn flakes is seen as taking a risk with your parents.'

The two friends giggled. Pippa didn't mind Tash ripping off her parents. She was almost their surrogate daughter so she was allowed to. Suddenly, an eardrum-rupturing alarm went off in the background.

'Oh, hell!' cried Tash. 'I forgot the lasagne in the oven. Got to dash, Pip. Speak to you soon!'

'Bye, Tash,' Pippa said to the dead line.

The new week brought with it a wet cold spell and Pippa had to scrape ice off her windscreen for the first time with her debit card. She took it easy driving to work, more in admiration of the countryside than in caution. On either side of the road the leafless branches of the trees were tinged silver and the grass glistened jade.

'I could probably get that using a slate grey and forest green. Maybe a hint of periwinkle,' she murmured. She had grabbed a couple of hours to start on *Hazyvale Dawn* over the weekend and, now that she had picked up her brushes again, it was like eating Pringles. You couldn't just have one, you had to stuff yourself until the whole tube was finished. Her inspiration was coming back in tidal waves.

The deep growl of a tractor coming in the opposite direction refocused Pippa's attention and happily she waved back at its driver. People didn't do that on her street in London, she thought as a flood of well-being gushed through her. All they did was hoot and crouch over their steering wheels, in too much of a hurry to take any notice of those around them.

She carried on to work, humming along to the crackling radio, satisfied with the mental photograph she had taken of her surroundings which would hopefully reappear on canvas later.

'Jack?' Pippa poked her head round his door.

Jack glared at her, his temper simmering beneath the surface.

'What?'

Pippa closed her eyes for a moment and took a deep breath. There was no point in both of them being in bad moods. Jack was still standing beneath the heavy black cloud that had emerged after Black Russian's defeat on Saturday in the Fighting Fifth Hurdle. The fact that Pippa was blissfully unaware of the crucial and unexplained result hadn't helped when she had cheerily asked how Aspen Valley had performed over the weekend. She decided in future that she was better off watching the races on TV herself so that she would be prepared for Jack's foul moods. The numerous calls from the media just seemed to feed the flames.

'Dan Cameron just rang to say he's got to rearrange your appointment today,' she said, naming one of Aspen Valley's premier owners. 'He can't do lunch so he said that you should meet him in Bath at half eleven.'

'What! You told him that was okay?'

'No, of course not. He didn't give me much choice though. He said that he wants to speak to you about Black Russian, as you know, and that half eleven was the only time he can see you.'

'Bloody ridiculous,' Jack muttered. He looked at his watch. 'Shit. I better get going then.' He downed the last of his coffee and snatched up his jacket. He strode towards Pippa. 'Here are today's entries. I haven't finished them. Put Leopard Rock in the two thirty-five at Huntingdon, Spurwing Island in the three ten, Carribea Bay in the four fifteen at Wincanton and Asian Dancer in the two fifteen at Chepstow. Can you remember that?'

'Don't worry - oh, Jack!' Pippa called as he disappeared out of the office. She dashed over to his desk. 'Keys!' Jack turned and caught them as she tossed them to him.

'See you later,' he said, giving the keys a twirl and shutting the door behind him.

Pippa grinned then ran to answer the phone.

'Right,' she said, five minutes later. 'Time for entries.'

# Chapter Nine

'Pippa. Can you come in here, please.'

Jack's command was barely audible, which was almost more unnerving than when he was yelling. Pippa rose on unsteady legs. Was this how it was always going to be? Would she live her days in fear of being told off? It wasn't much of a life. And Jack had been making hers hell for the past few days, with what seemed completely unnecessary provocation. She hadn't actually done anything wrong so far! Sighing, she left the safety of her desk and entered Jack's office. He was holding a piece of paper which he held up for Pippa to see.

'Do you know what this is?'

Pippa groaned inwardly. She hated trick questions.

'Entries ready to be declared,' she said cautiously.

'Can you tell me why Bajan Dancer is entered in the two fifteen at Chepstow tomorrow?'

A wave of uncertainty broke over her.

'Because that's what you told me.'

'No,' Jack said slowly. 'I told you to enter *Asian* Dancer in the two fifteen at Chepstow.'

'Oh. Sorry.'

'I don't think you realise the impact this has, Pippa,' he went on in a quiet voice. 'All my horses are primed for their particular races. I train them to hit their peak on the day of their race. Not the day before. Not the day after. Asian Dancer would be at his peak tomorrow. Next weekend he won't be as ready as he is now. Bajan Dancer would be at his peak in about six days providing his work goes to plan. Not tomorrow.'

Pippa gulped. Okay, maybe apologising wasn't enough to make things better.

'Oh.'

'This can't happen again, Pippa, do you hear?'

She felt like she'd been caught not doing her homework at school.

'It was a mistake, Jack.' She lifted her hands in a helpless gesture. 'I don't make mistakes on purpose.'

'You have to do better than that.'

'Mistakes happen, especially if you start yelling entries at me as you rush out of the door.' Indignation crept into her voice.

'I wouldn't have had to rush out of the door if you'd arranged a better time for me to see Dan Cameron!'

'That wasn't my fault, Jack. How can I help it if one of your owners decides the only time he can meet you doesn't suit your schedule, but says that it's of vital importance that he sees you?'

'You make a different plan!'

Pippa was about to retort when there was a knock at the main office door. She glared at Jack for a moment more, her chest hurting from the deep breaths she was taking.

Back in the reception, Finn O'Donaghue was waiting on the doorstep.

'Safe to come in?' he said in a stage whisper.

Pippa managed a smile, her spirits lifting at his arrival like a reflex action.

'Come in, Finn. What can I do for you?'

She liked Finn, the young wiry Irishman with equally wiry blond hair and crooked nose. Everyone liked him, despite, or perhaps even especially, because he always played second fiddle to Rhys Bradford. Rhys was apparently a better jockey; that was generally acknowledged – although Pippa couldn't comment on this – and he knew it, strutting around like a cat who'd just been spoon-fed a pint of cream.

'Just dropped in to see which nags we have runnin' tomorrow.'

Pippa gave a mirthless snort.

'Not Asian Dancer for one.'

Later that afternoon, Pippa relaxed in her chair, leaning back and gazing at the ceiling. Jack was out racing and it seemed the rest of the world had decided to give her ten minutes of peace and quiet. She looked around with displeasure. The room was drab. Boring. There was no colour, only bare white walls except for the framed photographs of Virtuoso's Gold Cup win and Black Russian's Champion Hurdle win.

She needed to get this horrible feeling of depression off her chest. She opened a new email window.

*Hi Tash,*

*How's you? You're not giving poor Liam a hard time I hope? I'm going to apologise now because I need to have a good rant and you're my only ally at the moment. Jack Carmichael is an absolute shit! He's bossy, miserable and shouts too much. Can you believe I've been here over a week and he hasn't said one nice thing to me? It's exhausting to have abuse thrown at you the entire time.*

*I cocked up on the entries this morning, which I feel bad about – really, I do – but Jack acted like it was either going to start a world war or someone was going to die because of it.*

*What have I done? Is Peace Offering really worth all this trouble? Life in London wasn't exactly rosy and I'm trying to enjoy the cottage even though it's hard work, but is this some sort of punishment for wanting to enjoy my life? I'm not surprised Jack's old secretary upped and left him in the lurch. I'd be inclined to do the same if it wasn't for Peace Offering. God knows he hasn't done anything to deserve any less.*

*"Jack fucking Carmichael is proven to be an extremely crazed bastard without question". That seems more appropriate than "Pack my box with five dozen liquor jugs".*

*Right, I feel better now. Thank you for listening to me. I'm now going to see out the rest of the afternoon in peace since thankfully, Jack is at the races. Speak to you soon.*

*Love ya,*

*Pip*

*xxx*

Pippa dropped her brush into the water-filled jar beside her easel. She rolled her shoulders and stretched, letting the last bars of Puccino's O Mio Babbino Caro seep through her aching muscles. Without glancing at the picture in front of her, she turned away to hunt her cigarettes down in the kitchen.

As she huddled beneath the front door's overhang in the dark she chewed her bottom lip, her thoughts still consumed by her day at work.

Was Peace Offering really worth it, she asked herself for the twentieth time? She sighed and tapped the ash from her cigarette, because, for the twentieth time, she couldn't come up with a definitive answer.

To say no would be to turn away from the magic she had seen in the racehorse's eyes and to turn her back on Dave's dream to run him in the Grand National.

To say yes, he was worth it, was to consider this new life an improvement on the one she had led in London. To say yes was to believe that Peace Offering could fulfil his late owner's dream.

Pippa took a deep drag, hearing the soft crackle of burning tobacco, such was the quiet of her surroundings, and she acknowledged that to say yes, meant the dream had to be her own as well as her uncle's. With a defeated shake of her head, she stubbed her cigarette out in an empty flowerpot beside the door and went back inside into the warm.

When she returned to the spare bedroom to look at her completed painting for the first time, she smiled with satisfaction. *Hazyvale Dawn* burst out of the canvas just as it had burst through the window on her first morning. The long sweeping watercolour strokes of peach and apricot mist swirled across the page; the sun was a soft gold orb as opposed to a hard amber ball as the moisture in the air blurred its outline.

'Perfect.'

Satisfied, Pippa picked up a fine-tipped brush and dabbed her signature in a red rosewood hue in the lower right hand corner. Holding the page with reverent care, she teased it away from the rest of the pad and laid it out on a table like a mother lowering her sleeping child into its cot. She sat back down on her stool in front of her easel, the urge to create still not quelled inside her. She twiddled the brush in her fingers, unsure what image could fulfil this craving.

She thought back to her first morning driving to work; how the frost had turned the countryside silver, of the tractor driver waving at her, but the pictures in her head refused to transfer to her hand holding the brush. Instead, she found herself dabbing delicate lines of a man leaning down to feel a horse's leg in the middle of a stable yard.

Pippa's breath shortened as the inspiration flowed through her fingertips and onto the canvas. Roused by the harrowing tones of *Tosca* from her CD player in the corner of the room, she nurtured the scene to life. The smell of turned straw brought to life the loaded wheelbarrows parked in the stable doorways, the sound of shod hooves on concrete transformed itself into saddled racehorses being walked along the concourse, the scent of warm sweating bodies recreated by their steaming flanks. The chatter of riders and grooms filled her head as she painted their faces, a splash of colour from their red anoraks catching the eye.

Pippa blinked and her brush stilled, poised millimetres from the canvas. Exhaling, she slowly withdrew her hand, placing the brush in the water jar. It was finished. She felt released, the tension in her body was gone. Her head felt clear again. As with the last painting, she turned away from it without studying its completion. She was too exhausted to go have her usual post-painting cigarette. She looked at her watch as she shrugged off her colour-spattered smock and gasped.

'Oh, God. I've got to be up in three hours for work,' she groaned. She rubbed her eyes with stained fingers. 'Where the hell did the evening go?'

She dragged her feet along the worn and balding carpet to the door, but paused before switching off the light. She looked back to the picture, which stood loud and alive on the easel in the middle of the room. Her breath caught in her throat as she noticed something for the first time. One stable on the far left stood free from the commotion and activity. Over the half door though, an equine head looked towards her with long ears pricked, stretched out from a thin bay neck.

Tears welled in her eyes as she took in the white blaze spilling down the horse's Roman nose and a glint in its pleading eyes reflecting the early morning sun. The horse stood alone, ignored and abandoned by everyone around the yard. She brushed a tear away with a hasty swipe and blamed it on being overtired. But as she switched off the light, blacking out the picture, Peace Offering still gazed after her, asking her for her support.

# Chapter Ten

Pippa made a bee-line for the office's kitchenette the following morning and scooped a double dose of caffeine into her mug. As she settled herself back at her desk, Jack walked in, shaking his sodden jacket from his shoulders and closing the door on the rain outside.

'Good morning,' Pippa said with a bright smile, making an extra effort to hide how tired she was.

'Nothing good so far,' Jack grunted in reply. His hair was plastered to his forehead and his nose was red from the cold.

'Hot drink to warm you up?'

'Okay. That'd be nice. Give Alan Warnock a ring at the vets to come down first though. Take Five is running a temperature and I'd like to check Try That's leg while he's here. The abscess in her foot has cleared up, but she's still lame.'

Pippa beamed and tapped her pen on her desk.

'On it right away.'

Jack shook his head at her cheeriness and stomped into his office, closing the door behind him with a thud.

'Hello, Mr Warnock. It's Pippa from Aspen Valley –' She paused as the main office door opened and Finn walked in. Pippa gave him a quick wave. 'Would you be able to come over? Apparently Take That is running a temperature and Try Five –' She stopped at Finn's desperate head-shaking and mouthing. 'Ooh, sorry, ignore what I just said. Take *Five* is running a temperature and Try *That* is still lame...'

A few moments later, she put the phone down and blew her hair off her forehead in a relieved sigh.

Finn leaned his folded arms on the tall reception counter and grinned at her, shaking his head.

'Thanks,' she said. 'I owe you one.'

'Not a bother. Although some might argue Take That might be running a temperature.'

Pippa giggled.

'I'll let that one slide on this occasion. How are you?'

'All the better now. A bit o' humour to lighten the mood, even if it was unintentional. You'da had ol' man Warnock scratching his nod wonderin' when in hell a pop band took up with Aspen Valley.'

Pippa lowered her voice.

'Can you imagine what *he* would have said if he'd heard?' she said, motioning to Jack's closed door. 'He certainly wouldn't think it was funny.'

Finn shrugged.

'Probably not, but now's not the time to be discussin' it with himself only ten feet away. What would be grand is if you can tell me tomorrow's runners. And don't be tellin' me your made up names like you've just done to Warnock. I'll be the joke of the weighing room if I announce I was riding Westlife in the next.'

With Finn dispatched back to the yard to saddle up for the next lot, Pippa knocked on Jack's door with a steaming mug of chamomile tea in her hand. She found him frowning at his computer screen and it was a moment before he registered her presence.

'Thanks,' he said, distractedly taking a slurp. The next moment he'd sprayed tea over his desk. 'What the hell is this?' he demanded, looking at Pippa as if she'd just fed him poison.

'It's chamomile tea. I thought it might be good for you.'

'Good for me?' he said, mopping his keyboard with a handkerchief. '*How?*'

Pippa hesitated, deliberating how not to upset him further.

'It's meant to have relaxing qualities. It's very healthy.' She gave him an encouraging smile.

Jack paused, his attention caught by his computer screen. He looked up at her, his lips parted and his brow furrowed. His gaze went back to the screen then across to the mug of tea. She noticed him hesitate, whatever sharp comment on his tongue withheld when he clamped his mouth shut.

'Er – okay. I guess I could give it a try,' he said.

'Great,' she beamed, relief that he wasn't having a complete meltdown. 'Alan Warnock is on his way. He asked if you'd isolated Take Five in case he has a virus.'

'Um, yes, of course.'

'Okay, then. Are these today's declarations?' she asked, pointing to a ring-bound tea-splattered notepad set aside on the heavy desk.

Jack nodded.

'Great. I'll get onto these right now.'

She turned to take her leave, but stopped as Jack called her name.

'Pippa. I'm going to give Peace Offering a fast workout later this morning. Maybe you'd like to come watch?'

A grin spread across her face and she clasped the notebook to her chest. Excitement burned through her, tingeing her cheeks. She hadn't been on the Gallops yet. Hell, she'd hardly had any contact with the horses since she'd been here. She wasn't sure what had caused this allowance in Jack's usually inhospitable nature (surely the chamomile tea wasn't that effective?), but she wasn't about to question it.

'I'd love to. Let me get these done. Just yell if you want anything. I'll be ready whenever you need me to be.' Without waiting for a reply, she hurried back into the reception to her computer to declare Aspen Valley's runners, a spring in her step.

'Ready?'

Pippa looked up from her emails an hour later to see Jack standing in his office doorway, his jacket zipped up and his hands in his pockets. She stopped typing mid-sentence and jumped to her feet.

'Absolutely.'

'Good. Bring your coat. You'll need it.'

The reappearance of his brusque manner did nothing to daunt Pippa's enthusiasm and she unhooked her red midi-coat from the back of her chair and trotted after Jack into the yard. The rain sluiced their hunched figures as they hurried towards his Land Rover in the car park. Pippa pulled her coat tighter around her in response to the brisk wind which reached its icy fingers into every available crevice of her clothing. Jack opened his door and was pushed aside by his arthritic black Retriever-cross, Berkeley.

'In the back today, buddy,' he said, unscrupulously downgrading the dog to the backseat.

Once inside the dry but decidedly dirty interior of the vehicle, Pippa was met with a blast of hot air as Jack turned on the ignition and the heater roared into life. With an uncomfortable shift, she removed a pair of binoculars from beneath her and tried, without success, to place her wet feet where they wouldn't dirty the carpet of *Racing Posts* littering the footwell. Under the loud drone of the heater she could just make out music playing from the rear speakers.

'Bruce Springsteen?' she said as they bumped over the uneven road.

Manoeuvring the Land Rover between the hay barn and the indoor school, Jack nodded, looking uncertain whether to turn it up or turn it off.

'Hmm,' Pippa mused, taking the initiative and increasing the volume. 'Makes sense.'

'Why?'

Pippa sang the chorus to *Born To Run* in an off-key baritone. 'It's apt.'

Jack snorted, a smile creasing the lines beside his eyes.

'I don't think Bruce had horseracing in mind when he wrote this, but okay. Do you like Bruce Springsteen?'

Pippa shrugged.

'He's all right, I guess. He goes on a bit about motorbikes and guitars and USA though.'

'So if bikes and guitars aren't your style, what sort of stuff do you listen to?' Jack asked, turning to glance at her.

'I don't know. Depends on what mood I'm in. Stuff like Bruce Springsteen and Meatloaf is great on the open road. When I paint, I listen to classical music, sometimes a bit of opera.' Pippa looked out of her window as they climbed the grey weather-blurred hillside along the Gallops. She thought of how Ollie had always mocked her taste in music, especially when she had been painting. So she had tried to paint when he wasn't around, but when acting roles had become few and far between, he had spent so much time at the flat, those snatched moments with paint and Puccini had lost their magic. She'd then tried to paint without music, but her inspiration had dwindled, as if the brush in her hand had been a conductor's baton, waving it around in front of an empty orchestra pit.

'Ah, yes. You're an artist. I forgot about that. How's that coming along? Have you had time to do anything since you've moved out here?'

'Some. Last night, I...' The words faded on her lips as she recalled the seemingly mesmeric trance in which she had painted the racing yard scene and the inadvertent inclusion of Peace Offering in the picture.

Jack took his eyes off the road to look at her, waiting for her to continue.

'Last night, I did some painting,' she said. 'I didn't get to bed until quite late.' Just the thought of how little sleep she had got made her yawn.

Jack's shoulders shook as he chuckled. He swung the steering wheel and brought the Land Rover to a halt halfway up the hills' incline.

'As long as you don't fall asleep on the job, you can stay up as long as you like.' He jerked the handbrake and twisted in his seat to reach behind them. 'Right. Binoculars for the owner. I'll take the ones you've got on your lap, if you don't mind. They're the ones I usually use.'

They swapped and Pippa fiddled with the woven black straps, excitement building up inside her again. She was here to watch *her* horse gallop. No longer was she Pippa Taylor, waitress at Vivace Restaurant and Ollie Buckingham's housekeeper. Now she was Pippa Taylor, racehorse owner and artist.

'Don't get too excited. This is just a pipe-opener for him –'

'A *what*?'

'To clear his airways,' Jack explained. 'He's up against three others, one of whom is Silver Dollar, who is a decent two-and-a-half-miler. Belongs to my favourite owners, Lord and Lady Pennington. Peace Offering's one asset is his stamina, not his turn of foot so I don't expect him to blaze the trail.'

'Okay,' Pippa said, nodding. 'Is that them at the bottom of the hill there?' She held her glasses up to her eyes for a closer look. 'Yes! There's Peace Offering! Are we going to get out and watch?' She turned to Jack, her eyes pleading.

He craned his head to look at the sky and grimaced.

'If you really want to.'

'Yes, please,' Pippa said, already halfway out the door.


With their collars turned up against the elements, they stood by the bonnet of the Land Rover, their binoculars both trained on the approaching horses. Pippa forgot how to breathe as the muffled drum of hooves drifted across the dank haze to them. Silver Dollar's grey face spearheaded the quartet and with a hop and a squeak of excitement, Pippa identified Peace Offering galloping hard about four lengths behind. The thunder of hooves grew steadily louder and Pippa lowered her binos as the horses neared them. The ground began to reverberate beneath them. In a heartbeat they had galloped past, the murk punctuated by their abrupt dragon-breaths with Silver Dollar still held up in front and Peace Offering pushed along in third.

Pippa gasped and jumped up and down, succeeding in planting her heels into the sodden ground and splashing mud on her legs. Overcome, she clapped her hands. Looking at Jack, she tried to rein in the wide smile

73

that lit up her face. Jack's attention was still held by the horses and as they galloped on, he picked up his glasses again.

By the time the horses had reached the top of the Gallops, Peace Offering had narrowed Silver Dollar's lead to just a length.

'Oh, my God,' Pippa cried. 'Did you see how fast they were going?'

Jack nodded.

'I saw. I'm more interested in how they pull up though. Come on. Let's get back in before we're both soaked.'

'Was that Emmie riding Peace Offering?' she asked as they got back into the vehicle.

'Yes. She usually rides out on him. She – and the others – can give us a better account of that workout when we're back at the yard.' Jack put his arm round the back of Pippa's seat and looked over his shoulder to reverse the Land Rover. Pippa felt the damp material of his sleeve brush the back of her neck and she looked across at him.

'Thank you,' she said, her voice soft with sincerity. 'I've really enjoyed this.'

Jack paused in manoeuvring the car to look at her.

Pippa was struck by the crystalline blue of his irises, encircled by a much darker shade. The colour wheel inside her head spun as she tried to pinpoint what paints she would need to mix to capture the distinct shades.

He averted his gaze first and removed his arm from behind her to change into first gear.

'It was just a gallop,' he replied. 'Lots of owners want to watch their horses do fast work.'

'And I can see why,' Pippa grinned. 'I can't wait to go racing.'

Jack's lips tightened into a grim line and he stared at the bumpy track leading down the hill.

'Let's hear what Emmie and the others have to say first.'

# Chapter Eleven

Pippa stood up straight, one hand holding a black bin bag, the other massaging the small of her back. She grimaced as her muscles took exception. With a weary sigh, she looked from the four bulging bin bags already lined up against the lounge wall to the detritus of old magazines and chipped bric-a-brac still littering the Welsh dresser. With a shake of her head, she picked one item up off the unit – what appeared to be a dirty rock about the size of her fist, and wondered what exactly it was that had made Dave want to keep it. She dropped it in the bag and picked up a crumpled piece of paper which had been flattened out again, a coffee stain ringing the upper right.

*Chepstow 1.15 – trifecta – Deuteronomy, Venetian Prize, White Fawn*
*Haydock 3.00 – Papago Prince e/w*
*Haydock 3.35 – Mister MacGuire*

The next was a bright yellow flyer announcing the 2001 Helensvale summer fete.

'God, Uncle Dave,' she moaned. 'You're worse than Mum when it comes to hoarding things.'

Dismissing the idea of going through each individual paper, she scooped the mass into one pile and pushed it all into the bag. The bag split and the papers slid onto the carpet. Pippa groaned. She closed her eyes and wondered if she should allow herself a break and make some dinner. At least the oven was clean now.

Her eyes shot open as the tinkling ringtone of her mobile sounded from the kitchen. Anything for a respite.

She hefted herself up onto the cracked kitchen counter then onto the windowsill, avoiding the row of chipped terracotta pots and brushed her hair behind her ear before answering the phone.

'Hi Tash,' she said, her tone cheerier now that she had an excuse not to clean.

'Yo, Pip. You all right?'

'Cleaning again, but much better than yesterday, thanks. How are you?'

'I need your advice. What would you do if you discovered one of the boys working in the Print Centre was mighty cute – think a young Orlando Bloom-cute – and you were tempted to ask him out for a drink?'

Pippa laughed.

'How young are we talking?'

'Maybe nineteen,' Tash said non-commitally.

'Christ, Tash. You cougar!'

'I'm only twenty-six! That's only...'

Pippa snorted as she imagined Tash counting out on her fingers.

'...only seven years difference.'

'Well, is that what's stopping you – the fact that he's younger than you?' she asked, trying to stop herself from laughing. 'If it is then you know age shouldn't make any difference.

'Yes and no,' Tash said in anguish. 'I'm also manager of his manager if you know what I mean.'

'Ah, hierarchy,' Pippa nodded. 'Going slumming, are you?'

'For want of a better word, yes.'

'Tash, you want my advice? Stop being a snob. If you like Orlando, ask him out. No one else has to know.'

'His name's Adam.'

'Okay. Ask Adam out then. Go for it, girl!'

Tash exhaled noisily into the phone.

'You're right. I will. Thanks. That's settled then. Now, more importantly, how are you and why has today been better than yesterday?'

Pippa grinned as she thought of the fun she had had that morning.

'Jack took me onto the Gallops to watch Peace Offering. It was so exciting. Peace Offering was fabulous, to the extent that even Jack was impressed. And Emmie – that's his work rider – said that when they'd ridden past us Peace Offering found another gear and took off with her.'

'Found another gear? What is he, a car?' Tash drawled.

'Apparently that's what they say when the horse starts going faster. Emmie told me she thought it might have been me jumping up and down in my red coat, but Jack's sceptical. Nevertheless, he said he's going to look at races for him next Saturday. Do you think you could come?'

'Depends on where it is, sweets. But I'll try.'

'Great. Anyway, that means Jack is back in my good books, you'll be pleased to hear,' Pippa continued, leaning her head back against the wall and thinking of the moody trainer. 'You can ignore that email I sent you yesterday.'

'What email?'

'You know. The one I sent you complaining what a prat Jack was being. I take it all back now.'

'Don't think I got that one. Maybe it disappeared into that big black e-hole. The same thing happened last week to me. Had a client supposedly send us confirmation on some proofs for a dinner menu, but did I get it? *Nooooo*.'

'Oh.' Pippa frowned and broke off a twig from one of the dead plants in the terracotta pots. She held it between her two fingers then looked around idly for her cigarettes. 'I did swear in it. Maybe your company's got a filter for rude emails. Never mind. I've forgiven him now –' She was interrupted by her phone beeping. She looked at the lit up screen and sighed. She had another call waiting. 'I've got to go, Tash. Ollie's trying to get hold of me. I'll speak to you soon.'

'No worries. Bye, Pip. Keep smiling.'

'You too. And good luck with Orlando.'

'Adam,' Tash corrected.

'Orladam.'


'Hey, Ollie. How are you, angel?' Pippa enthused a moment later. She had spoken to Ollie on a few occasions since she had left, but this was the first time he had actually called her.

'All right. Thought I might give you a ring now since I'm going out later. Didn't want you to call and interrupt dinner.'

Pippa pulled a face. She hadn't been planning on ringing Ollie at all.

'That's great. Who are you going out with?'

'Some people from the set. Rich Holden is coming along.'

Pippa scoured her memory for the name. By the tone of Ollie's voice, Rich Holden was someone she was supposed to know – or know of, she thought, remembering Ollie's tendency to name drop.

'An actor from *Holby City*?' she guessed.

'Yeah, you know him. He plays Doctor Feldman and is sleeping with his med student.'

'Of course. That sounds fun. Dinner, I mean. Where are you going?'

'Regan's and maybe The Watershed afterwards.'

Pippa felt a stab of longing for the buzz of London's bright lights and crowds.

'I miss you,' she said, tracing the twig still in her fingers down the window, keeping pace with a raindrop on the other side.

'I miss you too. It's not the same here without you. When do they collect the recycling here, can you remember? I put the rubbish out on Monday, but they only took the black bag.'

'Every second Monday. Make sure you put the tops off the plastic milk bottles in the black bag though. They won't take it otherwise.'

'Anal prats,' Ollie muttered.

Pippa snorted at his hypocrisy, but managed to turn it into a cough.

'Pippa, when are you going to give up smoking?'

'Soon. Listen, Jack's decided Peace Offering can have his first race next Saturday,' she said, changing the subject before Ollie could give her a lecture on the dangers of smoking. 'Will you come?'

She heard Ollie give an impatient sigh at the mention of Jack and Peace Offering's names. It was only because they both featured high on her current agenda of Life In The Country, she thought, trying to justify her reasons for always bringing them up in conversation with Ollie.

'I'll see. Depends on filming. My first episode is being shown around Valentine's Day. Gruesome love triangle, but I can't say much more. I'll let you know the exact date so you can record it.'

'I'm sure I won't miss it,' she reassured him.

'I know, but I want you to record it as well.'

The pride in his voice made Pippa smile and her heart softened.

'Okay. I'm proud of you, Ollie. I know things haven't been easy lately so I'm really pleased for you.'

'Me too. Anyway, I've got to dash if I'm going to make dinner. Rich hates people who are late. You should have seen him the other day when Jess, the make-up girl was late. She said her car had broken down, but she could easily have taken the Tube. Rich was furious –'

'Ollie,' Pippa interrupted, 'You'd better go. Tell me another time.'

'Shit. Look at the time. You're right. I'll speak to you soon.'

'Okay. Take care. Love you.'

'Me too. Bye.'

Pippa let the phone hang limply in her hand when the line was cut short then, with a sigh, she edged off the windowsill and counter. One of her buttock cheeks was numb. Rubbing some life into it, she wandered over to the fridge to fix herself some dinner.

# Chapter Twelve

The following Monday, Pippa was barely able to acknowledge Jack's entrance into the office as the phone trilled for about the twentieth time in as many minutes.

'Okay, if I can have your name and address I'll see what I can sort out for you,' she said to the caller. She saw Jack pause before going into his office as he stopped to listen to her conversation. 'Thank you, we're very proud of him too... Okay, Gerry. I'll make sure the farrier doesn't throw his shoes away. I'm sure there'll be a spare one for you... No problem. Bye.'

Jack raised an eyebrow and gave a mirthless chuckle.

'Souvenir collectors?' he said.

'Yeah. I've never known men get so excited about shoes before, and horseshoes at that. It's a pity Virtuoso's only got four feet.' She paused and grinned at Jack. 'Well done. Big race was it that he won yesterday?'

'Yes. A Grade One chase.' The frown lines on Jack's brow disappeared and Pippa was tempted to think that he might perhaps look *happy* for once. 'Did you watch it?'

'I did,' she replied, feeling smug. 'I might not know much about racing, but he certainly *looked* impressive. And by the sounds of it, the public think so too.'

'Won easily. Could have been more than twelve lengths if Rhys had asked for it.' His smile widened as he replayed the finish in his head. 'He did the right thing though, easing up like he did. We've got the King George next month and then another prep race before the Gold Cup at Cheltenham. We don't want to beat him up too much if we're to keep him fresh –'

The telephone interrupted him and Pippa reached for it.

'Wait!' Jack said, raising his hand. 'Before you answer that, if you have any calls from the press, just say Virtuoso has come out of his race fine and they can find my full statement in the *Racing Post*. I've got a telephone interview with them later this morning. Don't try answer any other questions. They're bound to ask for more.'

'Will do,' Pippa said, picking up the phone. 'Good morning, Aspen Valley Stables.'

Just before Jack turned away into his office, she saw him glance around him, a puzzled frown once more creasing his forehead. With a shake of his head, he left the reception.

Pippa smiled. She wondered how long it would take him to notice.

Five minutes later, Pippa knocked on Jack's door with his tea.

'That was the entertainment people just confirming they'll be round this afternoon to set up the marquee for the Open Day tomorrow.' She set his mug on a coaster. 'I hope the weather holds out.'

Jack peered at the chamomile tea then up at Pippa.

She held her breath.

Jack picked up the mug without comment and took a tentative sip.

She exhaled.

'Me too. Catering all sorted?'

'Yup,' Pippa said, pleased that for once she had completed a task without making a hash of it.

'That reminds me. Can I have a look at one of the owners' booklets? I just want to make sure the horses will be paraded in the right order for them all.'

Pippa hesitated.

'Owners' booklets?' she said, an icy tendril of fear contracting around her stomach.

Jack paused, his mug halfway to his lips. His eyes darkened.

'Yes, the *owners' booklets*, which everyone gets given tomorrow when they arrive so they know who they're looking at.'

Pippa gulped and moved her weight from one foot to the other.

'Um, was that something I was meant to know about, Jack? You never said anything about any booklets.'

Jack exhaled with dragon-force and put his mug down with a thud, slopping hot tea all over the desk.

'Jesus Christ! Haven't you had any deliveries?'

She shook her head.

Jack groaned.

'Gemma was meant to have organised it all before she left. Bloody hell. I should've checked before now, should've asked about them,' he muttered. He dragged his fingers through his hair and looked up at the ceiling, revealing tense muscles in his throat and neck. 'We've got a hundred and fifty people coming tomorrow to look at the horses and they're not going to know Virtuoso from fucking Peace Offering!' Jack's voice rose until he was shouting. 'Media! Owners! *Potential* owners!'

'Okay, okay, it might not be as bad as you think,' Pippa tried to placate him. The chamomile wasn't working its magic this time. 'Maybe Gemma has ordered the booklets. Which company is doing them for you? I can ring them and check.'

'Weatherbys did them last year for us. Jesus Christ. The Open Day is tomorrow.'

'Okay. Don't panic.' she said, backing out of the office. 'For all we know, Weatherbys have got them all ready and are just waiting for us to call. I'll just go do that...' Closing the door behind her, she dashed back to her desk.

Pippa's reappearance in Jack's office a minute later had him look up with hope. A wave of compassion swept through her when she saw his eyes, such a vivid blue, but now two shades darker with worry. Reluctantly, she shook her head.

Jack groaned and banged his head on his folded arms.

'What a fuck-up,' came his muffled response.

'There must be something we can do.'

'Like what?' he exclaimed, looking up. 'Scribble a hundred horses' names on a piece of paper and have you draw a picture next to each?'

Pippa bristled. Setting her jaw, she marched across the room until she was standing above her boss.

'Stop it,' she commanded. 'Right now –'

'Don't tell me what to do!'

Pippa raised a stern finger at him.

'*Listen to me, Jack,*' she said in a slow even tone. 'Do you have any booklets from last year? Give me one so I know what it looks like. Then give me the correct order you want them put in and I will sort it out –'

'You can't. You're only a bloody waitress!'

Pippa's blood began to simmer.

'I am also all you have right now. So do as I ask and stop wasting time.'

Jack glared at her and Pippa wondered if he was going to start throwing things around.

'What are you going to do?' he asked instead.

'I have a plan,' she said, not confident enough to say what exactly. 'Now, what about entries and declarations?'

'Only a handful, thank God. I'll have them ready for you in a few minutes.' He slid open a drawer and after rummaging around in it, retrieved a glossy A4 booklet. 'This was last year's,' he said, resigned.

'Fine.' She took it and walked away. 'One last thing, Jack,' she said, pausing at the doorway. 'Don't you *ever* talk to me like that again.'

Back at her desk, Pippa unearthed her mobile phone from her bag and with trembling fingers, scrolled through her address book.

'Hi Tash. It's Pip.'

'Hey, sweets! What're you doing calling me at work? Not another Jimmy Choos sale I've missed, is there?'

'Not quite.' She eased her quaking knees as she sank into her seat. 'I need to ask you a big big favour.'

'Sure. What's up? Are you okay?'

The concern in Tash's tone made Pippa want to cry.

'We've got an Open Day tomorrow and we've just discovered Jack's last secretary didn't order the booklets which get handed out. If I get all the info together, do you think you could bash something half-decent together before tomorrow?'

'Like what?'

Pippa flicked through the pages in front of her.

'Booklets. A4 size, colour with photos. About thirty pages. I guess about a hundred and fifty copies.'

'Blimey, Pip. I thought you were going to ask for a couple of flyers or something. But a hundred and fifty *full* booklets? In one day?'

Pippa felt the blood drain from her face. Tash was her one and only hope.

'Please, Tash. You have to help.'

'Design is backed-up at the moment. Your booklet sounds at least a full day's work for them. Then it's got to be printed. I'm sorry, Pip. Our schedule's manic –'

'What if I designed it then?' she said in desperation. 'What's the latest I could get it to you to be printed?'

'Well, ideally we ask for a week's notice, but I can see that not happening.' She paused and Pippa could imagine Tash's business brain clicking into gear. 'This is going to take you all day to do so it's not going to make print before close of business. What time does this thing start?'

'Half eleven.'

'Right. That's almost a full morning then. You do some artistic wizardry on your computer and get the design to me by half seven tomorrow morning and I'll slip it in the print queue and courier it over to you. We should make it.'

Pippa sighed with relief.

'Oh, thank you so much. I owe you big time.'

'So does Orladam in the Print Centre,' Tash drawled. 'This is called payback, baby.'

Pippa mustered half a smile.

'You went out with him then?'

'Yep. He was DJ-ing at a club over the weekend and he invited me to join him. He's twenty by the way.'

'Out of nappies then?'

'He was out of Calvin Kleins too, Saturday night. I'm thinking of changing his name to Aladdin rather than Orladam.'

Pippa laughed then covered her mouth so Jack wouldn't hear.

'You devil, you.'

'Pah! Devil nothing. Stop gassing. I've got work to do and so do you by the sounds of it. You can do it. Don't let that Jack Carmichael use you as a punching bag.'

'How –' It always amazed Pippa how Tash seemed to know exactly what was going through her head.

'I just do. Now go away and do some work.'


By lunchtime, Pippa had finished the entries and declarations, directed a call from the *Racing Post* through to Jack, promised six other people Virtuoso tail hairs and shoes, taken a call from the caterers asking whether she would prefer Winter Pimms rather than the summer variety, downloaded a programme off the internet on which she could design booklets and was now only just starting on the cover.

She looked at last year's cover, which was a simple photograph of two horses jumping a schooling fence out on the Gallops and "Aspen Valley Stables Horses In Training" written in plain black font. Pippa pulled a face. It was a bit... *boring*. She flexed her fingers and straightened her shoulders.

'Right.' If she was going to do anything with this booklet, then one thing for sure was that it would look good.

*

83

While snatching the occasional bite of her sandwich, she wrestled with the design programme, deciding on a photograph of Virtuoso clearing the water jump during his Cheltenham Gold Cup win last season. She saturated it with the red and white stable colours of Aspen Valley, the sun in the corner shedding pink rays across the background. She added a brush effect to both jockey crouching in his saddle and the horse stretching out to enhance the feeling of speed. In a bold Edwardian font she typed out *Aspen Valley Stables*.

Just as she tweaked the contrast and brightness of the picture to finish off the cover, the main office door opened and Finn stepped in. He scraped his boots on the wire mat and held up a piece of paper with a grin.

'Jack asked me to pass this on to you. It's a list of all our residents from Block A to Block H.' He handed Pippa the sheet of paper.

'Jack avoiding me, do you think?' she said. 'Who are the lucky ones to be kept in H Block?'

'By the look on your face, it should be Jack.'

She laughed and waved him away.

'Don't mind me. I'm just picking up on Jack's stress, is all. I don't know how tomorrow is going to pan out.'

Finn shrugged.

'It'll be good *craic*, I'm sure. Busy, but fun so long as the weather stays dry.' His eyes softened at her anxious expression. 'You'll enjoy it, I promise. Just serve them enough jars and they'll all be flamin' by two o'clock and then they won't care if a couple of things go wrong.'

'Oh, God. Don't say that. Enough has gone wrong already.'

Finn's laughing green eyes wavered from Pippa to the wall behind her.

'That's good.'

Pippa turned in her seat to look where he was motioning. *Hazyvale Dawn*, which she'd brought in with her earlier that morning, proudly adorned the wall.

'Thanks.'

Finn looked at her in surprise.

'You did that? Jaysus, what are you doing here sittin' behind a desk? You should be in a studio wearing a beret and smock, not here.'

'I wish. Maybe someday though,' she said, a trace of wistfulness escaping.

'What did himself think of it?'

Pippa giggled.

'Jack hasn't noticed yet. Well, I think he noticed *something* earlier, but he couldn't figure out what.'

'That's men for you, I'm afraid. I think it's grand. Will you be doing any more? It's brightened this place up, to be sure.'

Pippa thought of *Morning Stables*, but decided she would keep that picture for herself. The unintended inclusion of Peace Offering in it made it somehow more personal.

'I might do. The countryside around here is so beautiful. It's just finding the time.'

'Aye. Speaking of which,' he said, rolling up sleeve and looking at his watch. 'I've got to get on. Right ye be, Pippa.'

The clock on the opposite wall struck five o'clock and Pippa leaned back in her chair and stretched. Usually, around this time she would be packing up and thinking of dinner and what to tackle next in the cottage, but today those thoughts were far from her mind. At the forefront was the booklet, which she was still struggling with.

She groaned, knowing she would need Jack's help in order to complete it. Last year's version had a brief but fact-filled form write-up for each horse and she didn't have the faintest idea how to update them. Jack had promised to be back from the races by five, but there was still no sign of him or the horse lorry. Realising there wasn't much she could do until he returned, she dug through her handbag for her cigarettes and shrugging on her coat, headed for the door.

Outside, it was cold and already dark. By the glow of the electric light, she watched the stable staff finishing up their day. She needed a break, but for once, her cigarette tasted disgusting. She doused it in a puddle before throwing it in a nearby bin and retreating inside the office again.

She was rewording the introduction on the first page ten minutes later when Jack walked in. They looked at each other for a moment, an awkward silence filling the room.

'You're still here,' he said at last.

'No rest for the wicked,' she replied, attempting a smile. She needed Jack on her side if they had any chance of getting this booklet finished in time.

'How is the booklet looking?'

'Come see for yourself.' She pushed her chair back from her desk to make room for him. He walked around the reception unit and rested his hands on the desk, clicking on the different pages.

Pippa waited for his verdict, her hands intertwining.

'I-I need your help with the form write-ups,' she said, her voice quiet and humble.

Jack straightened up and nodded.

'Okay. Give me a minute.' He went into his office, reappearing a minute later, minus his jacket and wheeling his black leather chair to join Pippa in front of her computer.

Pippa edged sideways to make room.

'Right,' he said, once settled. 'Where shall we start?'

'With Box One would probably be best.'

Jack sighed and rubbed his eyes. Pippa noticed the dark circles beneath them. His hair was messy, making him look even more tired.

'Okay. Box One: Spurwing Island.' Jack picked up the old booklet and flicked through it. 'Lightly raced over hurdles. Has done well over fences, but doesn't like the ground too soft.'

Pippa bent over her keyboard, typing furiously to keep up.

'Am I going to fast?'

'No, you're all right.' She smiled at his concern. 'Carry on.'

'Er, doesn't like the ground too soft. Finished third in his last start in two-mile novice chase at Huntingdon. Ought to improve with step up in trip. Box Two: Dexter. Easy win on debut over hurdles in September after winning a bumper at Newbury last season. Stays well. Could be high class hurdler. One to follow...'

Three quarters of an hour later, Pippa stopped typing and flexed her fingers. Her eyelids felt lead-coated and her head hurt from staring at the computer screen all day.

Jack broke off mid-sentence.

'Do you want a break?'

'Would you mind?' she said, her eyes pleading.

'No. Go have a cigarette or something if you want to.'

'I'll make us a drink.'

She returned a couple of minutes later with two steaming mugs of coffee, placing one in front of Jack.

'I'm allowed coffee? What have I done to deserve such a treat?' he asked, raising a wry eyebrow.

The fact that for the past forty-five minutes he had been generally calm and courteous towards her had been enough for her to forgive him, at least temporarily, for being so rude.

'Figured you might need it. You look tired.'

'So do you,' he said, taking a noisy sip and looking over the rim at her.

'A bit. Today's been pretty hectic with everything going on.'

'You'll sleep well.' A faint smile parted his lips.

'Hopefully when I'm in my bed and not before,' she replied with a laugh. 'All I need is to fall asleep at the wheel. I could probably do with some caffeine tablets or something, but until then there's always this.' She held up her coffee, but paused when she saw Jack's face fall.

'Oh, shit,' he said, his tone thick with dread. '*Tablets*. I meant to stop off and pick them up on the way home. What's the time? Fuck, they're going to be closed soon.'

'What? Jack?' Pippa put down her mug and watched, speechless, as Jack hurtled out of his chair, making it crash against the back wall, and rushed into his office. 'What are you talking about, Jack?' she called after him. 'What tablets? Can't it wait 'til tomorrow?'

Jack appeared again, buttoning up his jacket and striding towards the exit.

'No. I've already forgotten twice. He's run out of his medication. Sorry, Pippa. I'll be back in half an hour at the latest. I've got to get his pills.'

'Whose?' Pippa cried, roused to her feet by the urgency in Jack's voice.

'Berkeley's!' he yelled over his shoulder as he ran out into the yard.

Pippa sat back down with a bump.

'The dog?' she said, feeling unimpressed.

Pippa sat in silence, finishing her coffee and listening to the whirr of the fan on her computer. She watched the hands on the clock-face fall past six then slowly start to rise towards the hour. She picked up her empty mug and Jack's untouched one and deposited them in the kitchenette's sink.

She was just fashioning an extra page of a lovely photo of the Gallops for the back of the booklet when Jack appeared at the doorway.

'Sorry about that,' he muttered.

Startled, Pippa leapt in her chair.

'Jesus, you frightened me,' she said, placing a hand on her chest.

'Sorry.' A mouth-watering smell wafted over to Pippa and she peered over the reception unit at the plastic bag he held. He lifted it onto the counter and began to unearth little plastic and foil cartons. 'Thought you might be hungry,' he mumbled, not meeting her eye.

'You bought us Chinese?' she said, a smile splitting her face.

Jack looked embarrassed and he busied himself placing the containers on the desk.

'We might be here for a while yet.'

'I'll go get plates,' Pippa grinned and hurried back to the kitchenette.

They ate in silence for a couple of minutes, interspersed by Pippa's giggles as she tried to master noodles with the complimentary chopsticks. A loop of sauce sashayed off one evasive noodle's tail and splattered her screen.

'Oops,' she said, stealing a glance at Jack as she wiped it clean.

Jack, perched on the desk, looked unmoved.

'Ollie and Tash were always wary of taking me out for dinner in public places,' she said.

'Tash your best friend?' Jack asked, trying to cut a spring roll in half with his chopsticks.

'Yeah. She's the one helping us with the printing of this damned thing.'

Jack nodded.

'And confidante?' He seemed to have lost interest in his food as he waited for Pippa to answer.

Pippa hesitated, struck by the almost hurt look in his eyes.

'Um, yes, I guess so. She's my best friend.'

'And your only ally,' Jack provided.

'Pardon?'

'Sometimes I shout because it's the only way I can be heard,' he went on, dropping his gaze and poking at his food. 'And if I come across as miserable to you then it might be because that way, if something goes wrong, it doesn't hit you in the gut as hard as if you went around thinking the world was full of roses.'

Pippa's hand flew to her mouth and she gasped.

'Oh, God. The email...' Her voice trailed off when Jack nodded. 'How?'

'You sent it to me by mistake.'

Pippa's heart dropped in mortification.

'I'm so sorry, Jack. I meant to send it to Tash. Really, I am so sorry,' she cried. 'It meant nothing, honest. I was just having a really bad day and needed to offload it onto someone, you know? I didn't mean all the things I said.'

Jack shrugged.

'Maybe it was for the best,' he said, popping a pork ball into his mouth and raising his eyebrows at her.

Pippa looked at him, wide-eyed and confused.

'*How?*'

'Maybe it's something I needed to hear –'

'But in that way? I'm sorry. It was hurtful and mean.'

'Maybe it was the only way I would have listened. On the other hand, it's good to know you aren't always the chirpy bunny. Your language is terrible by the way and what the hell does "Pack my box with five dozen liquor jugs" mean?' Jack delved through his noodles in search of another pork ball and to her disbelief, Pippa saw a smile start to tug at his lips.

'It's a typing exercise thing.' She paused, still uncertain. 'You mean you're okay?'

'I didn't go and cut myself some rope, no. I've grown a pretty thick skin. Having said that, it was a bit unnerving when I opened my emails in the morning and came across that. Then you arrived, smiling with a cup of that herbal concoction. It was a bit too Jekyll and Hyde for my liking.' His eyes twinkled as he watched Pippa's expression.

'I'm sorry, Jack,' she whispered.

'Forget it. Eat your food before it gets cold. And then we've got to finish this up,' he said, gesturing to the screen.

Pippa did as she was told. She tried to balance some soggy rice onto her chopsticks, her fingers shaking.

'Oh, fuck!' she blurted as the chopsticks clicked apart and the rice went flying. She bit her lips together to stop herself laughing as Jack peered down his front at the offending food now attached to his white shirt in a sticky brown glob. Without a word, he scooped it up with his forefinger and held it up to her.

'Would you like this back?' he said with a deadpan expression.

Pippa's resolve failed and she snorted.

'Um, no, thank you,' she giggled, trying – but failing – to mirror his expression. He ears burned and a flush crept up her neck.

Jack raised an eyebrow, smiled once and popped his finger in his mouth.

'And I'm the crazed bastard?' he said. 'I can see why your friends don't like to take you out.'

'Chirpy bunny?' Pippa retorted.

Jack covered his mouth with the back of his hand as he laughed.

A slow mocking rap on the reception door stopped them both. Melissa, her blonde hair wound in a stylish French roll above the fur lining of her coat, stood in the doorway.

'Is this a private party or can anyone join in?'

89

Jack choked on a rice grain.

'Melissa. Come in. There's no party,' he said, putting his plate down with a clatter and heaving himself off the desk. 'We were just – um, just...' He gestured to the cartons.

Pippa struggled to raise the smile only moments ago she had been unable to contain. Who was this woman who had Jack scurrying around like a naughty boy every time she appeared?

'Hello, Pippa. Working late?' Melissa said, raising an eyebrow, while at the same time offering her cheek for Jack's hurried kiss.

Pippa found the smile she had reserved for difficult customers at the restaurant.

'Hello. Just sorting things out for the Open Day tomorrow.'

'Leaving it a bit late, aren't you?'

'Just some last minute things,' Jack said with a vague wave of his hand. 'Couldn't be helped.'

'I see.' Melissa walked over to the reception unit and peered over, avoiding the rows of half empty takeaway boxes, to look at Pippa's computer screen.

Pippa tried hard not to glare at her and only just managed to stop herself from saying, '*It's porn*, Melissa. Yes, Jack and I were eating Chinese and looking at porn on the internet.'

'Were we meant to be going out tonight, Mel?' Jack said, scratching his head.

She gave him a thin smile, her red lipstick catching the gloss of the overhead light.

'No. I thought I would drop by on the off chance of a drink. I can't bear to go home. Daddy's having some dinner party for his French and Italian peers.'

'Well, we've still got a good couple of hours' work to finish off here,' Jack said doubtfully. 'You're welcome to stay though.'

Pippa gave a silent groan.

Melissa put her leather-gloved hand over Jack's arm and squeezed it.

'No. I can see you're both very busy,' she said, acknowledging the food cartons. 'So I'll leave you to it. Ta-ra, Pippa. Don't work my Jack too hard now.' She laughed and turned for the door. 'Walk me back to my car, Jack?'

Jack did as he was asked.

As they both disappeared round the corner, Pippa gave a sigh of relief so vast it could have revived a drowning whale.

When Jack returned, all their previous humour was now blatantly absent.

'Let's crack on, shall we?' he said, his manner brusque. With brisk movements, he stacked the plastic containers on top of one another and dropped them into the carrier bag and removed his plate from the desk. He sat back down without another word and sighed.

'Are you okay?' Pippa said, her tone gentle.

'I'm fine. Come on. If we hurry, we might get these done in an hour. What box are we on now?'

'Eighty-Two,' she said quietly.

'We've go to put in all the bloody horses for sale after that as well. Right. Eighty-Two: Think On Your Feet. God,' he muttered, reading the horse's form in the last booklet. 'This has got be the most inaptly named horse ever. Okay, here we go. Has run with promise, but has taken a knock to his confidence after a couple of falls last year. Switched back to hurdles, but disappointed on return at Exeter.'

'What does this mean in his last runs: 65RFU? Sixth, fifth, Royal Fuck Up?' Pippa asked as she typed.

Jack chuckled and shook his head.

'R means he refused, F means he fell, U means he unseated his rider. He can hardly put one foot in front of the other. Rhys says he updates his will each time he rides this horse. Eighty-Three...'

Pippa waited for him to continue then glanced at him when he didn't.

Jack cleared his throat.

'Eighty-Three: Peace Offering. Um, a sound jumper and stayer. Did not perform as well as hoped last year, but...'

'But?'

'...but has shown progress at home indicating potential for longer distance handicaps later this season.'

'And is a live Grand National contender?' Pippa prompted with a grin.

'Not yet, Pippa,' Jack replied, his voice grave.

'I know, sorry. I know you don't think he's good enough, but –' How could she convince him that having a dream wasn't a bad thing? A wave of exhaustion washed over her. She was suddenly too tired to press the matter. 'Never mind. Eighty-Four?'

Barely able to lift her fingers across the keyboard, Pippa clicked the pointer on *Send* and watched the email of attachments vanish from the outbox on her screen. With a groan, she folded her arms in front of her and let her head drop.

'I could sleep right now, right here.'

'Not advisable,' Jack said, standing up and wheeling his chair back into the office, colliding with the doorframe as he went. 'With the heater off, it's like an igloo in here.'

'You know, if an igloo is properly insulated, it's not actually that cold,' she said, still collapsed on her arms.

'I'll take your word for it,' he said, re-emerging. 'I, however, am going home.'

Pippa raised her head and scraped her curls out of her eyes, suddenly curious.

'Where is home, Jack?'

'On the other side of the hill past the Gallops. If you look closely, you can just see one of the outside lights on the brow, but the main house is on the other side. Are you going to be okay getting back?'

Pippa yawned and dragged herself to her feet.

'Yeah. If I can keep awake for another half hour, I'll be fine.' She shut down the computer and threaded her arms through her coat.

Jack waited by the door for her, ready with his keys.

Pippa rubbed her hands together as she stepped out into the frosty night air then stopped while Jack switched off the light and locked the door.

'Thank God that's done now,' he muttered as they walked to their cars.

'Yes. Now we've only got tomorrow to deal with. I hope Tash can get the booklets to us in time.'

'Yeah. I hope it doesn't rain either.'

They both looked up at the clear sky, alive with stars.

'Looks promising,' Pippa said. She rummaged through her bag for her car keys.

'You did good tonight, Pippa,' Jack said, his voice quiet. 'Thank you for your hard work.'

She grinned.

'No problem. Thanks for your help too.'

She unlocked the door to her Beetle and Jack held it wide for her as she stepped in.

'Well, goodnight, Jack.'

'Goodnight. Oh, and the picture in Reception? It's very good, Pippa. You're very talented.'

'Thanks,' she said with a shy smile.

Jack nodded and shut the door behind her.

# Chapter Thirteen

Pippa pulled into Aspen Valley's car park at eight o'clock the next morning, feeling surprisingly chipper considering her late night. As soon as she sat down at her desk, she telephoned Tash.

'No problem,' Tash reassured her. 'Aladdin is running it right now. I made a couple of adjustments, but nothing serious, don't worry. Should all be done in half an hour and the courier is on hold waiting for it.'

Pippa hugged herself with her free arm and gave an exultant sigh.

'Thank you, Tash. You've saved my arse.'

'Any time. Got to go. Call me later and tell me everything.'

'Will do. Thanks again. Bye.' Pippa hung up the phone and smiled at Jack's closed office door. He wasn't in yet, but she gave him a nod of satisfaction all the same. She got up and walked out into the yard.

Passing behind the far block of stables, she stopped to admire the billowing white marquee planted square in the middle of the lawn like a grounded spaceship. The horses whose stables opened out over this new spectacle looked on with interest at the dew-sparkling canvas flapping in the breeze.

'Ready for the masses?' a voice murmured in her ear.

Pippa jumped.

Finn grinned at her.

'I think so,' she said, recovering. 'It looks lovely, doesn't it, in the sunshine like that?'

'To be sure. And with the walking paddock not twenty feet away we'll be havin' a right time of it parading these horses, so. Eyes out on stalks at this contraption.'

'Oh, God,' Pippa laughed. 'I hope Peace Offering doesn't make a fool of himself.'

'Knowing him, he'll be more interested in the sausage rolls ye'll be serving.'

'That reminds me. Last night, I was thinking of what you said about getting the owners drunk and thought it might be nice if we could serve them mulled wine. I was going to give the catering company a ring to see if they could do it.'

'Good idea. The faster you get ol' man Mardling plastered, the better.'

'Mardling. That name rings a bell,' Pippa mused, thinking back to the booklet.

'So it should. He owns about a quarter of the horses here, including Virtuoso. Yer man, Jack is also walking round with Mardling's daughter on his arm.'

'Melissa? She owns Virtuoso? No wonder she's so up her –' Pippa stopped herself as Finn raised his eyebrows.

'Go on,' he cajoled.

'Nothing,' she said hastily. 'It just comes across as her walking about with Jack on her arm rather than the other way round.'

Finn laughed and wrapped his arm round Pippa's shoulders and steered her back towards the office.

'She's a man-eater. Of that, we're all in no doubt. She is her father's daughter.'

'What does Mr Mardling do?'

'Ken Mardling makes money,' Finn said with a shrug. 'He owns a textile business which he netted back in the eighties and made a fortune out of through Indonesian trade. Melissa is a fashion designer.'

Pippa was jolted by a stab of envy.

'How lovely to design clothes all day,' she murmured.

Finn chuckled.

'Don't you be getting jealous of Melissa Mardling. She has everything she wants, but is no happier than the rest of us.'

'Really?'

'Aye. You ever seen her smile?'

Pippa shook her head.

'Not a proper smile anyway.'

'And neither've I.' Finn nodded discreetly to someone just rounding the corner of the yard. 'And there's himself so we'd best be leavin' it there, so. Save me some smoked salmon snacks if there's any on offer.' He gave Pippa a friendly squeeze on the shoulder as they reached the racing office's door and walked away, his bow-legged stride sprightly.

Pippa leant against the cold brick of the office's outside wall and watched him stop at a stable to scratch the eager occupant behind the ears. She turned as Jack approached, his shoulders hunched as he spoke into his mobile phone.

'I understand, Lady Pennington, but Silver Dollar isn't due a fast work today and we only have time to watch the faster ones...' He raised his eyes heavenward as he passed Pippa and raised a finger in greeting before stepping into the office. 'No, I can't interrupt his programme by doing that. You're welcome to come watch him do his next fast work –'

Pippa followed him inside and grinned as he disappeared into his office with his fist clenched. 'Yes, I *realise* you're very busy...' He shut the door behind him, muffling the rest of his conversation.

By half past ten, the activity in the yard had doubled. The marquee company were back to finish setting up tables and chairs and the caterers had arrived with the buffet lunch and crates of glasses, plates and cutlery. After brief consideration, Pippa asked for a couple of long tables to be set up on the grassy centre of the stable block nearest the office and car park for welcome drinks to be served.

She looked on with satisfaction at the rows of gleaming glasses catching the morning sunshine set out on the starched white tablecloths, awaiting their patrons' arrival.

'Pippa, can you give me a hand?'

She turned to see Emmie, the stable lass, holding Peace Offering on the walkway. The horse's flanks steamed and a sweat-darkened imprint of a saddle stained his bare back. Pippa walked over and held out her hand for Peace Offering to sniff.

'Sorry. I know you're busy,' Emmie said. 'Can you hold him for a sec while I check his back foot? I think his shoe is loose and I was just about to put him on the walker.'

'Sure.' Pippa took the knotted lead rope offered to her. Peace Offering blew warm breath over her hand and nudged her arm. She grinned, remembering how nervous she had been that first day they'd met. It felt like an eternity ago. She watched as Emmie ran her hand down the horse's hindleg and he obligingly lifted it for her to inspect. Behind them, Pippa noticed one of the catering staff balancing three stainless-steel serving dishes in his arms on his way to the marquee. The young waiter could barely see over his load.

Suddenly, he tripped.

Pippa watched in horror as the dishes went flying. The crash resounded about the yard like a heavy metal band warming up for a gig. Her concern over the waiter was whipped away by Peace Offering, bounding forward in fright. Emmie sat down with a bump.

'Oh!' Pippa cried as the horse knocked her sideways too. Peace Offering threw up his head in alarm, whisking the rope out of her grasp and bolted. 'Wait!'

She watched helplessly as her horse galloped away. Despair turned to dread as she saw the direction he was heading for. The tables adorned with refreshments barred his way.

Peace Offering checked his stride, the lead rope looping wildly about his head, and gathered himself for take-off.

Pippa gasped as he arched over the neat rows of glasses and cups and saucers, folding his legs tight beneath him to avoid contact. She dug her nails into her palms, willing him to land clear. Her heart lurched as she saw the knotted end of the lead rope catch the underside of the table. The table flipped backwards. Amidst the shattering of glass, Peace Offering disappeared through a gap at the end of the walkway, his hooves skittering on the concrete as he escaped the chaos.

'Oh, my God,' wailed Pippa, running towards the wreckage.

Emmie, climbing to her feet, followed at her heels.

'Look at this mess,' Pippa moaned, gesturing to the glass fragments carpeting the ground.

'I'm so sorry, Pippa,' Emmie said, her eyes wide.

Speechless, Pippa looked at the girl then back to the debris.

'It – it wasn't your fault,' she managed at last. Swallowing hard, she paused for another moment. Thankfully, the adjoining table bearing the jugs of orange juice, Pimms and mulled wine had stayed upright, albeit with a serious amount of spillage. 'We've got to get this cleared up. And we have to find Peace Offering. Where's Jack?' She looked around warily.

'Up on the Gallops,' Emmie replied.

'Good. Best place for him right now. Emmie, you go find Peace Offering. Make sure he's all right. Billy? Tom?' she called out to a couple of stable lads standing with their mouths agape. 'Please can you help get this mess cleared up? I've got find us some more glasses.'

Pippa ran back to the office, struggling to keep her calm.

The woman on the other end of the line sucked her teeth.

'I'm sorry, Miss Taylor. We can't supply any more glasses. Not at this short notice. We've got other functions on today as well and we're only a small company.'

Pippa closed her eyes and dragged a hand through her discordant curls.

'Not even a few?' she asked, thinking they might be able to salvage some cups and glasses from the wreckage.

'Not even a few, love.'

'Okay,' she sighed. 'Thanks anyway and – um, sorry about the damage.'

'Don't worry. That's why we charge you a deposit.'

'Great,' she said through gritted teeth, thinking of what Jack's reaction would be. 'Bye.'

Putting down the phone, she snatched up her handbag and coat and dashed to the door. Billy and Tom were bent over in the middle of the yard with thick plastic grain sacks in their gloved hands, methodically dropping shards of glass and china into them.

She raced as fast as her heels would allow towards the car park. As she wrenched open her car door, a familiar bay head appeared from around the corner of the hay barn. Beside him, with the lead rope loose in his hand, was Finn.

'What's going on?' he said, frowning at Pippa's ashen face. 'I find this ol' boy stuffing his face in the barn and now you flapping around like a chicken.'

'Finn,' Pippa breathed in relief. 'I can't stop, sorry. Peace Offering got loose and knocked over one of the tables. I've got to go find some more glasses from somewhere. People are going to start arriving any minute. Are there any other catering companies in Helensvale?'

Finn chewed his lip then shook his head.

'Not as such, I don't think. Hang on, I'll come with you. In fact –' He paused, looking at Pippa's VW Beetle. '– we'll go in my car.'

Relief gushed through her.

'Aren't you meant to be riding though?'

'Not until later. Wait a minute while I get someone to take Peace Offering.'

He set off at a jog with the horse, who danced beside him, his head held high and ears pricked, oblivious to the mayhem he'd caused.

Pippa wavered by her open car door.

Finn was back in seconds and he motioned her over to his mud-splattered Honda Civic.

'Come on,' he said. 'We might get lucky with one of the pubs.'

Pippa was thrown against the passenger door as Finn pulled out of Aspen Valley and put his foot down. The countryside rushed past her in a blur of greens, blues and browns. She closed her eyes and gripped the edges of her seat with clammy hands as Finn rounded a blind corner in the middle of the road. In contrast, the jockey lounged in his seat, his left leg bent nonchalantly against the gear box and his fingers tapping the wheel.

'You okay?' he asked, looking at Pippa and grinning at her stricken expression.

'Just concentrate on the road, if you don't mind,' she replied.

'We'll be there in no time at all.'

True to his word, they were soon upon the small town of Helensvale. With little traffic around, Finn pulled into a parking space right outside The Plough.

'I'll try here,' he said as they reconvened on the pavement. 'There's an Indian restaurant a couple of doors down. The Moulin Raj. You go there.'

Pippa nodded and hurried down the street, skipping over the uneven paving slabs. She pushed the door to the restaurant and nearly head-butted the glass when it stayed firmly shut. She groaned when she saw noticed the skewed *Closed* sign swinging from the window. Praying that Finn was having more luck than she was, she retraced her steps back to the pub, reaching the entrance just as Finn walked out.

He shook his head.

'They won't do it,' he said.

Pippa's shoulders slumped.

'There's nowhere else around here that I can think of,' Finn went on. 'Bristol is the nearest place.'

'That's miles away though,' she said. 'The Open Day is meant to start in less than half an hour!' She looked around in desperation. On the opposite side of the road was the café she had visited on her first trip to the West Country.

'The caff,' she gasped, grabbing Finn by the arm and pulling him with her as she dashed into the road. 'We can try there.'

A jangling bell announced their entrance and Pippa recognised Wendy, the owner, look up from her stool behind the counter. With a grimace, the woman heaved herself to her feet and placed her hands wide on the linoleum tabletop.

'What'll it be?' she said in a bored voice.

'Well, this is probably a bit of an unusual request,' Pippa said, wringing her hands. 'But we were wondering if you might have any cups and glasses we could borrow – I mean hire – from you.'

Wendy looked at her as if she had just requested a hot air balloon ride. She folded her arms across her chest.

'This is a caff, love, not a caterers.'

Pippa fixed her with pleading eyes.

'I know. And we did have a caterers, but all the glasses got broken and now we've nothing to serve the owners drinks with. Could you help?'

Behind Wendy, the gawky figure of Randy appeared, the paper chef's hat lopsided on his head.

'You 'avin' a Greek party?' Wendy said.

'No, it's the Open Day at Aspen Valley. One of the horses got loose and smashed through one of the tables. Please say you can help?'

Wendy pulled a face.

'How many cups are we talking here?'

'As many as you can spare. We're expecting about a hundred and fifty people.'

Wendy's bosom shook as she laughed.

'Love, I couldn't lend you that many even if I wanted to.'

Randy peered over Wendy's shoulder.

'Ain't you the Styrofoam cup lady?' he said.

'Yes,' Pippa said, resigned.

'We just got a delivery of those type cups yesterday,' he said.

Wendy frowned at him, her arms still folded.

Randy stepped forward.

'We can let her have an 'undred and fifty of them, can't we?' he said to his boss.

'Well, I suppose we could do that,' she conceded. 'But they won't come free.'

Pippa thought fast. Her options were limited, to say the least. She looked at Finn and swallowed.

'Yes,' she said, mirroring his nod. She opened her bag to fish out her purse. 'Yes, that would be wonderful. Thank you ever so much.'

Jack pounced on Pippa the moment she walked back into the yard.

'Where've you been?' he hissed. 'People have already started to arrive.'

'I can see that,' she stage-whispered back, glancing at a well-dressed couple wandering along the stable walkway.

She fumbled with the awkward tubes of stacked Styrofoam cups in her arms as she stepped into the office.

'And what the hell are those?' Jack said, following her in.

'I'll explain everything later.' Her attention was caught by a messily-taped brown box sitting on the reception unit. 'Please tell me those are the booklets.'

'They arrived about five minutes ago,' Jack nodded.

Pippa let the cups roll out of her arms onto her desk and scooped out a booklet. The smell of fresh ink chemicals and gloss paper filled her nostrils. She stroked her fingers over the smooth red cover then flicked it open, scanning each page. She grinned at Jack.

'Looks pretty good if I do say so myself,' she couldn't help gloating. 'What do you think?'

Jack still looked flustered and he threw a hand in the air.

'Yes. Very good, Pippa. Well done.'

'No need to look so pleased,' she said, her pride dented.

Jack looked at her, exasperated.

'They'll be no good to anyone unless we get them out there,' he said, pointing to the door. 'Come *on!*'

Pippa kissed the booklet.

'Thank you, Tash,' she said, hugging it to her chest.

'Ah, yes. Tash. She put this note inside for you, by the way,' Jack said, his tone dry. He handed Pippa a compliments slip that had been lying beside the box.

*Here you go, Pip. I had to promise Aladdin a blowjob for this. You owe me, sweets. Tash xxx*

Pippa grinned.

Jack shook his head.

'I'm not even going to ask,' he said.

'I'll explain another time.' She lifted out more booklets from the box, balancing them against her chest.

Outside, she was relieved to see the tables were back in place. There was no evidence of the carnage from half an hour earlier. She did, however, notice Billy letting himself into a nearby stable with his hand now wrapped in a bandage. She was grateful to find a few lonely glasses and cups had been saved and were being passed, filled with the desired refreshment, to some newly-arrived owners by Emmie.

'Everything okay?' Pippa asked in a quiet voice as the owners drifted away. She placed the booklets on the corner of the table.

'So far, so good. Did you manage to find some glasses?'

'Of a sort,' she replied dubiously. 'I'm going to need your help though in a sec. Can you cover for me for just a short while longer?'

'Um, okay. I've got someone taking out my lots, but I'm going to have to ride soon.'

Pippa held up her hands.

'Just hang in there,' she said and dashed back to the office.

Scooting her chair close to her desk, Pippa opened a new document on her computer, selected a bold red font and began to type furiously. After a few seconds, she yanked open her stationery drawer and pulled out a wad of card paper and slotted it into her printer.

'Please work,' she murmured, pressing the Print button.

The machine hummed and hawed then mechanically began spewing out her typed document. Pippa banged the printed papers together on the desk to straighten them and ran over to Jack's office, where she had noticed before there was a miniature guillotine. Taking extra care of her fingers, she made a rough measurement and chopped the papers into thirds, wincing as the handle bruised her palm. Holding a strip of card up, she nodded, satisfied. She rushed back to the office entrance and called to Emmie, hurrying her over with her hand.

She split the pile of cards in half and handed one to Emmie then picked up a tube of Styrofoam cups and handed it to her like a soldier in a gun parade.

'Help me with these,' she said, giving the bewildered-looking stable lass a stapler.

'What is this?' She looked at the strips of paper and read it out loud. '*Aspen Valley Stables.* What are these for?'

'To stop your fingers getting burnt,' Pippa explained.

She held up a strip with the loopy red writing on it and folded it into a cylinder, then used her stapler to seal it. She took a cup off the top of the tube in Emmie's arms and slotted it into the hole.

Emmie looked impressed.

'Wow, were you a big fan of *Blue Peter* when you were younger?'

'I have all the badges,' Pippa winked. 'Come on. Let's get cracking. If we get these done in ten minutes, I'll buy you a round tonight.'

'You're on,' Emmie laughed and started folding.

With a couple of minutes to spare, Pippa and Emmie marched out of the office bearing the now brightly-coloured cups against their shoulders.

'Just in time,' Pippa murmured as a flock of new arrivals wandered in from the car park. With Emmie dispatched to saddle up her next lot, Pippa waited with a ready smile for her next guests. Walking towards her was Jack with Melissa and a much older man. His bald head, freckled with age spots, reflected the bright sunlight like a bowling ball. She recognised him from the trophy presentation she had watched on television when Virtuoso had won on Sunday. This must be Ken Mardling.

'Two Pimms please,' Melissa said.

*Nice to see you too, Melissa,* Pippa said silently. *Yes, everything got finished in the end. Thanks for your concern.*

'Of course.' The rebel in her made her hesitate as she reached for two of the few glasses still on the table. Instead she picked up two Styrofoam cups and poured warm Winter Pimms into them. She held them out to Melissa and her father with a gracious smile.

Jack looked on in horror.

Melissa took her cup between one manicured finger and thumb and held it up to read the writing.

'How very – *quaint,*' she said, smiling at Pippa.

Ken Mardling looked at his cup, turning it as he read the inscription and pulled an indifferent face before taking a long sip.

Jack stared at Pippa, dumbstruck.

'Mr Mardling,' she said, avoiding her boss' gaze. 'Congratulations on Virtuoso's win on Sunday. He was brilliant to watch. Rhys could so easily have won by further.'

Ken Mardling puffed out his chest.

'Thank you. It was a very satisfying result.'

'Would you like a copy of our Horses In Training booklet?' she said, picking up a copy and holding out to him.

He took it from her and held it at arm's length to peer long-sightedly at it. He beamed when he recognised Virtuoso on the cover.

'Very good, very good,' he muttered and turned to walk away with Melissa by his side.

Jack hung back and leaned over the table.

'We'll speak about this later,' he whispered through clenched teeth.

But not even his simmering rage could dampen Pippa's mood. The booklet might not be perfect, but it was decent enough, and more importantly it was *there.* The cups might not be what they had planned, but she had sorted it out and again, they were *there.*

Yes, Pippa glowed, she was very proud of herself.

# Chapter Fourteen

The Plough was crammed that night and toasting from its patronage of alcohol-warmed bodies. Pippa had to weave a sideways dance to get from the door to the bar counter. She struggled to remove her coat while she waited to be served. Not for the first time, she cursed her five-foot-three stature as she tried to spot Emmie. She balanced on the brass foot rail that encircled the bar and peered over the sea of bobbing heads. Amidst the throng, she glimpsed Emmie over at the pool table in the corner.

The stable lass stood against the patterned sea-green wall, her cue stick planted in front of her as she waited for her opponent to take their shot. Pippa squinted at the spirits bottle she raised to her lips, then, satisfied, she turned to make her order.

After tripping her way through the crowd, she felt almost isolated in comparison when she reached the pool table, people respectfully giving the players space.

'Pippa!' Emmie said, her voice raised above the chatter and music of the pub.

Pippa grinned and held up a bottle of WKD for Emmie.

'I promised you a drink earlier.'

'So you did. Ta – Billy, come on. You don't have to play like an idiot just because I'm a girl.'

Her opponent, his hand now only strapped with a plaster rather than a bandage, looked up, offended.

'I'm not. I'm just trying to pot the ball.'

'Oh. Okay.' Emmie lapsed into silence.

Pippa looked on with interest.

Billy, his short brown hair plastered neatly to his skull with gel, frowned in concentration. He tapped the ball and it rolled obligingly into the far pocket.

'Ha!' Emmie said in triumph. 'Thank you for that. Two shots to me.'

'What?' Billy frowned.

'I'm solids, you're stripes. Remember?'

'Aw, fuck it,' he scowled and withdrew to the table where Pippa had just placed her and Emmie's drinks to retrieve his own. 'All right, Pippa?'

'Can't complain. How's the hand?'

Billy flopped his hand around to show it wasn't painful.

'Got a shard of glass in it when cleaning up this morning. Ain't sore or nothing.'

'Thanks for helping,' Pippa grinned.

'No problem.' A scowl returned to his unlined face as Emmie sunk another ball. 'Here, give us a chance. I'm playing handicapped,' he called, holding up his hand.

Emmie, a wicked grin on her face, merely glanced in his direction before returning to her shot.

'Evenin' all,' a rich Irish brogue interrupted whatever Billy was about to rebuke Emmie with.

With an unfamiliar feeling of almost pleasurable surprise, Pippa turned, coming face-to-face with Finn.

'I didn't know this was your local, Pippa?' he said.

'First time in here,' she replied. 'Nice place.'

'Aye,' he nodded. 'But come the weekend, it can get a bit mad. Noisier than a skeleton wankin' on a tin roof when they've got a live band in.'

Pippa choked on her drink, trying to swallow and giggle at the same time. A groan from Billy beside her made her look back at the pool table. Emmie was busy sinking the black ball to win the game.

'Would you like a game, Pippa?' Billy offered. 'You and Emmie?'

Pippa shook her head.

'I'm useless, really. I don't even know how to hold the pole thing.'

'Called a cue stick, a thaisce,' Finn said. 'Whyn't we have a game of doubles? Me and Pippa against you and Emmie.'

'Okay, but I warn you, Emmie's a shark,' Billy said.

Finn grinned.

'Maybe so, but I'm just as savage. To the extent that I share the same name as part of a shark's anatomy.'


Pippa leaned over the table, the unfamiliar stick in her hands, and clumsily bounced it off her splayed knuckles. She felt her right hand become enfolded as Finn leaned over her. His thumb caressed the inside of her wrist and Pippa gulped.

'Just relax,' he murmured in her ear. His breath was hot on her cheek as he stretched forward to correct her bridge. The scent of his cologne was intoxicating. 'Think of it as playing the violin.'

'I don't know how to play the violin,' Pippa faltered.

'Neither do I, so, but this is how I'd imagine it works.'

Pippa's initial discomfort dissolved into giggles.

'That's better,' Finn said. 'Slide it over your bridge, rather than pushing it. Concentrate on the ball you want to pot, not the white ball. Then it'll be easier to hit.'

With Finn's body framing her own, his hands guiding hers, Pippa tapped the white ball, watching with bated breath as it kissed the side of another, which smartly rolled into a side pocket.

'I hit it!' she said, turning her face sideways to grin at Finn. Beneath the light hanging over the pool table, she noticed the tips of his dark eyelashes were tinged with a red blond.

His Adam's Apple bobbled as he swallowed.

'Aye, you've hit it all right,' he replied, his green eyes holding Pippa's in an intense fix. He loosened his grip on her hands, allowing her to straighten.

You still have a boyfriend, remember? a steely voice in her head cut through Pippa's haze of uncertainty. She gave Finn a weak smile and glanced at Emmie and Billy.

They were both staring, their drinks half-raised, their mouths open at Pippa and Finn. Emmie was first to regain her composure.

'Good shot, Pippa,' she said, nodding vigorously.

Billy joined in, even clapping to overcome his shock.

'Yeah, you're a natural, like. We might be in some trouble here, Emmie.'

# Chapter Fifteen

Pippa wasn't wholly sure Jack had forgiven her for the Styrofoam cup debacle. He certainly wasn't praising her for her ingenuity. Nevertheless, the day before Peace Offering's first run of the season he had dropped a couple of owners' badges on her desk and asked if she had needed a lift over to Ascot.

'Thanks, but I'm going to stay in London for the rest of the weekend,' Pippa had replied.

Now Saturday had arrived and Pippa sat in one of Ascot Racecourse's bars, her frozen hands wrapped around a glass of mulled wine. Somewhat apprehensively, she watched her fellow-racegoers while they referred to their racecards and studied the televisions mounted high on the walls showing the Tote betting. It was all a meaningless jumble of numbers to Pippa, but everyone around appeared to have no trouble deciphering them. She pulled up the sleeve of her beige and cream fake fur-lined coat and glanced at her watch for the 'nth time.

She was about to resort to checking her mobile for any missed calls when she heard her name being called.

Tash trotted towards her, dangling a vast black handbag from her shoulder.

Grinning, Pippa stood down from her stool and held out her arms to receive her friend's enthusiastic embrace.

'Ooh,' Tash cooed, hugging her from side to side. 'I've missed you so much. How are you, Pip?'

'Much better now you've arrived,' Pippa said. She cast a cautious look around the warm busy room as she sat down again. 'I feel a bit out of place here. I don't even know how to place a bet.'

'Probably half the people here don't know either. You've just got to look like you belong and no one will doubt you.' Tash smoothed her dark bob of hair away from her face and put her leather-gloved hands on her broad hips. She frowned at the screen closest to her, nodding with apparent knowledge.

Pippa laughed.

'That's all well and good until you get to the Tote window.'

Tash pulled out a stool from beneath the high oval table and sat down, crossing her legs and extending a black suede-booted foot.

'What do you think of these?'

Pippa scrutinised the boot's silver studs encircling the ankle and calf and nodded in approval.

'Very nice. I thought you already had a pair like this?'

Tash grimaced.

'I do, I know, but I got sick of the tassels on the last pair. So I bought these as my reward for asking Aladdin out. Do you have any shoe shops where you live?'

'One,' Pippa giggled. 'In fact, I bought a new pair of boots there a couple of weeks ago.'

'Nice ones?'

'They call them Wellingtons.' Pippa laughed at Tash's shocked expression.

Tash leant forward and held her friend's face in her hands with exaggerated tenderness.

'Sweets, are they turning you into a country bumpkin? Do you know how to milk a cow and drive a tractor yet?'

'No, not yet. I wouldn't mind learning how to drive a tractor though. It could be quite fun. Jack has one at Aspen Valley.'

'Ah. The man whose name is never far from your lips. Where is he?'

'That's not true, at least not for the reasons you would like to think,' Pippa said sternly. 'It's just that he's one of the few people I know out there. Anyway, I think he's probably with some owners. We've got a runner in the next.'

'When can I meet him?'

Pippa shrugged.

'He said he would come fetch us here before Peace Offering's race so I guess then.'

'Good,' Tash said, smacking her hands together in a gesture of anticipation. 'Now, in the meantime, I need a drink. What are you having?'

Half an hour later, her confidence bolstered by her friend and the alcohol, Pippa joined the queue in front of the Tote window.

'Um, twenty pounds – I mean quid – on Peace Offering, please,' she said, slapping a bank note on the counter.

The lady on the other side of the Perspex glass looked nonplussed.

'To win or to place?'

108

'Er, well, I hope he'll win,' Pippa replied, her bravado faltering. 'What's the difference?'

'Place odds are lower than a win,' the lady explained. 'That's because you get paid out if your horse finishes in the first three, regardless of which position.'

Reminding herself of Jack's less than enthusiastic belief in her horse, Pippa said,

'Okay, I'll go for a place then.'

'Place on Number Eight. There you go.' She slid a betting slip under the window to Pippa.

Pippa looked at it, her fingers trembling with excitement. She stood to the side while Tash placed her bet.

'The lady said place odds were lower than win odds, but this says I'll win a hundred and seventy-five pounds if he comes in the first three,' Pippa said once Tash had joined her again.

'Sweets, I don't know if that's very encouraging. How many horses is he up against?'

Pippa pulled her racecard out of her pocket and flipped it open to the 2.30 three-mile steeplechase.

'Says here there are thirteen runners. That's not too bad. He's only got to beat ten of them for us to win some money.'

After deciding against another drink so close to Peace Offering's race, the pair returned to their table to wait for Jack. Pippa was reading her racecard when she heard Tash give a long low wolf whistle.

'My, my, my,' she murmured. 'I see now why you can't stop talking about him. He's better in the flesh than he is on Google Images.'

'What?'

Pippa swivelled on her stool to see Jack standing at the doorway of the bar. His familiar Clint Eastwood frown creased his forehead as he scanned the sea of heads for her. Their eyes met and he strode towards them, the crowd of people around seeming to part before him like the Red Sea.

For a moment, Pippa allowed herself to see what Tash was seeing. She couldn't resist admiring his piercing eyes again and she conceded that he did exude an extreme amount of testosterone with his strong jaw framed by the upturned collar of his black Mafia-style trench coat. In one large hand, he grasped a pair of binoculars and the other, he lifted in greeting.

'Hello, Pippa,' he nodded as he reached them.

Tash shot out her hand, nearly falling off her stool in the process and Jack transferred his binos to his other hand to shake it.

'Jack, this is Tash Bradley, my friend. Tash, this is Jack Carmichael, my trainer and boss.'

Jack's eyes twinkled with mirth.

'So *you're* the infamous Tash?'

'Infamous in a bad way, I hope,' Tash murmured.

Pippa kicked her none too subtly on the ankle.

'Let's say an interesting way,' Jack replied, a smile playing on his lips.

Pippa could see him re-reading the compliments slip which had accompanied the booklets a few days ago in his head.

'I believe we owe you a big thank you for your help with our Open Day booklets. I hope it wasn't too much of –' He paused, searching for the appropriate word, '– an inconvenience for you.'

'No inconvenience at all,' Tash smirked. 'All part of the job.'

'Job being the operative word,' Pippa muttered. 'Shall we go see Peace Offering?' she suggested. She didn't know what was worse: Tash flirting with Jack or Jack flirting back.

'Good idea,' Jack said. 'I've got to go collect his saddle etcetera, but I'll meet you in the saddling area.'

They walked to the door and Jack stepped aside, holding the door open for them. He directed them where to go then departed towards the weighing room.

'My God,' Tash squeaked once he was out of earshot. 'How can you concentrate at work with that man – that sex god – next to you?'

Pippa wrapped her coat more firmly around her as a blast of cold wind blew across them.

'Believe me, his temper is much more distracting. Suggesting we go see Peace Offering is the first *good idea* he's ever said I've had.'

'Pip, if you can keep your muffs off that hunk until Grand National then you deserve a medal. In fact I will give you my new Jimmy Choos *and* pay for a psychiatric consult.'

Pippa shook her head and laughed.

'Not going to happen, Tash. Don't forget Ollie.'

Her friend raised her eyes to the overcast sky and held up her hands in defeat.

'How could I forget Ollie? Sweet devoted soul that he is.'

'Careful,' Pippa warned. She paused as they showed their badges to the paddock attendant and walked towards the boxes where horses were already being saddled for the next race. 'I know you're not keen on Ollie. You just don't understand what he's been through lately so let's not go down there.'

'Okay, okay. My bad. Where is he?'

Pippa puckered her lips before answering.

'He had to work.'

'Uh-huh,' Tash replied, sounding far from convinced.

Pippa stopped and gave her friend a meaningful look. Ollie's non-appearance was enough of a disappointment without her best friend rubbing it in.

'Tash, please can we leave it there?' She looked around the boxes and caught sight of Emmie standing outside one. Inside she could just see a bay head and white blaze. 'Look, there's Peace Offering. Come meet him.'

'Are you scared?' Tash asked as they shouldered their way through the throngs of spectators. Jack led them up the grandstand steps to a less crowded row.

'A bit,' Pippa grinned, her teeth clenched against the bitter wind which was sweeping through the stands. 'More nervous than anything. I hope he doesn't fall. How many fences do they have to jump?' she said, turning to Jack on her right.

'Thirteen and two circuits. Ascot's quite a stiff course, but he's a good jumper and Rhys Bradford's the best jockey around,' he replied. He held up his binos to watch the horses canter to the Start.

'So we might have a chance then?' Pippa said hopefully.

'A thirty-three-to-one chance, yes,' he replied, quashing her optimism. 'The favourite is Freewheeler and he's only carrying three pounds more than Peace Offering. He should be carrying more, but his jockey is claiming five.'

'Okay,' Pippa said slowly. 'Explain what that means, please?'

'Conditional jockeys are given a weight allowance because they're supposed to be less skilled than professionals. Rhys is a professional so he can't claim anything.'

'Oh. That's a pity,' she said, pulling a face.

'On the other hand,' Jack carried on, seeing her woebegone expression, 'he's still got the third lightest weight in the field and the ground is heavy. There'll be some tired horses by the end of this.'

'They're lining up,' Tash said, grasping Pippa's arm.

Pippa bit her lip and dug her fingernails into her palms as the thirteen horses grouped together and began to jog towards the starting tape.

'And away they go in this three-mile handicap chase,' the commentator announced, his voice echoing around the grandstand. 'Night Owl is first to show and leads them through the first furlong, to Raven's Way in second alongside Freewheeler, the four-to-one favourite.'

Pippa swayed back forth in time with the horses striding away from the stands to the far corner of the course. She could just make out Peace Offering and Rhys in his green and red-striped silks racing towards the rear of the bunched field.

'...They take the first...'

Pippa closed her eyes and clutched Tash's hand still holding her arm.

'...and they're all over safely...'

She opened her eyes again to see Rhys still riding high in his stirrups.

'...They approach the next plain fence. A big leap there from Raven's Way and he jumps into the lead. A mistake midfield from outsider, Blue Barney, who drops back to last...'

She darted a swift glance at the big screen opposite for a closer look and was relieved to see Peace Offering still travelling sweetly, his ears pricked and his reins flapping loosely in Rhys' easy grasp.

'...Now for the first open ditch. Another big jump from Raven's Way! Night Owl was a bit clumsy and forfeits second...'

'How are we doing?' Pippa hissed in Jack's ear.

'Okay,' he replied, not taking his eyes off the galloping horses. 'Early days yet. The next fence is the water.'

'Oh, God,' she moaned. 'I can't watch.'

Despite herself though, she leaned forward as Rhys gathered his mount for an almighty leap across the water and nearly fell over the chairs in front of her.

Jack and Tash hauled her upright.

'...So now, as they reach the top turn and start making their way back towards the stands, Raven's Way leads narrowly over Freewheeler. Two lengths back is Henchman on the outside of Night Owl with Spanish Hawk and Peace Offering racing just behind...'

Pippa squeaked at the mention of her horse's name and watched in breathless excitement as the strung-out field of horses thundered towards the next row of fences.

'...And Night Owl is a faller!' the commentator cried, making Pippa's knees give way. 'He's hampered American Smooth who has been making progress up the inside, but his jockey seems to have him back in a rhythm now. They round the turn into the home straight for the first time. Still two miles to travel...'

'Two miles?' Pippa quailed. 'Half of them already look knackered.'

'As long as Peace Offering isn't one of them, we don't mind,' Jack muttered. 'Shit!'

Pippa gasped as her horse put in an awkward stride and brushed through the thick of the next fence, sending the birch flying. To compensate, Peace Offering took off a stride early at the jump closest to the stands, stretching out his head and forelegs to clear it.

Pippa grabbed Jack's arm, unable to stand by herself. Unaware of the tight hold she had on him and Jack's tense glance at her, she watched, terrified and thrilled in equal measure, as the horses galloped away for the final circuit of the track.

'...Raven's Way is coming under pressure now as Freewheeler ranges up alongside. Back in third, Henchman still travels on the bridle with American Smooth on his inside. Blue Barney is being pulled up. Here's the next...'

Pippa squeezed her eyes shut.

'He's over safe,' Jack said.

'This is agony!' Pippa said. 'How many more?'

'Five. This is when weight comes into play.'

'Oh, God. Where is he? Come on, Peace Offering! Come on, Rhys!' she cried, seeing Rhys lower his posture in his saddle. With mounting excitement, she watched the bay stick his neck out and begin to move ahead of Spanish Hawk.

'...Now for the last open ditch. Freewheeler spring-heels it! Raven's Pass less fluent in second. American Smooth takes it in third. Henchman veers left and blunders badly, upsetting Peace Offering!'

Pippa sucked in her breath and hid her face against Jack's arm. She looked up in time to see Rhys pull his horse clear of their floundering rival. He pushed him forward in earnest.

'...They've only two more to jump!' the commentator said, his voice rising an octave.

Pippa began to jibber, hopping up and down in constrained excitement.

'...Freewheeler has extended his lead to three lengths. American Smooth joins Raven's Way in the air! That bump from Henchman has knocked the stuffing out of Peace Offering and Rhys Bradford is working hard to build up the momentum again. He might be too late though...'

'No!' screamed Pippa in reply. 'Don't say that! Come on, Peace Offering! You can do it!'

Jack was silent beside her, in contrast to Tash who was swiping the air with her fist and yelling like a football yob.

'...They're over the last and head up to the line!' shouted the commentator. 'Freewheeler still leads, but he looks all in! American Smooth can do no more two lengths back. Raven's Way is plugging on. Peace Offering is gaining in fourth! Rhys Bradford has found an extra gear and the horse is staying on well!'

Pippa whimpered, hugging Jack's arm to her like a life-buoy.

'Come on, Rhys! Come on, Peace Offering!'

Peace Offering, his head stretched low and his reins dangling, took giant strides, eating up the gap between him and the three in front. The finishing post seemed to stretch further and further away from Freewheeler as he cantered wearily towards it. Peace Offering closed in on Raven's Way's quarters just as the tired horse veered away from his jockey's driving whip. Rhys snatched up his reins to avoid going into the back of him.

'...And the line comes just in time for Freewheeler!' the commentator cried in triumph.

Pippa sagged.

'...Second is American Smooth. Half a length back to Raven's Way and an unlucky Peace Offering in fourth...'

'That was a good run, don't worry,' Jack said, giving Pippa's hand an awkward pat.

For the first time, she realised she was holding on to him. She disentangled herself, brushing the creases out of his jacketed arm, embarrassed. She cleared her throat.

'Sorry,' she mumbled. She turned away to be enfolded by Tash giving her a consolatory hug.

'Never mind, sweets. Maybe next time. He was unlucky, wasn't he, Jack?'

'He wouldn't have won. But yes, he was unlucky not to get third,' he conceded under Tash's reproachful look.

Pippa stepped out of Tash's embrace and straightened her coat. She threaded her hair behind her ears, squared her shoulders.

'Oh, well. Onwards and upwards, I guess,' she said with a brave smile. 'Let's go say well done to him. He tried so hard.'

# Chapter Sixteen

The next morning, Pippa lay on her side in her and Ollie's bed, her fingers caressing Ollie's abdomen in silky circles. She smiled when his eyes flickered open and he raised his arm to rub the sleep from them.

'Morning,' she murmured.

'Hmm,' Ollie grunted in response.

'Did you sleep well?'

He lifted his arm from over his eyes to look at her, heavy-lidded.

'Like a baby.' He gave her a wry smile. 'I don't know about absence making the heart grow fonder, but it sure as hell makes other things fonder. Last night, you were –' He paused to find the perfect word to describe the previous night's lovemaking, but shook his head in defeat. 'Did you sleep okay?'

Pippa nodded, unwilling to admit the ceaseless traffic outside and the adrenalin-filled memories of her day at the races had kept her awake until the early hours.

Ollie arched against Pippa's gentle stroking like a cat.

'Do you have to go back today? Can't you tell your boss that you're sick or something and can't come in tomorrow?'

'I couldn't do that to Jack, Ollie,' Pippa smiled. 'Besides, I've got loads to do at the cottage.'

Ollie rolled onto his side and raised himself on one elbow.

'Do you like living out there in the middle of nowhere?' he asked.

'It's very peaceful.'

'No. I mean do you prefer it to living here in the city?'

Pippa frowned.

'What do you mean?'

Ollie collapsed onto his back with a sigh.

'It's just that all you ever seem to talk about these days is your job, your horse and your cottage.'

'It pretty much sums up my existence at the moment.'

'When are you going to come back?'

Pippa chewed her lip.

'Well, when the cottage is finished, I'll be able to sell it. Then I'll be able to afford Peace Offering's training fees without having to work for

Jack. The sooner that gets done, the sooner I'll be back.' She waited, hopeful that Ollie might volunteer his services.

'How much work does it need?'

'The lounge only needs to be painted now, and I think I've done an all right job retiling the downstairs loo. The kitchen is having new worktops installed next week, then there's the two bedrooms and bathroom upstairs to sort out. Oh, and I haven't even touched the garden yet.'

'How long is all that going to take?' Ollie groaned.

'I'm going to try have it all ready by the end of the jump racing season. That way, I won't be leaving Jack in the lurch.'

'And when's that?'

'After the National. Sometime in April I think.'

Ollie groaned again and Pippa stifled a sigh. Ollie's scarce DIY skills weren't going to be forthcoming.

'But just think,' she carried on brightly. 'Once the cottage is sold, I can move back to London and maybe together, we can get a bigger flat. Somewhere I can have an art studio.'

Ollie's eyes brightened and he raised himself up again to look at Pippa.

'If we got a bigger place, we could have drinks parties too. I went to Rich Holden's place a couple of weeks ago for a party –'

'Your acting friend?'

'Yeah.' Ollie looked a little smug. 'My *friend*. His place is massive. He had twin three-seater sofas in his sitting room plus extra chairs and tables. And a huge garden by London standards.' A frown passed over his forehead. 'We would have to look at places in decent areas.'

'Well, of course,' Pippa agreed.

'No. I mean *decent* areas. Rich had his neighbours round for the party – which was just as well because it went on until about four in the morning. But they were the sort of neighbours whom you could invite to that sort of party, if you know what I mean.'

'Um...'

'We can't get a place in some backstreet if we're going to have parties like Rich does.'

Pippa stayed silent, thinking of what it would be like if she had a party at Hazyvale House. It would be fun. She could just imagine the driveway crowded with cars, guests in the lounge and kitchen, spilling out into the back garden. In her mind's eye, she could see Finn and Jack – minus Melissa – Emmie, Billy, Tash, maybe Randy from the café serving drinks... Disturbingly, when she tried to picture Ollie there, it wouldn't stick.

She became aware of the lazy circles her fingers were unknowingly still drawing on Ollie's body when he shivered. He shifted his body and his eyes sparked hungrily. She stroked her fingers down his waist and over his hips, brushing against the hard heat of his erection and feeling a confidence boost that she could still arouse Ollie, even when they seemed to be drifting apart.

Ollie removed the duvet which had been modestly covering her naked body and began his own explorations. He leaned over to kiss her, brushing a lock of her hair away from her face.

Pippa closed her eyes, arousal heightened by its lengthy absence.

'Do you want me?' Ollie murmured.

'Oh, yes,' Pippa said, writhing beneath his touch. She felt his weight upon her, his breath short and rasping in her ear as he nibbled her earlobe. Pippa's pelvic muscles spasmed as she felt his cock rub against the tender skin on the inside of her thigh. She rose up to meet him, a gasp escaping as he entered her, a familiar body made unfamiliar by absence. One thing that she would always compliment Ollie on was that he was great in bed. His rhythmic thrusts grew faster and more urgent and he muttered in her ear.

'Hmm?' she said, lost in a swirling pool of bliss.

'I said *call me doctor*.'

Pippa's eyes opened and briefly she lost her rhythm. Ollie, supported on his arms, was staring, his eyes glazed over, his mouth open to reveal clenched teeth. Was he having a heart attack? Why did she need to call his doctor?

'What?'

'Call me Doctor Fletcher,' he snarled.

'Doctor Fletcher?' Pippa echoed.

Immediately Ollie's lovemaking became more frantic.

'Yes! That's my name.'

Pippa couldn't help herself. She roared with laughter. Her eyes, which had been watering with arousal seconds earlier, now streamed with amusement.

Ollie rolled off with a huff, his proud penis now shrinking into a sulk.

Pippa reached out to him, trying to contain the giggles still bubbling out of her like champagne.

'I'm sorry, Ollie,' she chuckled. 'I am, really. We've just never played that game before. I mean, I've heard of Nurse-Patient, but not Doctor –'

Ollie shook her placating hand off his shoulder and sat on the side of the bed, his back to her. His neck was red, either with rage or embarrassment.

Pippa kneeled behind him and wrapped her arms over his shoulders.

He tried to shrug her off.

'Come on, Ollie. I'm sorry. I should be grateful you didn't want to play this game when you did that cameo of the vet on *EastEnders*. What role would you like me to play: nurse or patient?'

'Just forget it,' he muttered and got up to stride over to the bathroom.

Pippa's feelings of remorse and pity were once again replaced with amusement and she fell back onto the bed, smothering her giggles into the pillow.

# Chapter Seventeen

With the first week of December came the first snowfall of the season. The flakes began their silent descent as Pippa drove home from work on Thursday evening and she found Hazyvale House's swayback sprinkled with a light dusting when she pulled up in the rutted driveway. By the next morning a crusty carpet of untainted white blanketed the front garden, covering the messy tangle of flowerbeds and softening the general dishevelled image it hadn't yet managed to shake.

To be fair, Pippa thought as she wrenched open her car door and ripped the rubber lining from the frozen frame, she hadn't paid that much attention to the garden yet. That was something she was gearing up to tackle when the days were longer and less hypothermic.

She dragged her thoughts away from the cottage renovations as she made her slow journey to the stables, her first experience driving in snow. Whether the gritters had been caught napping or whether this particular part of the southwest didn't register as worthy on their routes, the narrow roads had been left unprepared.

Pippa chewed her lip and gripped the icy steering wheel as she manoeuvred the Beetle through the slushy ruts left by previous vehicles. When she pulled up outside the stables, she flexed her stiff fingers then blotted her damp palms on her trousers.

Snow was very pretty until you drove in it.

Aspen Valley's horse lorry was parked, ready to depart for the day's racing and she pitied whoever was responsible for driving its great bulk across country in these conditions.

When Jack arrived shortly after her, he looked like he was returning from a trip to the Arctic. His nose was cherry red and fat melting flakes clung to his jacket as he bustled into the office. A few minutes later, he handed her the list of entries and declarations.

'Could be a waste of time,' he grumbled. 'An inch of snow and everything grinds to a bloody halt. Wincanton have cancelled this afternoon's meeting because the track is frozen. Why couldn't they have put the covers on?'

Pippa had a sudden mental image of young Wimbledon ball boys running around the racecourse hauling tarpaulins after them, but swallowed the smile this brought to her face. Jack wouldn't see the funny side of it.

'Don't know, Jack,' she replied. 'Maybe they were given the wrong forecast.'

'And it's Cheltenham Festival Trials weekend! I've got both Dexter *and* Dust Storm running in the novice hurdle.'

'Maybe the ball boys will have a chance tomorrow then,' she murmured, concentrating on entering the runners in their designated races.

'*What?*'

Pippa stopped typing to look at Jack then realised what she'd just said.

'I mean the people who put the covers on the course. You know, like at Wimbledon. Maybe they've had enough warning to get them on.'

Jack shook his head.

'Pippa, sometimes I think you're in a different solar system, never mind a different planet to the rest of us.'

Poised over her keyboard, Pippa beamed at Jack heading back into his office, feeling strangely proud of her eccentricity.

With racing still hanging in the balance, Pippa wasn't surprised when, just before lunch, the office door was opened, admitting a blast of glacial air. But instead of a grumpy-looking Jack muttering about a wasted journey, she was greeted by a tall, mouth-wateringly sexy man followed by a young woman not much older than herself. Pippa's jaw fell slack when the man smiled at her. The crows' feet at the corners of his eyes deepened beneath a natural tan which was criminal to have in the middle of an English winter.

'Can I help you?' Pippa uttered at last, really meaning it.

'Good morning, *ma'amoiselle*. Is Jack here?' he asked, his French accent as soothing as a feline purr.

Pippa shook her head.

'No, I'm afraid not.' A nasty thought occurred to her. Her eyes flickered from the Frenchman to the office diary lying on the desk. 'Er, was he expecting you?'

'No. We stopped by on the off-chance.'

The woman, her long brown hair secured in a plait, smiled at Pippa.

'I don't think we've met. I'm Ginny Kennedy. My partner, Julien. Our horse, Caspian, is being stabled here for the winter.'

A light bulb pinged in Pippa's brain and she beamed at the two visitors. She might not know all of the horses at Aspen Valley yet, but Caspian stood out for a particular reason: he wasn't a jumper.

'Of course!' she said. 'I'm Pippa. I haven't been working here all that long. When Caspian arrived, you more than likely met Gemma, Jack's last secretary. He'll be disappointed to have missed you.'

'Likewise,' Ginny sighed, her tone receiving a quick frown from Julien.

'I'll just check where he's being stabled, and have someone take you to him,' Pippa said, clicking open a document on her computer of all Aspen Valley's residents.

As she waited for the page to load, she noticed Ginny hardly able to contain her excitement. 'Caspian's a bit of a celebrity around here,' she said. 'Everyone wants to look after him.'

'We miss him at home,' Ginny replied. 'But hopefully a good rest over winter means he'll come back next season bigger and stronger.'

'Here we go. Caspian's in Box 104. I'll just call someone to take you there.'

'Do you know where it is? Have you met Caspian?' Ginny asked.

Pippa paused as she rose to her feet. Would they take offence if she admitted that she hadn't been that bothered to meet what was obviously their favourite horse?

'Um, not officially, I haven't.'

'Would you like to? He's such a love. Isn't he, Julien?'

'More so since he won the Dewhurst,' he teased.

'Rubbish. Would you like to come along? He's favourite for next year's Derby, you know. If he wins, you could say you met the Derby winner.'

Far from sounding boastful, Ginny's voice softened with wistfulness as she imagined winning flat racing's most coveted prize. Pippa recognised what she felt about Peace Offering's bid for the National in her misty eyes, albeit Caspian was more like a handful of aces to her own Joker card.

'I'd love to,' she said. 'Follow me.'

The sound of Ginny's voice softly calling his name brought Caspian whickering to the door.

'He certainly knows who his owner is,' Pippa said with a smile.

The dark bay colt blew gustily over Ginny as she rubbed the small star between his eyes.

'Well, strictly speaking, my father is his owner,' Ginny said. 'But I'm his trainer.'

Pippa was taken aback for a moment.

'You're a trainer?' she said. 'Wow.'

Ginny grinned.

'You sound amazed.'

'I don't mean to. It's just that – I didn't think –' she stammered. 'Sorry, I'm pretty new to this game. Jack's the only trainer I know. I guess I just presumed all trainers were like him.'

Ginny and Julien laughed.

'No. We come in all shapes and sizes,' Julien said.

'You as well?'

Ginny chuckled at Pippa's astonished expression.

'Julien was my hottest rival last season.'

I wouldn't argue with that, thought Pippa.

'And this fella here,' Ginny went on, scratching her horse under his chin, 'was my deadliest weapon.' Her brow furrowed in puzzlement. 'Jack's at the top of his game. If you don't mind me asking, if you're new to this, how did you get the job as his racing secretary?'

Pippa batted her hand.

'Long story. The short version is that he trains a horse that I own.'

'How lovely. Have we heard of him?'

Pippa pulled a doubtful face.

'Probably not. Does Peace Offering ring a bell?'

Ginny shook her head and Pippa nodded.

'No, I thought not. He's not exactly the Kauto Star of the yard, as someone once said, but...'

'But?' Julien prompted.

Pippa felt embarrassed all of a sudden, telling two virtual strangers who must be experts in their profession, her naive hopes for her horse.

'I want to run him in the Grand National,' she said with a shrug. 'Jack isn't quite so optimistic. He's probably right. It is a bit pie in the sky.'

Ginny and Julien exchanged a small smile.

'Don't let that stop you,' she said to Pippa. She turned back to Caspian to fuss him some more before continuing. 'On paper Caspian didn't stand a chance in the Dewhurst Stakes. He was one of the outsiders in the race. But he made all the sceptics eat their words when he won.' She gave Pippa a warm smile. 'If you have a dream, don't let anybody talk you out of it. *Anything* can happen in racing.'

Looking at Ginny, Pippa saw the young trainer believed every word she spoke. And she *was* a trainer. She must know what she was talking about. A tiny ball of anticipation flickered inside her. What was it? Hope? Belief? She had an overwhelming urge to hug Ginny. Wrapping her coat more tightly around her, she restrained herself.

'Thanks,' she said. 'I'll remember that.'

The light snow was still drifting down that evening as Pippa closed the office door behind her and headed past the stables to her car. From within the nearer stables, she could hear the horses munching on their supper and the thought of them cosily wrapped up in their blankets and knee-deep in bedding brought new warmth to her bones. This feeling rapidly evaporated when she stepped into the Beetle, into temperatures that Health and Safety standards would have found acceptable for freezing meat.

Her teeth chattering, she turned the car down the long sloping driveway onto the main road. Against the murky darkness, the Beetle's headlights illuminated the white landscape, whipping up the peaceful descent of flakes in its slipstream. Pippa squinted through the foggy visibility. Her jaw ached from clenching her teeth.

Her tension eased as she pulled onto the main road that linked Helensvale to the rest of civilisation. It was still carpeted with snow, but at least the lanes were wider.

To take her mind off the cold, she switched on the car's disc player. Tapping her fingers on the steering wheel, she listened for a few moments to Take That tripping their way through *Patience* before her own gave out and she ejected the CD. Keeping one hand on the wheel, she held up the disc to check for dirt or scratches. She flicked her gaze back to the road. She breathed on the disc, a satisfying fog coating the shiny surface then rubbed it on her leg.

'Shit,' Pippa muttered as the disc slipped out of her hand and down to her feet.

Craning her neck so she could partially see the road through the steering wheel, she leant down to retrieve it. A movement up ahead caught her eye. She looked up, suddenly dazzled by the floodlight glare of an oncoming truck. It rushed past her, the wind and snowy debris on the road buffeting the Beetle.

Pippa blinked frantically, trying to adjust her vision to the pitch black she was now plunged into. The disc slipped from her hand again as the car's wheels caught a thick rut in the road. The car veered left. Pippa slammed her foot on the brake pedal.

Feeling the tyres begin to slip, she grappled with the wheel to straighten them.

'Shit! Shit! Shit!' she muttered through gritted teeth as she struggled with the car's momentum.

It was already in a slide.

She was powerless to stop it from skimming off the road.

Pippa opened her eyes. She removed her shaking hands from the wheel and leant her head back. The car tilted drunkenly into a ditch. With a sigh of resignation, she switched off the engine and unclipped her seatbelt. She pushed the door open, wincing as it bounced back and hit her on the shin.

Hugging her coat around her, she skirted the bonnet, pulling a face at the lone right headlight torching a beam of silvery light into a nearby hedge. A lethargic glow from the left headlight pierced through the dense snow packed around it. The whole car was pitched at a precarious angle.

Pippa wondered if she might be able to reverse out of the ditch.

'Nothing ventured, nothing gained,' she shrugged, turning back to the driver's side.

Easing back into her seat so she wouldn't upset the car's balance, she turned on the ignition and crunched the stiff gear lever into Reverse. Her heart skipped a beat as the wheels found traction and inched backwards, but a moment later it was gone again and the wheels spun on the packed snow.

'Bugger, bugger, bugger! Damn, damn, damn! Bloody hell!'

She leaned her forehead on the cold steering wheel. She didn't know if the AA would be able to find her out here, besides which, she thought with a grimace, she hadn't included breakdown cover in her insurance policy. She groaned. Jack would have a field day when he found out. She looked over her shoulder, relieved that at least the car was more or less off the road then tried to work out what to do next.

Call for a Helensvale taxi? Walk home? It would have been a ten minute drive from here, she figured. It would take her forever to walk, especially in the snow. Would she make it in the cold? She'd try for a taxi first.

She scooped her mobile out of her bag. She groaned again when she saw the stark text *No signal – Emergency calls only.*

Did this count as an emergency? Was one allowed to ring 999 to order a taxi? Probably not, she would have to be suffering from hypothermia and frostbite before she qualified.

She stuffed her phone back into her bag and got out of the car, slamming the door as she did so. With a rueful shake of her head, she watched the Beetle tip what few inches it had regained, back into the ditch. She tucked her chin into the upturned collar of her coat, plugged her hands into her pockets and trudged in the direction of Hazyvale, snowflakes tickling her frozen cheeks.

Pippa felt like she had walked miles, but when she turned to look back at the lonesome outline of her car, she realised with a sinking heart that she had barely gone two hundred metres. Hunching her shoulders, she pressed on.

Moments later, her shadow began to deepen in front of her as a car approached from behind. Pippa stopped, ready to wave them down. She saw it slow as it passed the Beetle then watched as it drove on towards her. A sigh of relief flooded her chest as she saw the indicator switch on just as it reached her. She pushed away the sliver of unease as she recalled the horror stories of butchered hitchhikers. The passenger door was pushed open and she bent her head to see the driver.

'Finn!' she cried. 'Thank God it's you!'

'Y' all right, Pippa? I thought that was yer car back there. Come, get in before you freeze yourself to death.'

Pippa didn't need to be asked twice. She hopped into the heated car and rubbed her hands together in an attempt to build some warmth.

Finn gave her a sympathetic smile and brushed a frozen tendril of her hair behind her ear.

'What happened?'

While he drove, Pippa explained.

'...And I couldn't see a thing. Then I lost control and it went into the ditch,' she concluded with a defeated shrug. 'I've never driven in snow. I didn't know what I was meant to do.'

Finn shook his head.

'An easy mistake to make if you're not used to this weather. By the sounds of it, you probably would have ended up in the ditch no matter what. Do you not have breakdown recovery?'

'No. I was trying to cut costs.'

'Not a bother. I'll drive you home and we'll sort your car out tomorrow.'

'Will it be okay, do you think?' she asked, wringing her thawing hands.

'Aye, for the night it will be. The traffic's not mad on this road, you know yourself, and there'll be even less in this weather.'

Pippa made a non-committal noise, wondering how on earth she would get around if her car was broken and couldn't be driven.

Finn turned off onto the single lane road leading to Hazyvale House and Pippa flashed him a grateful smile.

'Thank you for helping. I would have been out there walking for hours if you hadn't come by. I don't know what enjoyment Ralph Fiennes gets from trekking across the Arctic. I hope I haven't made you late for anything.'

Finn gave her a strange look, which was quickly replaced with his usual smile.

'No, I was headin' into Helensvale to see someone at The Plough – a friend. I'll only be a couple of minutes late.'

'Must be a special friend to make you drive on a night like this,' Pippa grinned.

Finn gave an awkward chuckle.

'Aye, special is one word to describe 'em.'

Pippa stopped him at Hazyvale's gate.

'Now don't you worry nothin' about tomorrow. I'll pick you up for work and we'll sort out a tractor or something to haul your car out as well.'

She felt so grateful she wanted to kiss him, but resisted the urge. Instead, she gave him her sincerest smile and let herself out.

'Thanks again. Enjoy the rest of your evening.'

'You too. Oh, and Pippa?'

Pippa paused as she went to swing the door shut.

'Yes?'

'Sir Ranulph Fiennes.'

'Sorry?'

Finn grinned.

'You said Ralph Fiennes enjoyed trekking across the Arctic. Yer Ralph Fiennes is an actor, you know. Sir Ranulph Fiennes is the mad git who walked everywhere in snow boots.'

Pippa snorted.

'Ah, yes. Quite right.'

Finn winked.

'Goodnight then.'

Pippa closed the door and wobbled in her heels up the uneven driveway. She turned as Finn tooted the horn and waved as he drove away. She sighed and continued on towards the front door. What a disastrous night. What more disasters would tomorrow bring?

# Chapter Eighteen

As promised, Finn was waiting for Pippa the next morning, the exhaust from his idling car belching out thick steamy fumes which drifted across Hazyvale's driveway. The snow had stopped falling and what had settled on the ground was beginning to turn to slush.

Pippa hurried from her front door into the front seat, sighing exultantly as she was met by the furnace blast of the heater.

'Thank you for helping me out.'

'Not a bother.' Finn patted her clasped hands.

She noticed the dark circles beneath his eyes and concluded whoever the 'friend' was that he had met up with last night hadn't let him get to bed until late. Or perhaps hadn't let him get to *sleep* might be more appropriate, she corrected her thoughts. Going to bed didn't necessitate sleeping.

'Good night last night?' she said as they swung onto the road.

Finn shrugged.

'Aye,' he replied non-commitally. 'I'll give you a number of a mate who can get your car out. He's got a garage not far from here. Better than any of the garages around, he won't cheat you so you'll be safe.'

'Thanks. I really appreciate it,' Pippa said as sincerely as she could.

His abrupt change of subject got her wondering though. He obviously didn't want to talk about his friend from the previous night, even though he'd never struck her as being a particularly private person. Their brief moment of intimacy at The Plough after Aspen Valley's Open Day had forged a friendship between them, which Pippa enjoyed, but was still unsure of.

Was Finn purposefully avoiding telling Pippa of his personal relationships in an effort to protect her? If he was seeing a girl then perhaps it would be better to tell him not to worry, she already had a boyfriend.

No, Pippa decided. To say that would give her away and if he was simply meeting up with an old friend then she would be left with a very red face.

*Or,* a sceptical voice in her head spoke up, *you enjoy Finn's attention and setting him straight would put an end to that.*

She blocked the voice from her thoughts and turned to her companion.

'It's the Cheltenham Festival Trials this weekend, isn't it?'

'To be sure,' Finn nodded. 'And if the course passes inspection this morning then it'll be a tough card to ride in.'

'Don't you get afraid?' she asked. Jump racing looked scary enough for the jockeys, especially when they took such crunching falls, but to ride in such awful weather she felt must be terrifying.

'No room for fear,' he grinned. 'The moment I lose confidence in myself is the moment I fall. The horse can tell, you know.'

'How can he tell?'

'Horses might be dumb, but they make up for it with their other senses. A horse can feel if his rider is wettin' his cacks. And if he senses you doubting a fence then he'll lose confidence in himself and will probably make a mistake.'

'You're very brave.'

Finn laughed.

'Or off my nut, one or the other.'

Pippa smiled, again noting the tired lines on his face. It was a young face, full of humour, made especially attractive by his laughing eyes, but the faint lines made him look older, more mature. He was probably no older than Pippa really, but he seemed so much more worldly to her.

'No, you don't look crazy. Brave suits you better,' she said before she could stop herself.

Finn glanced across at her and grinned.

'You're coddin' me. Me ma is forever tellin' me I was dropped on my head as a babby.'

'Does it frighten her when you ride?'

Finn shrugged.

'She gets uptight when I ride in the National. She doesn't want to lose her only child I guess. Otherwise, I guess she's used to it.'

'Is the National really that tough?' Pippa asked.

'Aye, but it's the one we all want to win. You don't become a mountaineer without wanting to conquer Everest.'

'I hope Peace Offering will cope,' she murmured, the first seed of doubt germinating in her mind.

Finn took his hand off the steering wheel and squeezed her knee.

'There's no horse I've ever felt safer on than he. He might not be the fastest, but he's a grand le'per. Clean jump a row of houses for the fun of it.'

*

Jack was outside, supervising the loading of horses into Aspen Valley's horse truck when they pulled up in the car park. He frowned at Pippa's arrival by Finn's side, his eyes narrowing with suspicion when he also noted Finn's lack of sleep.

'Racing still on?' Pippa asked optimistically.

Jack nodded.

'For now. The Met office are saying the snow will hold off for another day or so, but you can never believe a bloody word they say.'

Pippa couldn't argue with that, her confidence in weather forecasts was just as dubious.

'Let's hope it's worth it then,' she said and headed past him towards the office. She could feel his eyes burning her back. Seconds later, she heard the crunch of his footsteps on the gravel as he followed her. She didn't look back.

Let him think what he wants, she thought in defiance. What I do in my personal time is my own business and nothing to do with him.

She let herself into the office and was shedding her coat and handbag when Jack made his entrance. She waited for him to speak, looking at him expectantly and for the first time, saw him back down.

He stomped into his office, but reappeared moments later.

'Entries and decs for next week,' he said, holding out a ring-binder.

Pippa went to take it from him, but he didn't let it go. She was curious to see in his blue eyes a conflict going on, like stormy seas.

'Jack?' she prompted.

He let go of the notebook and pinched the bridge of his nose with his fingers, squeezing his eyes shut.

'Pippa, I'm not going to tell you how to live your life –'

'Good,' she cautioned.

Jack looked at her impatiently.

'– but mixing business and pleasure doesn't gel.'

Pippa folded her arms.

'What's that supposed to mean?'

'It means you work with Finn. What else could it bloody mean?'

'Ah, you think I'm sleeping with your jockey?' She gave him a benign smile.

'Well, aren't you?' Jack replied, lifting his hands in exasperation.

Pippa took a deep breath to contain the urge to throw the notebook in his face. She sat down at her desk without answering and rummaged through her bag for the piece of paper Finn had given her earlier. She picked up the telephone and began to dial out.

'What are you doing?' Jack demanded.

Pippa slammed down the phone and glared at him.

'I'm ringing a mechanic to go pull my car out of a ditch!' she threw back at him. 'If it wasn't for Finn, I'd probably be in some A&E with hypothermia right now!'

Jack took an unsteady step backwards, startled.

'You - you had an accident? Are you okay?'

The remorse in his tone flushed the anger out of Pippa and with a sigh, she nodded.

'Last night,' she explained. 'I lost control. It wasn't a bad accident really. I wasn't going fast or anything, but the car got stuck. Finn was passing by and gave me a lift home. Then he picked me up this morning to bring me to work.'

Jack's brow furrowed and his even white teeth bit into his lower lip.

'So, you're not - um - seeing Finn?'

'No, Jack.'

He rubbed his jaw and cleared his throat.

'Right. Well - er - I guess I owe you an apology then.'

'I guess you do,' Pippa said, turning her back to him and picking up the phone again. Not until Jack had looked so uncomfortable did she acknowledge her hurt pride.

Did he really think so little of her to assume she would jump into bed with anyone, especially when they were both aware she was dating Ollie?

She felt his hand close over her shoulder, his fingers briefly scorching her bare neck.

'I'm sorry I jumped to the wrong conclusions,' he mumbled and withdrew his hand.

He was already heading out the door before Pippa could decide whether or not to accept his apology.

By five o'clock, Pippa was more than ready to go home. She hadn't been able to shake off the chill that had settled over her that morning. Finn's mechanic friend had been in touch to say he was towing her car back to his garage to give it a proper look over, which meant she would have to ring for a Helensvale taxi.

She switched off the office lights and stepped out into the cold. It was already pitch black. The snow from the night before had turned to slush and only the occasional white mound in a drain corner, illuminated yellow by the dusky security light, gave away it had ever been.

Hugging her coat around her, she wandered down the row of stables towards Peace Offering's, returning the greetings of the few staff finishing up their duties as she passed them.

The lady at Helensvale Taxis had warned her there was a good half hour queue for rides on a Saturday night so she was in for a wait. Pippa leaned her arms on her horse's stable door and murmured his name. Peace Offering, snug in his winter rugs, was crunching on his hay at the back of the stable. At the sound of her voice, he looked up, long ears pricked, his white blaze glowing in the darkness, and walked over to the door.

Pippa stroked the soft skin between his nostrils, smiling as his hot breath blew up her coat sleeve. He pushed his head past her and Pippa leaned her cheek against the warmth of his neck, feeling safe and secure beside his solidity. She wondered how she could ever have been afraid of this gentle giant.

'Hey, Pippa,' a voice interrupted her thoughts.

She turned to see Emmie, bundled in a red Aspen Valley jacket and baseball cap standing a few feet away.

'All right, Emmie?'

'Yeah, can't wait to get home and have a hot bath though.'

'Hmm, me too,' Pippa agreed.

'I heard about your car accident.'

Pippa shrugged.

'It was so minor, I wouldn't even call it an accident.'

'Still. Can I give you a lift home?' she offered. 'I live in Helensvale, see, and your house isn't far out of the way.'

'Thanks, Emmie, but I've already called a taxi.'

'Rubbish, the taxi won't be here for ages, especially on a Saturday with everyone going partying in Bath and Bristol. Come on, just ring them up and cancel it. I'll drop you home.'

Pippa hesitated.

'You sure it's not out of your way?'

'Certain. And I like a bit of company in the car.'

Pippa grinned and dug her mobile phone out of her handbag.

'It happened somewhere along here,' Pippa said as they travelled down the road in Emmie's Punto. 'Everything looks so different when it snows. I wonder if I would've got lost trying to walk home.'

'You were walking?' Emmie asked in disbelief.

'Not for long. Finn picked me up. He was on his way into Helensvale.'

'That's right,' Emmie said. 'I saw him at The Plough –' She paused and glanced at her. 'Are you and Finn... you know?'

Pippa laughed and shook her head.

'You're nearly as bad as Jack. No, Finn and I aren't *you-knowing*.'

Emmie shrugged.

'It was just at The Plough that night after the Open Day, you and he seemed to be getting on really well.'

'We do get on well,' Pippa agreed. 'He's a nice guy, but we're not involved.'

'That's all right then,' Emmie breathed. 'Me and Billy saw him last night with some girl.'

Pippa's interest perked up. So he *was* seeing someone.

'Really?' she said, keeping her tone light.

'Yeah. Never seen her before. Very pretty like, all long blonde hair and nice figure, but not from around here.'

'Interesting,' Pippa mused. 'Are you and Billy seeing each other?'

Emmie threw her a quick look, hesitating.

'Well, almost. But please don't say anything to Jack about it; we're trying to keep it quiet.'

'Why?'

'Jack doesn't really approve of his staff dating. All that "not mixing business with pleasure" attitude.'

'So I found out this morning. He told me I shouldn't be sleeping with Finn.'

'But you're not,' Emmie pointed out.

'Yeah, but Jack just presumed that I was since we arrived together this morning. Besides, it's a bit pot calling the kettle black, don't you think? He's dating Melissa, after all. And he trains her father's horses. That's mixing business with pleasure.'

Emmie shook her head.

'Jack was dating Melissa *before* Mr Mardling moved his horses here.' She turned to grin at Pippa. 'And I don't know if I would call dating Melissa a pleasure, would you?'

Pippa giggled.

'Maybe that's why he's so against it then. He's realised his own mistake and can't get himself out of it. It would explain why he's such a misery all the time.'

Emmie shrugged.

'He isn't actually that miserable. He's just got a serious way about him.' She looked across at Pippa to see what sort of reaction her disagreeing was having. Pippa waited for her to continue. 'He's very fair unless he thinks you're not pulling your weight. *Then* he'll come down on you like a ton of bricks.'

Pippa didn't reply. In the face of Emmie's subtle defence over Jack, she felt a little guilty for slagging him off. She gazed out of her window at the high black hedges on the roadside merging with the inky sky.

Jack's comments deserved nothing less than her contempt, she told herself.

But he had apologised, and quite sincerely too, the other voice in her head argued. Maybe you just bring out the worst in him.

'Well, as long as my boyfriend doesn't come work for Aspen Valley, I should be in the clear then,' she said, trying to defuse the laboured silence.

'You have a boyfriend? I didn't know that.'

'He lives in London. Hasn't been down here yet – busy with work and everything,' Pippa explained. She didn't know how true that last excuse was, but it was the same one Ollie constantly gave her.

'What does he do?' Emmie asked.

'Acting.' She was tempted to add 'up', but refrained. Emmie would think her a right bitch if she started sniping her boyfriend as well as their boss.

'Ooh, how exciting. Have I seen him in anything?'

'Do you watch *Holby City*?'

Emmie stared at Pippa open-mouthed and wide-eyed.

'Road,' Pippa reminded her, pointing ahead.

'Don't tell me you're dating Rich Holden,' she breathed.

Pippa laughed.

'No, Ollie Buckingham. He's Doctor Fletcher.'

'Oh, my God!' Emmie squeaked. 'I don't know who Doctor Fletcher is, but how lucky are you, Pippa? Dating a *Holby City* doctor. Have you met Rich Holden?'

'No, but I believe we're going to his Christmas party according to Ollie. Road,' she prompted again, as Emmie's concentration lapsed once more.

'Wow,' Emmie sighed, relieving Pippa by looking ahead again. 'A Christmas party at Rich Holden's place.'

'Speaking of Christmas parties,' Pippa said, a thought popping into her head. 'Jack hasn't mentioned anything about a Christmas party for Aspen Valley. Don't you have one each year?'

'Kinda,' Emmie nodded. 'Usually between Christmas and New Year, we have a few drinks. Jack'll buy a couple of crates of beer and snacks and leave us to it. Mind you, the beer is usually drunk within an hour so you couldn't really call it a party, I suppose. And most of us are still sober enough to know we have to get up early for work the next day so it would all be over by about eight.'

'Sounds like a humdinger,' Pippa said with a dry smile. 'A party would be good fun. I'll have to ask Jack about it.'

# Chapter Nineteen

Monday morning found Pippa opening scores of Christmas cards addressed to Aspen Valley, Virtuoso and Black Russian, and Jack Carmichael (the sexiest trainer in National Hunt, according to one well-wisher) while forecast snow fell in sleepy abandon outside in the yard. Their success over the weekend at Cheltenham Festival Trials, which had reaped four winners for Aspen Valley, seemed to have unleashed a surge of Christmas spirit from racing fans.

Pippa hunted down some string and looped lines along the walls of the office, draping the cards over them. She stood back with her hands on her hips and surveyed her handiwork with satisfaction. The room looked alive and festive now with its brightly-coloured decorations. With Christmas only two weeks away, she could feel the child-like excitement, which always consumed her at this time of year, begin to bubble up inside.

Jack walked in, shaking snowflakes from his shoulders as he closed the door on the bitter weather. He did a double-take when he saw the Christmas cards looping across the walls.

'What the hell?'

'From your fans,' Pippa said with a grin. 'What do you think?'

Jack looked dubious.

'It's different,' he answered.

'It's festive,' she corrected him. 'Speaking of which, presumably you want me to organise a staff party?'

'Oh, that. Yeah, although don't get too excited. "Party" is probably too strong a word. Just order a couple of crates of beer.'

Pippa looked pained.

'But it's Christmas,' she pointed out. 'Why not have a proper party? Everyone would love a good ol' bash. Let them forget they're at work and at a proper party.'

'Because,' Jack maintained, 'all that will happen is everyone'll come to work the next morning with sore heads and end up breaking their necks out riding. They won't love you so much then.'

'If it's a really good party with a DJ and stuff then they might be more forgiving.'

'This isn't London. A few beers will do just fine.'

Pippa thought about arguing, but decided to leave it for now.

Jack gave her an expectant look.

'Now, any chance of some tea?'

She couldn't help the smile twitching her lips.

'Really? Did I just hear you ask for some tea? *Chamomile* tea?'

Jack averted his eyes, an embarrassed frown creasing his brow.

'It's not that bad, I've decided,' he mumbled.

Pippa grinned and made for the kitchenette, mildly surprised when Jack followed her. Usually he'd come in, grumble about the weather then shut himself away in his office.

'How's your car?' he asked, raising his voice above the noise of the kettle.

She grimaced in reply.

'I've got it back now. It needed a few things done to it like removing the dent on the front bumper and something about realigning the wheels or some such like. At least it's working again.'

'Did it cost a lot?'

Pippa shrugged and handed him his tea.

'It means I can't fix the kitchen cupboards or buy any paint until next month, but what can you do?'

Jack sucked his teeth in deliberation.

'Do you – er – need an advance? We can do that, you know, if you're in trouble.'

Pippa hesitated, recognising a more forgiving side to Jack's nature struggling to surface. She smiled and shook her head.

'Thanks, but I'm sure I can cope for another couple of weeks. Personally, I blame it on Take That,' she said, walking past Jack back into the Reception.

'Take That?'

'Yeah, if that CD I was listening to hadn't been skipping then I might have had more of a chance.'

Jack chuckled.

'Send them the bill. Ask them to *Reach Out*.'

Pippa looked back in surprise.

'Blimey, I'm impressed, Jack. I didn't think you would know who Take That was, never mind know one of their songs.'

Jack gave an awkward smile and looked at his feet.

'Comes from having a fanatical teenage niece,' he explained. 'She came to stay for a couple of weeks a while back while my brother and his wife went on holiday. All she ever listened to was bloody Take That. Drove me insane.'

'So I take it you won't want their CD as a Christmas present?' Jack grinned.

'Oh, I don't know. I am running low on coffee coasters, after all.'

Pippa shook her head and laughed. She wandered over to the window and gazed out. She blew on her drink, misting the glass.

'The Gallops look beautiful with the snow covering them,' she murmured.

Jack joined her, standing behind her shoulder.

'Yeah, also means we only get to use the all-weather gallop. Can't take the horses jumping on ground like that.'

'How's Peace Offering doing?'

Jack gave a half-hearted shrug.

'Okay, I suppose. All going well, he'll be ready to run again in two or three weeks' time.'

'God, it takes so long,' Pippa mused, turning back to the view.

'Some horses take longer to recover than others. Don't forget he had quite a hard race at Ascot.'

'Hmm. How are the horses that ran over the weekend? They must have had a hard time of it at the Trials.'

'Dust Storm is pretty stiff. We'll give him a few days to recover. But Dexter's bouncing around, looking for more hurdles to jump.'

Pippa noticed the satisfaction in his voice.

'He won, didn't he?'

'Yep, he's going to give Black Russian a run for his money next season when he's no longer a novice.' Jack chuckled. 'Emmie's going to have her loyalties torn.'

'Why?'

'She looks after them both. Black Russian is her baby. She was more pleased when he won the Champion Hurdle at Cheltenham last season than Dan Cameron was.' He shook his head, smiling at the memories.

The phone rang, interrupting their conversation.

Pippa looked out of the window one last time and heaved a sigh.

'I have to paint that,' she murmured to herself before turning away.

'Pippa,' Jack stopped her. He glanced at *Hazyvale Dawn* on the wall. 'What if I take you up onto the Gallops to watch the horses work in the snow? Would you be able to paint that?'

Pippa forgot about the telephone.

138

'Really? You'd do that for me?'

Her enthusiasm made Jack hesitate.

'I'll pay you for it,' he said. 'Like a commission. Maybe that'll soften the blow from your car repairs.'

Pippa tried to bite back the smile radiating from her face. She squeezed her fingernails into her palms to stop herself from hugging Jack.

'Thank you,' she squeaked.

Jack nodded, his expression becoming business-like once more, as if his generous nature had outstayed its welcome. He motioned to the phone.

'You'd better get that.' His more familiar frown settled on his forehead. 'I should go do some work.'

He set off abruptly for his office, leaving Pippa tingling with excitement.

'Aspen Valley Stables, good morning,' she carolled into the telephone receiver, more chirpily than usual.


Jack brought the Land Rover to a juddering halt three-quarters of the way up the Gallops. They sat in expectant silence, watching the distant speck of horses and riders preparing for their exercise at the base of the hill. The dark blobs against the white landscape blurred as the snow settled on the windscreen until the wipers cleared their view again.

'I suppose you want to get out and watch?' Jack said reluctantly.

'If you don't mind.'

'Very well.' He turned and reached onto the backseat. 'Binos for you,' he said, handing her a pair.

Stepping out of the vehicle, they crunched over the frozen ground to the running rail and held their binoculars up to their eyes. Pippa could feel the snow seeping into her shoes, numbing her feet. Her fingers burned against the icy textured metal of her field glasses. The four blurry blobs at the bottom of the Gallops suddenly became alive as she focused the lenses and she squeaked with excitement as they set off towards them. They were headed by a dark bay horse, his head, tucked into his chest, half-hidden by an encasing black blinkered hood.

'Black Russian, right?' she said.

'That's right,' Jack replied, his voice distracted as he followed the horses' progress. 'Can you name the rest?'

Pippa scanned the others: two chestnuts and another bay.

'Spurwing Island, Leopard Rock and, um...'

'Bold Phoenix,' Jack provided. 'Very good. I told you you'd know them all soon.'

139

Pippa laughed.

'Eventually.'

They lapsed into silence, Jack concentrating on his horses' performance, Pippa studying them with an artistic eye. A smile spread across her face as more details became apparent – the flapping multi-coloured saddle-cloths, the riders with the goggles fastened and helmets lowered, their startling red Aspen Valley jackets ballooning behind them as the rushing wind caught inside them. Black Russian, at the head of affairs, snorted with every stride, his forceful blows channelling two distinct plumes of mist from his dilated nostrils. The moistened air was whipped away, swirling, by his chasing stablemates. Their hooves, beating a dull drum which rode up the rise on the wind, flicked up snow and sand in savage disregard.

Pippa's creative brain whirred. The defined lines of the horses and riders were softened by the constant snowfall. Their misty breaths blurred the strapping, shuddering muscles. Her love for oil paints was overridden with the knowledge that a softer medium would be needed here. The washed-out sky blended with the ground and she considered whether watercolours would be a better option.

She moved from foot to foot, undecided, as the horses loomed larger. She lowered her binoculars to take in the entire landscape with the horses cutting their path through it. The undulations of the valley threw some of the glistening white into shadows of grey and purple. The divets left behind by the galloping horses lay in a churned passage of bruised pale blue snow, sprinkled with tan, like cinnamon dust on cappuccino froth.

*Yes*, watercolours, but using pastels as well to build depth into the horses' steaming bodies.

The horses thundered past, their hindquarters propelling them forward, but their speed kept in check by their poised riders.

Pippa found herself wishing she knew how to ride, just so she could experience the feeling of such accumulated strength.

'So much power,' she breathed.

'Yeah,' Jack agreed.

Pippa glanced at him, surprised as she hadn't realised she'd spoken aloud. Jack continued to watch the horses, letting her study his profile, unaware.

*Tash isn't far wrong*, she found herself thinking. She couldn't help but imagine what medium she would use to paint Jack. He stood tall and broad across the shoulders, his raised collar lining his strong jaw. Against the bright contrast of the background, his dark hair fused with his black

140

jacket. His features were rugged, and Pippa knew she would use oils to capture the raw cheekbones and jutting chin.

She chewed her lip as she tried to decide what skin tone he had. How the hell did he manage to get a tan in winter, she wondered idly?

He turned, catching her watching him.

Pippa was thrown off-guard.

The pupils of his eyes had contracted against the glare of the snow, revealing more iris, its shades of blue more astounding in the wintery brightness. Cornflower blue? Maybe, but no, she decided. There was more to them than that. Cerulean? Not quite –

He raised his eyebrows in question when she continued to stare at him, compelling Pippa to refocus.

'Um, thanks for this,' she said, gesturing with a vague hand.

'Did you see enough?'

For a frightening moment, she thought he meant of him, but then realised he was referring to the horses.

'What? Oh, yes! Perfect. I can't wait to get started.'

Jack grunted in acknowledgement.

'Come on, let's get back inside before you get hypothermia.' He nodded towards her with a faint smile. 'Your lips are turning blue.'

His mention of the cold brought reality rushing back to her and she noticed for the first time since she'd got out of the Land Rover just how bitter the weather was.

'Good idea,' she said. She turned back to the vehicle, but with a cry of alarm, she felt her ankle twist beneath her as she stepped in a hidden rut. Jack reached out to break her fall, his reflexes as sharp as his temper. Grasping his arms for support, she felt a volcanic flush burn up her cheeks and over her ears as her hormones instinctively approved of the hard muscles she could feel beneath his jacket.

'Sorry,' she croaked.

Jack's misty breath faded as he stopped breathing, suddenly aware of their awkward hold on one another.

'You okay?'

Pippa nodded fervently.

'Yes.' She let go of his arms, clumsily dusting the snow from them. 'Just practising my drunken Christmas party stumble.'

Jack raised a smile at her attempt to diffuse the atmosphere.

'Just so long as you're not practising the drinking right now,' he replied.

# Chapter Twenty

Wrapped in her dressing gown and slippers, Pippa tip-toed across the dark bedroom, dimly lit by the street light outside the window. She put two steaming mugs of coffee on the bedside table.

'Ollie,' she whispered, giving the mound cocooned in duvet that was Ollie a gentle shake. 'Ollie, wake up. It's Christmas!'

The mound grunted and snuggled deeper into the warmth of their bed.

'Come on, Ollie. It's time to open presents.'

'No,' he mumbled into his pillow. 'Don't have time. They need me in Trauma Two...'

Pippa giggled and switched on the table lamp.

Ollie sat up, startled.

'Wha-?'

She laughed.

'It's Christmas Day, Doctor Fletcher. You don't have to go into work today.'

Ollie looked sheepish.

'I was dreaming we had a mass casualty and you suddenly appeared in the ward and told me we had to open Christmas presents.'

Pippa chuckled and swept his messy fringe away from his forehead to give him a kiss.

'Merry Christmas. Here's some coffee.'

Ollie shivered audibly as he emerged from his cocoon to take his drink.

'Christ, it's cold. Get back into bed.'

'Let me go get the presents from the lounge then. We can open them in here,' Pippa said.

Excitement, like little bubbles of champagne, popped and fizzed in her chest as she gathered the modest bundle of colourfully-wrapped presents into her arms and skipped back into the bedroom. She spread the gifts at the base of the bed and hurried back under the covers beside Ollie. Her enthusiasm was contagious and Ollie hugged her close, kissing her temple and beaming at her.

'Here, you first,' he said, reaching out for his present to Pippa.

She flexed her fingers in anticipation as he handed her a clumsily-wrapped rectangular present. With her tongue cinched between her teeth, she teased the elf-decorated paper open. Inside was a Lee Child novel and three DVDs. She giggled when she noticed he'd forgotten to take the *3 for 2* label off one of them.

'Thank you,' she cooed, kissing him. 'I've never read any of Lee Child's books. I've heard he's very good.'

Ollie smiled back, looking smug.

'My pleasure. I thought a different type of book would be good to broaden your horizons. Plus I haven't read his latest book. What have you got for me?' He looked in expectation at the small jumble at their feet.

Pippa retrieved another present and handed it to him. Ollie took it and tore at the wrapping greedily. Inside were two silk shirts and a bottle of cologne. He held up the green shirt to admire then smoothed it against his torso.

'What do you think?' he said.

'Brings out the colour of your eyes.'

He nodded in satisfaction and picked up the cologne to read the label.

'*Armani Code.* Are we both trying to broaden each other's horizons this year?' he asked.

'What do you mean?'

'I usually wear *Versace Eau Fraiche.*'

Pippa frowned to herself as Ollie uncapped the bottle. Did he? She hadn't been able to remember his favourite brand when she had gone shopping in Bristol so rather than ringing him up to ask and ruining the surprise, she had smelt them all until she had found the right one. Maybe the two had similar smells, she decided.

As soon as he squirted a little of the scent into the air, Pippa realised her mistake. The fragrances were nothing alike. But instead, it was almost as if Jack had walked into the room.

'Hmm,' Ollie gave his approval.

Pippa swallowed hard.

'Let's see what else we've got!' she exclaimed, grabbing the closest present. 'Here, open this one, Ollie! It's from your parents.'

Ten minutes later, fifty pounds wealthier in department store vouchers and with a new bookshelf worth of gifts, Pippa and Ollie relaxed back in bed to finish their tepid coffee. Ollie happily started on Pippa's new Lee Child novel, while she leafed through the *DIY for Dummies* book Tash had given her, trying to ignore the lingering scent of her boss' cologne hanging in the air and cursing herself for her stupidity.

How *could* she have made such a blunder? It looked like she had got away with it, but what would happen if Ollie ever met Jack? Would he realise they were wearing the same cologne? Did men notice those sorts of things? The potential situation made Pippa giggle nervously.

Wait until she told Tash.

The following day, Ollie was almost hyper with excitement at the prospect of going to Rich Holden's Boxing Day party. He had informed Pippa that only the elite were invited so they should both be very grateful to have made the guest list. The more he enthused about the A-list party goers, the less Pippa wanted to go.

Ollie walked into the lounge where she was lying on the sofa. He held up the two shirts she had given him the day before.

'Which one?' he asked, holding each against him in turn.

'They're both nice,' Pippa said, tearing her attention away from the television. 'I like the green one best. It really brings out the colour of your eyes.'

Ollie pulled a face as he deliberated.

'Yeah, but the blue one would look better with my grey trousers. I'll go with the blue. I wonder if I should wear a suit. What do you think?'

'What?' Pippa turned her head towards Ollie without taking her eyes off the screen.

'I said *I wonder if I should wear* – Pippa, you're not listening to me! What are you watching, anyway?'

'The one fifty at Kempton. It's the big Boxing Day meeting today. We've got the favourites in the two main races. Virtuoso in the King George VI Chase and Black Russian in the –'

'Pippa!' he interrupted her. 'We've got to be at Rich's place at six. You're not even dressed yet! You don't have time to watch the racing.'

'I just want to see how Virtuoso and Black Russian do, then I'll get ready,' she said, attempting a placating smile. 'We won't be late, I promise.'

Ollie closed his eyes and shook his head. Marching back into the bedroom, Pippa could hear him muttering mournfully,

'What has that bloody horse turned you into?'

She turned back to the television only to find the race had ended. With a sigh, she heaved herself off the sofa and went in pursuit of Ollie. She found him flicking through his wardrobe. She wound her arms around his waist from behind and planted a kiss on his tense neck.

'I'm sorry,' she murmured. 'Black Russian runs in the next and Virtuoso's race will be over by three thirty. After that, you have my undivided attention and I promise not to speak another word about horses.'

Ollie turned around to face her, still looking annoyed, but with a trace of forgiveness visible.

'Okay. Only if you wear that red number tonight that you wore on my birthday.'

Pippa camouflaged a grimace with a forced smile. The number he was referring to was more suited to summer-wear. It was a lovely dress, she was the first to admit, and very sexy, but she would freeze in it.

'Deal.' She kissed him to seal it before returning to the lounge.

The racing presenter was interviewing Jack and Dan Cameron, Black Russian's owner, before the next race.

Fumbling for the remote, she turned up the volume to hear the conversation. It felt a little peculiar sitting in the London flat with her boss' voice booming around it, debriefing the viewers on his horse's chances.

'Pippa,' Ollie said, stomping back into the lounge, 'must you have it on so loud – hey, is that Dan Cameron?' His jaw dropped.

'Yeah, do you know him?'

Ollie sat down beside her on the sofa, his eyes trained on the screen.

'Only of him. What's he doing there?'

'He owns Black Russian, one of Aspen Valley's horses.'

'Do *you* know him?' Ollie said in awe.

'Well, we've spoken over the telephone. Why are you looking so amazed?'

'Oh, my God. You don't know who Dan Cameron is? He's only one of the biggest directors in Britain!' Ollie cried. 'And you say he's a racehorse owner?'

'Want to watch the race with me?' she grinned.

Ollie shifted in his seat, looking perturbed.

'Well, it would be useful to know the result since he *is* in entertainment. It can be a topical conversation this evening, especially as you know him.'

The nine runners in the Christmas Hurdle milled around by the starter's platform, waiting to be called into line. The camera zoomed in on a dark bay horse, his face half-hidden by the black blinkers he wore, looking almost sinister. His jockey, Rhys Bradford, looked equally formidable in his black and yellow silks and gaunt serious expression.

'That's Black Russian,' Pippa informed Ollie, pointing excitedly at the pair. 'Ooh, they're about to start! Come on, Black Russian!'

She leaned forward in anticipation as the horses jogged towards the starting tape. The roar from the Kempton crowd drowned out the commentator's *'They're off!'* and the horses thundered towards the first hurdle.

Rhys found a cosy position one off the rail behind the pacesetters and hardly moved in the saddle as they cleared the first. The field were still tightly grouped together as they rose over the second and rounded the turn to pass the grandstands for the first time. The cheering of the crowd followed them round the next bend, where Rhys eased Black Russian towards the inside rail. Against the cold and dank winter backdrop, the pair glided stealthily up to challenge the leading group like a pickpocket sliding through an oblivious crowd on the street.

Pippa started drumming her slippered feet on the floor as the Aspen Valley representative got his head in front.

The commentator's voice rose a decibel.

'Black Russian moves effortlessly to the front as they make the long run to the third. They've still a circuit to go, but Rhys Bradford is sitting pretty aboard the favourite. They're over safely – Jeeves is a faller!'

Pippa gasped, but let out her breath when horse and rider clambered to their feet, muddied but none the worse. She clutched a cushion to her chest, willing Black Russian to keep going. Some of the other horses were being niggled along, their jockeys lowering their posture. Still Rhys sat motionless, his rear tilted arrogantly high in the face of their opponents. He sat back down with a bump as Black Russian made a mistake at one of the hurdles in the backstretch, paddling his forelegs through the jump.

'Oh, come on, Rhys!' Pippa cried. 'Keep going!'

Black Russian appeared to lose his momentum somewhat and his two length lead was shortened to one by High Scribe in second. Rhys shook his reins at Black Russian. The two horses sailed over the fifth flight, one after the other, well clear of the chasing pack and began the frenzied drive around the turn into the home straight.

Pippa bounced in her seat and thumped the armrest, urging Black Russian to see off his challenger.

The running rail became a blur as the camera kept pace with the sprinting leader. The second last loomed. Rhys, crouching low in his saddle, fanned his whip alongside Black Russian's eye and asked for a bold jump.

146

Pippa leaned forward with them. With a cry, she threw her weight back as Black Russian caught the top of the hurdle and nose-dived into the ground. His giant athletic body somersaulted over his head, half-buried in the hoof-pocked ground. Rhys was flung mercilessly from his back like a discarded banana peel into the path of High Scribe.

Pippa clung to her cushion, her lips trembling with shock.

'Please get up,' she whispered. Tears filled her unblinking eyes as both horse and rider remained on the ground. Not even the chasing field, making hasty manoeuvres to avoid the stricken pair, made them stir. 'Maybe they're just winded.'

Even to her own ears, her words sounded doubtful.

'And you call yourself an animal-lover?' Ollie scoffed.

She'd forgotten he was there. She looked at him with distaste.

'Do you get altitude sickness?' she asked sarcastically.

'Eh?'

'Sitting up there on your moral high ground.'

His mouth fell open at her blatant contempt, but she ignored it. She looked back at the television. She pulled a face as the camera pulled away from the fallers to follow the conclusion of the race. High Scribe won by a distance, but the result barely registered with Pippa. Down the bottom of the screen, she saw the distressed figure of Emmie, in her red Aspen Valley anorak, sprinting down the side of the course.

'Oh, poor Emmie,' Pippa asked, her chest constricting with anguish for the stable lass.

A head-on view of the winner showed, in the background, the foreboding erection of the tarpaulin screens around the seventh hurdle and a waiting ambulance parked beside it.

Pippa chewed the corner of her cushion, hardly able to breathe as she waited for the winner's interview to finish and for them to update the viewers on the casualties. At last, the racing presenter who had interviewed Jack earlier on, appeared on the screen.

'We're very sorry to inform you that unfortunately Black Russian's fall was fatal...'

Pippa's breath caught in her throat and she gave a whimper. She dug her teeth into the cushion to stem the tears.

'...I have Jack Carmichael, his trainer, with me now,' the presenter continued. 'Jack, please accept our condolences. Can you give us any more information?'

The camera swung right to focus on him and the expression on his face released Pippa's tears. He looked a wreck. His face was pale, his hair dishevelled from running his hands through it. He addressed the camera with dry but dejected blue eyes.

'We're not sure of the extent of Rhys' injuries, but we should know more in the next few hours. He's being airlifted to hospital as we speak.' He paused, his composure faltering ever so slightly. 'And yes, I can confirm Black Russian's fall was fatal. I'm very sorry that this has happened to such a talented and popular horse. Not only was he a firm favourite in the yard, but I know he had many fans out there. The only consolation I can offer is that he wouldn't have suffered. His death was immediate, caused by a broken neck.' He frowned and cleared his throat.

'Poor Black Russian,' Pippa said, her voice muffled from behind the tear-dampened cushion. 'Poor Jack.'

'I'd like to thank all his followers for their support over the years,' Jack went on. 'He has been a great horse to watch and a privilege to train –' His voice caught and he cleared his throat again. 'Excuse me.'

Jack turned and walked away from the camera.

'And you call this a sport?' Ollie tutted.

Pippa's patience at Ollie's unsympathetic nature ran out.

'I have to go,' she announced, standing up.

Ollie stared at her.

'Go? Go where? We've got Rich's party in a few hours.'

'I have to go back to Aspen Valley,' she threw over her shoulder as she marched into the bedroom. She heard Ollie scramble off the sofa and come running after her.

'What? Why?'

'Because, Ollie!' she exclaimed, whirling around to face him. 'Because they're going to need me. Jack, Emmie, the entire yard are going to feel like shit! When horrible things happen in racing people like you simply sneer at those involved and accuse them of being murderers. You've no idea how much they love their horses. Their jobs are gruelling hard work in punishing weather – I know, I've seen it! Nobody does all that and *enjoys* it if they didn't love horses. Now they've lost the thing dearest to them and you are just going to make it worse by throwing mud at them. They need me.'

Ollie's face turned puce.

'*I* need you, Pippa!' he retaliated. 'What about me? What is it about this job that has you dropping me and scurrying back during our Christmas holiday when a horse dies? What about the party tonight?'

'Is that what you're worried about – Rich Holden's party?' Looking at his desperate expression, she wasn't sure whether to feel pity or contempt. 'Ollie, you don't need me for that,' she said, shaking her head. She went to pull her suitcase out of the wardrobe. 'The yard needs me a lot more than you do right now.'

Ollie stayed silent, watching her shove clothes into the open case.

When she glanced up at him to question his sudden lack of objection, she noticed a change in his demeanour. It was almost as if leaving now to support Aspen Valley in their hour of need held a deeper significance than usual. She felt like she was leaving her relationship with Ollie as well this time. Her priorities had changed somewhere along the line.

The look on his face mirrored her feelings.

But she didn't have time to discuss where their relationship was going and she wasn't about to give him the chance either. Tugging the zips closed, she heaved the case off the bed and headed for the door.

Ollie made no move to follow her. His deadpan expression registered no anger, no boyish sulk, just a detached observation of her movements.

'I'll call you,' she said, pausing by the doorway.

He nodded once and Pippa exited the room.

# Chapter Twenty-One

When finally she pulled up in Aspen Valley's car park, Pippa was surprised to see some members of staff still wandering around the darkened yard. The cold drizzle which blanketed the night seemed to accentuate their hunched dejected attitudes. She recognised Billy standing beneath the tack room's overhang, his fists deep in his pockets while he idly kicked the ground with his muddied boot.

'Billy,' Pippa called, hurrying over to him.

He looked up, shadows from the nearby security light making him look even more desolate.

'All right, Pippa?' he said without enthusiasm.

'I saw the race. I'm sorry, Billy. Are you okay?'

He shrugged and kicked at the ground again.

'Been better,' he replied.

'Is everyone back from the races? Where's Emmie and Jack?'

'The lorry got back about ten minutes ago. Jack's gone off to the hospital in Bristol to see Rhys.'

'How is he? How's Emmie?'

'Dunno about Rhys. Can't be that bad if they brought him all the way back here. Emmie's gone home. Nothing more for her to do here today.'

Pippa winced as she imagined the long journey home the stable lass must have had in a lorry without her horse.

'How is she holding up?'

Billy shrugged again.

'Said she wanted to be alone.'

'Oh, Billy. She must be so upset.' She paused to consider how she would feel in the circumstances, both in Emmie's shoes and Jack's. 'You should go to her,' she said.

'She said she wanted to be alone.'

'I know, but really she needs someone to comfort her.'

He looked at her, expression doubtful.

'You think I could comfort her?'

Pippa rubbed his slouched shoulder.

'You especially. Are you done here for the day?'

'Yeah, was about to head off home.' He bit his lip. 'But what good would I be to her? I don't feel so great right now either. Why don't you go?'

Pippa took a deep breath as she made her decision. Her own weariness after her long drive from London raised its head before she quashed it. Her own needs could wait for the time being.

'I'm going to Bristol to check on Rhys and Jack. Emmie needs you, Billy,' she urged.

Billy shrugged again.

'I guess a bit of company might help. For both of us, like.'

'That's right.' She gave his shoulder a squeeze. 'Please go to her, Billy. I'd better get moving if I want to get to Bristol before midnight.'

Billy gave her a twisted smile and nodded.

'If you're intending to comfort Jack, I reckon you got the harder job.'

Pippa gave a mirthless chuckle.

'I'll see you tomorrow,' she said before heading back into the rain towards her car.

The hospital reception was all but deserted when Pippa stepped through the automatic doors. The small internal bookstore and gift shop in the lobby had their shutters closed and the woman sitting behind the reception desk leaned over some paperwork, oblivious to the occasional passers-by.

'Excuse me,' Pippa said when she didn't raise her head. She smiled a greeting when the woman looked at her above her glasses.

'A and E's round the back, love.'

'No, I don't need to go to the A and E. You have a patient here, Rhys Bradford. He would've been brought in earlier. I'm not sure what time,' Pippa explained.

'You family?'

'No, he's a friend – well, we work together,' she corrected herself. She didn't really know Rhys well enough to class herself as a friend.

'Visiting hours are over. You'll need to come back tomorrow after two o'clock.'

Pippa pulled a face. She'd driven all this way in horrible weather. Her eyelids felt coated with lead, she was so tired. And now she had to go all the way home again?

'But I just need to find out if he's okay and to find Jack –'

'Sorry, love.' The receptionist shook her head. 'Not unless you're family.'

Pippa dragged her fingers through her hair and looked around her, searching for a good enough reason for the woman to let her in.

'He's a jockey,' she tried again. 'He had the most awful fall. Our boss should be with him –'

The receptionist tapped her pen against a sign on the desk.

'That's our visiting hours. Come back tomorrow at two.'

Pippa opened her mouth to protest, but the woman's telephone rang and with a meaningful look towards the visiting hours sign, she turned away from Pippa to answer it. Pippa's shoulders sagged as a resigned sigh escaped. Maybe she could try calling Jack on his mobile. She rummaged through her handbag and scrolled through her address book to find his number.

*'The number you have called is unavailable. Please try again later. The number you...'*

'Damn,' Pippa muttered under her breath and punched the cut-off key. She dropped her phone back into her bag and, dragging her feet across the stark clinical hospital flooring, made her weary exit. So much for flying in to the rescue. Now all she could do was go home and wait for tomorrow. The chivalrous automatic doors whooshed open as she neared them, letting in a blast of cold wet air.

Out of the corner of her eye, she saw a familiar figure walking down a side corridor before turning through a doorway. Pippa stopped short.

'Jack!' she cried. She made a dash to follow him, clattering past the reception desk.

'Here, you can't go through there!' the receptionist barked after her, futilely holding her hand over the telephone receiver.

'It's okay! It's Jack! I know him!' Pippa threw over her shoulder. 'Jack!'

A sudden awareness of the silence around as her voice and heels echoed down the corridor made her lower her voice. 'Jack?' she called quietly. She nipped through the doorway out of sight from the reception and saw him at the far end, standing in front of a vending machine. He pushed a couple of couple of buttons then rattled the machine with force. He was about to give it a kick when Pippa spoke again.

'Jack.'

He whirled round.

'Pippa! What are you doing here?'

Up close he looked even more haggard than he had earlier on television.

'I came to see if you – if everything was all right,' she replied, carefully rephrasing her answer. It seemed so inadequate when things were obviously very wrong.

'No, everything is not all right,' Jack replied. He turned back to the vending machine and delivered the threatened kick to its metal gut. 'Ow, fuck,' he muttered, leaning down to rub his toes. 'And you can't even get any bloody food here either.'

'Let's go find a canteen or something. There must be something still open,' Pippa said, taking his arm gently.

Jack scowled at her, but let himself be led away. They walked back towards the main foyer and Pippa avoided meeting the receptionist's glare.

'There,' she said, pointing further down the room. 'That looks like a café. Let's get a coffee and a muffin and you can tell me how Rhys is.'

Pippa ordered their drinks and two Chelsea buns from the café's limited menu and glanced across to Jack, sat in the corner booth. He had his head in his hands, his elbows resting heavily on the linoleum table. In the near-deserted room, he looked the picture of desolation.

Why wasn't Melissa here to support him? If you loved someone, you wanted to be with them, especially when they needed you most. Not for the first time she considered the complexities of Jack and Melissa's involvement.

With a shake of her head, she shoved her change into her handbag. For a start, she knew next to nothing about their relationship, she chided herself. Secondly, what business was it of hers?

Jack looked up as she arrived at the table and slid onto the plastic-cushioned bench opposite him.

'So, how's Rhys?' she said.

Jack picked up his Chelsea bun, but dropped it again with a bleak sigh.

'Broken his leg in three places,' he replied, shaking his head. 'He's waiting to go into theatre now. They say he's going to be out for at least three months.'

Pippa grimaced. To break your leg once sounded painful, but to break it three times in one go sounded agony. The broken toe she had incurred when she'd fallen down the steps outside Brannigans' Nightclub last year had been bad enough.

'Poor guy. But otherwise alive?'

'Just about. He's so pumped full of painkillers it'd make you wonder though.'

'Well, that's the main thing,' she said, trying to look on the bright side.

Jack wiped his sticky fingers on a paper napkin before throwing it down.

'Yeah,' he snorted. 'Where does that leave us though? He'll be out for the rest of the season. Finn's good, but how can I run a stable with one jockey?'

'It'll be fine,' she reassured him. 'There's loads of jockeys out there, really good jockeys, who'd jump at the chance of riding for you.'

'I wouldn't be so sure about that after today's performance,' Jack said in a morose tone, his head drooping. 'God, I can't believe he's gone.'

'It wasn't your fault, Jack.'

He looked up at her, his blue eyes desperate.

'What if it was though? I shouldn't have run Black Russian when we haven't had a chance to do some proper schooling over hurdles at home. He made mistakes when he lost the Fighting Fifth. I *knew* he needed more work. Even a couple of jumps in the indoor school, but I didn't do it. I still entered him at Kempton and now – now he's dead.' His face drained of what little colour it held as he said it out loud.

'It was just an accident,' Pippa insisted, 'a terrible, terrible accident. He'd been jumping fine before he fell. It wasn't anyone's fault.'

'He was so good,' Jack continued. 'He would have won, you could see him stepping up a gear and pulling clear of High Scribe. He would have had a great chance to win at Cheltenham again next year.' He shook his head. 'Does that make me a bad person because I'm feeling worse over his death since he was such a talented horse?'

The insecurity in his eyes made Pippa's heart twist in anguish.

'No, of course not,' she said gently. 'It always seems to hurt more when we lose a real talent. It doesn't make you a bad person at all.'

Jack didn't say anything. Instead he frowned at his clasped hands resting on the table.

Pippa realised she'd reached across and was covering his hands with her own. She eased her hands away. She felt a sudden surge of anger towards Melissa for not being here to hold Jack when he so obviously needed it, but which she, Pippa, wasn't allowed to do.

'Where's Melissa?' she said.

Jack blinked as if trying to recall her existence. He gave a sardonic smile.

'Virtuoso won the King George with Finn aboard. She's in London with her father.'

'Oh,' Pippa replied, thinking that she'd been in London too and it hadn't stopped her coming back. Maybe it was different for Melissa. She knew the King George was a big race – maybe the winning owners were expected to attend some sort of royal banquet afterwards.

'You shouldn't have come,' Jack muttered.

'I had to.'

'You're meant to be celebrating Christmas with your family and your boyfriend.'

'How could I, Jack? How could I stay in London after seeing the race on TV and knowing how awful everyone would be feeling?'

'You've got your priorities wrong.'

Pippa thought of Rich Holden's party, which would be well into its stride by now and the pretence she would have had to keep up the entire evening to impress Ollie's co-stars and peers. Not to mention the red dress that Ollie had wanted her to wear.

She shook her head and smiled.

'I don't think so.'

Jack looked at her with a steady gaze, a glint of curiosity in his eyes.

Pippa readied herself for the explanation he was bound to ask for, but the question never arrived. He just nodded.

'In that case, I'm glad you came.' He broke eye contact and cleared his throat.

Pippa bit back a smile. She wanted to gather his hands in hers again to show how those few words had made her four-and-a-half-hour journey back on the dark and wet M4 in holiday traffic worthwhile. Instead, she picked up her coffee and took a sip.

'Urgh, the coffee here is awful,' she said, grimacing.

Jack raised a smile for the first time.

'It's a government incentive to never end up in hospital,' he replied. 'Think of Rhys. God knows how long he's going to be subjected to it for.'

Pippa laughed in sympathy, which soon became a yawn.

'You look done in,' Jack said.

'So do you,' she replied.

'Shall we go? Presumably you've got your car.'

Pippa nodded.

'Come on, then.' Jack shifted along his seat to get up. 'I'll follow you home. Just to make sure you get back all right.'

155

'It's okay, I got rid of my Take That CD. That was my only hazard while driving.'

Jack chuckled and waited for Pippa to stand up before guiding her to the exit.

'Nonetheless, for my peace of mind then.'

They walked in silence out of the hospital and into the damp winter outside.

'I'm over there,' Jack said, pointing to a section of the car park.

'I'm just here,' Pippa replied.

'Well, see you tomorrow then.'

'Yes, see you tomorrow,' she echoed.

'I'll be right behind you.'

She watched him walk away across the car park to his Land Rover, feeling a warmth inside fill her from within. She wasn't anxious about her drive back to Hazyvale, more dreading the fact that she wouldn't be able to curl up in bed for at least another half hour. But the thought of having Jack drive behind her leant a curious feeling of comfort to her. Whether it was simply having his company, albeit in a separate vehicle, for the duration of the journey or his small gesture of protectiveness, she was too tired to decide.

With a shrug, she delved into her bag to find her car keys.

# Chapter Twenty-Two

Pippa arrived at Aspen Valley Stables the next morning feeling exhausted. She stood near the entrance to watch the yard activity as she had done on her first morning. With a sad acknowledgement, she saw the vitality and buzz that had captured that original moment was absent. The lads and lasses still went about their duties, but without any spark or enthusiasm. There were no jovial shouts and chatter. Even the horses looked miserable, their heads lowered away from the constant rain that plastered their manes and forelocks to their skin in rats' tails.

Pippa hoped the Christmas 'party' scheduled for tonight might help lift everyone's spirits. Before she became soaked through, she walked on to the office.

Her emails were taking so long to load, Pippa was able to make herself a cup of coffee in the meantime. Jack's office door remained firmly locked and she imagined him, sitting in his Land Rover halfway up the Gallops in dejected solitude, watching the horses work in the rain. She wished she could go deliver him a coffee just to warm him up, to let him know that she was on his side. Her longing to do this became even more acute when she finally sat down to read through the hundred odd emails they'd received over the last forty-eight hours.

*So sorry to hear about Black Russian. He was my favourite horse...*

*Murdering hypocrite. How can you say you like horses? You killed Black Russian by forcing him to race...*

*R.I.P. Black Russian. A true hero of National Hunt racing who brought great pleasure to his many fans...*

*Have you recently been hurt or injured at work? If so, you may be entitled to claim compensation...*

*You bastard, Jack Carmichael. Any fool would have seen Black Russian wasn't fit to run in the Christmas Hurdle. I put my faith in you with a two grand bet that Black Russian could win at Cheltenham two years running and he would have if you hadn't been so blind...*

And so they went on. Tears sprung in Pippa's eyes as each well-wishing email was interspersed by angry punters and animal activists. She hoped Jack's mobile was unlisted. Methodically, she deleted the hate mail and after a moment's deliberation, opted to keep the condolences for Jack to read if he wanted to.

When Jack did appear, he looked tired and grumpy.

'Morning,' he grunted in reply to Pippa's greeting and shut himself away in his office.

For once, his abruptness evoked sympathy in her. What personal hell was he putting himself through?

She glanced down at the box canvas leaning against her desk drawers, trying to sum up the courage to intrude on Jack's dark mood. Perhaps a hot drink would help ease things along, she thought, getting up and heading for the kitchenette.

With difficulty, she knocked on Jack's door a couple of minutes later, a cup of tea and the canvas in her hands.

'Tea to warm you up,' she said as she entered. 'How are you doing?'

Jack looked up from his computer, his expression pained and Pippa guessed he'd received some pretty unpleasant emails to his personal address.

'Like Santa's forgotten me this year,' he replied. 'What have you got there?'

Pippa placed his mug down on a coaster and fingered the canvas nervously.

'It's the painting I did of Black Russian and the other horses working in the snow. I finished it a few days ago, but didn't get a chance to give it to you.' She turned the painting round and held it up for Jack to inspect. She heard him catch his breath.

He got up and skirted the desk, his eyes never leaving the picture.

'I'll understand if you don't want it anymore. I know it might not be the happiest painting to look at now,' Pippa babbled when he didn't say anything.

Jack traced his finger down the fluid muscular outline of the dark bay horse in the lead, almost bursting out of the canvas against the contrasting pale background. He frowned and shook his head.

'No. It's perfect. It's a great tribute to Black Russian.' He sighed and let his hand drop. 'God, he was some horse.'

Pippa bit her lip at the emotion in his voice.

'I want you to have it,' she blurted.

Jack's brows knitted in confusion.

'I mean as a gift. I don't want to be paid.'

He stared at her then shook his head again, this time more vigorously.

'No, this was a commission. You need the money. Of course I must pay you for it.'

'No, Jack, please,' she persisted. She held the picture out for him to take. 'It's the least I can do. I feel so bad over his death. Please take this as a gift.' She tried to smile. 'Santa hasn't forgotten you.'

Jack took a step back, leaving her to hold the picture. He walked away and threaded a hand through his hair.

'No, Pippa. I can't,' he said, turning to face her again.

She gazed at him, confused, searching for an explanation.

'But why?'

Jack looked at her, his steely eyes intense.

'I can't accept this as a gift. I haven't got you anything. I didn't even think to get you anything.' His eyes darkened as she became more bewildered. 'Exchanging Christmas presents is what friends and family do. I – I'm your *boss*.'

With a stab of torment, Pippa realised she'd crossed the line. She'd made the mistake of caring too much. She swallowed with difficulty, embarrassment mingling with the hurt. She bent down and leaned the painting against the desk, trying to mask her feelings. She couldn't look him in the eye.

'Yes, of course you are. There you go then.' She kept her gaze down, hiding behind her auburn curls and hurried towards the door.

'Pippa,' Jack called after her.

She ignored him.

'*Pippa!*'

No matter how hard she tried, she couldn't ignore that tone. She stopped, unwilling to face him.

'I'm sorry,' he said, his voice gentler. 'You understand though, don't you?'

She set her expression and looked back at him. To give him his due, he didn't look that comfortable either.

'Yes, I do.' She stepped out of the office, clicking the door shut behind her.

What had she been thinking? She was beginning to scare herself when she couldn't come up with a definitive answer, especially as Jack's abrupt clarification of their relationship had impacted on her so forcefully. Everything he said was true. He was her boss, nothing more. All the small allowances like trips onto the Gallops and this art commission and his following her home last night meant nothing more than general goodwill.

159

As she sat back down at her desk, she chided herself for forgetting that. She wouldn't make that mistake again in a hurry.

Emmie walked into the office at lunchtime, making Pippa jump up and rush round her desk to console her, her own jumbled feelings at once put aside. The girl's drooping posture and sad eyes were more befitting to someone who had lost a close family member.

Emmie attempted a brave smile, but in the face of Pippa's obvious concern, her lower lip trembled and her eyes glistened with tears. She tried to wave away Pippa's support.

'I'm sorry. I didn't come here to be a burden,' she whimpered.

'Nonsense. You're never a burden.'

Emmie sagged and allowed herself to be hugged.

Pippa felt a hard lump swelling in her throat as she felt the distressed sobs of the stable lass buffer against her.

'I loved him so much,' Emmie croaked. She stepped out of Pippa's arms and folded her hands against her chest. 'My heart feels like it's breaking.' She gulped. 'I never understood the – the magnitude of that expression until now.'

Pippa hugged her close again, rubbing her back in comfort.

'You probably think I'm being silly,' Emmie sniffed. 'Maybe I am. He was just a horse. But not to me. To me he – he was my best friend.' She choked as a new wave of sobs shuddered through her.

Pippa's eyes filled with tears as she realised the enormity of the girl's grief. The horses outside weren't just animals or products of their work. They were friends, companions, confidantes and were just as capable of invoking love in a person as any other human could.

'I know,' she replied into Emmie's shoulder. 'And it's not silly at all. In fact, it might be considered silly if you weren't upset.'

Jack's office door opened, interrupting her. He started to say something then noticed Emmie weeping onto Pippa's shoulder. For a long moment, he watched them, his expression guilt-ridden before quietly closing the door again.

When the tears started to subside, Pippa felt Emmie's body straighten as her composure reasserted itself.

'I'm sorry,' Emmie apologised again. She gave Pippa a weak smile. 'I didn't mean to cry like that. What I really came in for was to let you know that I don't think I'm going to make it this evening for the drinks do.'

'But Emmie, it might make you feel better. It might take your mind off things,' Pippa reasoned.

Emmie shook her head.

'I don't think so. I'm sorry.'

Pippa rubbed the lass' shoulder.

'It's okay. Go home and watch *Something About Mary* or *When Harry Met Sally*. Those are my two cheer-up movies.'

Emmie smiled, this time stronger and wiped her swollen eyes with the back of her sleeve.

'I'll see if Blockbusters have them,' she said.


Pippa tilted her watch towards the light as the last member of staff wheeled their bicycle out of the yard. It wasn't even seven o'clock. She looked glumly at the rows of unopened drinks still lining the table in the tack room and the bowls of snacks hardly touched. With a shrug, she set about repacking the bottles of beer. Hopefully, the dingy off-licence in Helensvale's back-end might give them a refund for the three untouched crates.

After heaving the crates onto the backseat of her car, Pippa locked up the empty yard and headed back to the car park with a heavy heart. Of the fifty odd members of Aspen Valley staff, only a handful had stayed on for their Christmas celebrations.

Had she expected any more though? The mood of those who had made the effort was subdued and was more like a bad wake than a Christmas party. She hadn't known them very well and her attempts at making light conversation had been stilted and forced. Jack hadn't come, but he'd told her beforehand that he was meeting Dan Cameron to discuss their 'situation'.

Pippa's loyalties were torn. Jack had a commitment towards his staff and should therefore be present at the party. On the other hand, he also had a business to run and Dan Cameron was still very much a part of that, Black Russian or no Black Russian. Despite her earlier promise not to take a personal view on Jack's circumstances, Pippa hoped Dan wasn't meeting him to tell him he was removing his remaining horses.

She was further upset by the absence of Finn. She'd relied on seeing him at the yard, a cheerful face amidst the gloom to lend his support. But even he hadn't bothered to pitch up.

Pippa's feelings spiralled south as she drove through the dark narrow lanes towards Helensvale. As well as the party being a resounding failure, it also meant she'd be home early and would therefore not have any excuse not to call Ollie like she'd promised.

What would they say to each other? She knew the inevitable was looming. The pleasure their relationship had once thrived on was just a faraway memory. In her mind's eye, their happier times were almost sepia-coloured they were so distant. The optimistic belief that their 'rough patch' would be temporary was fracturing. It seemed every time she returned to London, those cracks became even more cavernous. She wasn't happy in their relationship. Ollie obviously wasn't either. Why didn't he break up with her then?

Pippa sighed as she pulled up in front of a small restaurant a little way down from the local off-licence. She switched off the engine, still deep in thought. She didn't want to live a lie, but neither did she want to be the one to shatter this fanciful dream she and Ollie had created. She hated breaking up. She remembered how she'd cried for days on Tash's shoulder when Dean Mason had broken up with her when she was fifteen because she'd refused to have sex with him. After that, the only other long-ish term relationship she'd had she'd broken off because she had met Ollie. On that occasion, Craig, the dumpee, had cried. She didn't expect Ollie to cry, but still, why did she get to be the bad guy?

Pippa frowned, suddenly aware, as she was sitting in her car, of a familiar face inside the restaurant in front of her. Through the window, his sandy blond hair fell across his furrowed forehead as he nodded at his companion seated opposite. The thick burgundy curtains were partly closed and Pippa craned her neck to see who was dining with Aspen Valley's newly appointed number one jockey. The frosted window blurred the person's face, but Pippa could make out long blonde hair and a tailored blouse.

Was this Finn's mystery partner?

If it was, then judging by his expression, it wasn't a particularly romantic evening they were sharing. The woman slid something across the table towards him, her elegant fingers capped with dark red nail varnish. She stood up and Pippa's mouth dropped in surprise. Melissa Mardling swung her Louis Vuitton bag over her shoulder and sauntered away from the table and out of sight.

'No way,' Pippa breathed. Surely not. Melissa was dating Jack. Would Finn be so stupid as to have an affair with his boss' girlfriend?

She shook her head.

He wouldn't be that careless nor that conniving. Besides, he'd always given Pippa the impression that Melissa wasn't one of his favourite people either. Had he been saying that to throw her off the scent perhaps?

Theories whirred round Pippa's brain as she continued to stare, mouth agape, at Finn. He was looking down at a piece of paper – the bill maybe, which Melissa had pushed towards him.

He shook his head and ran his fingers through his hair. Melissa obviously wasn't a cheap date.

# Chapter Twenty-Three

Back at Hazyvale, Pippa opened the fridge, not particularly hungry, but in need of something to distract her. Even though she'd spent most of her working life in restaurants, she was far from adventurous when it came to cooking, well aware from her past efforts that she was more than capable of giving herself food poisoning.

She was just considering chicken risotto when her mobile phone trilled from its usual resting place on the windowsill. She grabbed a half-finished tub of potato salad and went to answer it.

Her thumb paused above the answer button when she saw the caller ID. She took a deep breath and prepared herself for the worst.

'Hi Ollie,' she said in a tentative voice.

'Hey Pippa!'

Taken aback by his cheery greeting, Pippa's spoon halted in mid-descent towards the creamy potatoes.

'You okay?' she asked. She considered whether he'd been drinking, but dismissed it immediately. Ollie was not a happy drunk.

'Not bad, not bad. How is everything with Dan Cameron?'

A frown passed over her forehead. Maybe with her emotions running high when she'd abandoned him in London, she'd misread the situation. Perhaps she'd been too hasty with her supposition that she and Ollie were about to break up.

'Um, not the greatest. Black Russian, as you know, died. Rhys broke his leg. Jack's meeting with Dan this evening,' she replied.

Ollie chuckled.

'First name terms now, eh? Next time you speak to him, make sure you pass on my condolences.'

Her frown deepened in confusion.

'Okay,' she said. 'Listen, Ollie, I'm sorry for walking out on you like I did. I know how much you were looking forward to Rich Holden's party. It was selfish of me.'

'Don't worry, Pippa. I went anyway. Rich was well impressed that you knew Dan Cameron.'

'Well, I don't really *know* him, Ollie.' She bit her lip. With Ollie obviously trying to make amends, it probably wasn't the best plan to start contradicting him. 'Did you have a good time?'

'Yeah,' he enthused. 'When I said we had a racehorse, it was a surprisingly popular topic. Rich said he was thinking of getting into racing. Peace Order is going to win the Grand National, right?'

'Peace Offering,' she corrected. 'He's got an entry in the race. Obviously I can't say whether he's going to win it or not.'

'You've got to be in it to win it.'

'We've still got to make the cut,' Pippa said.

'When's he next going to race? I thought I might come along.'

A rush of warmth flooding through her body at the thought of Ollie taking an interest in Peace Offering crashed against the cold incoming tide of alarm that she'd already invited Tash to Peace Offering's next start.

'Next Saturday. But it's down at Wincanton and I thought you'd be working,' she went on quickly. 'You usually work over the weekends.'

'I'm sure we can sort something out. Where's Wincanton?'

'South of here. Near Glastonbury, I think,' she said, vaguely recollecting her own search for the racecourse on a map. 'Miles from London,' she added.

She cringed in anticipation of his reply. It wasn't that she didn't want Ollie to come along. On the contrary, if this was an opportunity to revive their stagnant relationship she was ready to grasp it with both hands. But it would mean Ollie and Tash would be in each other's company and that probably wouldn't be as therapeutic.

'But it can't be far from where you are. We can make a weekend of it,' Ollie said, not put out at all. 'I'll get to see our house in the country. Did I tell you Rich has also got a country pad down in Dorset?'

'No-o-o,' she replied, not entirely certain. When Ollie started talking about his co-star these days she had a habit of switching off.

'That's settled then. I'll drive down for the weekend and we'll go racing. Will Peace Offering be favourite?'

'I don't know. Probably not.' She dabbled her spoon in the tub of potato salad with discomfort as she realised Ollie would get to meet Jack as well. 'Are you sure you want to come, Ollie? I mean I don't want to get your hopes up. Peace Offering might not win and this place is still pretty shabby.'

There was a brief pause before he answered.

'Pippa, look,' he began in a humble voice. 'Maybe I was a bit unfair to you on Boxing Day. I was nervous about going to Rich's party and when you left, I might have panicked a little. I didn't necessarily think about it from your point of view.'

Pippa smiled in concession. She missed this part of Ollie's nature. Maybe their relationship wasn't doomed just yet.

'I'm sorry too,' she said. 'You'll love Hazyvale. And Peace Offering's a gorgeous horse. You'll love him too.' She couldn't help the enthusiasm creeping back into her voice. Optimistic thoughts of the pair of them laughing and having fun at the races and the opportunity to reveal the charm of Hazyvale to Ollie was too much to resist.

All was not lost, after all.


Jack walked into the office the next morning as Pippa put the telephone receiver back in its cradle.

'That was Emmie,' she told him. 'She's calling in sick.'

Jack's mouth twisted in dissatisfaction.

'Black Russian-sick?'

'No. Bad tummy she said.'

'Damn, I wanted to give Asian Dancer a schooling session today and she's just about the only person who can control her,' he muttered. He scraped his hair away from his forehead with a sigh. 'Is she hung over from the drinks last night?'

Pippa shook her head and motioned to the three crates stacked against the wall which the off-licence had refused to refund her for last night.

'No. She didn't come. Only about five people stayed on. It probably would've been a more popular party if I'd been handing out nooses rather than beers.'

Jack didn't look surprised.

'I told you not to expect much.'

'No, but there are bad parties and then there are sad parties. Last night was a sad party.'

He gave a resigned sigh.

'Did Emmie say if she would be back tomorrow?'

'She didn't know, but she said she'd try. Even if she is fibbing and she really is Black Russian-sick, maybe a day away from here would be good for her,' Pippa said. Emmie had sounded uneasy over the phone, but she knew from past experience that even the most genuine absence excuses left the convalescent feeling guilty.

Jack didn't say anything. He just stood, looking nonplussed at the three crates of beer lining the wall. Pippa's thoughts strayed to the restaurant

166

scene she had witnessed last night. How much lower could things get for Jack to find out his girlfriend was more than likely having an affair with his jockey? As much as she'd like to know the truth behind it all, she didn't dare mention it to him.

'Well, we can't leave these here.' He bent down and picked up the first crate, making it seem as light as if the bottles were empty.

'I'll help you,' Pippa said, sympathy getting the better of her. She pushed her chair back and went to assist.

'You don't have to. I can do it –' Jack paused as raised voices from out in the yard drifted through the window. He and Pippa looked out to see Billy and another lad arguing outside Black Russian's empty stable. Finn was jogging across to break it up.

'He'd no right to take that head collar without asking!' Billy fumed when the Irishman asked what the matter was. 'It's still Black Russian's tack even if he's not using it no more!'

Jack turned away from the window, the crate now appearing much heavier as his shoulders drooped.

'I thought maybe Virtuoso's win might be enough to lift their spirits,' he said. 'Doesn't seem to be working though.' He set off towards the kitchenette with a shake of his head.

Pippa readied herself to pick up one of the other crates, mindful of bending her knees, especially when wearing heels.

Jack reappeared in the doorway, still holding the crate. The expression on his face made Pippa pause.

'I decorated the splash-back tiles behind the sink,' she said sheepishly. The patterned tiles which she'd created in Hazyvale's kitchen had turned out so well she hadn't been able to resist doing the same with the bland kitchenette at work. 'I hope you don't mind.'

'What?' Jack glanced distractedly behind him. 'No, that's fine. I was just thinking...'

'Yes?' Pippa prompted when he didn't continue.

'You suggested having a proper staff party with a DJ would make them forget they were at work. Maybe it's still worth a go.'

Pippa grinned.

'It'd take some of the monotony out of their present lives,' she encouraged.

'Maybe a good shake-up will snap everyone out of this bloody awful gloom we're all stuck in,' he added.

'And it'd get the beers drunk.'

167

The gleam in Jack's eyes, which Pippa was tempted to say almost looked like excitement, reflected in her own.

'Do you think you could still organise it?' he asked. 'Where would we have it? Do you think we should hire the church hall or something in Helensvale?'

'No need. We've got the hay barn right here. Just a bit of rearranging and we'll have our very own disco. Leave it to me!' she beamed.

Ten minutes later, Pippa wasn't feeling quite so confident. She riffled through the Yellow Pages, but couldn't find any DJ or disco companies in Helensvale. Mind you, it was such a small community that The Plough and its Thursday karaoke evenings was probably sufficient for the residents' musical needs. She pulled out the heavier Yellow Pages for Bristol.

After her fourth attempt had laughed at her openly for wanting to hire a discotheque at short notice over New Year, Pippa stilled her drumming fingers on the open page for a rethink. She wasn't envisaging flashing strobe lights and glitter balls, but a DJ with a decent sound system was a must. For the briefest of moments she yearned for London, with its superfluous productivity and immediate availability of everything from kebab shops to pirated porn videos (neither of which she was particularly keen on).

Her thoughts turned to Tash, for what reason she wasn't entirely sure since she didn't see how her best friend would remind of her of kebabs and porn. She slammed the Yellow Pages shut and reached for the phone. Of course!

'Oh, boy,' Tash answered the phone in a wry drawl. 'A phone call mid-morning from work. You don't have another Open Day which you've forgotten about, have you?'

Pippa laughed.

'Merry Christmas, Tash. How are you?'

'I've got a hangover from hell and I feel like a blue whale with jaundice. Next time somebody suggests playing Ring of Fire, take my advice, sweets. Say *no*. It's a bad bad drinking game.'

'Oh, Tash, feeling a bit green? What are we going to do with you?' Pippa giggled.

'Send me home with some hangover pills would be my recommendation, but I doubt whether that'd pass muster. How are you and your scrumptious boss?'

168

'Well, now that you mention it, not so great. You know I told you we lost one of our best horses on Boxing Day?'

'Yeah, sorry to hear about that. The public have gone right for Jack's jugular on that one.'

'Tell me about it,' she agreed. Despite filtering calls and emails, anti-racing activists had still found ways of kicking Jack when he was down. 'Everyone's really low here so Jack and I have decided that having a proper Christmas – or probably New Year's – party would be good to give them a boost. The only problem is, I can't find a DJ who's willing to do it at such short notice.' Pippa wound the telephone cord around her finger. 'And I remember you saying Aladdin did a bit of DJ-ing on the sidelines...' She left Tash to fill in the blanks.

'How short a notice are we talking here?'

'About a week?'

She heard Tash sigh with relief.

'Thank God for that. I thought it was going to be another twenty-four hour jobby. Aladdin can't do it though I'm afraid. He's up in Yorkshire for two weeks.'

'Oh.' Pippa couldn't help the despair in her tone.

'But he's got connections, sweets, don't panic. And I'm sure some of them can be found near you. Leave it with me.'

Pippa closed her eyes and thanked God for creating Tash and allowing her to be her friend.

'I owe you again.'

'Hmm, maybe. I don't know. The last time you owed me, Aladdin was good enough to repay in kind.'

Pippa snorted.

'Say no more. I don't want to hear about your indiscretions.'

# Chapter Twenty-Four

'You off your fuckin' 'ead, yeah?' DJ John the Boptist looked at Pippa incredulously beneath the rakish tilt of his New York Yankees gangster cap.

Feeling uncertain, Pippa stood in the doorway to the hay barn, the late afternoon sunshine casting long shadows into its dusty interior.

'Um, I don't think so,' she said in a hesitant voice.

'You fink I'm gonna set up my decks in 'ere with all this straw around?'

'Hay,' she corrected.

'Whatever. It would be a major fuckin' fire 'azard, is what I'm saying. Now, my gear is safe an' all that, yeah, but the wirin' can get bare 'ot.' He took off his cap and smoothed his dark shaven head before reapplying it at a more acute angle.

'We'd clear a space obviously, so you wouldn't have any hay where you set up your – your decks,' Pippa tried to placate him.

Dread seeped through her as he shook his head.

'No way, man. Too dangerous. I ain't taking no chances.'

Pippa's dread began to turn into panic.

'No, please don't say that. You can't cancel on us now. The party's going to start in three hours!'

John the Boptist shrugged.

'Forget it. If I knew this was gonna be some sorta barn dance, I woulda said no right off, like.' He walked away, the chafing of his low-slung jeans grating in Pippa's ears as she watched on, helpless.

'Wait!' she cried. 'Don't go!' She ran after him, her heels plugging into the soft ground outside the barn.

He stopped and gave her an impatient look.

'Maybe we could have it outside,' Pippa suggested. 'I'm sure we could find some extension cords somewhere.'

'And if it rains? Only 'alf my decks are insured. I could do with the gig and all that, but I ain't gonna risk my decks.'

Pippa looked up at the sky, a weak buttery blue punctuated by the odd fluff ball of cloud.

'It might not rain.'

'Sorry, mate. You find a proper venue and I'll be 'appy to jam for you.'

He began walking away again and Pippa felt her panic flood down to her feet. She'd persuaded nearly the entire Aspen Valley staff to attend with the promise of some music. She'd even found a store in Helensvale that would supply some coloured lights to set the scene. Some of the staff had actually brightened at the idea of having a proper party.

How could she let them down at this late hour? It would turn into the same disaster as the original Christmas drinks do had been last week only with fifty people more.

John the Boptist shuffled round the corner into the car park and out of sight. A few moments later his van roared into life, accompanied by a loud backfire. A startled neigh from a horse nearby responded, followed by a muffled stream of expletives from its handler.

Pippa glanced, distracted, towards the sound coming from the next building along. She gasped and sprinted in the direction of the car park.

'WAIT! STOP!' she yelled.

The van jerked to a halt as it made a cumbersome three-point-turn. The window was wound down and John the Boptist leaned his head out.

Pippa panted to a stop beside the vehicle.

'The indoor school – we can have it there! We can move the jumps and clear it out. We could probably even squeeze you onto the platform bit at the end.'

'No straw?'

'Not even a blade.'

The DJ gave her a mirthless smile.

'Definitely no blades. That's why I got outta London.'

Pippa leaned her hands on her knees to catch her breath. Her New Year's resolution to give up smoking hadn't begun paying dividends just yet. She grinned.

'Thank you,' she breathed.

Pippa accepted her third cup of punch from Randy, the acting barman behind the precarious-looking table laden with refreshments, and made her way in the semi-darkness round the edge of the indoor school. She perched on the top pole of one of the jumps which had been pushed to the sides and watched, with satisfaction, the lads and lasses of Aspen Valley dancing and chatting, the coloured lights flickering off their animated faces. The atmosphere was so different from the week before, any reservations she might have harboured had evaporated with the warmth of the party.

'Hula Hoop?' offered a voice, raised above the thrashing of Scissor Sisters.

Pippa looked up to find Finn standing beside her, a littering of snacks on his outstretched palm. She gave him a grateful smile and took a couple, popping them into her mouth. She hadn't spoken much to Finn over the past week. It seemed that in the absence of Rhys, his role as first stable jockey took him away from the yard more. Although she'd missed his good-natured presence, a feature that had been in desperate need since Boxing Day, she wasn't altogether sorry their paths hadn't crossed. She still didn't know what to make of his and Melissa's rendezvous. It even scared her a little that such a likeable person as Finn could do anything so devious. If indeed, he was doing something devious, Pippa reminded herself.

Finn sat down beside her and took a nonchalant swig of his beer.

'Good *craic*,' he said, gesturing towards the dancing crowd. 'It was an excellent idea.'

'Jack's idea,' she said.

Finn choked on a Hula Hoop and Pippa grinned.

'Jack? He suggested all this?'

'Well, I suggested it originally, but he didn't take to it. Then of course, the Christmas Hurdle happened and he decided it *would* be a good idea,' she explained.

'Looks like he still can't make up his mind,' Finn said, nodding towards a group of people.

Pippa smiled as she recognised two lasses, probably emboldened by the liberally-spiked punch, pulling Jack towards the dancing area. His stance was of one being dragged to the galleys, but his half-hearted protests were uttered with humour.

'We also had three crates of beer left over from last week's drinks do. Had to think of something to get them drunk,' she went on, still watching a self-conscious Jack now trying to dance to Black Eyed Peas. 'I tried to return them to the off-licence in Helensvale, but they wouldn't take them back.' She bit her lip, realising she was moving onto potentially awkward territory.

Finn turned to her in a swift movement, nearly overbalancing on the pole and clicked his fingers.

'Last Tuesday evening, you were in Helensvale down by the liquor store?'

Pippa nodded, not quite able to meet his eyes.

Finn wagged a finger at her.

'I thought I saw your car outside!' he said in triumph.

'You were in town that evening?' Pippa tried to sound nonchalant, but her heart began to thud. Was he going to deny being with Melissa?

'Aye, at that lousy Turkish bar. You'd think with it being Christmas, they'd have turkey on the menu, wouldn't ye?'

Pippa couldn't help giggling. Damn, this punch was strong.

'I thought I might have seen you through the window,' she admitted with a vague wave of her hand.

Finn threw the last of his Hula Hoops into his mouth and crunched on them, his eyes glinting with wicked humour.

'Ye did, didya?'

'Yes, okay. I saw you,' she surrendered with a defeated sigh. 'And Melissa. But you don't have to explain anything, Finn. I didn't mean to see you. It's none of my business what you get up to.'

Finn leant his head back and roared with laughter.

'And what did you think I was getting up to?' he chuckled.

Pippa looked down at her drink in embarrassment.

'I don't know. I guess the obvious came to mind, really.'

Finn wrapped his arm around her shoulders, jogging her as he shook with laughter.

'You thought I was doing a line with Melissa Mardling? Pippa, *a thaisce*, what sort of chancer do you take me for? Riskin' a pummelling from Jack for *Melissa*?'

A flush burnt Pippa's cheeks and she shrugged.

'What were you doing then?'

'You forget now with Rhys up to his clackers in plaster, I'm riding all of the mighty Mardling horses, including Virtuoso. She just wanted to talk a few things over about them.'

Pippa sighed with relief and searched Finn's eyes in the dim light for reassurance.

'Really? That was all?'

Finn squeezed her shoulder.

'Yes, that was all.' He chuckled and shook his head. 'Now, don't let that be botherin' you. I believe this is Take That playing and with you being a fan, I think we should take to the floor.'

Dizzy with alcohol and relief, Pippa let Finn lead her into a hub of dancing stable lasses. With a laugh, she saw Jack valiantly trying to escape the group as Take That bounced their way through *Shine*. She grinned and mouthed 'Okay?' to him.

Jack gave a wry smile in reply and shrugged in defeat.

Caught up in a moment when everything seemed good again – Finn wasn't sleeping with Jack's girlfriend, Aspen Valley were enjoying themselves and Jack looked relaxed – Pippa laughed out loud, moving her feet in the springy sand in time with Finn's and sang along to the chorus.

Her flushed cheeks were aching from smiling so much by the time the song finished. She paused for breath and tried to empty her open-toed shoes of sand, waiting for the next track to begin. The lulled electric guitar chords and drumbeat of Prince's *Purple Rain* resounded about the building. Pippa looked up, her eyes locking with Jack's. She gulped.

He stood, three feet away, an inevitable invitation to join him issued by body language as other parties coupled together.

She hesitated before taking a step forward. In a convoluted way, it felt right to dance with him. She stopped. On the other hand, it was absolutely absurd that she should dance to such a number with her boss.

A hand slipped into hers and pulled her away. With a slight start, she found herself in Finn's arms, staring into his smiling eyes.

'Dance with me?' he said, cradling her waist.

A sudden relief swept through her as she nodded. What had she been about to do? Distracted, she nestled into his arms, swaying to Prince's haunted yet melodic longing tones. She looked over Finn's shoulder at Jack.

He was walking away.

A pang of disappointment twisted in her stomach. If she wasn't mistaken, the look on his face before Finn had swept her away had shown a part of him had wanted to dance with her too. An irrational part. Jack stopped by the wide entrance to the indoor school and turned back, his face half-lit by the moonlight beaming through the doorway.

Without embarrassment or discomfort, Pippa watched him watching her. Finn, moving her body in a gentle rhythm, was forgotten to her. Jack's face was almost statuesque with the silvery light cast against it, but his eyes bore into hers with penetrating intensity. She felt she was almost dancing with *him* instead. Like a rabbit being hypnotised by a snake, she couldn't bear to break his gaze. And amidst the stillness of his expression, a feeling very much alive projected itself across to her. *Wanting*.

As Finn guided her round, she was forced to tear her eyes away from Jack. The moments that she had her back to him dragged by, made longer by the mesmeric tune of *Purple Rain*. When at last they'd turned a three-sixty and she could look at him again without banging heads with Finn, her heart dropped.

The doorway was empty, the place where Jack had stood looking lonelier for his absence.

Pippa's eyes darted around the room. Beside them, Billy and Emmie were locked in a slow dance shuffle. A few other couples were scattered around the dance area whilst others converged on the drinks and snacks tables. But Jack wasn't among them.

Pippa stepped out of Finn's embrace as the song faded to its conclusion. She made the conscious effort not to be hasty, lest the jockey take it personally.

'Thanks, Finn,' she smiled. 'I - um, have to go.' She gave an embarrassed giggle. 'Nature calls, you know.'

'Oh, aye. Thank you, *a thaisce*,' he replied, giving her a genteel bow with one hand behind his back.

Pippa hurried to the exit. She wasn't sure why she needed to find Jack and even less idea what they would possibly say to each other, but the urge to just *see* him was overwhelming. He wasn't outside the building though. Hugging her arms around herself to fend off the cold, she made her way over to the office, ignoring the inquisitive equine heads looking out over their stable doors at the unusual events going on. The office lay in darkness.

Pippa stopped. She sighed, her breath escaping in misty clouds. What was she thinking running after Jack like that?

She gave herself a shake to jog herself out of this dazed aura and walked along a row of stables towards Peace Offering's box. Like many others, he was alert and looking over his door, his ears flicking to the sound of the music from the nearby indoor school.

Pippa wrapped her arms around him and rested her cheek on his warm neck, breathing in the heady aroma of bedding and horse.

A beam of light projecting across the mist-veiled Gallops to her right caught her eye. Looking up, she watched the headlights of Jack's Land Rover swing across the rolling landscape, rousing the slumbering steeplechase fences out of the shadows, and vanish over the brow of the hill towards his house.

She exhaled in defeat. This was where her party ended too.

She continued to gaze at the spot where the vehicle had disappeared, a slow realisation that probably Jack had made the right decision by leaving when he did, settling inside her.

A shooting star winged across the horizon and Pippa's grip on Peace Offering's mane tightened. She closed her eyes. She pressed her cheek against the soft strength of her horse and mouthed the words,

*'I wish I didn't care so much.'*

# Chapter Twenty-Five

From the deep murmur of his voice emanating from beyond his closed door, Pippa was uncomfortably aware of Jack's presence in the office when she walked in the next morning. She read Aspen Valley's emails, seeing the typed words, but not concentrating on their context as, hearing the tone of his voice winding up his telephone conversation, she readied herself for the inevitable encounter. With an attempt to keep her face devoid of expression while her heart thumped in her ears, she watched the interleading door click open.

Jack hesitated when he saw her seated at her desk before walking through and giving a brief nod.

'Morning, Pippa.'

'Morning, Jack.'

The silence that followed was punctuated by the tapping of Jack's Entries and Declarations notebook against his palm.

'Good party last night,' he said.

'Yes, I think so. Everyone seemed to enjoy it.' A small smile lit her face as she thought of the numerous lads and lasses who had stopped her on her way from the car park this morning to thank her for the occasion.

'Seems most have turned up for work today as well despite their hangovers,' Jack nodded. 'I've already caught two people hurling their guts out behind the stables.'

Pippa's smile broadened.

'Kills two birds with one stone then,' she replied. 'Not only has it lifted their spirits, but the riders are always trying to keep their weight down.'

'Did you - er - stay late?' Jack probed.

Pippa guessed the slight frown settling on his forehead was directed towards himself rather than any judgement being passed on her social escapades.

'Not too late,' she said. She hesitated, the question on her tongue burning to be asked. 'You left early as well?' Damn! She bit her lip until it hurt. She hadn't meant to say that out loud.

Jack's frown deepened.

'Yes. I had to go because I - er - had to go.' He cleared his throat and dropped an envelope on her desk. 'Owners' passes for Wincanton on Saturday. We've got the Penningtons' Smoking Ace in the same race as

Peace Offering so can you get two of those passes posted Special Delivery to them?'

She nodded, anything to change the subject.

'Sure.'

She slit open the envelope, letting four passes fall out. Her stomach leapt in anticipation of taking on the role of racehorse owner once more. Being so involved with the horses sometimes made her forget that she owned one of them. The reality check of Peace Offering's infrequent visits to the racecourse was enough to bring the excitement of ownership rushing back to her.

'Who are you bringing along? Your friend, Tash?'

Her excitement ebbed at his question and she struggled to meet his eyes.

'No. Ollie's coming down for the weekend...'

Jack gave a deliberating nod of his head.

'Oh, yes. Ollie.' He smiled sardonically. 'I'd forgotten about him for a moment.'

If it hadn't been quite so awkward, Pippa was tempted to agree with him. Ollie had featured less in her thoughts these past few months than could be considered healthy for any relationship.

She fingered the passes, searching for something else to say that would diffuse the strained atmosphere. The office door opened and she looked up, exhaling with relief then inwardly cringing when Finn stepped into the room.

'Mornin',' he grinned. 'With faces like that, you'da thought it was the two of you partying 'til dawn and not the rays of sunshine out there.' He leaned up against the reception unit and chuckled at Jack and Pippa's sober expressions. 'And you, Miss Taylor,' he said, wagging a finger in her direction. 'There we were enjoying a slow number and next thing you were after disappearing.'

Pippa darted a panicked look towards Jack.

He stared at her, his face immobile, but his throat muscles tense.

'I had to go. Sorry,' she mumbled hastily. 'I remembered something I needed to do at home.'

'Your presence would've been handy a little later when we had to cart Billy off to Bristol A and E.'

'Oh, God. Is he okay? What did he do this time?' Pippa asked, aware of Jack shaking his head.

'Was tightrope walkin' along one of the jumps and o' course went arse over tit. Thought he'd broken his wrist, but turns out 'tis only a sprain.'

Pippa closed her eyes, relieved he hadn't broken any bones, but at the same time cursing him. He was a walking, breathing illustration of why Jack hadn't wanted to have the party in the first place.

'Who took him to hospital?' Jack asked. 'You must have all been over the limit.'

Finn shook his head.

'Emmie was off the booze. She donned the adult role. Nevertheless, I thought I'd report it and see if it needs to go in the Accident Report Book.'

Pippa looked at Jack, unsure.

Annoyed, he shook his head.

'It wasn't a work-related accident. Bloody idiot,' he muttered. He was about to give the Entries and Declarations book to Pippa when he paused and turned to Finn. 'I've put you down in the entries aboard Smoking Ace rather than Peace Offering. Presumably, you'd rather be on the more fancied ride?'

Pippa looked away, stung. When she raised her gaze, she found Finn looking at her, a mixture of pity amidst the humour in his eyes.

'Well, I don't know,' he said to Jack. 'I wouldn't say Peace Offering was without a shout now. If you're givin' me the choice then I think I'll opt for him instead.' He winked at Pippa and she gave him a grateful smile.

'Fine,' Jack said curtly. He tossed the book onto her desk and strode back to his office. 'Pippa, make sure you get those passes sent out,' he threw over his shoulder. 'I hope your boyfriend enjoys his first day out as an owner.'

She stared, her mouth open half in surprise, half in disgust as the door slammed shut behind him.

What was his problem?

'Boyfriend, eh?' Finn recaptured her attention with a raised eyebrow. 'That's something you didn't mention before.'

Pippa squirmed in her seat.

'There never seemed a good opportunity to mention him,' she replied.

Finn's green eyes danced with mischief.

'And where is the lucky man? I sure haven't seen him with you at The Plough. Keepin' him locked away in the cellar?'

'He lives in London,' Pippa explained. 'He's not really a country kind of guy.'

179

'Then I won't be complainin' about that. The more we have of yerself in the sticks alone, the better.'

Pippa snorted and shook her head.

'Do you still want to ride Peace Offering?'

Finn looked affronted.

'Of course I do. It'd give me a legitimate excuse to kiss you if we win.' He gave her a lazy smile. 'You do know that it's customary for the winning owner to kiss the jockey, don't you?'

'I guess so,' Pippa laughed.

'Plus, Smoking Ace has a fair chance of winning too and that means I'd have to kiss Lady Pennington,' he added in a stage whisper.

'Is she really that bad?' she giggled.

Finn pulled a face.

'If you've ever tried to kiss a cow on its nose, you'd know what I mean.'

Pippa covered her mouth to conceal her laughter.

'That's a terrible thing to say.'

'Aye, but not a word of a lie in it,' Finn shuddered.

# Chapter Twenty-Six

Pippa drummed her fingers on the freshly varnished wooden windowsill and looked out over Hazyvale's shaggy front garden. Through the foggy glass, she searched for the first flash of red entering the driveway amidst the bleak leafless shrubbery. Apart from a shivering rabbit hopping among the tangles, nothing stirred. She glanced at her watch, sucked her teeth in impatience and dipped into her handbag for her mobile to see if she'd missed any calls from Ollie.

Nothing.

She smoothed her booted sole across a dimple in the worn lounge carpet where it was curling away from the skirting board to reveal dirty oak floorboards. She idly wondered if it was worth leaving the floor bare and just giving it a sanding and a varnish rather than re-carpeting the whole thing. She could discuss it with Ollie and perhaps tomorrow he'd help move the furniture. Otherwise, Tash was coming to stay next weekend.

Pippa's mouth twisted into a grim smile as she recalled how her best friend had cried off from Peace Offering's race when she heard Ollie would be in attendance. Of course, Tash's excuse had been completely different, claiming she had been shagless for nearly three weeks with Aladdin being away and was desperate for his return this weekend.

'And you know what I can get like if I don't get my full dosage of sex, Pip,' Tash had added. 'Especially if your boss is going to be there looking as desirable as banoffee pie and custard is to a struggling weight watcher.'

Pippa did know so wasn't quite sure whether to believe Tash's excuse or not. On the other hand, she was rather relieved that she wouldn't have to cope with Ollie, Tash and Jack all at the same time. Tash was never shy when it came to telling Ollie what was on her mind and she doubted whether Jack would be either.

A glint of sunlight on metal caught her eye through the trees bordering the garden and Pippa's pulse quickened. She watched as Ollie's red Alfa Romeo turned into the driveway, bumping and dipping its way towards the cottage. She rushed to the front door, fumbling with her keys then hurtled down the two stone steps.

Ollie had got out and was looking, nonplussed, at the underside of his car.

'Ollie! Where've you been?' Pippa cried.

'Traffic on the M25 was horrific,' Ollie replied. 'What's the rush?'

'It's nearly two o'clock. Peace Offering's race is at three-thirty!'

'We've got plenty of time. Wincanton's not that far from here.'

'But we have to get our badges and see Peace Offering before the race, watch him in the paddock –'

'Do we have time for a hello, happy to see you kiss?' he asked.

At once, Pippa felt bad. Ollie had come all this way to see her and she was already having a go at him. He looked very boyish, but very dapper in his dark suit with pale blue silk tie and shirt, his hair, waxed and combed, now a little messed from the journey. He was obviously making an effort for the races.

She rounded the front of the car and took his hands in hers.

'I'm sorry,' she said, kissing him.

'I know.' He arched her hands wide so he could look at her outfit and nodded his approval. In her black knee-length boots, topped by a red and black Grecian-style dress and stylish tartan coat, she curtsied to him.

'You like?' she giggled.

'Oh, I like,' Ollie nodded with conviction. He gazed longingly at the cottage. 'You sure we don't have time?'

'Quite sure. The grand tour will have to wait until later, I'm afraid.' She gave his hands a last squeeze and headed round to the passenger's door.

'A grand tour of the house wasn't exactly what I had in mind,' Ollie mumbled.

Pippa proudly held up her star-shaped owners' badge for the course attendant to inspect before entering the paddock enclosure with Ollie beside her. Her nerves were resurfacing again and she sought out Ollie's hand as they stepped across the springy grass. She scanned the groups of people within the ring.

'There's Jack!' she said, pointing to the distant figure of the trainer, standing beside two other people, and quickened her step. Jack had the same harassed look on his face that he wore whenever he took phone calls from Lady Pennington. She scrutinised his company. The man was small and slight, his lizard-like throat raw from his too-tight collar and his mouth in a wide line of meekness, reminding Pippa of a hand puppet. The woman resembled a grizzly bear just back from the salon in her enormous fur coat and rouged cheeks and lips. A huge peach rose sprouted from her black Cossack hat like a crooked miner's lamp.

'That must be Lord and Lady Pennington,' she whispered as they approached them.

'Rubbing shoulders with aristocracy as well as the rich and famous?' Ollie replied, sounding impressed.

'Ooh, here come the horses,' Pippa squeaked as the first horses were led into the parade ring by their handlers. She clutched Ollie's hand and bounced on her toes with excitement for a couple of steps. Eagerly, she awaited Peace Offering's entrance. 'There he is!' She pointed avidly to the tall bay horse strolling through the gap in the hedge. She tore her eyes away to gauge Ollie's reaction.

He looked confused.

'Why's he half-shaved?' he asked.

'They're clipped during the winter,' Pippa explained. 'Otherwise they would be too furry and sweat too much during hard workouts.'

She watched Peace Offering saunter around the outer edge of the ring, occasionally bashing against Emmie as he tried to take a mouthful of hedge leaves, and her chest swelled with pride. His close-cropped coat rippled sleek and tight over the long lean muscles and his black tail, trimmed and unknotted for the occasion, floated behind him like a princely cape.

They reached Jack and the Penningtons just as the jockeys spilt into the ring from the weighing room in a flood of colour.

'Hello, Jack.'

Jack wheeled round, his expression a mixture of desperation and fury.

'Where've you been?' he demanded, not quite concealing the trauma in his tone.

'Delays on the motorway,' she said. 'Jack, this is Ollie. Ollie, this is Jack Carmichael.'

Regaining his composure, Jack nodded and held out his hand.

'Nice to meet you,' he said. He turned to the couple standing with him. 'May I introduce Lord and Lady Pennington. This is Pippa, my secretary, and her partner.'

They shook hands then Lady Pennington turned her back on them in order to watch the horses and in a loud whisper in her husband's ear commented,

'What an unusual arrangement, inviting one's staff along to the races and giving them *owners*' badges. Makes you wonder what sort of relationship he has with his secretary.'

Jack rolled his eyes. He'd obviously had his fill of the Penningtons already.

'Actually, Lady Pennington,' Pippa raised her voice, 'I do own a horse. Peace Offering, the horse Finn O'Donaghue chose to ride instead of your Smoking Ace, is mine.' She gave the surprised woman a beaming smile.

'Pippa,' Jack growled beneath his breath.

Once the jockeys had mounted and were filing out of the ring towards the track, Pippa and Ollie followed the others towards the packed stands. With Lady Pennington clearing their path like a bulldozer, sending spectators sprawling, they climbed the steps of the Club Stand opposite the winning post. There wasn't room for all five of them and Pippa had to settle for the row beneath the others. She shuffled along with Ollie on her left until they were directly in front of Jack and the Penningtons.

For the first time, Pippa looked out over the course, catching her breath as she did so. The sunshine, which had prevailed for the last few days, bathed the track's inner golf course in a fresh emerald glow, the sand bunkers peeping out like pockets of gold. Behind the backstretch, the Somerset countryside rose up in a patchwork quilt of farmland to the pale blue sky. The huge screen opposite the stands showed the ten horses cantering down to the Start with their betting odds moving across the bottom.

'Isn't it beautiful,' Pippa breathed.

'Bloody cold,' Ollie replied as a gust of wintery wind buffered the grandstands. 'A pity we didn't have time to put any bets on. Looks like Peace Offering is third favourite. He must have a chance.'

'I hope so, although with no rain lately, Jack says the ground might ride a bit quick for him. I think the odds have been swayed since Finn opted to ride Peace Offering rather than Smoking Ace.'

'Well, that's a good sign. He must have reason for wanting to ride our horse.'

Pippa refrained from telling him Finn's excuse. Ollie might not appreciate it as much as she had. Instead, she watched the horses circling at the Start, loosening their muscles, their opaque breaths accumulating in a thin cloud around them. She glimpsed the starter climbing his rostrum.

The jockeys gathered up their reins, jogging towards the tape in readiness for the off.

Pippa took a deep gulping breath as they set off towards the first, Peace Offering's white blaze bobbing in and out of sight in midfield. The first three jumps down the homestretch came in quick succession, the thunderous rumble of hooves being drowned out by the cheering crowd. The horse in the lead, which Pippa quickly identified through her racecard as Town Crier, swung the chasing field away from the enclosures at a brisk gallop towards the water jump. Peace Offering, with Finn aboard, was being niggled along as he struggled to keep up with the pace.

'Come on, Peace Offering,' she whispered, scrunching her racecard in her clenched fist. The bay horse pricked his ears approaching the water and lengthened his stride, soaring over while Finn sat motionless on his back. She beamed with pride as the commentator mentioned his impressive jump.

'He's a bit far back, isn't he?' Ollie shouted above the roar of the crowd.

'I don't know,' Pippa shrugged in reply. 'There's still another two circuits to go.'

She chewed her bottom lip as Ollie's observation became more apparent when the field of horses raced along the back straight. Town Crier led by four lengths, followed by the grey favourite, Smoking Ace. Another cluster of horses followed in his wake, behind which Peace Offering galloped hard to stay in contention. Only two other horses kept him company. The leader rounded the turn furthest away from the stands and headed downhill towards the obstacle that would take them into the homestretch again. Peace Offering was just landing after the previous open ditch, trailing by at least fifteen lengths.

'Town Crier is keeping up a strong gallop here,' the commentator's voice could barely be heard above the noisy spectators. 'With one circuit complete, the field is well strung out. Smoking Ace, in the hands of Mick Farrelly races handily in second. Three lengths back, Pastiche, Lumberjack, Silver Rock follow – Town Crier makes a bad mistake! Nods on landing. Smoking Ace closes the gap! Further back, Peace Offering heads a group of three and Fisherman's Son brings up the rear and looks like being pulled up.'

Pippa hugged Ollie's arm as, unblinking and breathless, she watched the horses tackle the three steeplechase fences in front of the grandstand once more. Smoking Ace drew up alongside Town Crier as they headed into their final circuit and the pair stretched over the water jump in tandem. The gap to the chasing field widened as they drew away.

Pippa cringed, noticing Finn start to push his mount for more speed. She compared her horse to the others racing around him. Some were beginning to drop back, their heads bobbing heavily as they tired. Peace Offering took off well away from the next open ditch, ballooning over. He didn't seem tired at all, he just wasn't fast enough, thought Pippa in anguish.

'Smoking Ace now takes the lead as they jump the last in the back straight,' cried the commentator, a renewed urgency creeping into his voice. 'Town Crier blunders! Back in third, Pastiche is gaining. Silver Rock is upsides him. Next is Lumberjack – Lumberjack falls!'

Pippa moaned as the runners made hasty manoeuvres around the horse and jockey as they climbed to their feet, unharmed. Peace Offering, now in fifth was far enough back to avoid the pair without being hampered.

'Now they enter the home straight for the last time!' yelled the commentator. 'Smoking Ace is all out and leads by four, make that five lengths. Town Crier is spent, He's dropping back! Pastiche now moves into second as they take the third last – he's given that fence a hefty clout! Peace Offering is battling it out with Silver Rock for fourth place...'

'Come on, Peace Offering!' Pippa cried, unable to contain herself any longer. 'Go on, Finn! You can do it!' She jumped up and down as the distance and strong early gallop now started to tell on the runners' weary legs.

Peace Offering's stride was lengthening. With the freedom of a loose rein, he stretched out his neck, eating into the gap between him and the three horses in front. In giant strides, he passed a wobbling Town Crier. Smoking Ace jumped the second last, brushing through the top and stumbled on landing. Pastiche wasn't much more fluent. Finn sat tight on Peace Offering, keeping him balanced as he tackled the fence.

Behind them, Pippa was vaguely aware of other tired horses being pulled up or making such ghastly mistakes that their riders were tossed over their shoulders and into the ploughed up turf. The last jump loomed and the gap between Peace Offering and his two rivals ahead dwindled as he went into overdrive. Smoking Ace got in tight, but cleared it. Pastiche, a length behind, did the same. Another two lengths back, Peace Offering, feeling the sting of Finn's whip, took off a stride too soon and paddled his way through the birch.

Pippa gasped and clung to Ollie's arm for support. Finn sat back in his saddle, pulling on the reins and threw out an arm to keep from overbalancing. The bay horse scraped his nose along the churned up ground as he fought to keep his feet.

With a sigh of relief, Pippa watched them regain their balance and set off after the leaders once more. But their momentum was gone. After galloping three miles, it was an impossible task for them to build it up again with less than a furlong more to go.

The favourite, Smoking Ace, pulled further ahead and to the welcoming roar of the crowd, passed by the winning post two lengths clear of Pastiche. Another four lengths back, Peace Offering crossed the line, his neck stretched low and his nostrils curled wide to gulp in the cold air, out of gas, but still full of heart.

Pippa sagged, exhausted, and looked at Ollie.

He looked disenchanted.

'Sorry,' she said.

'How much do we win?' he replied.

Pippa shrugged.

'Prize money won't be huge. Maybe a grand then there's jockeys' and trainers' percentage to be taken off that too.'

Ollie shook his head and Pippa exhaled with resignation. Was she going to get another lecture on how racehorses were a waste of money? Didn't he understand? Couldn't he see what a huge achievement a third place was! She felt a hand close over her right shoulder, a brief reassuring squeeze. She looked behind her. Jack gave her an almost indecipherable nod. She'd almost forgotten he was there. She smiled, but didn't know if he caught it. The Penningtons were already hustling him away so they could go greet their winner.

# Chapter Twenty-Seven

Pippa and Ollie strolled along the Bristol Harbour promenade, whiling away the time before their appointed dinner reservation. Bundled in her coat, Pippa huddled against Ollie for warmth as they stopped to admire the night time view. Misshapen reflections from the lights of bordering restaurants and pubs rolled in the rippling black inkwell of the tide. The boats, floating weightless on the water, thudded against their moorings like dozy hobbled donkeys, the occasional flap of a canvas sail catching the night breeze like an indolent flick of the ear. Nearby, a dull heartbeat of musical bass pulsing through its nightclub's soundproof walls lured the Saturday night revellers to its hub.

'So pretty, isn't it?' she murmured. 'I wish I could paint this.'

'It'd be a bit dismal, wouldn't it?' Ollie said. 'I mean it's so dark it wouldn't exactly brighten up somebody's living room, would it?'

'Hmm,' Pippa agreed half-heartedly. 'On a sunny day, it'd be lovely.'

'I'm getting sea-sick just looking at those boats. Come on, let's go find this restaurant. Rich says it's where all the cast from *Casualty* hang out. Maybe we'll spot a few faces.'

'They may recognise you too,' Pippa said, giving him a teasing nudge and linking her arm through his.

Ollie smiled modestly.

'Maybe.'

Pippa blinked as they entered the restaurant, the galaxy of ceiling lights making her shy away after the soft darkness of the harbour. They were met by the maître d'.

'We have a table booked for seven-thirty under Oliver Buckingham,' Ollie said.

The woman referred to her reservations book and gave them a thin smile, reminding Pippa of her old boss, Jayne.

'I'm afraid your table won't be available until the appointed time. Perhaps you would like to wait in the lounge for the remaining twenty minutes,' she said, gesturing to a long glass-fronted room overlooking the harbour.

They stopped en route at the bar and ordered some wine before weaving their way between the brown leather lounge chairs to find vacant seats.

'I think we might have to stand at the bar,' Pippa said, casting her gaze over the fashionable clientele.

'Look! Over there,' Ollie hissed.

'Where? Can you see some spare seats?'

'*There*,' Ollie nodded his head sideways. 'I can't point. I'm sure that's Jess Heffernan from *Casualty*.'

Pippa refrained from rolling her eyes.

'Ollie, we're meant to be looking for seats. Let's head back to the bar.'

'No, wait! Isn't that whats-his-face?'

'Ollie, please. My feet are killing me. At least let me prop myself up on a bar stool,' Pippa groaned.

'No. It's your boss or your trainer or whatever he is.'

Pippa whirled back and scanned the room.

'Jack?'

'Yes. I'm sure it's him. There, with some blonde woman.'

Her stomach lurched as she realised he was correct. Jack was indeed relaxing into an armchair, one ankle crossed casually over his knee. Opposite him was the striking figure of Melissa Mardling.

'And look!' Ollie went on. 'They've got a spare couple of seats at their table. Let's go join them.'

'What? No –' Pippa tried to grab Ollie's arm, but he was already walking purposefully across the room. 'Ollie, no,' she muttered, hurrying after him.

'Evening, folks!' Ollie said in a loud jovial voice, coming to a standstill above the couple.

Jack looked at him blankly. Melissa looked bemused.

Pippa sidled up next to Ollie.

'Hello, Jack, Melissa,' she said awkwardly.

Jack spilt his beer on his thigh.

'Pippa! And yes, of course, Ollie. Sorry, wasn't expecting to see you here.'

'Just treating Pippa to a decent meal,' Ollie beamed. 'Mind if we –'

'Sorry to have disturbed you,' Pippa interrupted and gave his arm a subtle yank. 'We were just on our way to the bar.' She gave them an apologetic smile and tried to guide Ollie away.

'No, please. Have a seat,' Jack said, half-rising in politeness.

'We really don't want to intrude,' she insisted.

'Don't mind if we do, thanks,' Ollie grinned, stepping around the table to an empty chair.

Pippa hesitated. She noticed a small frown flit across Melissa's unlined forehead as Ollie passed her and the woman tilted her nose to sniff the air. Pippa cringed. She'd almost forgotten about the potential matching cologne issue. Jack didn't appear to have noticed. He was busy dabbing the wet patch on his thigh with a paper napkin.

'Pippa, are you going to sit down? I thought you said your feet were hurting.'

Three faces looked up at her in expectation. Feeling like she was about to step into a minefield, she took her place next to Ollie.

Jack cleared his throat.

'Melissa, you remember Pippa, my secretary? And this is Ollie. Ollie, Melissa.'

'Nice to meet you,' Melissa conceded. 'I didn't realise you had a *boyfriend*, Pippa.'

'Ollie still lives in London,' she explained. She glanced at Jack, trying to gauge his reaction to them crashing their party. His expression was of controlled neutrality.

'And what do you do in London?' Melissa asked.

'I'm an actor.' Ollie smiled modestly at the impressed raise of her manicured eyebrows. 'One of my co-stars on *Holby City*, Rich Holden, recommended this restaurant. What line of work are you in?' he continued, sensing a potential fan.

Melissa gave a nonchalant wave of her hand and re-crossed her long legs.

'Fashion. I design clothes. Not a huge label; I prefer to cater for the select.'

This time it was Ollie's turn to look impressed.

'And no doubt you're very good at it,' he replied, nodding in appreciation at her stylish woollen twill outfit. 'Have you ever thought about acting? The camera would love you.'

Pippa's eyes widened at his blatant flirting and darted a panicked look towards Jack. The trainer sat, very still and watchful, reminding her of a hunter awaiting its prey.

Melissa laughed, placing an elegant hand at the base of her throat and fingering her necklace.

'Pippa,' she smiled, a trace of misguided pity in her tone making her feel even more humiliated. 'Jack tells me you're quite the artist. Do you intend to make a business of your talent?'

With an awkward chuckle, she shrugged.

'I don't know –'

'It'd be a pretty precarious business, wouldn't you say?' Ollie snorted. 'When was the last time you sold a painting?'

'Not so long ago, in fact,' Jack spoke up. 'She did a commission just before Christmas.'

For a moment, Ollie looked wrong-footed.

'You never mentioned it,' he said, frowning at Pippa.

'Didn't I? It was the one of Black Russian on the Gallops.'

'Ah, that name rings a bell. Dan Cameron's horse, wasn't it?' Ollie directed his question at Jack.

'Yes, that's right.'

'Bet he won't be commissioning Pippa to paint any more of his horses if that's the outcome,' Ollie chuckled.

Jack remained silent, a muscle now jumping in the hollow of his jaw.

'Why don't we go see if our table's ready yet?' Pippa suggested.

Ollie waved her away.

'No, they said at least twenty minutes. Look how full this place is. Anyway, please pass on my condolences to Dan, won't you?'

'Of course,' Jack nodded.

'You don't happen to know what projects he's got in the pipeline, do you? I mean, they've extended my role in *Holby City* indefinitely, but it's good to know what else is on the card.'

Jack took a long level sip of his beer before answering.

'No, I'm afraid I don't. I'm not in the habit of delving into my owners' affairs. My interests in them only go so far as their horses.'

'Well, maybe next time he calls, Pippa can do a bit of delving,' Ollie beamed.

Pippa closed her eyes, wishing her chair would swallow her up.

'Ollie, I don't think that'd be such a good idea.'

'Why not? You roped him into letting you paint his horse, didn't you?'

Pippa's ears burned, but Jack intervened before she could reply.

'That painting was commissioned by me actually.'

Pippa's focus swung from Jack to Ollie via an entertained-looking Melissa.

Ollie regained his composure and chuckled. He looked at Melissa and threw a thumb towards Pippa beside him.

'There's your answer then about making a business out of her paintings. Pippa, you can't seriously consider making a living out of it when it's friends and family who buy your stuff.'

Pippa clenched her teeth. Ollie's pride, which Jack had just dented, was becoming a bit too precious for her patience.

'I didn't say I was going to –'

'She's more than capable of earning a living off her art,' Jack said quietly.

Pippa gulped.

Jack's eyes had turned indigo.

Oh, God, she knew that look more than any other.

'I think we should go check on our table,' she blurted. 'Like you say, they're very busy. We wouldn't want to miss our booking.'

'No, don't go. Twenty minutes hasn't gone by that quick,' Melissa said, sounding almost genuine.

Pippa was surprised to see open amusement on her face. She was actually enjoying the encounter. Ollie, misinterpreting the request for sympathy, relaxed back into his chair.

'Quite,' he replied, his feathers soothed. He took a gulp of his wine then held up the glass to reflect on its empty contents.

'Why don't you go get us another drink then, Pippa, if you're so keen to go?' His mouth twisted into a nasty smile.

Pippa set her jaw. She would not make a scene in public, especially in front of Jack, but by God she was going to have it out with him when they got home later.

'No, I think we'd best wait until we've had some food. You probably haven't eaten since you left London this morning and we've already had a couple of drinks at the races.'

Ollie's eyes glittered dangerously, but he didn't argue. Instead he placed the empty glass on the table then lounged back, linking his hands behind his head.

'I have to say hats off to you, Jack, for taking on Pippa.'

Jack frowned.

'And why do you say that?' he said quietly.

Pippa was past caring why. She recognised the solemn tone of Jack's voice, which others fortunate enough not to have been on the receiving end of his temper might not. It was like earth tremors which are only felt

192

by animals. The imminent earthquake would hit the unaware all the harder.

'Well, she's a feisty thing, isn't she?' Ollie laughed. He winked at Pippa. 'Strong-willed yet away with the fairies most of the time. And you, brave enough to take her on knowing she's just a waitress –'

'Ollie!' Pippa exclaimed.

'What?' he said, raising his hands in innocence. 'That is what you are, Pippa. You'd never worked in an office before a couple of months ago. I'll bet she's given you a few grey hairs since she joined the ranks, eh, Jack?'

Jack exhaled with difficulty.

'Pippa is one of Aspen Valley's best assets,' he said, his voice straining to keep level. 'She's resourceful and hardworking. If anybody is to be deemed brave, then it's her, not me.'

Melissa looked less amused.

Ollie snorted.

'How so?' he asked in a patronising tone.

Pippa gasped as Jack slammed down his drink. He leaned forward in his seat and glared at Ollie.

'Because she's taken on a new career, wanting to support her horse whilst juggling a massive renovation of her cottage. And what's more she's succeeding.'

Pippa's discomfort over Ollie's manners fell by the wayside as she stared at Jack in wonder of his rigid defence of her.

Ollie laughed, any caution now a distant speck of dust in the wind.

'Ah yes, her horse. This whole racing venture isn't brave, Jack. You, of all people, should know that. It's foolish, plain and simple. Look at today, for instance. That horse, which Pippa is so convinced is going to win the Grand National, couldn't even win some low class race out in the middle of the sticks.'

'Enough, Ollie!' Pippa cried. She snatched up her bag, but Jack was already on his feet, towering over the table and pointing a menacing finger towards Ollie.

'The only foolish thing I've seen Pippa do is date you!' he shouted, his body trembling with rage.

Ollie's sardonic smile disappeared. A blaring hush fell over the lounge. All eyes turned on Jack, his fury sending shockwaves through the room.

The surprise on Ollie's face altered and his wide-eyed gaze flickered between Jack and Pippa, a dawning. Pippa felt it too and by the not-so-amused-now look on Melissa' face, she did as well.

'It's time we left, Ollie,' Pippa said, her voice shaking. She leapt up and, grabbing a shell-shocked Ollie by the sleeve, pulled him after her.

'What the hell is that guy's problem?' Ollie exclaimed, finding his voice as they burst out of the restaurant onto the harbour promenade.

Pippa whipped around and stared at him, incredulous.

'You, Ollie!' she said. 'You are the problem! How dare you speak to me like that in front of Jack and Melissa!'

Ollie glared back.

'What did I say that was so wrong? Or so inaccurate?'

'In the space of five minutes, you managed to insult me, Jack and Peace Offering!' she said, jabbing the air with her finger at every name.

'Everything I said was true though!'

Pippa's breath came in short shallow gasps that pooled in foggy clouds in front of her.

'What gives you the right to dismiss me like that, huh?' she said, her voice lowered to a steel iciness. 'You sit there shamelessly flirting with my boss' girlfriend in front of me –'

'I wasn't flirting!'

'Yes, you were,' Pippa snapped. 'And to rub in that humiliation, you insult my secretarial skills and fob off my artwork.'

'You never painted in London!' Ollie said in defence.

'I used to though, didn't I?' she challenged him. 'Have you ever wondered why I stopped painting?' A sudden urge to punch him swelled inside her as the bitter reason exposed itself to her.

'It was a hobby. I thought you lost interest.'

'No, Ollie!' she cried, stamping her foot. 'My art was *not* a hobby! And if you weren't so wrapped up in your own little world, maybe you would've seen that, would've encouraged me rather than slagging me off the entire time! That's why I stopped painting! I loved my art. I wanted to make a career out of it and *you* stopped me!'

Ollie glared at her, insult etched across his face.

'I never stopped you from painting!'

'No, not physically. But psychologically, that's another story. You managed to make me think your career was more important, your happiness was more important.' She gulped as a ball of tears rose in the back of her throat. She pointed at him accusingly. 'And for three years, my life has been non-existent. It has merely revolved around yours.'

'Well, if that's the way you feel. Personally, I think you should take a good long look at yourself, Pippa. Look at reality, if you've got the guts to. You deserted me in London to live out some stupid fantasy. Don't you think that was pretty fucking selfish of you?'

'Selfish to want to live my own life?' She shook her head. 'No, Ollie. I think it's selfish of you not to have let me.'

Ollie opened his arms wide.

'So where does that leave us? You've said some pretty unforgivable things to me, Pippa.'

The swelling in her throat subsided and she couldn't help uttering a short burst of laughter.

'It leaves us with nothing, Ollie. I have no wish for your forgiveness because quite simply, I don't respect you anymore. You've done nothing to earn it.'

He gaped at her.

'*You're* breaking up with *me?*'

'Yes, Ollie,' she laughed. 'This useless away-with-the-fairies waitress girlfriend is dumping her hot-shot Hollywood-here-I-come actor boyfriend.'

'Well, you beat me to it then because don't think anybody can talk to me like that and get away with it!' Ollie replied, folding his arms across his chest, his rigid stance making her think of someone with a carrot stuck up their arse.

'I can't believe your arrogance,' Pippa snorted in disbelief.

'I'm not arrogant!' he retorted. 'I know when I'm right, I – I just have difficulty proving it sometimes, that's all.'

'Go on then,' she said, gesturing him away with her hand. 'Go back to London. I'm not what you need nor do I want to be that person anymore.'

Ollie nodded and took a hesitant step away.

'Fine, I'm going. Have a nice life, Pippa.'

'Bye, Ollie. Have a good one too.'

In the amber lighting along the quay, she watched Ollie stride away without a backward glance. She turned to go in the opposite direction, hugging her coat around her as she became aware of the icy wind coming off the water. Like a popped beach ball, her almost hysterical triumph of finally breaking up with Ollie started to deflate, replaced with a pitiful low. Pity for herself and pity for him as well.

As she wandered aimlessly and alone along the row of restaurants and nightclubs, she realised that she was stuck in Bristol. Ollie had been her lift home.

'Oh, fuck,' she muttered. 'You and your big mouth, Pippa. Why couldn't you have broken up with him tomorrow or something? Now you've got to get a taxi all the way back home.' This rather conniving thought brought a smile to her face as she realised that now she really was on her own. Ollie was no longer a part of her life. Her smile widened and her step quickened. *Oh, the relief!*

She passed the fountains and headed for a long queue by the taxi ranks. The boisterous shouts of drunken Saturday nighters bounced off the stone Georgian buildings leaning over the steep cobbled streets as she took her place at the back of the line.

She supposed about a quarter of an hour had passed, shuffling along the barrier on cold aching feet as the taxi queue wobbled forward, when she heard her name being shouted. She looked up.

'Do you need a ride?' Jack asked from the open window of his Land Rover.

Pippa didn't think twice. Flashing him a grin and amidst the jovial shouts of 'Ey there, love, give us a ride too! I'll give you one in return', Pippa ducked beneath the metal railing and pulled wide the passenger door which Jack had pushed open for her.

'Thank you,' she gushed. 'God, it's freezing out there.'

She rubbed her hands together and blew on them as they set off down the street.

'Where's Ollie?' Jack asked, his expression grave.

'On his way back to London, I expect. Where's Melissa?'

'She had her own car with her.' He paused. 'Pippa, I'm sorry for my – my outburst. It was completely out of line and totally unprofessional.' His frown deepened as he stared resolutely at the road ahead and gripped the steering wheel for emphasis on each word.

'No, please. Don't apologise,' she said, full of remorse. 'It was Ollie who was out of order. I'm sorry he was so rude.'

'I hope I haven't caused any long-lasting damage by what I said.'

She looked ahead again, unsure how to answer him without making him feel even guiltier.

'Ollie and I have decided to call it quits.'

Jack's head snapped sideways in surprise.

'Jesus, Pippa! I'm sorry. I didn't mean for it to go that far. I just saw red and I couldn't stop myself. You know how I can get like.' He shook his head and banged his palm against the wheel. 'Me and my bloody temper. I'm sorry.'

Pippa ventured out a placating hand to his arm.

'Don't be,' she said. 'It was already on the cards.'

'Are you – um – are you okay?'

Pippa shrugged and let her hand drop away.

'Well, I don't feel great, but on the other hand it's actually quite a relief now that it's over.'

'You deserve better than him. Does he always treat you like that?'

'It hasn't always been this way,' she reasoned. 'I guess it's been a gradual thing, kind of like wrinkles. You don't notice them until one day you have a particularly bad hangover and then they're glaring at you from the bathroom mirror. It's only lately that I've come to realise just how much of a wrinkle Ollie is.'

Jack gave a mirthless chuckle.

'There's a lot more appropriate and less complimentary words I can think of to describe him than *wrinkle*.'

'He's not entirely to blame though. I've pandered to his every need these past few years to avoid his temper tantrums. I'm just as much at fault.'

'I doubt that. You never stood up to him?'

'No, it was easier not to.'

'That surprises me. You don't think twice about standing up to me.' He shot her a wry smile.

'Well, you're different. Ollie's ego is a lot more delicate than yours. And contrary to what you might think, I *do* think twice before standing up to you.'

'Really? Why?'

'I don't know. You can be a bit intimidating.'

They pulled up at a stop-light and Jack's frown returned.

'Can I? You've no reason to feel intimidated by me.'

'When you're angry with me it's hard not to be a bit frightened,' she said diplomatically.

Jack looked at her for a long moment, his expression a mixture of offence and distress.

'I've never been angry with you, Pippa,' he said quietly. 'Maybe I've been angry at circumstances involving you, but I've never been angry at *you.*'

# Chapter Twenty-Eight

'Then what happened?' Tash asked, as captivated by Pippa's recount of the previous Saturday's events as a five-year-old with her first picture book.

'Then nothing. Someone hooted at us because the light had turned green and we just carried on home.'

Pippa wiped her brow and moved to the opposite end of the Welsh dresser in the lounge.

'You must have spoken about something after that. What else did he say?'

'Lift on three?'

'That's an odd thing to say.'

'No, the dresser, doofus. One, two, *three!*'

The girls staggered under the weight of the cabinet before half-carrying, half-dragging it towards the dining room to join the rest of the living room furniture.

'Really, all that happened after that was Jack got all impersonal and started speaking about the horses and Cheltenham Festival in March. And then we were back here and he left.'

'You didn't give him a kiss to say thanks for the ride?' Tash grinned. 'I would have.'

'No – ow, fuck. Mind your fingers going through the doorframe there. No, even if I'd wanted to, Jack would probably have sprinted in the opposite direction or more likely, fired me. He's very against relationships in the workplace.' With a sigh of relief, they lowered the Welsh dresser to the ground. Pippa sprawled out on the sofa, also randomly positioned in the dining room. 'Shall we have a break before we start ripping up that carpet?'

'Sounds like a plan. I'll go grab some of that wine I brought along.'

Tash reappeared a couple of minutes later, her fingers wrapped around two wine glasses, a corkscrew and a bottle of rosé.

'Sounds to me like your Jack Carmichael doesn't know what he wants,' she said, joining Pippa on the sofa. 'First he insists you and he are purely employer and employee, the next minute he's springing to your defence and by the sounds of it, ready to clobber your boyfriend. Although I'm rather pleased somebody stood up to Ollie for once. No offence, Pip, but

I've been driven crazy by the amount of times I've wanted to shout at you 'strap on a pair, will ya?'.'

Pippa curled up in the corner of the sofa in a chuckle-attack.

'Hmm. Always wanted to do that,' she giggled.

'What – strap on a pair?' Tash passed her a glass of wine.

'Yeah.'

Tash laughed.

'Really? *Why?*'

'Well, it'd give you something to do when you're standing in queues.' With a grin she rescued the wine from Tash's hand.

'One thing's for certain though,' she said. 'Jack doesn't go for the whole mixing business with pleasure. Finn took me out for a drink on Wednesday to cheer me up and Jack wasn't terribly happy about that.'

'Poor thing,' Tash said, reaching out to hold Pippa's chin with her thumb and forefinger. 'Get this down you. Here's to a new chapter in your life, filled with freedom and irresponsibilities – or should that be no responsibilities? Rest assured, there is life after Ollie Buckingham.'

They clinked glasses and Pippa took a slug, half in need to quench her thirst, the other half in reinforcement of Tash's toast.

'You're not sorry that I've broken up with Ollie, are you?'

Tash looked offended before her expression became a bit sheepish.

'Am I sorry that you're no longer seeing that knob? I'll be honest with you, Pip. No, I'm rejoicing he's now out of your life. On the other hand, I'm very sorry he upset you. Even if I didn't exactly love him to bits, I know you did.'

Pippa nodded, satisfied.

'Like I said to Jack, it's quite a relief that it's over. What Ollie has ensured is that I'm in no hurry to get into another relationship.'

'So this Finn character is chasing down a dead end?'

'I don't know that that is what he's after. He's just very good company. And I *do* like him, don't get me wrong. But Ollie's put me off boyfriends for a while.'

'What you need is to have a bit of fun. To get out there, have a couple of one-night-stands, get Ollie out of your system for good.'

'Doesn't sound a bad idea,' Pippa conceded.

'Good, we can start tonight. I've come all this way over here to act as slave labour, I expect a bit in return. So I insist you take me out and show me the bright lights of the country.'

'They're not that bright, believe me,' she warned. 'But The Plough is usually buzzing on a Saturday night. We can go there, maybe go out for dinner beforehand.' She sat up to face Tash and held up her depleted wine glass. 'Okay, here's the deal. I'll treat you to an Indian for dinner if you help me get the carpet up in the lounge *and* the stairs.'

'You're on,' Tash replied, tapping her glass against Pippa's. 'Let's finish the bottle first. It tastes so much better chilled.'

Pippa was just blotting her lips on a piece of tissue paper when she heard the toot of a horn outside.

'Pip!' Tash yelled from downstairs. 'The taxi's here!'

With a last glance in the mirror to make sure she'd mascara-ed both blue eyes and rouged both cheeks (learnt from experience when getting ready with a bottle of wine), she skipped out of the bathroom and clattered down the now stripped and dirty stairs in her high-heeled boots. She had forgotten how noisy bare wooden floors could be. She'd nearly reached the bottom, her hand skimming the oak balustrade when a crack and a dry splintering of wood interrupted her descent. With a cry she grabbed wildly at the bars as her footing vanished. Her elbow smashing into the lip of a higher stair, making her eyes water.

'You lightweight, Pippa,' Tash said, appearing over her crumpled position. 'We've only had a couple of bottles and you're already falling over.'

Pippa rubbed her elbow and sat up with a groan, trying the disengage her boot from the gaping hole where a stair had once been.

'Oh, fuck, look what I've done,' she moaned, her pain forgotten as she examined the broken step.

Tash leaned forward for a closer inspection.

'Jesus, you just broke an oak floorboard. What did you do? Jump from the top of the stairs?'

'No,' Pippa giggled, her anguish softened by rosé. She ran her fingers along the splintered hole, brushing bristles of old blackened wood from the main. 'I might have been a bit heavy-footed, but not enough to *break* this, surely.'

'Well, that wood does look a little rotten. How old did you say this place was?'

'A couple of centuries, I imagine.'

A more impatient toot from the taxi outside caught their attention.

'Come on, we can worry about this later,' Tash said. 'Can you walk or do I have to carry you to the car?'

The taxi deposited them outside Moulin Raj, Helensvale's local Indian restaurant and Pippa led the way up the few steps to the entrance. Inside, with the heating on tropical, the restaurant manager still wore a scarf and gloves. He nodded when they requested a table for two, the soft lighting bouncing off his neatly combed black hair.

'Please take a seat. I will see what we have available, please.'

Pippa and Tash made themselves comfortable on the sofa in the entrance room whilst their host disappeared through a beaded curtain beneath an archway into the main dining area. Tapping her boot idly against the carved chest-like table in front of them, Pippa glanced around the room, her gaze alighting on the diners she could see through the flimsy beads. With a gasp, she looked round for somewhere to hide, settling for a poster-like menu on the table.

'What the fuck?' Tash looked at her as if she was mad.

'Ssh,' Pippa hissed. She peeped around the dog-eared corner of the menu held up to her and Tash's faces, to certify what she had glimpsed. 'It's Finn.'

'Ooh, your admirer. Put this thing down before you take my eye out, sweets, and let me see. Why don't you want him to see you?'

'Because he's with someone else,' she replied in a grating whisper.

Emboldened by Tash, who was craning her neck to get a better view, she lowered the menu so she could see over the top. Finn, dressed in casual jeans and collared shirt was leaning his arms on an intimately-small table, nodding as his companion spoke. Pippa couldn't hear what she was saying, nor was she that interested. All she could do was stare at the girl's almost angelic beauty. Honey blonde hair which glowed beneath the restaurant lights, framed a slim heart-shaped face, milky white and pure in complexion. Matched with Finn's attractive bone structure, they were a perfect pair.

Pippa felt a pang in her gut.

'Oh, I say,' Tash drawled. 'They do raise rather dishy stock out here in the country.'

'He's Irish.'

'That's mostly countryside, isn't it? Who's that with him?'

'Dunno. I've never seen her before. She must be the girl Emmie saw him out with a while back. She's not from around here.'

'I'm sure I've seen her somewhere before. Hang on.' Tash looked puzzled. 'I thought he was chasing after you.'

Pippa shrugged.

'Well, he's always been very *affectionate* towards me. I'd stand no chance next to her though.'

The pair ventured a bolder look over the menu at the dining couple before their focus was cut off by the restaurant manager's frame.

'There is a table available if you would like to follow with me, please,' he beamed at Pippa and Tash.

'No, no, no,' Pippa shook her head. 'We can't eat here anymore.'

Tash looked pained.

'Oh, come on. What harm will it do? They might not even notice us.'

'I'll notice *them* though,' Pippa insisted. 'I'll buy you some dry-roasted peanuts at The Plough.' She turned to the confused-looking manager. 'I'm sorry, there's someone in there I'd rather not see – oh, shit!' She ducked. 'He just looked this way.'

Grabbing Tash by the arm, she dropped to the floor and crawled towards the exit, shielded by the carved table then made a dash for the door.

Once outside, Tash leaned against the metal railing alongside the steps and clutched her sides, heaving with laughter.

'What are you like, girl?' she said, 'Do you think they'll ever let you back in there?'

Pippa conceded to see the funny side and half-supporting, half-being supported, she held onto her friend's shoulder, wracked with giggles. The pavement swam in front of her feet and a vague voice in her head told her she should really get some food inside her before she drank any more.

They weaved a path down the High Street, arm in arm, towards The Plough.

'That's the café across the street there,' Pippa pointed out, her finger bobbing like a buoy on stormy waves. 'That's where we got the cups to replace the ones Peace Offering broke.'

'Pip, I know you love your horse, but I shouldn't need to tell you, a bucket will do just fine for him. He doesn't need to drink from cups.'

Pippa doubled over. Tash pointed further up the street.

'Oh, look. Your local fire crew are out on display.'

The garage doors were open, beaming light onto the pavement and a fire engine stood docile in the entrance while its crew, their overalls lowered to their waists to reveal fit torsos in slick t-shirts, sprayed and polished its flanks.

'Come on, lads! Show us your hose!' Tash bellowed.

Pippa dragged her friend through the front door of The Plough.

They shed their coats as they were enveloped in the thick warm air and hung them on a floundering coat stand by the door. They shouldered their way to the bar, deciding to order a bottle of wine rather than have to keep ordering it by the glass and stocked up on peanuts and crisps. Using Tash's shoulder for support, Pippa climbed onto the footrest of the bar to look around the pub. The whole room was jammed with people, even the pool table was being encroached upon. At the other end was the lounge area and with a triumphant smile, she spotted the familiar faces of Emmie and Billy sitting beside the cast iron fireplace.

'Come on,' she said. 'Come meet some friends.'

With introductions complete, they settled down, Pippa perched precariously on the arm of Tash's chair and shared the snacks with the Aspen Valley grooms.

'We were going to eat at Moulin Raj, but Finn was there with his mystery woman,' Pippa explained the heap of food. 'We didn't want to interrupt.'

'She's back, is she?' Emmie said. 'Finn won't tell us who she is. Says she's just a friend.'

Billy snorted.

'With legs like that and a face like an angel, no guy would want to be *just friends* with her,' he said, then catching Emmie's disapproving eye continued swiftly, 'is how some men would see it. Personally, she's too skinny for my tastes.'

He busied himself with picking up the fire poker to rejuvenate the smouldering logs in the grate, but dropped it with a hiss and plunged his burning fingers into his beer.

'Maybe she's an owner or something,' Pippa suggested. 'I saw him out with Melissa a couple of weeks ago.'

'Is this the Melissa Jack's dating?' Tash asked.

'Yeah, but her father also owns half the horses at Aspen Valley –'

'Including Virtuoso,' Billy added with extra emphasis.

'Honey, I'm sure that would impress anyone who knows anything about racing, but I work at a London advertising agency,' Tash replied. 'What's so great about him?'

204

Billy looked taken aback.

'He won last year's Cheltenham Gold Cup *and* the King George! He's evens favourite to do the same thing this year as well.'

'Sounds impressive. And what does this Melissa character do when she's not accepting gold cups and deceased kings?'

'She has some fashion label or other,' Pippa said. 'But my point is Finn said he'd met up with her to discuss her father's horses since he's riding them all now. Maybe this girl is also –'

'I've got it!' Tash said, sitting up and nearly dislodging Pippa from her perch. 'I knew I recognised her from somewhere. She's Cara Connolly, an Irish model. She's the new face of Skylark!' She stared at the three blank faces before her. 'Come on, Pip, you know who Skylark are. They're an accessories chain doing handbags and jewellery and stuff. No? God, a few months in the country and I've lost you already. Anyway, Cara Connolly is their latest discovery. We've been doing an advertising campaign for them and she's all over it.'

Pippa let this information sink in, feeling a tiny twinge of regret knowing that this girl wasn't just a pretty face, she was obviously successful too. Looking at it from that angle, Finn's attentions were sure to be further diverted away from herself.

'Did I say something wrong?' Tash asked when her only response was silence.

'Oh, no,' Emmie reassured her. 'It's just not Finn's style, that's all. He's usually happy to hang out with us at the pub. If he's dating celebrities... well, he probably won't want to do that anymore.'

Pippa munched on some peanuts and washed them down with the last of her wine. She leaned over to retrieve the bottle, steadied by Tash, and refreshed their glasses.

'Maybe they're better suited than we think,' she said, masking her disappointment with a smile. 'At least they can watch their weight together.' She took another gulp of her drink and beamed at the other members of the party.

Emmie looked troubled, Tash looked bemused and Billy plain confused.

'Strange that,' he piped up. 'You say she works for a handbag shop called Skylark? That's the name of Virtuoso's biggest rival in the Gold Cup.'

# Chapter Twenty-Nine

Pippa had little time to ponder over Finn's escapades over the next few days as the trail leading up to Cheltenham Festival began to hot up. The following Thursday, she'd only just managed to get the entries and declarations done by the deadline in between telephone calls from press and jockeys' agents. She was just about to take a break for lunch when another call came through.

'My name's Seth Rutherford. Could I speak to Jack Carmichael, please?' a pleasant cultured voice spoke.

'I'm afraid he's not in the office at the moment, Mr Rutherford. Is there anything I can help you with?'

'If you have a persuasive nature, perhaps you can. I'm raising funds for some charities by enlisting the help of some of the more celebrated faces of racing in the run up to Cheltenham and was hoping Mr Carmichael would be one of them.'

'I'm sure Jack'd be happy to help providing it doesn't clash too much with his schedule,' Pippa replied confidently, knowing Jack already did a fair amount for charity. 'What does he have to do?'

'Well, with the past success of the charity single *Cheltenham* based on Petula Clark's *Downtown*, we've decided to do the same thing, but this time using The Beatles' *Ticket to Ride*, with a few lyrics tweaked here and there, obviously, to make it Cheltenham-themed. We have a number of high profiles already lining up to help. Do you think Mr Carmichael would be keen to do the same?'

Pippa paused.

'Um, well,' she began, 'personally, I think it's a marvellous idea. I'm sure Jack will do too. I'm just not sure if he'd be so keen on the singing bit.'

'It'd only be the chorus and the odd line here and there. We're literally going to record it in one evening and with twenty or thirty other participants, so it'll be minimal fuss and he wouldn't exactly be standing out from the crowd,' Seth Rutherford was quick to reassure her.

She glanced at the entrance door in Jack's general direction, wondering how on earth she might be able to coerce him to sing. She gave a start as it was wrenched open. Jack strode in, talking on his mobile phone.

'Melissa, can we discuss this later? I don't want to –' His nostrils flared as he was interrupted.

Pippa saw her chance.

'Just bear with me for a moment, Mr Rutherford,' she said quietly then folded her palm over the mouthpiece.

'Jack,' she said in a stage whisper.

He stopped outside his office and pointed to the phone at his ear.

'I know. Just a quick question. Can you do a bit for a racing charity?'

Jack frowned at her, distracted as his ear received a pummelling from Melissa.

'Doing what? No, I wasn't talking to you, Mel. I'm at the office... Yes, I'm listening to you.'

'Just have to lend your voice one evening. It's no big deal.'

'What? Fine, whatever. Yes, I'm still here, Melissa! I can hear you loud and clear!' Jack exclaimed, slamming the door behind him.

Pippa grinned.

'He'd be happy to, Mr Rutherford.'

'Really?' Seth Rutherford sounded aghast.

'Yes, really. Just tell me where and when and I'll stick it in his diary.'

She opened the calendar on her computer and typed in the details.

'My pleasure,' she responded to his thanks. 'Bye now.'

She put the phone down and looked at her computer screen. Wow! Abbey Road Studios in London to do a recording session. Jack was so lucky. An appointment box popped up with a beep making Pippa's smile disappear.

'Oh, shit,' she gasped, her gaze darting to the clock.

In one swift movement, she hurtled out of her chair and into her coat, swiping up her handbag as she went. She was due to meet the builders at Hazyvale to discuss the broken staircase in ten minutes. Skirting the desk, she tripped over a pile of jockeys' silks, the colourful shirts baked in dried Chepstow mud from the day before.

'Fucking hell,' muttered Pippa through gritted teeth.

She bundled the clothes into her arms and hurried through to the kitchenette and shoved them into the washing machine, chucking in a washing tablet and swivelling the dial. Without a second glance, she tore back through the office.

'Just shooting out for lunch, Jack! Won't be long!'

*

An hour and a quarter later, Pippa swung her car back into Aspen Valley's driveway, narrowly missing the gatepost. What she had imagined would be a five minute conversation and an immediate quote for fixing the broken stair had turned into a forty-five minute examination of the rest of the staircase, which was now deemed 'unsafe'. Pippa wasn't surprised. If there'd been any indecision over it before, it was certainly a hazard now. The guy had pulled up every other stair, pointing out the rotten wood, and the whole structure was now about as stable as a see-saw factory.

She winced when she saw Jack's Land Rover still in residence, although she knew he wouldn't have left the office unmanned.

Jack burst out of his office as soon as Pippa made her arrival known.

'Where've you been?' he demanded.

'Sorry. I got delayed,' Pippa said, sitting back down at her desk. She stood up again when she heard the beeping of the finished wash cycle in the kitchenette. 'I had to show the builder the staircase and he took forever. He couldn't even give me a quote at the end of it.'

'I've got to get down to Newton Abbot for the three-forty!'

'Sorry, Jack. I tried to be as quick as I could. You shouldn't have waited for me. You knew I'd be back.'

Jack followed her into the kitchenette.

'I've just been told Finn's appeal on the three-day ban he picked up the other day has been turned down. The ban falls over next weekend.'

Pippa paused before opening the washing machine door and looked at him blankly.

'Next weekend is the Denman Chase!' Jack raked his hands through his hair. 'It's Virtuoso's last prep before the Gold Cup and now he's going to have another different jockey on board. It'll be the third change in three races!'

Pippa pulled an anguished face, half in sympathy for Finn missing out on a big ride and half for Jack's obvious distress.

'That's a bugger. Why did they turn it down?'

'Because it's meant to be a punishment,' Jack said in a mocking tone, obviously quoting the authorities. 'Jockeys' convenience isn't high on their list. They don't bloody think of other people's convenience either though!'

Pippa attempted a consolatory smile.

'At least the ban didn't fall over Cheltenham week.'

'I need you to get Mick Farrelly on the line. ASAP. See if he can take the ride.'

'Will do,' Pippa replied, turning back to the washing machine. 'Just as soon as I've taken these...' The words died on her lips as she extracted the wet tangle of clothes from the washer. The delicate white silks with green stars on the sleeves were now a washed out pink decorated with excrement-coloured blobs.

'Whose the hell are those?' Jack said, looking at them in distaste.

'Er –' Pippa unwound a couple of red Aspen Valley jackets from the mass. 'I think they're Leopard Rock's colours. Or they were at any rate. The colour seems to have run from these jackets.'

Jack groaned and stalked out into Reception.

'Can anything else go wrong today?' he roared.

He reappeared a moment later, his eyes so dark there was almost no distinction between iris and pupil. 'Sort that out before next weekend. We've got another runner in those colours on Sunday.'

Pippa didn't have the faintest idea how, but she nodded anyway and dumped the sodden clothes on top of the washing machine.

'Of course I will.'

'But after you've rung Mick Farrelly. Getting that sorted is more important.' He looked at his watch. 'For fuck's sake. I should have left half an hour ago.'

Pippa followed him back into Reception, indignation rising in her chest.

'I do know how to prioritise,' she flung at him.

Jack stared at her as if she'd just sworn at him.

'Don't look at me like that, Jack. You're the one walking around like a bear with a sore head yelling orders and blaming everyone else for making you late –'

'Bear with a sore head?' Jack ridiculed. 'If you say so, but with bloody good reason! This is the third day in a row Emmie has called in sick. Melissa has been giving me an earful about some stupid fashion show she wants me to go to. I don't know what her problem has been this past fortnight; she hasn't retracted her claws once! Then I hear we have to change Virtuoso's jockey and you're nowhere to be seen,' he exclaimed, counting each point on his fingers. 'And now you've ruined some of the silks!'

'You are not the only one with problems!' Pippa cried, stamping her foot. 'For your information, I *am* entitled to a lunch break. As for problems, this staircase looks like it's going to cost me a fortune. I've yet to hear from Ollie about what he's going to do with the last of my stuff in London – burn it probably! But you don't hear me ranting and raging about it!'

They glared at each other, the silence only broken by their shallow breathing. Jack raised a finger.

'You *are* entitled to a lunch break,' he said in the quiet even tone which Pippa dreaded. 'A one hour lunch break. Anything more, tell me because I need to know.'

For a moment she quailed. In his present mood, he was more than capable of firing her for bad time-keeping and damaging work property – if that's what silks were. What would she do without a job with what looked like more unforeseen expense looming on the horizon? Suddenly, she felt close to tears. Why did he get her so worked up?

'You'd better get going if you want to make Newton Abbot in time,' she said stiffly and walked past him to her desk. She was aware of him watching her, motionless for a long moment before he turned and strode out the door, letting it slam behind him.

She picked up the telephone to ring Mick Farrelly's agent, but replaced it again. She covered her face with her hands, fighting back the tears which pricked her eyes. She leapt in her seat when the office door opened once more.

Jack faced her, looking harassed.

'Pippa, please can you move your car? I can't get out.'

'Oh!' Pippa jumped up, the urgency of his request stemming her tears.

She trotted after Jack into the car park, aware by the stiff set of his shoulders that his patience was hanging by a thread. Without her coat on the wind funnelling from the yard's walkways gnawed through her top, making her shiver. She fumbled with her keys in the lock, scraping against the paintwork in her haste. Out of the corner of her eye she saw Jack look at his watch before he got into the Land Rover in front of her.

Her car gave a half-hearted wheeze like an old man clearing his throat when she switched on the ignition. Pippa's fingers trembled.

'No, don't do this now,' she muttered. 'Come on. You've just had a good warm up.' She turned the key again and pumped her foot on the accelerator like a demented rhino putting out a campfire. The Beetle roared into life, the high revs rattling through every loose fitting, including Pippa. Slugging it into gear, she turned in her seat to see behind her and put her foot down. Her ear thudded painfully against the headrest as the car shot forward instead. A crunch sounded before it stalled.

A sickening dread diluted Pippa's blood. Groaning, she leaned her forehead on the cold steering wheel and wrapped her arms limply around it for comfort. A car door slammed and Jack's footsteps crunched on the gravel. She lifted her face to peep over the steering wheel to see him standing by the bonnet, his hands thrust deep into his pockets. She didn't know whether to feel cheered or not that he wasn't roaring his head off, such was the look of disconsolateness on his face.

She pushed open her door and stepped out into the bitter weather. A light drizzle was beginning to fall. Jack didn't look up, even when she went to stand beside him to inspect the damage.

Wincing, Pippa saw one of his rear brake lights lay in a jigsaw of red glass amongst the gravel. The Beetle looked surprisingly unscathed, the new bumper doing a proud job. She ventured a sidelong look at her boss.

Only the muscle in his jaw moved.

'Sorry,' she tried. 'Volkswagen really should redesign the gearbox so First and Reverse aren't so close together.'

Jack looked at her with as much humour in his face as a disgruntled silverback.

'Shall we try that again?' he said. 'I'm late.'

Pippa nodded and scampered back to the driver's seat. She carefully selected the correct gear and eased the car backwards, cringing when she heard another tinkle of glass as the two vehicles detached.

Once she had found another parking spot (beside the drainage ditch she had been trying to avoid in the first place), she got out, shifting from foot to foot and fingering her car keys and watched Jack turn his Land Rover around.

He pulled up level with her and leant out the window.

'We'll discuss this later.'

'Sorry, Jack.' Pippa couldn't help herself, but her words were drowned out by the spewing of gravel as the vehicle roared off down the driveway. Pippa stood in the rain, her shoulders heavy beneath the damp clinging of her shirt and watched him disappear behind the scraggy roadside hedges. 'Way to go, Pippa,' she muttered. 'You sure know how to keep the boss sweet.'

211

# Chapter Thirty

By "we'll discuss this later", what Jack meant in fact was that he was going to ignore Pippa for the next week. When she'd broached the subject and said her insurance would cover the costs, he'd merely nodded and carried on reading the *Racing Post*. And apart from the bare communication necessary in their jobs, he hardly said another word. Not that she wanted any great heart-to-hearts, Pippa thought as she sat at her desk after completing that day's declarations, but a little interaction would be nice. Just to reassure her that he didn't really despise her.

'Pippa,' Jack broke into her thoughts from his office doorway, 'what is this thing I've got in my diary about going to Abbey Road Studios next week?'

Oh, fuck, said courage and promptly deserted Pippa.

She put on a bright smile.

'It's the recording of the Cheltenham charity single that you're doing.'

Jack looked at her as if she'd just informed him he was going to front the opening gig at Glastonbury.

'*What?* I never agreed to that!' he spluttered.

'Um, well, yes, you did.'

'When? I would never agree to do this! I can't sing, Pippa!'

She looked at him, feeling the first twinge of guilt.

'You might have been a bit distracted when I asked you. You were receiving an earful from Melissa at the time.'

Jack ran both hands through his hair, making it stand on end.

'Story of my bloody life at the moment. I can't do this. Ring them up and cancel. Say there was a misunderstanding or something.'

'But we can't cancel,' cried Pippa. 'It's for charity. And it's not like you're the only person who's doing it. Seth Rutherford, the guy who's organising the whole thing, said there was about twenty or thirty of you all singing together.'

'Like a choir?' Jack looked horrified.

'More like a really big backing group. You're singing *Ticket to Ride*.'

'Oh, no,' Jack said, backing away. 'No way. I am not singing a Beatles song.'

'Why not? It'll be fun. Come on, Jack! Where's your sense of adventure? You'll get to go round one of the biggest recording studios in the world.

212

They'll give you a set of those great big earphones and you can sing while holding just the one piece to your ear like all the big artists do.'

Jack leaned up against the doorframe in surrender.

'Pippa, why are you doing this to me?'

'Doing what?'

'Turning everything upside down.'

'Everything?' She frowned dubiously. 'Am I?'

'I'm a horse trainer, not a singer.'

'It's for charity,' she urged.

Jack exhaled and Pippa beamed. He might not be hugely enthusiastic, but it looked like he was going to do it.

'This is a one-off, you hear?' He fixed her with a cautionary eye. 'Next time you ask me to do something make sure I'm paying attention.'


Pippa was halfway through her roast beef and mayonnaise sandwich when Emmie appeared at the door after over a week's absence. She was shivering, her nose as red as an alcoholic's against the pallor of her cheeks.

Pippa dusted the crumbs off her fingers and went round to greet the stable lass.

'Hey, stranger. You don't look like you should be back here,' she said with a gentle smile and closed the office door, shutting out the cold. 'How are you feeling?'

Emmie averted her gaze, her puffy eyes circled with purple rings as she looked down. She scuffed her booted toe against the carpet.

'I don't know, to be honest,' she said in a trembling voice. 'I went to see the doctor yesterday.'

Pippa took her arm and led her to a couple of Reception seats. Emmie looked on the verge of collapse.

'What did he say?'

'He said –' Emmie licked her lips and took a deep breath. 'He said I'm pregnant.' She gave a frightened chuckle. 'Six weeks to be exact.'

Pippa stared, her brain completely void of anything to say. What could she say? Congratulations, even if it's unplanned? Express her condolences on the creation of life? Who's the father?

'Wow,' she settled on. 'Um, how do you feel about it?'

Emmie shrugged. She attempted a weak smile.

'Scared,' she said. 'I've had my suspicions for the past few weeks, but having the test and getting a scan has really hit home.'

Pippa gazed at her in sympathy, feeling the girl's fear. She was also itching to ask if Billy was the father. As far as she knew, the two of them weren't officially a couple. For Emmie to be six weeks pregnant, she would surely have known by now.

'Have you told anyone else?'

Emmie nodded and brushed a stray tear away with a shaking hand.

'Billy knows. He's taking full responsibility.' She smiled. 'He's being very supportive even though I know he's scared too.'

'Oh, so it's Billy's,' Pippa said before she could stop herself. 'Sorry, that was rude. Of course it would be Billy's. I just didn't realise you and he were – you know, *involved* six weeks ago.'

'We weren't really. But it was Boxing Day and he came round to see if I was okay after work. And well, one thing led to another and you know what happens next. Neither of us were exactly *prepared* and it's the only time we've been so careless. What are the odds, eh?' Emmie gave a mirthless chuckle.

Pippa's eyes widened in horror. This whole thing was her fault! She had talked Billy into visiting her after Black Russian's fall and now Emmie's life was about to change completely. And at nineteen years of age, Pippa couldn't see how it would be for the better.

'Have you discussed what you're going to do?'

'I'm going to keep it. There's no two ways about that,' Emmie said. She looked down at her hands. 'But the doctor told me I should stop riding out in case I have a fall. He said I can still do stable duties though.'

'Oh, God, we're going to have to tell Jack,' Pippa shuddered. How would he take it, she wondered, losing one of his best riders because she was having a relationship with another member of staff? Not too kindly, she imagined.

'He's going to kill me.' Emmie shook her head. 'Or Billy.'

'No, he won't,' Pippa tried to reassure her. 'Why would he? You're a woman. You're bound to have babies at some stage. He knows that.'

'Yes, but a mistake like this? And with Billy?' she quaked. 'I'm more terrified about telling Jack than I am about telling my parents.'

Pippa took a deep breath.

'You don't have to tell him then. I will.'

A wave of relief washed over Emmie's face before she shook her head.

'No. You shouldn't have to. It's my responsibility. I should tell him.'

Pippa shifted awkwardly in her seat.

'Well, to be honest with you, Emmie, I feel partly responsible. See, I kind of encouraged Billy to go see you that night.' She rubbed the girl's slouched back comfortingly. 'Let me deal with Jack. You've got enough going on to keep your mind occupied.'

It wasn't until the following morning that Pippa got the opportunity to speak to Jack. Laden with two mugs of tea, she knocked on his door and shouldered her way inside.

'Morning,' she greeted him.

Jack looked up from his paperwork and Pippa tried to gauge what sort of mood he was in.

'H'ro,' he grunted.

Not great, she ascertained. Oh, well, it didn't really matter what mood he was in now. It certainly wasn't going to be very chipper in a couple of moments' time.

She waited until Jack had taken a tentative slurp of his drink. She wasn't going to have him with third degree burns as well if she could help it.

He looked up at her when she remained standing by his desk then darted a look sideways.

'Can I help you with anything?' he said.

Pippa took a deep breath.

'Perhaps put your drink down first.'

Jack frowned, but did as he was bade. Pippa's hands were shaking so much she did the same.

'What have you done?' he asked warily.

'Me? Nothing... for a change. Emmie came in yesterday after you'd left for the races.'

'Is she better? When is she coming back?'

'Well, there's the thing. It's all dependent on how you take things.' Pippa bit her lip and wrung her fingers.

'What? Stop talking in riddles, Pippa. Take what?'

'Oh, hell. I'm not doing this very well. Okay, here goes. Emmie's pregnant.'

Jack sat up in his chair as if she'd just pulled a gun on him, making her glad she'd asked him to put his tea down.

'*Pregnant?*' he spluttered. 'How?'

'In the usual way I imagine. I didn't ask for details.'

'No, I mean she hasn't got a boyfriend.' Jack frowned. 'Has she?'

215

Pippa closed her eyes and asked God to protect Billy.

'Yeah, she does. It's Billy.'

Jack's nostrils flared and his eyes turned a thunderous shade.

'Billy? Billy from here?'

Pippa grimaced and nodded.

Jack stood up so fast his chair fell over. In two strides, he was already past Pippa and heading for the door.

'I'm going to kill that little shit,' he growled. 'Stupid idiot doesn't know the difference between his dick and his brain. Wait until I get my hands on him.'

Pippa was struck dumb by his fury then instinct kicked in. She caught hold of Jack's arm and dragged him to a stop.

'No! Stop it, Jack. Just calm down for a minute.'

'Calm down? CALM DOWN?' he fumed, his shoulders shaking. 'Don't you see what that little fucker has done because he couldn't keep his dick in his pants? He's fucked up Emmie's life! And he hasn't done me any favours either. Emmie can't ride out when she's pregnant!' He shook off Pippa's hold, but she was quick to bar the doorway.

'Just wait, please,' she said, her eyes pleading. 'Just sit down and take some deep breaths. You going out there and giving Billy a boxing isn't going to help anything.'

'No? It'll make me feel better though.'

'Look, he's feeling just as scared as Emmie is right now. Don't make it any harder on him. He went over to her place with the best of intentions –'

Jack snorted in derision and Pippa gave him a withering look.

'– He went over with the best of intentions after Black Russian was killed. He wasn't taking advantage of her.'

Jack's eyes were still stormy, but Pippa was relieved to see he wasn't shaking quite so much. She stepped away from the door and held his arms in an effort to calm him further. She felt his muscles tense beneath her grip and he drew his head back.

'He could still have used some common sense,' he said.

'Jack, this is Billy we're talking about.' She rubbed his arms in a consoling gesture.

Jack tore his eyes away from hers and looked down at her hands.

'Proves my point though, doesn't it?' he said, his tone hoarse. His Adam's Apple bobbed as he swallowed and he stepped away from Pippa. 'Relationships in the workplace always end in a mess.'

Pippa felt her cheeks burning. What was he implying?

'Their relationship hasn't ended,' she retorted, more severe than she had intended to cover up her embarrassment. 'So they made a mistake. Would it have made a difference if the baby's father was someone we didn't know?'

'Oh, God,' Jack groaned, squeezing his eyes shut and pinching the bridge of his nose. 'Emmie's going to have a baby. She's just a kid!'

'They're both kids. That's why they need your support, not your hostility.'

Jack gave a thunderous growl and thumped his fist on the desk, making Pippa and the tea-cups jump. 'God, nine months then she's going to have to go on maternity leave. Who's going to ride Asian Dancer for the year and a half that's she gone, huh?' he ranted at her. 'She's already thrown two lads off in the past week. I can't get a decent workout into that bloody horse because most of the time she's tearing around the Gallops without a rider.'

'Make a plan then,' Pippa replied, her patience gauge hitting E. 'Maybe one of the other lads will learn to stay on her. Maybe you shouldn't be so reliant on one rider.'

'Are you trying to tell me how to do my job, Pippa?'

'No, Jack! Of course not!' she snapped. 'But at the very least I would expect a man of your experience not to lean so heavily on one person. Do you know Emmie was more scared of telling you than she was about telling her parents? What does that say, huh? Don't you think she can feel how heavily you rely on her?'

'I don't rely on her that much! She's just a bloody good rider. I'd be a fool not to take advantage of that. I was going to help her get her amateur's licence. Now what is she going to do?'

'She's going to do stable duties until it's time for her to go on maternity leave.'

'Oh, she is, is she?' Jack chortled, crossing his arms across his chest.

'Yes. Wouldn't you rather she was doing that than nothing at all? She needs your support.'

'Yes, I heard you the first time,' he snapped. He shook his head and went to pick up his chair. As an afterthought he scribbled a couple more lines in his Entries and Declarations notebook and tossed it onto the other side of the desk.

Pippa snatched it up and stalked towards the door.

'Bloody stupid kids,' she heard him mutter.

She stopped by the door and turned to him, the last of her patience evaporating.

'Jack, have you never made a mistake in your life? If I recall, you blamed yourself for Black Russian's death because of mistakes *you* had made in his training, right?'

Jack stared at her.

'And I'm sure I don't need to remind you that you were feeling pretty shit after that, weren't you?' she continued. 'Just imagine what Emmie and Billy are feeling right now.' She turned on her heel and left, tempted to slam the door behind her.

Sitting down at her desk, she picked up that morning's post and began to sort through them, too distracted to start on entries. She paused as she flipped over one envelope. It was addressed to her. The return address was Stairway to Avon.

Realising it was her long awaited quote, she slit open the seal. Her hands shook as she read the contents, panic drawing from her limbs and gathering in a hard ball in her stomach as she absorbed the figures. This was not good. Maybe they'd made a typo and put an extra zero on the end by mistake? She knew the cost of replacing Hazyvale's staircase wasn't going to be cheap, but...

'Nine thousand pounds?' she croaked.

'What?'

She looked up to see Jack had appeared from his office, his jacket zipped up, ready to ward off the raw February wind outside. Still stunned, Pippa couldn't speak. Jack frowned at her.

'What's nine thousand pounds?'

'My quote,' she managed. 'For the staircase. N-n-nine grand.' She looked up, her eyes wide with panic. 'I can't afford that.'

Jack looked far from sympathetic.

'I guess you're going to need to make a plan then,' he said, quoting her earlier words.

She watched him walk out of the office then looked down again at the piece of paper, the typed words blurring before her eyes.

Nine thousand pounds? Something would have to give.

# Chapter Thirty-One

Pippa walked along the row of stables towards Peace Offering's box, the gaiety of the stable staff's farewells to each other as they looked forward to the weekend lost on her. Peace Offering was looking over his half door, the blaze down his face luminous in the darkness, a scarecrow's hand of hay poking from either side of his mouth.

He pricked his ears and tossed his head at her approach.

She smiled at his comic appearance before a blanket of sadness wrapped itself over her shoulders. Did he know she was his owner? Did he realise how his entrance into her life had turned it upside down? Was it all about to come crashing down around her?

She rubbed her fingers between his nostrils and looked into his glistening eyes.

'Peace Offering,' she murmured, 'whoever named you got it right, didn't they?'

He butted her hand and resumed his chewing, his lips skewed to capture the strands hanging from the corners of his mouth. With a smile, she helped move the hay into a more accessible position.

'What am I going to do with you, boy?' she sighed. Her sinuses filled with the tangy comforting smell of warm hay and horses. Looking around, her gaze followed the silvery snail-trail of the Gallops' running rail lit by the rising moon. At the crest of the hill, she could just see a light protruding through the skeletal trees from Jack's house. 'What am I going to do *without* you?'

Her shoulders sagged as the inevitable became clearer in her mind. Peace Offering was a luxury and in her current financial crisis, luxuries would be the first to go.

'Now there's a sad stance if I ever saw one,' an unmistakable Irish voice broke into her thoughts.

Pippa gave Finn a weak smile of greeting as he strolled towards her.

'Oh, hello.'

He stopped beside her and arched a quizzical eyebrow. Unearthing a hand from his pocket he raised her chin with his thumb and forefinger.

'What's ailin' ye, *a thaisce*?'

Pippa shrugged and looked away.

'Just some personal problems. Nothing to worry about,' she replied. He wouldn't want to hear her financial woes.

'Nothing to worry about?' Finn echoed. 'With a face longer than Peace Offering's here, it doesn't sound like it's nothing. Want to tell Uncle Finn about it?'

Pippa's next attempt at a smile was more successful.

'No, it's okay. Thanks though. I think I'm just going to go home now and have some hot chocolate. That'll cheer me up I'm sure.'

Finn cocked his head to try get Pippa to meet his eyes.

'Hot chocolate nothing. By the look of things you need a bottle of Jameson's. Let me take you out for dinner.'

She shook her head. In her vulnerable state of mind, she was likely to become fonder still of the sympathetic Finn and knowing he was seeing this Cara Connolly character already would just complicate matters further.

'Thanks, but I won't. I've already got some food defrosted for tonight.'

'Away with ye. You'll be doing me a favour at the same time, you know. I'm at a loose end, another two days of my suspension to serve thanks to Leopard Rock's attempt at dodgems the other day, so. You need some cheering up. At least let me take you out for a jar.'

Pippa wavered. Maybe unburdening all her worries onto Finn wasn't such a bad idea. There was always Tash at the other end of the phone, but Tash always got Pippa's burdens.

'I have to cook that fish tonight otherwise it'll go off,' she tried once more.

'Well then, you go home and have your tea and freshen up. I'll do the same so I don't smell like a stable and I'll pick you up at eight. How's that sound?' His green eyes searched hers for a positive answer.

Yes, maybe telling Finn would be a good idea.

She nodded, grateful for his kindness.

Back at Hazyvale, Pippa trudged through from the kitchen to the lounge in her dressing gown and Snoopy slippers with her dinner. Sitting cross-legged on the sofa, she balanced her plate on her lap and switched on the television. She gasped. The image which greeted her saw her fried fish slide off her plate onto the floor with a wet slap.

How could she have forgotten this?

She watched, transfixed as the action unfolded onscreen.

'He's bleeding out! BP is one-eighty over one-twenty. Where is Feldman?' cried the pretty paramedic rushing around a gurney and crazily beeping machines.

'Last I saw of him he was shepherding a med student into the maintenance closet,' replied a casual voice stepping into shot. 'Maybe I can lend a hand in his absence.'

'Who the hell are you?'

Pippa's lip trembled as she waited for the response. The actor sauntered forward, his attitude in suave contrast to the panicked paramedic.

'Doctor Fletcher,' she whispered in unison with *Holby City*'s newest addition.

Her appetite lost, she watched the rest of the medical drama in numbed silence. Ollie was heroic, saving two critical patients, snubbing a curt senior character with witty responses and she had to admit, looking very sexy in blue scrubs and stethoscope draped round his neck. Tears sprung from her eyes, blurring the credits as they rolled up the screen.

What was she doing? She'd thrown away her life in London all for a horse and now even that looked in jeopardy. Self-pity and loathing crumpled her face and she curled up on the sofa, hugging a cushion to her chest.

A rhythmic tap on the front door dragged Pippa from her well of gloom and, with a groan, saw it was ten past eight. She opened the door to Finn, looking down at her fidgeting Snoopy slippers.

'My opening line was gonna be "Are you ready to paint the town red", but I see I might be getting ahead of myself,' he said, looking her up and down.

'Sorry, Finn. I – I just got sidetracked. I'm sorry you've come all this way for nothing. I wouldn't have been much fun anyway.'

'Who says I've come all this way for nothing?' He rubbed his arms and looked at Pippa hopefully. 'Are you going to invite me in or leave me on the doorstep to catch my death?'

'Sorry. Come in,' she said, unable to keep the despondency out of her voice. She didn't feel like playing the role of hostess. Nevertheless, she stood aside for her guest.

'Stop apologising and tell me what the problem is – Jaysus! Have you been takin' your frustrations out on your staircase? It's got more loose boards than a jockey who's had his teeth kicked in.'

Pippa followed his look of amazement at the offending bomb site. It really did look a mess. She looked away again and wandered into the lounge.

'That's what the problem is,' she said over her shoulder. 'We pulled up the carpet and found all the wood is rotten. I got a quote yesterday to replace it and it's going to cost nine thousand pounds.'

Finn followed her to the sofa and removed her plate and fish fillet where now a fish-shaped patch of grease marked the newly sanded floor. He sat beside her.

'Nine grand? That's a bit steep.'

Pippa gave a mirthless snort.

'It's a staircase. Bound to be steep. But I can't afford it *and* keep Peace Offering in training. So my only option is to sell him.'

'But you can't sell him,' he protested. 'Can't you get a loan or something?'

'No,' she sighed, pulling at a thread on one of the cushions. 'I've already got one which is going to be used up replacing the stairs, but I've still got the whole of upstairs to refurbish and the bank won't lend me any more. I've got no choice.'

'But Pippa, you can't sell him. You had such big plans to run him in the Grand National. You've come this far, you can't throw it all away now.'

Pippa shrugged.

'I was being silly thinking he could win the Grand National. I was looking at the antepost betting the other day and there's about two hundred horses listed! One bookmaker was quoting Peace Offering at five-hundred-to-one. Some other firms weren't even giving a price, that's how confident they are that he'll even make the final cut.'

'You're not being silly at all,' Finn said adamantly. 'Peace Offering has got just as good a chance as any. Much of it is down to luck on the day.'

'But we can't even be certain that he'll *be* there on the day. If there's only forty places available, he might not even be good enough to get an entry.' She looked at him, her swollen eyes swimming with despair.

'All he needs is one good result and his handicap rating will shoot him right into contention,' he insisted.

'Still, it's useless even talking about it. I can't afford him,' she sighed.

'Have you spoken to Jack about it?'

She shook her head.

'I'm not Jack's favourite person at the moment. This cottage is stressing me out so much I haven't been the best secretary in the world. It wouldn't surprise me if he fired me even.'

'Nonsense. Now you're being silly. Jack wouldn't fire you.'

Pippa snorted.

'I wouldn't be too sure about that.'

'Believe me, Pippa, since you arrive at Aspen Valley, Jack has become a hundred times easier to work with. He'd have a mutiny on his hands if he let you go. Your smile is a little light relief for us all.' He reached out and stroked her cheek. 'You don't know how unhinging it is seeing you without it now.'

'I always seem to make Jack mad though,' she said, dropping her gaze. She could feel the tears threatening again. 'I mess up on the entries and declarations and appointments. Then just last week, I not only took out the brake light on his car, but I ruined Leopard Rock's silks and then had the cheek to give him a bollocking about Emmie and Billy –' She bit her lip, realising she had probably said too much.

'Ah, Emmie and Billy,' Finn smiled. 'Yes, I hear you're not the only one messing up.'

'What do you mean?' she feigned innocence.

'I believe Billy has been doing some entering and declaring of his own.' He gave a wicked smile and winked. 'Don't fret, you haven't given away any secret. Billy told me he got Emmie up the pole.'

Pippa raised her hands and let them flop down on the cushion in resignation.

'They've got such massive problems and here I am crying over this measly staircase and Ollie –'

'Ollie?'

'Well, not over him as such,' she relented. 'It was his first appearance on *Holby City* tonight and seeing him again just reminded me of what my life used to be like. It might have been a bit mundane, but at least it was simple. I didn't have to worry about anything really. But now...'

'You changed your lifestyle. It was bound to come with its own set of challenges,' Finn reasoned. 'It hasn't all been bad though, has it? You met me, after all.' He gave her an encouraging smile and she managed a half-hearted laugh.

'Yeah, what would I have done if I hadn't met you? I know, the country hasn't all been bad. I've had the chance to do some painting and I've had fun watching Peace Offering race, even if it is about to come to an end.'

'Don't be talking like that. It doesn't have to end.'

'But there's no alternative,' she said with a futile shrug. 'I need to replace the staircase if I'm to sell the cottage and the only way I can do that is by selling Peace Offering. How else will I get the money?'

Finn thought for a moment, his brow furrowing.

'I don't know,' he admitted.

Pippa shook her head, the half hope that Finn could think of some way she could keep her horse extinguished. The thought of him being owned by someone else, who was bound to love him less than she did, made the tears well up.

'I'm going to miss Peace Offering. He's such a kind horse even if he isn't the most talented. Even if he doesn't win another race, I'd still want to keep him, but...'

'Don't cry, *a thaisce*,' Finn said, tucking a curling lock of her hair behind her ear. 'Come here.'

Pippa allowed herself to be hugged, finding comfort in his sympathy. She felt another rush of self-pity flood through her as she thought how, had circumstances been different, she could let Finn become so much more than a friend. His shoulder was warm and strong, his arms around her gentle, his light touch stroking her hair so supportive. The silent tears were now laced with regret. She couldn't have Finn even if she wanted him. Not only would it end when she sold the cottage and had to move, but there was Cara Connolly to think of as well. Pippa would never be The Other Woman.

Squeezing her eyes shut to stem the flow, she disengaged herself.

Finn cupped her face, brushing away a stray tear and shook his head.

'You really don't know how hard this is seeing you in this way. You're too good a person to be made to feel this sad.'

'I'm not good, Finn. Everything I've done these past few months has been for myself. Ollie was right. I have been selfish.'

'I'm glad I never go to meet him properly otherwise he'd be sportin' a socked jaw, you know. Did he really tell ye that?'

Pippa nodded pathetically.

'Yet he never contributed by coming down here to help with the cottage or give you any support,' he summed up. He stroked her cheek again. 'He sounds about as useful as a chocolate teapot, to be sure.'

Pippa gave a watery smile.

'There. That's more like it,' Finn encouraged. His eyes flickered to her lips and he leaned forward.

Pippa hesitated.

Finn paused and redirected his intended kiss to her forehead.

'There now. I think you should get some sleep. You'll feel better in the morning.'

Pippa could feel a blush start to rise from her dressing gown collar and she got to her feet before it showed.

'Maybe you're right. Thank you for sitting here and listening to my problems. I'm sorry I haven't been very good company.'

'Stop apologising!' he said, following suit.

She led him to the door and gave him a grateful smile.

'Thank you.'

'No, thank *you*.' He grinned at her confused grin. 'What firm did you say it was that quoted Peace Offering at five-hundred-to-one?'

Pippa's returning smile was the most genuine of the night.

'Good night, Finn.'

'Good night, Pippa. Sleep well.'

# Chapter Thirty-Two

With the most pressing duties of a Saturday morning completed, Pippa leant back in her chair and watched the rain through the office window blur her view of the yard. The telephone had been strangely quiet all morning and apart from the usual calls from jockeys' agents and a reporter who wanted a last minute quote from Jack on Virtuoso's chance in that afternoon's Denman Chase, there'd been nothing else to distract her. She'd tried to talk to Jack before he left for Newbury, but he was so preoccupied with his star horse that he'd told her it would have to wait until Monday. A whole day and a half of waiting to drop the bombshell loomed ahead.

Although, to be fair, Pippa reasoned with herself, it was more of a bombshell to her than it would be to Jack. Peace Offering's presence at Aspen Valley probably wasn't quite so important to him as it was to her. According to the internet there was a couple of National Hunt sales coming up and this time they must ensure his reserve was low enough for him to sell.

Pippa sighed, the sodden weather outside the office reflecting her mood inside. How would she cope with Peace Offering running in someone else's name and colours? Would he even race again or would he be sent to sale after sale until he was a broken wreck like Black Beauty? Uncle Dave had given her a copy of *Black Beauty* for her tenth Christmas. The tears had begun when Rob Roy was killed and were substantial enough to warrant flood warnings in the Taylor household when Ginger died. Needless to say, Dave was far from popular with her parents after this.

Feeling a lump swell in her throat as she realised how disappointed Dave would have been not to run Peace Offering in the Grand National, she bit her lip and clicked on her computer's calendar for next week to distract herself.

She grimaced.

Jack was due to go to London for the charity single recording on Tuesday. That wasn't going to improve his opinion of her.

The telephone rang and she welcomed its interruption.

'Pippa? It's Jack.' He sounded breathless, his voice raised above the background roar of traffic. 'I need your help.'

Pippa frowned. He'd left over an hour and a half ago.

'What's the matter? Have you broken down?'

'No, no. I've just arrived at Newbury Racecourse. Is Finn around?'

Oh, God, Pippa quailed. Mick Farrelly hadn't turned up. She reassured herself that she had definitely booked him to ride Virtuoso that afternoon. She couldn't be blamed for this.

'I don't know. He might be. Do you want me to go get him for you?'

'No, don't do that. There isn't time.' Jack sounded almost panicked. 'I need you to do something for me, Pippa. Right now, please. I've forgotten Virtuoso's passport. He can't run without it.'

'Bloody hell, Jack,' Pippa groaned. She opened her desk cabinet where all the horses' passports were kept and flicked through to V's folder.

'Yes, I know. I'm not so proud of it myself, but I might not live to tell the tale if Virtuoso doesn't run. Newbury are sold out with people coming to see him race. I need you to find his passport, find Finn and get him to drive over here with it. It's too late for me to come all the way back.'

'But where is it?' she exclaimed as she unearthed only Victory Speech and Viscount Camperdown's passports. 'It's not here in the folder.'

'It's at my house. Bloody fool that I am, I had it out last night and forgot to put it back with the others this morning.'

'Your house? Is it locked? Can I get in?'

'In the bottom drawer of my desk in the office, there's a spare set of keys. The passport should be in the lounge. Get it and go find Finn! Please, Pippa. As fast as you can!'

'I'm gone. Where will Finn find you?' Pippa said, standing up and threading her free arm though her coat sleeve.

'In the saddling enclosure. He's a jockey so he shouldn't have a problem getting in.'

'Okay, don't panic, Jack. Everything will be fine. You'll have the passport in no time at all.'

'Now!'

'Okay! Good luck!' Pippa slammed down the phone and grabbing her handbag like a relay runner's baton, sprinted for the door. 'Oh, shit. Need the keys first,' she said, guiltily back-tracking to Jack's office.

There was no obvious sign of Finn in the yard. Most of the staff had either finished work for the morning or were taking cover from the rain. Pippa flicked up her collar and dashed to the car park. She scanned the few cars left hunched in the drizzle for Finn's Honda Civic.

Her heart plummeted.

227

Finn had obviously already left.

'Only one thing for it,' she muttered, hurrying over to her car. 'How do you fancy a trip to Newbury?' she asked the Beetle.

It felt strange to pull up outside Jack's house, which she'd never really seen before. The solid stone walls of the converted barn were stained a dark grey by the rain, the trellised creeper draped soggily over the front door. It felt even stranger letting herself in the house with the spare keys and entering Jack's personal space. Despite the urgency of her mission, Pippa stopped to gape at the mammoth open-plan lounge-cum-dining room spread out before her. It was as big as a church, fit for a king, with dark wooden beams overhead like arched swords held aloft in reverence.

A soft whine from the opposite side of the room caught her attention and Pippa noticed Berkeley, Jack's aging Retriever in a wicker basket thumping his tail at her.

'Great guard dog you are,' she said, walking further into the room. 'Don't you ever get claustrophobic?'

In spite of her casual irony, she was struck by the solitary place setting at the six-seater dining table, in the lounge only one empty glass on a table beside a leather recliner chair. There were no family photographs above the open stone fireplace, only brass and stone sculptures of horses and a carriage clock frozen in time.

It felt lonely.

She ran her hand along the mantelpiece, unable to stop the smile of amusement when she saw an open CD case of the Beatles' album *Help!* lying next to the hi-fi cabinet.

Her gaze travelled along the walls and stopped at the picture opposite the recliner. She gulped. It was the picture of Black Russian on the Gallops, framed in dark wood to match the beams.

A deep gong emanated from the depths of a grandfather clock made her jump and she shook herself back to the present. Jack was waiting for her. She had to find Virtuoso's passport. She sifted through the haphazard pile of thriller novels and *Racing Posts* littering a central coffee table. A booklet slipped out between two newspapers. Pippa exclaimed with triumph.

'Right!' she said, snapping it in her fingers and addressing a bemused-looking Berkeley. 'Newbury, here we come!'

*

228

Pippa fidgeted as she stood in the queue waiting to enter Newbury Racecourse, ignoring the boozed-up party behind her all dressed as John McCririck. Such was their presence that the ticket man at the turnstyle didn't notice Pippa at first.

She tried to walk through 'like she belonged' as Tash had taught her, but the man held out his arm at the last second.

'Hold on, can I see your ticket?'

Pippa gave him her most helpless big-blue-eyed look.

'I don't have a ticket. I'm just here to drop something off.'

'Sorry, I can't let you through without a ticket,' he said, shaking his head.

'No, you don't understand. I'm not here to watch the racing.' She pulled Virtuoso's passport out of her bag and pushed it towards him. 'I just need to drop this off. It's a horse passport.'

The man gave her a bored look, which became pained when the John McCririck impersonators started getting fractious at the delay.

'Nobody comes through here without a ticket. No exceptions, I'm afraid.'

'Bugger. Okay then. How much is it?'

'Everything's sold out. If you'd come earlier or booked online you'd have been fine, but now...'

'But I was never intending to come!' Pippa cried, panic beginning to rise. She did not want to have travelled all this way to be turned away for something as mundane as a ticket. 'Don't you see? This is a horse's passport, *Virtuoso's* passport! It was left behind.'

The ticket man sucked his teeth.

'That means absolutely nothing to me. My instructions are to not let anyone in without a ticket.'

Pippa bit her lip, her gaze darting from the man's obstinate face to the throngs of warmly-dressed race goers milling on the other side of the gate. Weak sunshine split the overcast skies, reflecting off the windows of the grandstand beyond.

'Please, you have to let me in!' she begged. 'If I don't get this passport to Jack Carmichael, Virtuoso won't be able to run in the Denman Chase. He's the reason why you're sold out!'

The man folded his arms across his chest.

'Like I said, I don't know what you're talking about. I don't know who Virtuoso is –'

'But you work here! Surely you must know who he is!' Pippa exclaimed.

'Sorry, miss, you're holding up the queue,' he replied, gesturing to the party behind her. 'Now, if you don't have a ticket, please can you move aside before you create a traffic jam.'

Panic got the better of her and she stamped her foot.

'You're going to have more than a traffic jam on your hands if I can't get this passport through. You're going to have a bloody riot! Everyone's come to see Virtuoso race, but he won't unless you let me through!'

'Miss, I don't want to have to call Security on you –'

A deerstalker-capped man with fake ginger sideburns, part of the group standing behind Pippa, poked into her line of sight.

'That really Virtuoso's passport? Let's have a look, love?'

Pippa sighed and held it out for him to see.

'Yes, it's his.' A thought occurred to her and she smiled at the young man looking cross-eyed at the booklet. 'You're a big fan, right?'

'Oh, yeah,' he enthused. 'We've come all the way down from Liverpool to see him win.'

'I'm so sorry to hear that,' she said, shaking her head.

'What d'you mean?'

Pippa gave a forlorn shrug.

'Well, Virtuoso won't be able to race unless I can get his passport inside. And the gentleman here won't let me in without a ticket.'

'Oy, let her through, mate!' the deerstalker said.

'No, please don't blame him. He's only doing his job. Such a pity, really. For everyone. Your wasted journey, Virtuoso's wasted journey. God knows what effect this will have on his Cheltenham Gold Cup chances.'

The deerstalker and his now attentive friends all squared up to the ticket man who took an uncertain step backwards.

'It's against the rules to let anyone on course without a ticket,' he defended himself.

'Yeah, and it's also against the rules to retract the star attraction when we've paid to come all this way,' the deerstalker retorted.

'Look, fellas, just calm down a minute. I'll call a steward to help us sort this out, shall I?'

Pippa looked at her watch. Jack had twenty minutes in which to declare Virtuoso as a confirmed runner for the Denman Chase.

'That might be too late,' she said.

'Aw, fuck,' yelled one of the deerstalkers. 'An' it's Barry's stag do. Don't spoil it for us, mate. Just let her through and stop dicking around with your stupid rule book.'

'You must understand, I can't *do* that,' the ticket man replied, looking more frazzled. 'My job is to only let people through with valid tickets.'

'Fuck that, mate! Let her through!'

'Yeah! Let her through! If you don't, Virtuoso's not gonna race!'

Heads turned as the John McCriricks raised their voices.

'What? Virtuoso's not going to race?'

'Only because this dick-wad won't let this girl through. She's got the horse's passport.'

'What! Let her through!'

'Yeah, don't be a tosser! Let her through!'

The ticket man paled as his objectors swelled in numbers.

'Oh, Christ,' he faltered. 'You promise you're telling the truth?'

Pippa nodded, beaming and flapped Virtuoso's passport in front of her. 'Proof's all here.'

The ticket man closed his eyes for a brief moment then waved her through.

'Go on, then. Go do what you have to do. Just don't mention me.'

'Thank you!' Pippa skipped through the gateway feeling like Lassie escaping from the dog pound, the yells of well-wishes from the group of John McCriricks ringing in her ears. She turned to wave at them. 'Send the stables an email! I'll get one of Virtuoso's horseshoes sent to you!'

Pippa slipped through the gateway towards the pre-parade ring, unnoticed. Amidst the calmer atmosphere of the saddling enclosure she spotted Jack pacing back and forth outside the stalls, his trench coat flapping around him.

'Jack!' she called, trying to run across the grassy interior while her heels plugged into the soft ground.

The trainer whirled round at the sound of her voice.

'Pippa! Thank God you're here. Did you find it? I thought Finn was bringing it?'

'Right here,' she said, handing over the passport. 'I couldn't find Finn so I came myself.'

'Thank God,' Jack said, holding it to his heart. 'Thank *you*, Pippa. I've got to go declare him, but thank you.'

She watched him stride away, relief that she had got here in time now replaced with awkwardness as she fiddled with her coat buttons. With her task now complete she suddenly felt superfluous to proceedings. A sinking feeling set in as she realised she would never get to stand in the saddling enclosure ever again with Peace Offering's inevitable departure.

As abruptly as he'd set off, Jack stopped and turned back. He strode towards her and guided her into an empty saddling stall. He cupped her face with his warm hands and looked down at her, his eyes intense.

For a wild moment, Pippa wondered what he was going to do next.

By the fleeting expression on his face, the same irrational thought seemed to cross his mind too. He transferred his hands to her shoulders.

'You have saved my arse today, all of ours in fact,' he said soberly. 'I don't know what I would have done if you hadn't come all this way.'

Pippa attempted a modest smile, unused to receiving flattery from Jack and even more unsettled with him standing so close to her.

'You would have thought of something,' she said.

'We'll never know, but I *do* know you went beyond the call of duty to help me out. Pippa, listen,' he said, tightening his hold on her shoulders. 'Finn spoke to me this morning and told me about your concerns over keeping Peace Offering –'

'He did what?'

'No, don't be angry with him. I'm glad he told me. My point is, I know Peace Offering is the one thing that keeps you with us at Aspen Valley. If I have to train him for free and pay for his entries to keep it that way, then that's what I'll do.'

Pippa forgot how to breathe.

'You mean that?' she squeaked.

'Yes. This time I *am* paying attention,' Jack answered with a small smile. 'You're not going to sell Peace Offering. Not if I have anything to do with it.'

'Oh!' She hadn't realised just how heavy the blanket of gloom had been until it slid off her shoulders. Without thinking, she flung her arms around Jack's neck, squeezing him tight with joy.

'Thank you,' she whispered in his ear.

She felt his arms fold around her, a feeling of strength and solidity adding to her relief. She closed her eyes and inhaled a deep lungful of his damp trench coat. She pressed her cheek, cold from the chilly wind blowing across Newbury Racecourse, close to his neck, finding comfort from his warmth and faint graze of his skin. She felt his chest swell

232

against her as he breathed, his embrace tightening before relinquishing her in an unhurried, almost reluctant manner.

'I've got a horse to declare,' he said needlessly.

With the faint tang of his cologne still lingering in her nostrils and the heat of his skin still warming her cheek, she gave him a shy smile and nodded.

'Good luck.'

# Chapter Thirty-Three

Pippa couldn't help the grin spreading across her face as she opened her emails. A haphazard photograph of the John McCririck impersonators she had met five days ago greeted her with a polite request for some Virtuoso memorabilia.

'What's so amusing?' Jack asked, on his way out to watch the horses work.

'Wait. Don't go anywhere,' Pippa said, shoving some gloss paper into her printer and switching it on.

Jack looked at her with suspicion.

'What are you doing?' he asked as she cropped the resultant photograph with her scissors.

'This.' She handed him the photo. 'Can you write something nice on it for these guys?'

'Who are these idiots?'

'These idiots are the people who helped me get into Newbury on Saturday.'

Jack pulled a face.

'Do I have to? I can't even write a birthday card without getting stuck on the message.'

'Please,' she urged. 'If they hadn't bullied the guy at the gate, I'd have never got Virtuoso's passport to you in time.'

Jack looked disgruntled.

'I suppose we owe them then. What should I say?'

Pippa grinned.

'They won us the Denman Chase. Just tell them that. They'll love it.'

'Correction: *Virtuoso* won us the Denman Chase.' He held up his hands in surrender at Pippa's imploring expression. 'Fine, fine. I guess they played a hand in it too.'

He leant over Pippa's desk and took a pen off her keyboard and after a pause, scrawled a message across the top of the photo.

Pippa stole a glance at his frowning expression, her pen lid clamped between his teeth.

'How did yesterday go?' she ventured.

'Abbey Road Studios, you mean?'

She nodded.

Jack shrugged.

'Okay.'

'Just okay?'

'Pippa, I can't sing. Not even in the shower.'

Pippa felt herself blushing to her roots as a very vivid image sprung to mind. She knocked her computer mouse off the desk and bent to retrieve it in an attempt to hide her embarrassment. A fleeting glance at Jack saw a hint of amusement in his eyes.

'It was very long,' he said.

'Pardon?'

'The recording session. It went on for a long time.'

'Oh! Oh, yes, of course. Yes, I suppose it would,' she babbled.

'Which reminds me. Have you got plans at lunchtime?'

Aware she was still tomato red in the face, Pippa shook her head, not meeting his eye. She didn't like the way he was grinning at her.

'Good. Be ready to go at eleven-thirty.' He dropped the pen back on her keyboard and headed for the door.

'Go? Go where?'

'You'll see,' Jack said over his shoulder.


'My mother always told me never to accept rides if I wasn't told where we were going,' Pippa said as she climbed into the Land Rover's passenger seat beside Jack three hours later.

'Doesn't she mean strangers?'

'Those too. She liked to cover all eventualities.'

Jack swung the vehicle round and they bumped down the driveway to the road, sunlight bouncing off the bonnet.

'Were you a bit of a liability when you were younger?'

'I don't think so, but my parents did. They still think I am.'

'Couldn't argue with that,' Jack grinned.

Pippa gave him a dark look, but couldn't maintain it. To see Jack in such a good mood was too uplifting to get cross with him now.

'My parents just err on the side of caution whereas I like to take a few risks, that's all.'

'How did they handle you keeping Peace Offering?'

Pippa shrugged.

'I haven't spoken to them much for the past few months. They've been away cruising. Whenever we do speak they pretend Peace Offering doesn't exist.'

'That's a pity. Did they do the same to your uncle when he was around?'

Pippa chewed her lip.

'He wasn't the most popular with my folks. I think I inherited the same set of genes as him, whereas my father scooped his from a completely different pool.'

'Dave was an eternal optimist,' Jack nodded. 'The same as you.'

'Yeah, but not so great when you've got a gambling habit.' Pippa watched the fields flash by through the naked trees and tried not to think about Dave Taylor and his errant lifestyle. 'Where are we going?'

'To help you out of Dave's debts,' he replied.

'What?'

'Have you ever heard of Aaron Janssen?'

'Don't think so,' Pippa said after a moment's thought.

Jack looked at her in mock surprise.

'Really? A trendy person like yourself and you've never heard of him? He's a fashion mogul who owns racehorses. He was at the recording studios yesterday.'

'And he wants to pay for Dave debts?' Pippa said dubiously.

'*No.* Open up the glove compartment there.'

Pippa did as he instructed and pulled out a heavy camera with a fat lens which extended out about a foot when she switched it on.

'He wants portraits of his horses done. I thought we'd go along and take some photos for you to get started from. They're stabled not far from here.'

Pippa sat limp in her seat, staring at Jack, the urge to kiss him almost overwhelming. Inadvertently, she took a photo of his lap.

'Hey, careful where you aim that thing. You'll get me in trouble with Melissa.'

She bit her lower lip.

'You got me a commission?' she whispered, hardly hearing him.

'A couple at least,' he nodded, smiling at Pippa's expression. 'I know two of his horses are fairly decent. He's still quite new on the racing circuit though.'

'Thank you.' She gave him her most sincere smile.

'No problem. Don't get too excited. It won't be a huge amount, but it should replace a few roof tiles or something.'

'Who is he again?'

'Aaron Janssen. Only met him recently when Melissa dragged me to another of her dinner parties. She's trying to sweet talk him into combining both their labels in some big fashion show coming up.'

Pippa might not have been terribly fond of Melissa, but she had respect for anyone who did their best to succeed in their business.

'That'd be good if she gets it,' she said. 'Do you think she will?'

Jack grunted.

'I don't know. I think Janssen likes her because she's ambitious. When she goes after something, it's rare that she doesn't get it. She's strong like that.' An unmistakable note of pride and respect marked his tone. 'He strikes me as being very similar so she might get her big break, you never know.'

'Did she introduce him to horseracing?'

'Nah. I don't think she's known him personally that long. I don't know that he even likes horses that much. I mean he's a nice enough guy I suppose, but judging by the names he gives his horses it's more of a marketing ploy for his fashion label than anything else.'

Pippa giggled.

'Really? What does he call them? Naomi and Kate?' She imitated a racing commentator's voice. '*And it's Naomi and Kate on the run in, stride for stride. Kate gets her head in front, but wait! Naomi won't go down without a fight! Here comes the finish! Naomi pushes Kate off her line! Kate stumbles! Naomi wins, but there'll be a stewards' enquiry on this one too I expect – possibly a suspension or community service at the very least.*'

Jack's shoulders shook as he laughed.

'No,' he said. 'The two that I know of and that he wants portraits done of are Trendsetter and Skylark.'

'Skylark?' she said, the name jarring in her memories.

'Yes. Heard of him before?'

She opened her mouth to recall the evening they had spotted Finn and Cara Connolly at the Moulin Raj, but stopped herself. Finn wasn't the most popular with Jack at the moment after his three-day ban over the weekend. Telling Jack about him fraternising with the opposition wouldn't be doing him any favours.

'Kind of. Isn't he running in the Gold Cup against Virtuoso?'

Jack nodded.

'And in the Grand National against Peace Offering by the looks of things.'

'Really?' Pippa pulled a face. Winning the Grand National seemed so much simpler when she wasn't aware of who they would be up against.

Jack glanced at her.

'They're two very different races, don't worry. Even if Skylark is good enough to give Virtuoso a run for his money in the Gold Cup, it doesn't necessarily mean he'll be as big a threat in the National.'

He gave her a heartening smile, his usual frown erased.

In a moment of recklessness, Pippa pointed the camera at him and snapped a picture, wanting to capture this unusual event. Jack's frown reappeared with a vengeance.

'Pippa, do you mind?'

She grinned.

'Sorry. Couldn't resist.'

Despite his reassuring words, Pippa's doubts over Peace Offering's Grand National bid resurfaced when a tall handsome chestnut horse was led out of a stable for them to look at. In stark contrast to Aspen Valley Stables, Bracken Fields was home to a large American-style barn, with two rows of steel-barred stables on either side of a walkway. Pippa, who hadn't known yards to be any different from the traditionalism of Aspen Valley, felt over-awed by Bracken Fields' ultra-modern features, only enhanced by Skylark's considerable presence.

The horse pawed the rubberised floor with a soup plate hoof and Pippa moved closer to Jack. A wizened-face groom stood beside Skylark, waiting for both of them to pass judgement.

'He's very big,' Pippa said.

'Very strong too,' Jack said, casting an experienced eye over the horse's body. 'Needs to be to carry that frame. Can we take him outside to take these photos?' he asked the groom.

'Right, y'are, Mr Carmichael,' he nodded. He led a jig-jogging Skylark past them, making Pippa step back. She felt a reassuring hand on her back.

'Don't be frightened. Joe here has been looking after horses longer than I've been training. He won't let Skylark get loose.'

Pippa gave him a pathetic smile and shrugged, finding comfort more from his hand than his words. They followed Joe and his charge out into the crisp sunshine in which the horse's chestnut coat fairly gleamed with health. She wrestled with the camera strapped around her neck, trying to focus its protruding lens.

Jack reached over and adjusted the zoom for her, his calloused fingertips brushing against her hands. She gulped and gave herself a talking to. She wouldn't allow her gratefulness to transpose into any other type of attraction. It was easily done, but gratefulness was all it was, she told herself firmly.

'Are you going to take any photos or are we just going to pretend?' Jack's voice interrupted her thoughts.

'Sorry. Was just – um – trying to decide  on angles and – um – stuff.' She hoisted the heavy camera to eye level and smacked it against the bridge of her nose. 'Ow, fuck.'

Aware of Jack laughing quietly at her, Pippa got to work, walking around the horse, snapping him from this angle and that before asking for him to be turned to face a different light.

A voice from behind them made her pause.

'Ah! Jack! Good to see you could make it.'

Walking towards them was a rotund middle-aged man with thinning fair hair, dressed in a tailored violet-stitched suit and purple velvet waistcoat. He held out his arms in greeting.

Jack held out a hand in return.

'Aaron, thanks for having us. I'd like you to meet Pippa Taylor, the equine artist I was telling you about. Pippa, this is Aaron Janssen, Skylark's owner.'

It felt to Pippa as if her hand was being swallowed by a lump of dough, cool but comfortingly soft as it was enveloped by Aaron Janssen's paw.

'Pleasure to meet you. Thank you so much for commissioning these pictures to me.'

'Not at all. You came very highly recommended,' he replied.

Pippa shot Jack a grateful smile.

'I see you have already met Skylark,' Aaron went on. 'Isn't he beautiful?'

'Yes, very,' she agreed. 'And not small either.'

'In my experience, small is a downfall. No offence.' He patted her arm sympathetically. 'But tall has always done well for me.'

Pippa smiled.

'None taken. You're in fashion, after all.'

'In today, out tomorrow, darling. You have to do all you can, not just to keep up with the trends, but to *lead* them. Skylark will have a specially-made winner's rug put on him if he wins the Gold Cup. But it's all marketing. There is meaning behind the madness.'

239

'As long as you don't give him a handbag and a pearl-studded noseband I think you should be okay,' she replied.

Aaron laughed, again touching Pippa's arm.

'A handbag? Darling, that's priceless! I like the sound of the noseband though. Hold that thought.'

Pippa darted a look of uncertainty towards Jack who gave a brief shake of his head.

'I think I've taken all the pictures I'll need for Skylark. Perhaps we could see Trendsetter now?' she asked.

Joe nodded and led the horse away, leaving Pippa aching to get her paint brushes out immediately so she could capture the sun bouncing off the horse's copper-coloured coat.


Beneath the glare of artificial lighting, Pippa sat on her stool, an inviting blank canvas in front of her. Her fingers, balancing a broad ochre-tipped brush, hesitated before making contact with the sheet. Puccini's *Manon Lescaut* punched the musty air in Hazyvale's spare bedroom-cum-studio. Pippa glanced at the photographs she had printed off before leaving work that evening. Skylark stared back at her and again she went to dab the first spot of paint on the clean canvas. She frowned when her fingers refused to comply. A restlessness forbade her from focusing on the horse.

With a sigh, she surrendered the brush to a jar of water and picked up the photos from the table beside her. She flipped through them, pausing over the last one. Her agitation calmed. She bit her lip. She hadn't intended to print this particular picture, but when she'd imported all the others, she hadn't been able to stop herself. She had stuffed it into her bag after a guilty look around before carrying on as before.

Sitting on her stool, classical music curling around her like a masseur's kneading, she touched the image on the glossy card, tracing her finger along the strong jaw, across his hairline where a wisp of dark hair fell out of place, as if to move it aside. Jack's eyes, focused beyond the camera, sparkled like an island shore postcard.

Pippa picked up a finer brush and began to paint. She dabbed a vague outline of his profile before turning to his eyes. She cleaned her brush and dipped it into a blob of cornflower blue. She frowned after a few small strokes on the page and selected another, darker blue. No, now that made him look angry.

Swilling her brush in the water, she tried a mixture of blues. Navy, azure, baby and powder.

She tutted. None of them were quite right. She opened a tube of sky blue and tried again.

With a sigh of frustration, she looked down at the photograph again.

Her hand stilled as an icy feeling shimmied up her spine. What was she doing? She was painting her *boss*. There was something distinctly unhealthy about that. She slapped the photograph faced down on the table, revealing another of Skylark.

In strokes bordering on panic, she painted over Jack's face, the broad sweeps of sky blue removing all evidence as she painted the background for the horse. When no hint of curving cheekbone or straight brow remained, she relaxed.

'There,' she whispered. 'No one needs to know about that. It never happened.'

Picking up the ochre-stained brush, she began on the horse's chestnut head.

# Chapter Thirty-Four

Shivering in her coat, as much from nerves as from the cold, Pippa stood on the grandstand step huddled between Jack and Tash. The weak February sunshine of the week before had given way to a cold wet spell and looking out over Chepstow Racecourse, she could see evidence of the early week's snow still built up against the hillside hedges like fluff escaping its cushion cover. With the constant rain, the ground was saturated with slush, making the going as thick as the visibility.

Chewing off her lipstick, she squinted through the murk at the horses cantering down to the three-and-a-half mile start, barely able to identify her green and red racing silks worn by Finn.

'Sweets, I thought you said going racing would be fun,' Tash said, giving her a nudge. 'The two of you look like you're at a funeral.'

'There's a lot at stake today,' Pippa replied, not taking her eyes off the twelve horses now circling at the Start.

'Care to expand on that?' Tash prompted when she didn't elaborate.

'If Peace Offering doesn't pull it out the bag then he probably won't make the cut for the National,' Jack explained. 'And he's going to have it all to do against Solar Flare.'

'Which one's he?'

Pippa opened her racecard and with a trembling finger pointed out the favourite's name and racing colours in the form guide. Staring at her finger quivering over the list of wins beside Solar Flare's name, her stomach clenched at the prospect of her high hopes being dashed in under five minutes.

Jack placed his hand, warmed from his pocket, over hers to still her shaking and gave it a reassuring squeeze. She gave him a grateful smile, but recognised her own fears in his eyes.

The cheer of the crowds wrenched her focus back to the horses just in time to see them bound forward into the drizzle. She offered up a silent prayer on behalf of Peace Offering and Finn, held up in mid-field, awaiting the threat of the first daunting fence. She held her breath as the horses, already strung out, sailed over.

A whimper of fear escaped her throat as the horses tackled the next open ditch, claiming its first victim, and she inadvertently leaned into Jack for support.

'He's going good,' he murmured, his eyes trained on the field of runners surging over the next. 'Finn's got a handy position on the rail.'

Even with the cheering of the crowd reverberating in her ears, Pippa could still hear the dull rumble of hooves on the sodden ground as they passed the winning post for the first time and headed uphill for the final circuit. Peace Offering, his white face mud-splattered, galloped on a loose rein with a relaxed-looking Finn rocking in the saddle.

They jumped the next on an awkward stride and Pippa groaned, seeing the margin between Solar Flare and her horse widen. The naked trees bordering the back straight seemed to claw at Peace Offering's progress whilst ushering the favourite further ahead amongst the leading group.

The pacemaker of the field blundered over the next, interfering with his rivals, but giving Solar Flare the opportunity to take the lead.

Pippa darted her attention between him and the twelve-length gap back to her horse. Peace Offering soared over the water, as graceful as a stag, gaining impetus from his leap and narrowed the margin. Pippa bounced discreetly on her knees and clutched Jack's arm.

'Oh, God!' she cried as the next downhill fence had her horse twisting his body in an attempt to stay upright. Finn threw out an arm to keep his balance before gathering up his reins and pushing for more impulsion.

With the undulations of the course taking its toll on its travellers, Peace Offering moved up into fourth. His strides ate up the ground and Pippa leaned sideways as horse and jockey followed the leading trio round the turn into the home straight.

'Please, Finn!' she said, a spark of hope stirring in her chest as she realised the gap was closing. As if hearing her pleas, the jockey used his whip for the first time, inciting another spurt from his mount.

Solar Flare led them over the fourth last, his stride uncompromising. Peace Offering joined the third horse in mid-flight, forging clear as his neighbour floundered.

Pippa grasped Jack's hand, her hope strengthening with every step her horse took.

'Come on, Finn,' Jack growled, returning Pippa's grip.

Solar Flare brushed through the second last. Five lengths back, Peace Offering drew alongside the second horse, his head bobbing as he battled the uphill climb. The incomprehensible roar of the crowd urged the horses home.

'Go on, Peace Offering! Keep going!' Pippa cried, unable to stop herself.

Solar Flare cleared the last fence. His weary legs plugged into the thick turf. Peace Offering gathered himself for the leap just behind, his long ears flicking towards the cheering grandstand.

'Oh, my God! Oh, my God!' Pippa exclaimed, her eyes widening as the spark of hope burst into a ball of fire. Peace Offering was gaining ground on the tiring favourite, his muddied nose now bobbing beside his rival's flank. 'Come on, Peace Offering! Come on, Finn!' she yelled, jumping up and down.

The winning post slowly reeled in Solar Flare. Beneath Finn's desperate urges, Peace Offering lowered his head and stretched out his neck. Solar Flare's stride wobbled. Peace Offering drew up to his shoulder. Pippa clasped her fingers between Jack's. The winning post beckoned. Peace Offering drew level. The favourite faltered, his last energy reserves sapped, and forfeited the lead. Pippa's knees gave way as her green and red silks passed by the post half a length clear. Jack grasped her around the waist to stop her falling and Pippa clung to him for support.

She looked at him shell-shocked.

'Did he – did he...'

Jack flashed her a grin and nodded.

'Oh!' She collapsed into his arms, a ball of tears swelling in her throat. She hid her face in Jack's coat, overwhelmed with joy and relief.

'I think you've just booked your ticket to the Grand National, Miss Taylor,' Jack murmured in her ear.

Pippa met Finn and Peace Offering as they entered the winner's enclosure. Speechless, her ear-splitting grin said it all to Finn. He kicked his feet out of the stirrups and gave her a wink. Emmie wrestled Peace Offering to a standstill, trying to curb the adrenalin still pumping through his body.

Pippa reached out and patted his sweat and rain-slicked neck, feeling the burning heat in the wormy veins bulging beneath his skin. His ears flicked to and fro, catching the sounds of the crowd surrounding the enclosure. His eyes flashed and he side-stepped in nervous excitement.

'It's okay, boy,' Pippa whispered, stroking his cheek. 'They're cheering for you. You're a winner.' She exhaled a ragged breath, her emotions a whirlwind of excitement, pride and the sudden thought of her uncle smiling down on them standing in the rain in the winner's circle almost overwhelming her.

244

Finn dismounted after giving Peace Offering a last pat and pulled Pippa towards him. Holding her face in his gloved hands, he kissed her, his lips lingering over hers.

Pippa closed her eyes, her senses consumed by the smell of fresh earth and horses and the press of the jockey's cold nose beside her own.

'Okay, Finn,' Jack's gruff voice interrupted them. 'You've given the press plenty of time to get their cameras out. Tone it down, will you?'

Finn came up for air and gave Pippa a charming smile.

'I don't mind getting mud kicked in my face for three and a half miles when this is the reward,' he said.

'Finn!' Jack snapped. 'Unsaddle your horse so Emmie can get a rug on him. Pippa, come stand on this side of Peace Offering so the press can take their pictures.' His frown softened as she skipped around her horse to stand beside him. 'You've got mud on your cheek now.' He raised his hand to wipe it clean, but withdrew it before he touched her, glancing at the squatting photographers poised in front of them.

Pippa giggled and raised her sleeve to wipe her cheek clean.

'Thank you.'

'Pleasure,' he nodded. He paused, sensing Pippa wasn't just thanking him for pointing out the mud. He gave her a warm smile. '*Pleasure*. And if you think you can behave yourself, I'll take you and Tash out for a drink after this. It's not every day you get a horse breaking his duck after nearly three years.'

Pippa leaned back against the spongy bench cushion, the comforting crackle of an earthen log fire somewhere in the wood-panelled Welsh pub thawing her bones. She watched Jack disappear in the direction of the Gents, leaving her alone at the table with Tash. A yawn shuddered through her.

'You look done in,' Tash said. 'Has something or some*one* been giving you sleepless nights?'

Pippa smiled lazily.

'No. Work's crazy busy at the minute. Cheltenham Festival is just round the corner and it seems the entire world wants something with Aspen Valley.' She pondered her friend for a moment. 'What about you? I have to admit I was a little surprised you could make it this weekend at such short notice. Didn't think you could drag yourself away from Aladdin.'

Tash flopped her hands down on the armrests of her chair in dramatic fashion.

'I think I've finally realised that I'm twenty-seven and not nineteen anymore,' she said. 'All the partying and stuff was fun for a while, but whereas he can get away with coming to work with a hangover five times a week, I can't.'

'Oh, dear. Is old age creeping up on you?'

'I don't know about creeping, sweets. It gives me a wake-up call every morning when I look in the mirror. It would send me screaming if I had the energy.'

Pippa laughed, but her concern remained.

'Things not going so well then?'

Tash pulled a face.

'He's a lovely guy, don't get me wrong, but I just don't see the point in getting shit-faced on vodka shots every time we want to go out. I know I sound like a prude and you know me, I enjoy going out and having a few drinks. I just don't like alcohol being the sole intention of enjoyment. You know what I mean?'

'Tash, that's not being a prude. That's called maturity.'

Tash nodded, reluctant agreement twisting her mouth.

'I guess. Maybe age *does* count for something. In all honesty, I'm becoming quite jealous of you.'

'Of me?'

'Yeah. Out here in the country, living the rural life like something out of a Katie Fforde novel. With eye candy galore to top it off.'

'Jack, you mean?'

'And that Irish jockey who's so fond of you. You didn't give me much of a chance to gawk last time we saw him. I thought he looked rather buff in his boots and body armour today.'

Pippa snorted as an image of Finn clanking around in a suit of armour sprang to mind.

'Body *protector*. Although he probably is rather fit beneath that.'

'You see?' Tash said. 'Who needs the millions packed into London when you've got it all here in one small town?'

Pippa smiled.

'It's not as easy as all that. And I do miss London sometimes.'

'You seem so much more content though out here.'

'For now I am,' she shrugged. 'I'm getting there slowly with the cottage and I've got a few art commissions, but when the cottage gets sold I'm probably going to come back to London.' A familiar figure standing at the bar waiting to order their drinks caught her eye. A smile warmed her face. 'Then Jack can get a proper secretary.'

A smile danced across Tash's lips.

'Care to tell me what's going on between you two?'

Pippa looked down at the table, unable to meet her eyes. It was wonderful having a friend who knew you so well they could tell when something was wrong, but it had its drawbacks too when you didn't want to divulge other feelings.

'Nothing. Nothing at all,' she said, keeping her tone light. She looked up and beamed at Tash. She received a sceptical look in reply.

'Okay, I'll grant you that,' Tash conceded. 'By the little things you do to each other, it doesn't look like you've slept with him yet –'

'Tash!' Pippa hissed. 'He's standing just over there!'

'He can't hear us. So, come on, maybe you haven't slept with him, but you admit now that you wouldn't kick him out of bed for dropping biscuit crumbs, would you?'

Pippa gave her an anguished scowl.

'Tash, don't make me say it.'

'You fancy each other, don't you?'

She sighed.

'I guess you could say my opinion of Jack has somewhat changed over the past few months,' she said. 'But I don't know about Jack. You'd have to ask him – *don't* even think it, Natasha Bradley!' she added quickly, seeing Tash's eyes light up.

'Sweets, I don't need to ask Jack how he feels. He's got it written all over his face.'

Pippa felt her stomach disappear and she darted another quick look at Jack still standing at the bar.

'What do you mean?'

'Well, for starters, Finn kissing you like he did went down like a pork chop in a synagogue with him.'

'Only because of the media around. Rumours run like wildfire around here.'

'If you say so. Didn't you notice how pleased he was when you won?'

Pippa fiddled with a thread on her sleeve. She couldn't look Tash in the eye. She would surely see how much she wanted to believe her.

'He does train Peace Offering,' she argued benignly.

Tash leaned forward and tried to get her to meet her gaze.

'Do you honestly think that's it?' she probed.

247

Pippa sighed.

'I don't know. Sometimes I think yes, there is something between us. But there's no point in even thinking about it. Jack would never do anything. Not while I'm his secretary. He's already made it perfectly clear that the only type of relationship we can ever have is employer-secretary.'

'How did you find that out? Did you make a move on him?' Tash snorted.

'No, of course not,' Pippa giggled. 'I tried to give him a gift – a painting, at Christmas and he wouldn't accept it.'

'That was two months ago. A lot of water has flown under the bridge since then.'

Pippa sighed, her gaze returning to the figure across the room now talking to the barman.

'Jack has very strong moral values, relationships in the workplace being one of them. And even if he did let himself slip up, as tempting as it would be, I have to agree with him. I wouldn't want to be the stereotypical secretary who sleeps with her boss.'

'It wouldn't be like that though, Pip. You've got to be the least devious person I know.'

'Yeah, I know it wouldn't be like that. But that's not how other people will see it.'

'You shouldn't care what other people think,' Tash remonstrated.

'I know, but when those other people are the ones you're working with, then it becomes a bit more delicate.'

'Do you mean people like Finn?'

'Amongst others.'

'Ooh, that reminds me,' Tash said, unzipping her handbag. She pulled out a dog-eared copy of *Heat*. 'Check out Page Four.'

Pippa flicked through the magazine. A familiar face jumped out at her. She read the caption beneath.

*Skylark Fashion's new sweetheart, Cara Connolly, was spotted leaving a secluded Bristol restaurant with jump jockey, Finn O'Donaghue. The couple enjoyed a romantic dinner before leaving together. Connolly could be jeopardising her purist image by associating with O'Donague, who has a reputation for living life in the fast lane, but seemed happy enough to take that chance.*

With a frown puckering her brow, Pippa examined the photo once more. The pair looked to be sharing a joke, unaware of the paparazzi. He had his hand at the small of her back, assisting her down the restaurant steps.

'What do you make of that?' Tash prompted.

Pippa chewed her lip.

'What do they mean "living life in the fast lane"? I wouldn't describe Finn like that.'

'Sweets, if he's had a speeding ticket for going thirty-five in a thirty zone or has got drunk at a party, then as far as gossip mags are concerned, he's got a drink problem and is a danger on the public road.' Tash grimaced, seeing Pippa's expression. 'Oh, no, I've upset you, haven't I? I'm sorry, sweets. I shouldn't have shown it to you. I didn't think you liked him like *that*.'

Pippa shook her head and gave her a reassuring smile.

'No, you're right. Finn's just a friend.' She hesitated. 'But I just got the impression that he's not being entirely straight with me. Or with her for that matter. Today wasn't the first time he's tried to kiss me –'

'Who's been trying to kiss you?' Jack interrupted, placing three drinks down on the table.

'Oh – um, er –' Pippa gawped like a goldfish.

'Finn,' Tash supplied helpfully.

Pippa bared her teeth at her.

'What?' Jack gave her a stern look. 'I thought you told me you and him weren't seeing each other.'

'I wasn't. I mean, I'm not.' In a panic to clear her name, she thrust the magazine towards him. 'Look, I'm not the one Finn's dating. *She* is.'

Jack frowned at the article and Pippa realised she'd probably done the wrong thing. He looked up, puzzled.

'Skylark?' he said.

Pippa nodded reluctantly.

'I'm sure it's just a coincidence,' she said. 'They're both Irish and both live in the same part of England now. It'd make sense, I guess. A little taste of home and all that.'

Jack folded the magazine closed with a slow nodding of his head. After a pause, he even managed a grim smile.

'You're right. Finn's smarter than he lets on,' he said. He picked up his drink and held it aloft. 'But more importantly, here's to Peace Offering breaking his duck.'

'To Peace Offering,' she and Tash echoed.

Pippa sipped her drink and returned his smile, still warily observing the darkening shades of his eyes.

# Chapter Thirty-Five

With the onset of Cheltenham's four day festival, Pippa had little time to dwell on Peace Offering's future. Even her tumultuous feelings towards Jack took a backseat as she struggled to keep abreast with the action. Jack, when he wasn't at the Festival or doing previews and interviews for the racing press, was distant when he did make an appearance. Pippa had persuaded him to set up a television in Reception and by Friday lunchtime, alongside the stable staff, had celebrated Dexter's success in the Supreme Novices' Hurdle and Silver Dollar taking the spoils in the Festival Trophy Chase.

She was aware of great tension in the yard come the final day of the big meeting as everyone's thoughts centred on Virtuoso's bid to retain his Gold Cup crown. Despite not having known Virtuoso existed before a few months ago, she felt herself caught up in their anxiety and excitement. She'd learnt that being a Gold Cup hero was the highest accolade in National Hunt racing; to win it again deserved reverence of the highest order.

Through the window she watched the staff hurrying around the yard, trying to finish their duties before they could all squash into the office for the afternoon's racing.

The grimy pairs of boots mounted up by the doorway as they all converged and Pippa, seeing a pallid-faced Emmie walk in with Billy, pulled up a chair for her to sit on. The first race of the day, the Champion Hurdle, was watched in sombre silence, a stark comparison to the yells and cheers which had accompanied the previous days' events.

Pippa opened her mouth to ask why the long faces, when she recognised the name of the winner. High Scribe. She closed her mouth again, understanding now. The ghost of Black Russian hung over the shoulders of the staff, the thought in her head surely running through theirs as well. Had he not met his death on Boxing Day, he would have been running in the Champion Hurdle and if the winner's form was anything to go by, then he probably would have retained his title too.

The mood was lightened an hour later when Dust Storm, Aspen Valley's outside chance ran a close second in the next Grade One novice hurdle. Co-workers gave each other congratulatory pats on the back before their attention was once more drawn back to the screen. There was now nothing between a year's hard graft and the Gold Cup.

Pippa's stomach tied itself in knots. The room hummed with nerves. Like attentive school children, the staff shushed themselves when the presenter cornered Jack for a pre-race interview.

He looked relaxed, his expression neither over-confident nor diffident.

'We've enjoyed a good prep leading up to this race so it's fair to say we've got a decent chance,' he told the camera. 'Virtuoso is as fit as I can get him and he's shown us already that he's capable of winning this race. I'm very happy with how he is today.'

To Pippa though, his eyes betrayed him. Jack was a lot more nervous than he was letting on. The camera switched back to the horses parading before the giant Cheltenham stands and the commentator went through each runner's credentials.

Out of the corner of her eye, Pippa saw Billy wipe his clammy hands on his jeans. She smiled at his obvious apprehension. As the horses lined up before the starting tape, the office telephone rang and a universal outlet of held breaths flooded the room.

'For fuck's sake, who calls during the Gold Cup?' someone exclaimed. 'What planet are they on?'

Pippa reached over from where she was sitting to answer it, but another staff member was too quick for her. A stable lad picked up the receiver.

'Do you mind? We're watching the Gold Cup here, mate.' He slammed down the phone, creating a ripple of giggles through the room which suddenly became a cheer, joining the wall of sound coming from the television, as the horses were sent on their way.

'Go on, Finn!'

'Come on, mate!'

'All right now, Vertie!'

'You can do it, Virtuoso!'

Such was the adoration and support of Aspen Valley's staff, Pippa felt moved. She'd never known people to be so dedicated to their jobs. Her gaze flickered between the horserace and their rapt expressions. If the Pope had walked into the room right now, no one would have given him a second glance.

A unified intake of breath refocused her. Virtuoso had made a first mistake.

'Don't shut him on the rail, Finn, you prick!' someone yelled.

'Button it. Finn knows what he's on about. He's saving ground, can't you see?' came a reply.

The horses rounded the highest point of the course, thundering down to the next, led by the tank-like Skylark. Finn had Virtuoso tucked into a pocket of runners on the inside amongst the tightly bunched field.

'Skylark steps it up another gear as they pass the stands for the first time,' the commentator droned. 'Skylark leads from Sir Robbo, Kupala, Monsieur Le Cure, Virtuoso, Baker Street, Indigo Time, King Lear, Flying Scotsman, Zodiac and bringing up the rear is Killaloe.'

With each jump, the runners began to string out, the taxing undulations and stiff birch fences taking their toll. The field was reduced to ten as the longshot Kupala tipped up at an open ditch.

The camera zoomed in on the horses as they completed their first circuit, its main focus on the defending champion.

'Finn's niggling at him!' someone cried.

'You're seeing things. Vertie's going like a train.'

'Yeah! Look how easy Finn's riding!'

Virtuoso closed the gap between him and the leaders, drawing up alongside Monsieur Le Cure and passing him as fresh as when they'd started. Pippa crossed her fingers. Her pulse quickened as the commentator's voice rose an octave. Skylark had gone for home, his jockey pushing and scrubbing for every effort as they rounded the last turn. Finn lowered himself in the saddle, accepting the challenge in front of him. Sir Robbo's effort in second faded out and Virtuoso passed him in mid-air over the fourth last. The third last loomed and the noise in Aspen Valley's office swelled as they cheered on their horse.

He cleared it, not very fluently, but it was obvious to all that he was going better than Skylark. The thunderous roar of the crowd drowned out the commentator's frantic voice as Virtuoso drew level with his rival.

'Come on, Finn!' 'Come on, Vertie!' 'Get in there! Go on!'

The yells of the staff rang in Pippa's ears. Virtuoso eased ahead as they approached the second last, his head bobbing, the first real signs of fatigue starting to show. Pippa watched Finn glance behind him before asking for a big effort. Virtuoso hesitated and put in a short stride. His momentum carried him through the thick of the birch. A despairing cry cut the air as Finn was pitched onto his horse's neck. The defending champion rallied to keep his feet on landing, but gravity was too strong for Finn. The Irishman was jolted out of the saddle and tumble-turned into the churned ground.

Aspen Valley groaned, followed by a shocked silence.

The commentator, nearly whimpering with excitement, carried on regardless.

'Virtuoso has unseated Finn O'Donaghue! The favourite is out of the race! What an upset! He surely had it in the bag! He leaves the door open for Skylark to lead over the second last. O'Donaghue is climbing to his feet, he looks to be okay. Skylark is safely over! Just one fence left and the Cheltenham hill to contend with. King Lear is now promoted to second position. Zodiac, the twenty-to-one outsider, is making up late ground. Here comes the last. Skylark clears it! Zodiac is flying up the outside! He's passed King Lear. Can Skylark hold on? It's a weary climb up that hill! Zodiac draws level! He goes clear! Zodiac wins the Cheltenham Gold Cup!'

Pippa looked around at the shell-shocked faces. No one spoke. Some looked close to tears. She imagined that despite his heavy favouritism, a few weeks' worth of wages had gone on Virtuoso's number at the bookies.

'Aw, fuck it,' someone said.

The door was yanked open and a disheartened stable lad walked out. Like zombies, the rest began to follow. Some forgot to pick up their boots, walking across the yard in their socks. Pippa turned to Emmie still sitting down. The lass looked worryingly pale.

'Are you okay?' she asked.

Her heart skipped a beat when Emmie's face contorted with pain.

'Not really,' she said through clenched teeth.

Pippa whisked down beside her.

'What's wrong? Are you hurting? Where does it hurt?'

Emmie placed her hand over her stomach.

'It's just a twinge. It's probably nothing.'

Pippa met Billy's stare of horror. She licked her lips, trying to keep her cool and placed a comforting hand over Emmie's.

'I'm sure you're right. But to make certain, I think we should take a quick trip to the hospital. Okay?'

Emmie darted her a look of panic.

'Do you think something's wrong with the baby?' she said, trembling.

'No, no. I'm sure the baby's fine,' Pippa lied. She hadn't felt less sure of anything in her life. 'Blame me for being over-cautious, that's all.' She gave Emmie a quick smile then went to fetch her handbag and car keys. Her hands shook. Her head pounded, the already adrenalin-fired blood in her veins taking on a more urgent flow.

'You coming, Billy?' she said.

Billy, wide-eyed with fear, nodded.

'I'm coming.'


Pippa sat in the hospital's waiting area, chilled to the core. She pinched her eyes, trying to relieve her headache from the glare of the overhead lights. The sound of Billy's footsteps as he paced up and down the aisle throbbed in her ears as they awaited the verdict on Emmie in the adjoining examination room. To distract herself she pulled out her mobile phone to check for messages. There was nothing, not even an acknowledgement from Jack to the text she had sent earlier telling him she was taking Emmie to hospital. She grimaced at the thought of what he must be going through, wading through the aftermath of Virtuoso's defeat.

Billy's footsteps jarred her thoughts as he passed by once more.

'Billy, why don't you come sit down?' she said, patting the chair beside her.

The lad threw an anxious glance towards the closed door before complying.

'Do you think she'll be okay?' he asked.

Pippa nodded and squeezed his hand.

'I'm sure we would have heard something by now if it was anything serious.'

'But she said she was getting cramps. That can't be good, can it?'

Pippa tried to give him a reassuring smile, but felt fraudulent.

'I don't know much about pregnancy, to be honest with you. But I do know that if something bad was happening then there would be nurses and doctors rushing in and out of here.' She looked around and gave him a wry smile. 'I don't see much of anything going on, do you?'

Billy nodded with a sigh.

'It's all bloody Finn's fault, upsetting her like that.'

She frowned at his vehement statement, a barrier of defensiveness rising up inside her.

'I'm sure he didn't mean to fall off.'

'Yeah, I know,' Billy sighed. 'But he only fell because he made a stupid mistake. He shouldn't have asked Virtuoso for such a big jump after such a long race.'

'I don't know then,' she said with a resigned shrug. 'But if Finn did make a bad judgement call then he'll be kicking himself now. He'll know what he's done wrong.' She thought of the media frenzy he and Jack must be experiencing right now and how far removed it was from the isolation of Bristol's hospital waiting area.

'If anything happens to Emmie, then he'll get to know a whole lot more about what he did wrong,' he muttered.

Finn had Pippa's sympathy, but Billy's concern touched her.

'You and Emmie make a good couple.'

Billy dropped his gaze and she saw a ghost of a smile ball his cheeks.

'I love her, you know.'

Tears pricked Pippa's eyes and she blinked them back.

Really, she scolded herself, she must get a grip on her emotions. She'd recently gone back on the Pill to regularise her cycle, but it'd been playing havoc with her hormones ever since. Hormones and overtiredness is what it is, she told herself. She felt herself smiling as a voice in her head responded, *Oh, just admit it. You're a sap when it comes to love.*

'So I see,' she said out loud, giving him a teasing grin.

Billy's cheeks pinked and he fiddled with his hands.

'We were gonna get a place together. You know, before the baby comes and all that, just so we could get used to living with each other before everything changes.' He sighed. 'Don't know if that's going to happen now.'

Pippa opened her mouth to reply, but was forestalled by the adjoining door opening. She and Billy sprang to their feet. A nurse motioned them forward.

'Would you like to come see Emmie?'

'Is she okay? Is the baby okay?' Billy barraged her.

The nurse smiled kindly.

'Nothing to worry about. Cramps aren't unusual in early pregnancy. We've done an ultrasound just to be safe, but everything appears to be fine.'

Pippa sank against the wall and breathed a sigh of relief. Billy gave an anguished snort, biting down on his fist then hugged the nurse.

'She's okay? Can I take her home?' he asked as the nurse extricated herself.

'Yes, she's free to go, but she must take it easy for a while. She mentioned you both work at a horseracing yard?'

Billy nodded.

'Well, my advice is she should take some time out. Hard manual labour is the last thing she should be doing right now.'

255

Billy nodded again, more emphatically.

'I won't let her do a thing, don't worry. I'll even cook for her –'

The jingle from Pippa's mobile intervened, earning a disapproving frown from the nurse. With a guilty smile, Pippa fumbled for it in her pocket. Her thumb paused over the cut off key when she saw the caller ID.

'Sorry, I'd better take this,' she said. 'I'll be back in a minute, Billy. Go in and see Emmie. I won't be long.' She hurried down the corridor towards the exit, her heart doing random backflips as she answered the call.

'Jack?'

'Pippa. Where are you?'

'At the hospital. Hold on, let me just go outside... Ooh, fuck, it's cold out here.'

Beneath the entrance's overhang, she hunched her shoulders against the biting wind, wrapping her free arm around her body.

'What's happened to Emmie? Is she okay?'

'We've just spoken to the nurse who examined her. She's going to be fine.'

'What happened?'

'We were watching the Gold Cup and she started getting stomach cramps.'

'Jesus Christ. Is the baby okay?'

'They're both fine. Apparently cramps aren't that unusual. Scared the hell out of us though. Billy was ready to kill Finn not so long ago.'

'Hm,' Jack grunted. 'He's not the only one.'

His voice was hoarse, as if he'd been speaking or shouting for a long time without a drink to relieve his throat. Pippa ached to be back at the office and able to make him a cup of tea.

'I'm sorry about Virtuoso,' she said gently.

'Yeah, so am I. It wasn't the result we were hoping for.'

'How did Mr Mardling and Melissa take it?'

'Ken Mardling's been in racing long enough to know anything can happen. He's disappointed, I suppose, but that's to be expected.' He exhaled, weary and defeated. 'And Melissa, I don't know. She just seems... *distracted*. I don't know anymore.'

Pippa chewed her lip as she considered his words. A sudden image of Melissa and Finn in Helensvale's Turkish restaurant flashed into her mind. If there'd been more to that meeting than what Finn had said, could Melissa have been distracted because of Finn's fall?

Her eyes widened.

Maybe she'd got Melissa wrong. Did the fashion designer care for him more than she should? Oh, hell, that's all Jack needed now, she inwardly groaned.

'Pippa? Are you still there?' Jack's strained voice jogged her back to the present.

'Yes, I'm here.' She hesitated. 'Jack?'

'Yes?'

'Jack, are *you* okay?' she asked in a small voice.

A silence greeted Pippa's tender question. Her pulse racing, she wondered what was going through his mind. At last, she heard a faint chuckle.

'If you carry on talking to me with that voice, I will be very *unokay*. But I think for now, I'll survive. You go take care of Emmie and I'll see you in the morning.'

'All right. See you tomorrow then.'

'Sweet dreams, Pippa,' he rasped, his voice almost resigned.

He cut the call before she could reply.

Distracted, she put her phone into her handbag. Jack's voice echoed in her ears. Very *unokay*? What did he mean by that, she wondered. She leaned against the damp hospital wall, ignoring the wet seeping through her collar. *Unokay* if anyone showed sympathy? She knew what that felt like. She recalled the times she had bravely held her emotions together until the moment Tash would show compassion. *Then* she would break down. Or *unokay* because *she* was the one giving him sympathy?

She gulped and took and deep breath, knowing for certain which option she wanted it to be.

# Chapter Thirty-Six

Pippa was greeted by the deep murmur of Jack's voice the next morning when she walked into the office. His door was ajar and she poked her head round to signal her arrival. Jack, the telephone receiver pressed to his ear, distractedly acknowledged her.

'No, you can't print that, even if it is off the record, because it's not true,' he said patiently. 'In my opinion, Finn didn't have a chance of staying on when Virtuoso hit the fence. I don't think any jockey would have... No, his job as Aspen Valley's retained jockey is not in jeopardy. I still have every faith in him as a rider...'

His defence became muffled as Pippa retreated to the kitchenette to make him some tea. She picked up a copy of the *Racing Post* which had been left on the draining board as she waited for the kettle to boil. She sighed at one of the headlines '*Is Aspen Valley Finn-ished?*' She scanned the article, shaking her head as the columnist ripped into Finn's Gold Cup ride, calling him a poor replacement for the injured Rhys Bradford and criticising Jack for not letting Mick Farrelly, the jockey who'd steered Virtuoso to such a decisive victory in the Denman Chase, take the ride.

When she returned with a steaming mug of tea, Jack was winding down his conversation. His strong deliberate voice was in stark contrast to his dishevelled hair and the etched lines beside his eyes and mouth.

'Who's to say he would have won or not? Zodiac was a surprise winner, so who's to say he wouldn't have beaten Virtuoso as well? There, I think all that needs to be said has been said. You can use what you like from this conversation to put in your report.'

He put the phone down, exhaling noisily and looked up at Pippa.

'Bad day?' she said, passing him his tea.

'Cheers. Bad season more like it. First Black Russian, now Virtuoso.'

'He's not dead, is he?' Pippa said in horror.

'No, no, not dead. Just the media abuse we get, we might just as well have shot him in front of the grandstands.'

'Shame, Jack. You don't deserve this stick. I see in the paper Finn's getting much the same treatment.'

'Serve him right,' Jack muttered.

Pippa frowned at him, confused.

'But I thought I heard you say you didn't hold him responsible?'

258

'Ever heard the expression "live together, die alone"? Well, it's something like that. There's no point in severing ties with your allies when you need to stick together.'

'Right,' Pippa said slowly, trying to get her head round his reasoning. 'So you do think Finn is to blame?'

Jack raised his palms in indecision.

'Maybe, maybe not. Would he have stuck on if he'd tried a bit harder? Probably not. Should he have let Virtuoso pop over the fence instead of thinking he was riding Pegasus? Absolutely. He fucked up *before* he fell off.'

Pippa wrung her hands, troubled by Jack's verdict.

'He made a mistake.'

'Yes, but he made that mistake in the Gold Cup! A mistake which could have been avoided!' Jack exclaimed.

Pippa took a step back, shocked by his outburst.

'Well, we learn by our mistakes,' she replied, recovering her composure. 'Finn will think twice next time.'

'Damn right he will. I hope his ear is still burning from the bollocking he got yesterday.'

Pippa's heart went out to Finn, imagining him on the receiving end of Jack's fury. That on top of his own disappointment couldn't be an easy burden to bear.

'You shouted at him? He's already got enough on his plate. Don't you think that's a bit like rubbing salt into the wounds?'

A muscle jumped in Jack's jaw as he ground his teeth.

'Would you be quite so forgiving if it'd been Peace Offering in the Grand National that he'd fallen off? Don't you understand what the Gold Cup means, Pippa?'

She dug her fingernails into her palms and glared at Jack.

'Of course I do! Just looking at you shows how much the Gold Cup means to you. But it would have been worth just as much to Finn.'

'He's cost me the Champion Trainer's title!'

'But the season's not over yet. There's still the National to come.'

'Pippa, I'm not relying too heavily on the National to win me the trainers' championship,' Jack said through clenched teeth, making a sword of hurt pierce Pippa's chest. 'Why are you sticking up for Finn like this?'

'Maybe because I feel he's the underdog.' She looked at him with distaste, struggling to keep her emotions under wrap. 'And maybe that's why I'm sticking up for Peace Offering too. You obviously don't think much of him either –' She bit her lip as her voice began to tremble and turned away. Behind her, she heard Jack give a frustrated sigh and get up from his chair.

His hand closed over her shoulder.

'Pippa, I'm sorry.'

She stared hard at the floor, trying not to cry.

'Pippa?'

She raised her head and turned. Jack's hands folded over her arms and he gently pulled her round to face him.

'I'm sorry,' she said, wiping away a stray tear. 'I don't know why I'm crying. What are we even arguing about?'

Jack's face contorted with anguish. Like someone who has broken their favourite piece of china and tries to collect all the fragments, Jack brushed the moisture from her cheek with his thumb. He tucked a curl of her hair behind her ear. Pippa's heart began to thump, constricting her chest.

'I hate myself for upsetting you,' he muttered. 'I don't mean to. I – I have to vent my frustration and you – well, sometimes I guess you're just an easy target.'

'I'm probably oversensitive,' Pippa said. 'I know really that you're right about Peace Offering, but he does hold a special place in my heart.' She lifted her hands to her chest as the tears resurfaced. 'And Dave believed in him so much.'

'I know, I'm sorry,' he said, rubbing her arms. 'Please don't cry. You'll make me cry.'

Pippa smiled at the thought of him in floods of tears.

'You don't cry, do you?'

'Trust me. Watching *Marley and Me* was one of the most traumatic experiences of my life. I cry, let there be no doubt.'

Pippa gave a weepy chuckle.

'There, that's more like it,' Jack said, tilting her chin up with his finger.

As her eyes cleared, Pippa became more aware of Jack's proximity, the intensity of his gaze. She forgot how to breathe as she watched him. Her eyes flickered involuntarily to his parted lips, making her wonder what they would feel like to touch.

Slowly, tenderly, his fingers traced the curve of her jaw, the roughness of his fingertips rasping against her skin. The hold he had on her arm with his other hand intensified and Pippa stepped forward to keep her balance. Her senses reeled as his cologne filled her sinuses, the heat of his masculinity pulsing out of his every pore. She heard his shallow breathing match her own as he stroked her hair, his touch trembling.

Pippa swallowed hard, temptation pulling her towards him like a vacuum. Jack tilted his head slightly, in an almost curious gesture as his eyes travelled over her face, her eyes, her hair, her throat. He licked his lips, the pink tip of his tongue making Pippa's mouth water.

'Hello! Anyone in?'

A voice calling from Reception sent them both staggering backwards, as if they'd been rebuffed by a force-field. Pippa blinked and took a deep breath, trying to get her bearings back. She stared at Jack. If the terror on his face looked anything like her own, he must be feeling the same hurricane of emotions rampaging through his body.

'Hello?'

'Yes!' Pippa called out. 'Just a moment.' She tore her eyes away from Jack and fled back to the safety of Reception. Aspen Valley's head lad was leaning over the desk, looking at the two Aaron Janssen horses' portraits, which Pippa had brought in earlier with her.

'Can I help?' she asked, hoping nothing on her face would betray what had just happened.

'Yeah, can you tell Jack the racing at Ffos Las has been called off this afternoon? Track's waterlogged.'

Pippa nodded.

'Of course. Thanks.'

The lad gave her a curious frown, but didn't add anything. He nodded once and turned to leave.

Pippa sat down on her chair with a bump and blew a wisp of her hair out of her eyes. She tucked the curl behind her ear, but paused, cupping her jawline where Jack's fingers had travelled. What the hell *had* just happened?

'Pippa?'

She jumped like a startled rabbit at the sound of Jack's voice. He stood in the doorway to his office. She searched his face for a clue as to what he might say next.

'Yes?' she squeaked.

He lifted a notebook in his hand and walked towards the desk.

'Entries for next week. What did I hear about Ffos Las?'

Pippa didn't know whether to be relieved or disappointed that he was pretending nothing had happened at all.

'Racing's been called off. The course is waterlogged apparently.'

'Damn,' Jack tutted. 'I thought that might happen.'

He stood with his hands on his hips, his fingers tapping against his belt. He looked around him, distracted, until his gaze alighted on Pippa's paintings.

'Those Aaron Janssen's?'

'Yes,' she nodded. 'He asked if I could drop them round his house in Bristol this afternoon, if I can find the place.'

'I've been there a couple of times. Do you know where the Suspension Bridge is?'

Pippa shook her head.

'Okay, do you know where The Green is?'

'No,' she replied, looking apologetic. 'But I was going to look it up on Google maps. I just hate navigating. I usually get lost no matter how easy it is to find.'

Jack looked at her, somewhat cautious.

'I could take you. I mean, I know where it is and I've got a free afternoon ahead of me now.'

*Ah*, the voice in Pippa's head resolved, so he hasn't blocked it out completely. Did she really want be in such close proximity to him again so soon though? As spacious as Land Rovers were, they weren't designed for the space Pippa felt was needed between her and her boss.

'You don't have to. I'm sure I'd find it eventually.'

'No, really. It'll give me something to do and I'd get a chance to congratulate Janssen on Skylark's second place.'

Pippa felt reassured by the lack of awkwardness in his tone. Maybe a journey into Bristol sitting beside him wouldn't be so excruciating after all. Plus, she could do without the trauma of navigating through the city.

'Well, only if you're sure.'

Jack nodded.

'Sorted then. I've obviously got horses to see to now, but I'll catch you at lunchtime.'

'Okay. Thanks, Jack,' Pippa said with a grateful smile.

He responded with a brisk nod.

'See you later.'

Balancing the two canvases in her arms, Pippa followed Jack up the stone steps to the front door of Aaron Janssen's three-storey Victorian townhouse. Jack's knock was answered by a housekeeper, who led them through into a high ceilinged drawing room, where the lavishly decorated panelled walls and cornices provided an almost uncomfortable contrast to the huge plasma television and modern leather lounge suite, long enough to home an entire baseball team.

The fashion mogul was reclining in a chair, an idling cigar wedged between two plump fingers. His face lit up when their arrival was announced and he greeted Pippa and Jack like long-lost friends. Like a child at Christmas he urged her to reveal his horses' pictures.

'But darling, they're stunning!' he exclaimed, clasping his hands together and knocking ash onto the carpet. 'Oh, you are clever to catch such a likeness. Isn't she fantastic, Jack?'

'Very good,' Jack agreed obediently.

'Thank you,' Pippa said, a blush warming her cheeks. 'And thank you for commissioning –' Her rehearsed speech faded as a figure appeared through a doorway at the far side of the room. Surprise stalled her voice and she darted a look towards Jack.

He looked just as taken aback.

'Melissa?' he uttered.

For a moment the young woman hesitated, but regained her composure quickly.

'Jack,' she smiled. 'And *Pippa*. What a surprise.'

'What are you doing here?' Jack asked.

Pippa noticed the almost imperceptible nervous tension in her twisting fingers. Melissa opened her mouth to reply, but was interrupted by Aaron.

'Just an informal business meeting before I leave for Dubai Fashion Week.'

Melissa smiled in agreement and strode across the room towards them, lithe and feline.

'And what are *you* doing here?' she said.

'I – er – Pippa needed to drop these pictures off and racing was cancelled so I – er – I knew where Aaron lived...' His excuse sounded forced, provoking compassion from Pippa and a glare from Melissa.

Aaron clapped his hands.

'Well, isn't this nice. Everyone knows each other already.'

'Yes. Pippa is Jack's *secretary*,' Melissa said, giving them both a challenging look.

'Really? Where did you find the time to do these then, darling?' he asked Pippa. 'Oh, I do love the colour of this one! The copper in his coat set against that vivid blue blackground. What do you think, Melissa?'

263

Melissa glanced briefly at the picture.

'Hmm, they're good. A bit contrived maybe.'

'Melissa!' Jack admonished.

'What? I'm sure Pippa appreciates an honest opinion. Don't you?' She smiled at Pippa, her red lips cutting a sheer path across her face.

Pippa gave her her best waitress smile. She did appreciate honesty, but somehow Melissa didn't seem to fall into that category in her book.

'Of course,' she replied.

'Well, I think they're wonderful!' Aaron gushed. 'And since I'm paying for them, that's the main thing you need to worry about. In fact, if you don't mind, I'd like you to do some more for me.'

Pippa's smile blossomed into a genuine grin.

'Really?'

'I want a room dedicated to the horses here with their pictures on the wall and their trophies in the cabinets,' he said, his hands gesticulating as he described the scene. 'Winners' rugs draped like curtains, like a - like a...'

'Like a shrine?' Pippa said hesitantly.

'Yes! That's the word. Doesn't that sound wonderful?'

'Um, I guess so,' she replied, catching a glimpse of Jack rolling his eyes.

'Now, do you two need to rush off anywhere? I'm particularly glad you brought Jack along, Pippa,' said Aaron with a mischievous smile, 'because look what I received in the post yesterday!' He skipped over to a writing desk and flapped a DVD at them. 'It's the charity single we did! Have you received yours yet?'

Jack frowned.

'Yeah, it arrived a couple of days ago.'

Aaron's eyes twinkled with excitement.

'Ooh, have you watched it? I'm a teensy bit nervous about which clips they showed of me. I was getting the words wrong half the time.'

Jack shifted uncomfortably.

'No, I haven't seen it yet. Haven't had the time really with the Festival and - and things.'

'Nonsense! It's only four or five minutes long,' he said, batting the DVD case in Jack's direction.

'I'd like to see it,' Pippa heard herself say.

Aaron beamed at her.

'And so would I, darling. Come take a seat, you two. Melissa, be a doll and close the curtains?'

For a millisecond, Melissa looked anything but doll-like then nodded demurely. Aaron fiddled with the DVD player and stereo-system built into the wall then came to join Pippa and Jack on the long couch.

Pippa couldn't stop her grin of amusement as the recording began. The camera swung over the assembly of racing personalities in the huge recording studio.

She glanced at Jack, sitting beside her, looking less than impressed. An unseen voice led them through the first verse before the entire cast joined in the chorus. Jack was the first person they zoomed in on, looking stiff and self-conscious, sporting a pair of earphones. Interspersed with shots of the singers, replays of the previous year's Cheltenham Festival lit up the screen, showing predominantly Virtuoso's Gold Cup win. The image of Jack, with an ear-splitting grin that Colgate would have killed to sponsor, congratulating Rhys Bradford was replaced with Jack in the recording studio, seeming to have relaxed by the second chorus and joining in with more enthusiasm.

Pippa grinned at him, seeing the embarrassed smile on his face.

'They plied us with alcohol for most of it,' he murmured in her ear. 'We're nothing more than a bunch of drunken karaoke singers by this point.'

She giggled.

By the images chosen of the last Festival, of Virtuoso annihilating his rivals, Black Russian being embraced by an hysterical Emmie, crowds cheering, urging on their favourites, newspapers being flung in the air as winner after winner crossed the line, the magic and historicism of Cheltenham finally hit home for Pippa.

By the smile on his face, she could tell Jack was reliving last year's successes.

'I understand now,' she whispered back.

Warmth filled his eyes and he nodded.

'Good.'

A feeling of discomfort overshadowed her enjoyment of the DVD and she glanced up to find Melissa looking at her. No frown creased her brow, no sneer disturbed her lipstick. But her eyes burned into Pippa's in an icy stare crystallising her grey eyes.

# Chapter Thirty-Seven

Pippa wobbled down the step ladder and massaged her lower back. She grimaced as the moody pain voiced its disapproval of her painting the spare room walls at something past midnight. She'd only intended to do the one, maybe two walls that evening, but as she'd hauled all the old mismatched furniture and her easel onto the landing, she'd realised what a mission it would be to put everything back and then go through the whole process again.

She gave the blotchy marigold walls a dubious look then shrugged. It would need a second coat anyway. Squeezing past the buckled mattress and other bedroom items, she plodded down the stairs. An appreciative smile warmed her face. The novelty of the new golden varnished oak boards still hadn't worn off.

Her mobile phone, lying in its usual spot on the windowsill gave a plaintive beep as she wandered into the kitchen.

Pippa frowned at the message on the screen: two missed calls from ten minutes ago. She glanced at the clock on the wall. What was Tash doing ringing her at this hour? Maybe she was out on the booze and hadn't realised the time, she decided, hefting herself up onto the draining board and redialling. It was Saturday night after all.

'Hey, sweets. I hope I didn't wake you,' Tash answered, her voice raised above a busy background.

Pippa grinned. It was Saturday night all right.

'No, I was upstairs painting the spare room. Everything okay?'

'Well, I don't want to worry you or anything, but –' Tash hesitated, and the concern in her voice immediately made Pippa's worry meter shoot up to critical. 'But I'm at a party – well, a *function* more like it. I've been to wakes more festive than this. Anyway, the thing is your friend Finn is here.'

'Finn?' Pippa said in surprise. 'What's he doing in London?'

'I don't know, but he's not exactly selling himself.'

Pippa frowned.

'What do you mean?'

'Uh, he's a little bit *drunk*. And he's not creating a very good impression. He's cornered my CEO right now and is moaning about how he's a bad person. He's not making much sense.'

'Oh, God. Poor Finn.' Her heart contorted in pity. 'He fell off in the Gold Cup. He must still be upset about that, poor soul.'

'That's it? He fell off in a race?' Tash's tone was disparaging. 'By the looks of it, I'd have said someone had died.'

'The Gold Cup is rather special to racing. Jack gave him a bit of a bollocking afterwards too.'

'I guess each to their own. But what I called you for, sweets, is do you do you want me to do anything? I mean, he's making a bit of a spectacle of himself.'

'Is he that drunk?'

'Pip, he's about as legless as a day-old tadpole. Shit, he's trying to hug my boss' wife now.'

'Bloody hell. Um, yes, I think you'd better do something, if that's okay,' she fretted. 'We don't want Finn getting into any more trouble.'

'No problem. It gives me an excuse to leave this sad excuse for a party too. Incidentally, who's his sister? By the way he was going on, I thought she must have died or something.'

'*Sister?* God, he must be drunk. Finn's an only child if I recall correctly.'

'Hmm, maybe I mis-overheard. He hasn't launched his woes on me yet, but he's been working the room, that's for sure.'

'Christ. If the papers get hold of this, they'll take him to pieces.' Pippa chewed her fingernails, but stopped when a flavour of marigold paint matted her dry palate.

'No worries, sweets. I've donned my blue lycra jumpsuit and red Speedos and am flying in to the rescue. I'll take him home.'

Pippa closed her eyes.

'What would I do without you, Tash? Thank you. And don't be too tough on him. Yesterday will have hit him really hard and the media haven't exactly been kind either.'

'Don't worry – shit, I'd better go. He's moving in on Dame Rosa Lyle, the animal rights activist. I'll speak to you later. *Ciao.*'

Pippa held her phone in a feeble grip and looked blindly at the cut call, concern over Finn compounded by gratitude to Tash. Pursing her lips and taking a deep breath, she told herself not to worry. Tash would take care of things. Tash was rock solid.

For the remainder of her weekend, Pippa divided her time between the spare room's second coat and checking her phone for updates from Tash. She'd tried to call earlier in the day, but had only got her friend's

267

voicemail. She tried to reassure herself that no news was good news. Tash had the gift of the gab and she would surely have been able to smooth over any ripples that Finn might have created last night.

Later that evening, Pippa answered a loud knock on the front door. A sheepish-looking Finn stood on her doorstep.

'Word is you don't turn away waifs and strays such as myself. Can I come in?'

Shaven and tidy, the only evidence of his drunken debacle was the bruised bags beneath his eyes and hunched posture. Feeling reassured that perhaps it had all been a storm in a teacup, Pippa stepped aside.

'Come on in. Do you want a coffee?'

'No, you're all right. Thanks all the same,' he said, following her into the lounge. 'Tash has been spoon-feeding me caffeine since the wee hours.'

Pippa sat down on the sofa and after switching off the television, patted the seat beside her.

'Spoon-feeding? She's been gentle with you then?'

'Aye,' Finn grinned, taking his seat. 'Not that I've done anything to deserve her kindness. Or yours.'

'Who said anything about me being kind?' she teased.

'Well, you didn't slam the door in my face so that's a start. I'm sorry about last night, making a holy show of myself. I'm sorry Tash had to look after me like she did.'

Pippa's heart softened at the genuine apology in his eyes.

'Forget it. It was understandable considering everything.'

Finn looked at his lap and fiddled with the hem of his shirt.

'It's been a desperate couple of days, to be sure.'

'Hey, these things happen. It wasn't your fault, Finn.'

'But it was.' Finn looked up at her. 'I know it, Jack knows it, the papers know it. I've let everyone down.'

'Jack was upset. I don't know what he said to you, but I'm sure he didn't mean it. Not really,' she said, torn between her loyalties.

'I wouldn't be surprised if he jocked me off now.'

'Jack wouldn't do that,' she said sternly. 'He might get a bit hot under the collar, but he's still fair. I know the Gold Cup means a lot to everyone, but come on, we all make mistakes. Jack knows that. It's not the end of the world.'

'I was wishin' it was last night,' he said, shaking his head. 'I've made a right pig's arse of everything.'

Pippa reached over and squeezed his hand.

'You're a good person, Finn. The press are a fickle bunch. Just watch, they'll have forgotten about this whole thing within a week.'

Finn shook his head sadly.

'It's kind of you to say, but I'm not a good person.' He sighed. 'I – I haven't been entirely honest with you either.'

Pippa paused.

'Are we referring to Cara Connolly in this respect?' she asked in a gentle voice.

His green eyes widened.

'You know already?'

She shrugged and gave him a pathetic smile.

'I pretty much figured it out. It's okay, you know.'

'But it's not okay,' he insisted. 'You won't say anything, will you?'

Pippa hesitated, disturbed by the fear on Finn's face. She definitely wasn't going to tell him his secret had already been broken by *Heat* magazine.

'It's none of my business. Don't worry.'

Finn dragged his fingers through his hair.

'Why are you so understanding? After all that I've done?'

'You'd have to do a whole lot worse to make me hate you,' she reassured him.

Finn squeezed her hand back and leant over. He cupped her face in his other hand, his fingers chilled against her warm cheek.

'The world needs more people like you, *a thaisce*,' he murmured.

Pippa dropped her gaze, but couldn't stop the flattered smile curving her lips.

'It'd be a bit chaotic, I'd say.'

She looked up again to see his gaze flitting over her mouth.

'You've a beautiful smile, you know?'

The springs in the sofa groaned as he leaned forward. His hand slid from her cheek to the back of her head, his fingers threading through her hair. With gentle pressure, he coaxed her closer until his lips pressed over hers.

Pippa closed her eyes, enjoying his warm breath tickling her upper lip. They flickered open though as reality overwhelmed her. She turned her face to the side, making Finn sit up.

'We can't do this,' she mumbled, her cheeks burning.

Finn frowned at her.

'It's Jack, isn't it?' he said. 'Tash hinted at something between you two.'

'What? No!' Pippa bit her lip, still moist from Finn's kiss. 'I don't know.' Panic surged through her at the thought of anyone but Tash knowing about her feelings towards Jack. 'There's Cara to think about as well!'

Finn's frown deepened.

'Yes!' Pippa said. 'We can't do this when you're dating someone else.'

Finn's hand loosened in her hair and he withdrew it, disappointment clouding his eyes.

Confused, she tried to understand what was going through his mind. He looked almost resigned. As flattered as she was by Finn's attention, she didn't want to believe that he was a cheat. Perhaps this look of resignation, of sadness, meant he wasn't really?

'You're right. I'm sorry. I just forgot myself for a moment,' he said.

'Me too,' she replied in a small voice, guilt that perhaps her pity over Finn's troubles had been misinterpreted. She'd taken advantage of the young Irishman in a weak moment.

'I'd better go. I'm sorry to have interrupted your evening.' He stood up when Pippa nodded.

She followed him to the front door, her chest constricting in anguish when he bade her a sad farewell.

'I'll see you tomorrow at work,' she said.

'I'll be there. Goodnight.'

She closed the door and leant against it with a heavy sigh. Was this how it was going to be from now on? Would she never be able to feel anything for another man while Jack was still fresh in her mind? Had she messed up her friendship with Finn?

She looked around her sullenly. The sooner the cottage was finished, the sooner it would be sold and she could escape to London and forget Jack Carmichael. She knew loads of owners hardly ever spoke to Jack, content to let him get on with training their horses. She could be one of them. If not, she could always move Peace Offering to another stable.

# Chapter Thirty-Eight

Pippa was met with silence when she stepped into the office for the new week. Opening Jack's door and seeing his empty chair confirmed he was probably already out on the Gallops. She flicked through the Entries and Declarations notebook on his desk, but left it where it was when she read question marks beside Jack's scrawl. She busied herself back at her own desk, sorting through the weekend's emails and answering the persistently ringing telephone.

Jack walked in half an hour later, closely followed by Melissa. On the receiving end of a diatribe of abuse from Lady Pennington, Pippa was barely able to acknowledge their arrival.

'I completely understand where you're coming from, Lady Pennington,' she said patiently when the owner paused for breath. 'But when Aspen Valley advertises its services in the paper, there is only so much information we can include – yes, I'm sure Mr Carmichael appreciates what good owners you are. I'll let him know you'd like your name *as well* as Silver Dollar's to be included next time we announce our winners...' She rolled her eyes as Lady Pennington hammered home her point before letting Pippa go.

'Tea? Coffee?' she offered when she was finally allowed to hang up.

'Coffee. No milk or sugar for me, thank you,' Melissa said with a benign smile.

Pippa hurried away from the phone before it could ring again.

'Here you go,' she said, handing over the steaming mugs a couple of minutes later.

Jack took a slurp and sighed exultantly. Melissa sniffed the air as the scent of chamomile wafted across her.

'What are you drinking, Jack?'

'Chamomile tea. Pippa's idea. It's very nice.'

The bubble of pride swelling inside Pippa at this praise was popped by the daggers Melissa's eyes threw her. Nevertheless, the blonde woman didn't comment. Instead she took a tentative sip and looked pained.

'No decaf?'

'Um, no. Sorry,' Pippa said. Her tongue itched to say it. She bit it, but no, she couldn't resist. 'Would you like some chamomile tea instead?'

To give Melissa her due, the iciness in her eyes didn't carry to her voice.

'Thank you, Pippa,' she said graciously.

The telephone rang again and Pippa hesitated.

'Busy this morning?' Jack asked.

'Busier than the Samaritans hotline was when Take That broke up.'

'I'll go make the tea then. You grab that.'

Aware of Melissa's watchful gaze as she discussed veterinary procedures with Mr Warnock, Pippa doodled in the margin of her notepad to dispel her discomfort. Melissa leaned over the desk and gave a small laugh at her mindless sketchings, covering her mouth with her matching blood-red nails. Pippa frowned at her desk in annoyance.

'That was Warnock,' she said, her telephone conversation finished, when Jack reappeared with Melissa's tea. 'He's given me a list of the horses who need their 'flu jabs and has asked you to go over them and take out the ones which are due to run soon. And he's advised we get a physiotherapist and nutritionist to come see Dust Storm since he keeps tying up.'

'Okay,' he nodded. 'Anything else?'

Pippa referred to her jotted notes, holding back a sigh at the length of her 'to do' list.

'You've got an appointment with Mr Cox this afternoon to discuss keeping Lugarno in training. Channel 4 wants to do a feature on you for the Grand National. A couple of other magazines and newspapers want comment on how Cheltenham was for you...'

'Dammit. They're never bloody satisfied.'

'Why not just issue a press release?' she suggested.

Jack perked up.

'That's a good idea. Can you do that?'

She nodded and added it to her list.

'Are there any entries to be done?' she asked, glancing at the clock on the wall.

'Yes, I'll get those to you in a minute. You'll probably have to rush to get them in on time, I'm afraid.'

Pippa failed to camouflage her grimace of exhaustion.

'You okay?'

'Yeah. Don't worry about me.'

Jack frowned.

'You look tired.'

'It's my own fault,' she said, with an airy wave of her hand. 'I spent most of the weekend trying to paint the cottage. And now spring is really here, I can't put off sorting out the garden anymore.'

Jack gave her a sympathetic smile.

'Not green-fingered then?'

'Only when I'm painting landscapes or aliens.'

'Maybe we can sort something out then. Some of the lads here can spare an afternoon and help straighten things out for you. Billy's keen on gardening and he owes you, I'd say.'

'That would be lovely!' Pippa said, brightening at the thought of not having to tackle Hazyvale's jungle all by herself. Her grin faltered as she noticed Melissa glaring at Jack. Now was probably a good time to change the subject. 'Have you heard from Emmie?'

Jack's expression became serious again.

'She can't work in the yard anymore. Doctor's orders. But apparently she doesn't want to stop working - finances and all that.' He paused. 'I was thinking maybe if things are really hectic here in the office, she could come work in here. You'd have to show her how to do things, but I'm sure she'll pick it up quickly - she knows about horses after all. It would take some of the pressure off you.' Jack hesitated as he became aware of the laser-burning look he was receiving from Melissa. 'It would help you both out.'

Pippa ignored their disapproving audience and beamed at Jack.

'Good idea! Emmie'd be great to have around.'

'I'm not giving her this role for you two to sit around chatting all day.'

Pippa grinned at him, recognising the subtle touch of humour in his eyes.

'Let me get those entries done,' he went on. 'Then I'm off to see Melissa's father.'

He disappeared into his office, leaving Pippa sitting in awkward silence with Melissa. She wracked her brain, trying to think of a neutral subject with which to make conversation.

'So, Melissa, Jack told me you were hoping to join fashion forces with Aaron Janssen. How's that going?'

Melissa leaned over the reception unit and raised a menacing finger.

Pippa sat back in surprise.

'I know what you're trying to do,' Melissa hissed. 'Stirring things up with Jack and now Aaron.'

'What?'

Melissa sneered at her.

'Is that the look you give Jack when you fuck everything up for him? This wide-eyed oh-so-innocent look? Well, it might work on some, but it won't work on me.' A smile parted her lips. 'You're jealous, aren't you?'

'What?' Pippa said, astounded.

'That's why you've got Jack bending over backwards trying to help you out of your own shitty life. And why you went begging to Aaron so you could draw pictures of his horses.'

'Wh-what are you talking about?'

'Well, you might have got your way with Aaron, but you're not having Jack,' she spat.

Pippa stared at her. Oh, God, she despaired. It's one thing for Tash to notice, but if a virtual stranger like Melissa can see what's going on, then I really am up shit creek. Was she that bad at hiding her feelings?

Her look of horror turned to a returning Jack, armed with his notebook.

Melissa straightened and gave Jack a wide smile.

Jack hesitated, his focus flashing from his girlfriend, patting her kempt blonde hair, to his secretary.

Pippa swallowed and looked down at her desk, her composure still shaky.

'Right then,' he said slowly. 'Here you go.' He passed the notebook to her and frowned at her flushed face. 'Hang on. I think I forgot one.' He took it back and scrawled another entry into it before flipping it shut. 'There you go. I'm out of here. See you later, Pippa. Melissa, are you ready?'

'Whenever you are, darling. Ta-ra, Pippa,' Melissa said cheerily, hooking her arm inside Jack's and fluttering her nails at Pippa.

With a blush still burning her face, she watched them go. She opened the book of entries and declarations and turned to the last page. At the bottom, Jack's last entry read: *Whatever she said try not to take it personally. Her business has just taken a knock. Chin up, A.V. still loves you.*

Pippa forced herself to blink as she closed the notebook and held it to her chest. It would be difficult to construe Melissa's warnings as anything but personal. She *must* be that bad at hiding her feelings.

The town of Helensvale lay unperturbed as its inhabitants returned home from work. It seemed to Pippa, as she walked down the High Street, to embrace their presence. Far from the cold practicality of

London streets, the town's benches and striped canvas overhangs almost proffered a welcome, encouraging commuters to stop and chat.

She smiled, feeling the welcome extended to her then laughed at herself. Personifying Helensvale was another box ticked on her Insanity Checklist.

Her phone vibrated deep inside her handbag and she scrambled through its messy contents to find it. She peeled a tenacious chocolate wrapper from the handset.

'Hey Tash,' she greeted her friend. 'Was going to call you later.'

'All right, sweets? Guess who I got a call from last night?'

'Dunno. Do I know them?'

'I should say so. Better than most because they are quite famous. Come on, guess.'

'I don't know.' Pippa pulled a doubtful face. 'Ollie?'

'Hmm, is Ollie that famous? Gold help this world if he is ever called a celebrity. Although I'd love to see him do a bush tucker trial on *Get Me Out Of Here*. No, it's not Ollie.'

'I dunno,' she shrugged. She homed in on the nearest bench and plonked her bag down beside her.

'*Finn* called me,' Tash said.

Pippa chewed her bottom lip, thinking of his less than successful visit last night.

'What did he have to say?'

'Just rang to thank me again for stopping him making a fool of himself. Mind you, I think he'd already done that by the time I got my mitts on him, but I didn't say that. He sounded down enough as it was.'

'Yeah. He came round and visited me last night as well. It was all a bit strange.'

Tash burst into song, bellowing out the first few lines to Frank Sinatra's *Strangers in the Night*. Pippa laughed.

'Tash, I don't know what's more worrying: what you're implying or that that you know the words to that song. Where are you, just out of interest?'

'Just in Tesco picking up some food. Why?'

Pippa shook her head.

'No reason,' she chuckled.

Tash's next comment was lost as an ice-cream van rattled past, playing its jingle.

'Sorry,' she raised her voice above the noise. 'Hang on a sec while it passes.'

'Why do ice-cream vans always play Greensleeves, of all tunes?' Tash asked.

A mischievous smile lit Pippa's face.

'I don't know. Maybe it was a modern tune back in Tudor times so they played it on their vans.'

'Hmm, yeah. That's probably it.'

Pippa snorted.

'Ah, Tash. You sure you're not blonde?'

'What? Oh, you meanie!'

Pippa doubled over with giggles.

'Huh,' Tash grunted. 'Anyway, back to what we were talking about – what were we talking about?'

'Finn.'

'Oh, yes. So, what did he say that was so strange?'

'Well –' Her smile faded and she sighed. Unseeingly, she watched a greengrocer retrieve his sandwich-boards advertising freshly harvested rhubarb, radish and sorrel. 'Tash, is it that obvious what I feel about Jack?'

'That depends, Pip. What *do* you feel?'

She sighed again. The million dollar question and she was too afraid to answer it to herself, let alone her best friend.

'A lot more than I should.'

'Okay. So it shows that you care for each other,' Tash said diplomatically. 'Why? What did Finn say?'

'First, he apologised for his behaviour then he tried to kiss me. I don't know, maybe I gave him the wrong idea. I was only trying to be supportive. Then when I didn't kiss him back, he asked if it was because of Jack. And I thought maybe you'd said something to him, but then Melissa all but said 'Hands off my man' to me this morning at work.'

'Ooh, that sounds juicy. Tell me more.'

Pippa raised her free hand in a helpless gesture.

'I was trying to make conversation and I asked how her fashion business was going. The next thing I know she's leaning over me saying I might have got my grubby hands on Aaron Janssen, but that Jack was hers.'

'Wow,' Tash breathed. 'I can't wait to meet this Melissa. Was Jack around?'

'No, he was in his office. But then he came out and...' Pippa frowned at the ground, rereading the Entries and Declarations notebook in her mind.

'And? Come on, Pip. Your life is better than *EastEnders*. What happened next?'

'He gave me the entries like he usually did, then I think I must have still looked quite – I don't know, shaken? Shocked? – because he took the notebook back, said he'd forgotten something and wrote '*Chin up. A.V. still loves you*' on it and passed it back to me.'

'A.V.? What's that? I get that on my telly when I want to watch a DVD.'

'Aspen Valley, I should think.'

'Wow. You serious?'

'Yeah,' Pippa sighed.

'Bloody hell, Jack's got it bad. You sure he didn't write J.C., not A.V.?'

'What do I do?'

'Doesn't sound like much you can do. Although steer clear of Melissa, that's one piece of advice I can give you.'

'The sooner the season is over the better, I think.'

'When does that happen?'

'About six weeks' time. It's the National soon as well. Are you going to be able to make it? I know Aintree's quite far, but it'll be massive. I had to book hotel accommodation for everyone today. Jack's letting me have Friday afternoon and Saturday off so I can enjoy it all.'

'How soon, sweets?'

'Three weeks on Saturday.'

'Count me in, although I won't be able to make Friday night. It'd be pointless trying to get there in London traffic. How are you travelling?'

'I don't know. Car, I guess.'

'What if I drive up and you get the train or go with Jack or something then both of us can go back in my car to your cottage afterwards to celebrate Peace Offering's success? And you can get as tonked as you like since you won't be driving.'

Pippa laughed.

'I think he's about a hundred-to-one at the moment, but that sounds like a plan. The staircase has been replaced, you'll be glad to hear.'

'Good stuff. I'll get my bets on now. Is Finn riding?'

'I hope so.'

'Hmm. Me too,' Tash murmured. 'Anyway, sweets. I'm at the till now. I've got to pay for all this food. You can tell me off later for buying a whole cheesecake. I tell you what, I have no idea where the last one got to. It just seemed to disappear.'

'Oh, dear. Are you midnight snacking again?' Pippa giggled.

'Right, here's the burning question, Pip: if we weren't meant to have midnight snacks, why is there a light in the fridge?'

Pippa snorted.

'So you can see your way down to the wine cellar and drink yourself back to sleep?'

Tash roared in response.

'Good call. If I become an alcoholic, I'll blame Whirlpool. Anyway, gotta go. Speak to you later, Pip.'

'Cheers, Tash.' Pippa cut the call, still smiling and looked around as Helensvale dimmed in the dusk. Her gaze was caught by the lit window of a nearby bookmaker. It was showing antepost odds for the Grand National. Skylark was joint favourite at eight-to-one with Okay Oklahoma. Peace Offering's chances were so slim that they weren't even advertising his price.

Pippa sighed and got to her feet. She also had shopping to do and cheesecake didn't sound such a bad idea, come to think of it.

# Chapter Thirty-Nine

Feeling restless, Pippa closed her book and gazed around her. Her hotel room was small but cleverly furnished, making it feel much more spacious. Opposite the bed where she lay, a large oils of Liverpool's most famous steeplechase hung on the wall. The splashes of colour from the jockeys' silks clashed together as the forty-odd horses hurtled over a fence. Pippa stared at one horse crumpling on landing, his hind quarters displayed at an unnatural angle whilst his head disappeared into the turf. His jockey lay curled beside him, his knees drawn up and arms held protectively over his head, waiting for the other thirty-nine horses to land upon them.

Pippa gulped. The outstretched hooves of the horses in mid-flight looked certain to end it all for the stricken pair. The balled-up jockey became Finn in her eyes and Peace Offering, the horse. What if they met the same fate tomorrow? What if one of them was killed? Would she hold herself responsible?

'Of course you would,' she said with a sigh and tore her eyes guiltily away from the painting. She hoisted herself off the bed and slipped on her shoes. She was due to meet Jack in a quarter of an hour for pre-dinner drinks and if she left herself in her own company for much longer Peace Offering would end up scratched from the Grand National.

Maybe having Finn in the next room was a good thing, she thought, picking up her handbag and making for the door. She didn't know how she was going to cope with her nerves at the same time as have dinner with Jack and Melissa. Finn was off the carbs and the booze, frantically trying to get down to the featherweight the handicapper had allocated him and Peace Offering, so his minibar was bound to be full.

She let herself out into the warmly-lit hallway, tempted to tip-toe amidst its tranquillity. Her mobile buzzed as she reached Finn's door and she dipped into her bag before knocking. There was a text message from Tash.

*So sorry, Pip. Can't make tomorrow. Stupid fucking CEO has got us pitching for big deal so noses are at grindstone all weekend. Working right now even. Very best of luck tomorrow. I know you can do it. Wish I was there to share the experience. T xxx*

Pippa groaned and leaned against the doorframe. Of all times for Tash's boss to cancel their weekend, it had to be this one. The one when she most needed her friend's support. She took a deep breath before replying to the message. Acting whiney like she felt wasn't going to help anyone and Tash didn't exactly sound thrilled either.

As her thumbs skittered over her phone's keypad she became aware of movement on the other side of the door. At least Finn was in. She smiled as his Irish accent became more distinguishable through the partition. Judging by the one-sided conversation he was having, she guessed he must be on the phone.

*No worries, Tash. Sorry you can't make it. Am about to raid Finn's minibar before dinner*

She paused mid-sentence as the tone of Finn's voice became clearer. She frowned at the door, but looked away again, trying not to listen in on his conversation. He was moving about the room, sounding even more restless than she and now, with his voice almost perfectly audible, he must be right by the door as well.

'Calm yourself, Cara. Screaming like a banshee at me is not doing any good,' he said. 'Haven't we done all that was asked of us? There was only so much I could do in the Gold Cup. I kept my end of the bargain.'

Pippa's eyes widened and despite herself, she leaned closer to the door to hear better, her half-composed text message lying forgotten in her hand.

'What *about* tomorrow? I couldn't do it, no.'

Pippa's chest contracted, squeezing all the air out of her lungs as the seriousness of what she was overhearing dawned on her.

'Look, if they couldn't fix the Gold Cup then they've no chance fixing the National. This race is a lottery to begin with. I couldn't do that to Pippa anyway.'

At the mention of her name, her phone slid out of her hand. She grimaced as it bounced off the door. The ensuing pause from Finn sent a flash flood of panic gushing through her. She hastily bent down to retrieve the phone and do a runner.

'Shit,' she mouthed as her unzipped handbag upended half its contents onto the carpet. Footsteps on the other side of the door had her scrambling for random lipsticks and petrol receipts. The door opened as she sprang away back to her room. She gasped as his fingers fastened around her wrist.

Finn's eyes flashed.

'How long have you been standing there?'

Recognising the fear in his eyes made Pippa even more flustered.

'Not long at all, I promise. I –'

'How much did you hear?'

Pippa gaped as his grip tightened on her wrist.

'How much did you *hear*?' he snarled.

Tears filled her eyes as her fear was replaced with sadness.

'How could you, Finn?' she whispered.

His hold on her arm softened and he dropped his gaze.

She stepped back, her personal space violated by this stranger.

'You lied. You're – you're a fraud, aren't you?' Her heart twisted in anguish. She so wanted the façade which he'd been upholding to have been real. 'You bastard, Finn. Look at me, dammit!'

He raised his eyes, but couldn't hold her accusing gaze.

'You deceived me. You deceived *Jack*,' she said, tears bubbling at the back of her throat. She backed away from him. 'You can't ride Peace Offering tomorrow. I can't trust you.'

'Wait, Pippa!' Finn exclaimed as she tried to escape to her room. He grasped her by the tops of her arms and looked at her with a deep intensity. 'You *can* trust me. If you'd just let me explain –'

'Finn, you're fixing races. What is there to explain?'

He glanced nervously over their shoulders to check for stray ears and licked his lips.

'Let me explain, please. Come into my room and let me explain.'

For the first time in Finn's presence, Pippa felt a pang of fear for her safety. Locked in a room with a man whom she thought she knew, but had now turned out to be a criminal?

Finn's brow furrowed in hurt as her hesitancy betrayed her feelings.

'*Please*? I won't hurt you, Pippa. You know that, *a thaisce*.'

Reluctantly, she allowed Finn to guide her into his room, making sure the door was left ajar in case she needed to make a hasty escape.

'Take a seat while I get us a couple of drinks,' he said, gesturing to the small lounge suite.

She perched on a chair, her fingers gripping her handbag and watched him pour two generous whiskies and sodas. Her mind swirled with questions, most of which she was too afraid to hear the answer to.

'What's going on, Finn?' she asked at last.

Finn handed her a drink and sat down opposite her.

'Nothing anymore,' he replied with a sigh.

'Are – are you fixing races?'

'It was only the once, I swear, Pippa,' he said, leaning forward in his seat. 'I didn't want to do it. But I had to. You must believe me.'

'Why? Why must I believe you? Why did you have to?'

Finn sighed again and swirled his drink around the glass.

'I couldn't let Virtuoso win the Gold Cup,' he mumbled, looking down at his hands.

Pippa's hand trembled as she took a gulp. Her eyes watered as the fiery spirit burned her throat.

'You fell off on purpose?' she whispered.

Finn nodded.

'It was the only way I could let Skylark win –'

'Skylark?' Pippa interrupted. 'You were on the phone to Cara just now, weren't you? She works for Skylark. Did she make you do this? Why are you dating her, Finn?'

Finn held up his hand at her barrage of questions.

'I'm not dating her,' he said patiently. 'She's not my girlfriend, Pippa. She's –' He paused and bit his lip. 'She's my sister.'

Pippa choked.

'Your *sister*?' she echoed. 'But I thought you said you were an only child.'

'I know,' he nodded. 'It's a long story. My father was a well-respected jockey. Sportsman of the Year and all that. He was clean as a whistle. Then when I was just a lad, he went AWOL, had an affair with a model from Dublin. Cara was the result. I didn't know about it at the time. Hell, I was only knee-high. Nobody knew. My da had a reputation to uphold. My mother took him back and Cara was brought up by her mother and took her name. Then when she was old enough, she came looking for her real father. And that's when I found out I had a half-sister.'

Pippa stared, wide-eyed. She tried to imagine what it must feel like to have grown up thinking you are the sole progeny of your parents, only to find out you've had a sibling all along.

'Anyway, Cara became a model like her mam. But it's a tough business, Pippa, you have to understand. She did some stupid things when she was a teenager. She was taken advantage of.'

'What happened?'

'Some sleazy photographer persuaded her to do a glamour photo shoot, told her he'd make her famous. The usual shite.' Finn shook his head. 'Cara believed him. But he never published the photos so she moved on. Then she got a break with Skylark and moved over here. She met Melissa at a fashion gig and she was so excited to have found a connection with me that she told her about us being brother and sister.'

Pippa forgot how to breathe.

'Melissa knows?'

'Aye. And when Melissa pretended to be her friend, Cara told her about the dodgy photos. She was worried they'd come back and bite her on the arse.' His lip curled into a distasteful snarl. 'Melissa must have thought all her Christmases had come at once. She'd been trying to persuade Aaron Janssen to go into business with her for ages when Rhys Bradford broke his leg, putting me in the driver's seat. She tracked down the photos and told me if we wanted Cara's past put to bed then I should let Skylark win the Gold Cup. Everyone knows Janssen is just using horseracing as a marketing strategy so Melissa fixing the Gold Cup for him to win allowed their business venture to go ahead.'

'Melissa fixed the Gold Cup?' Pippa cried. 'No way, Finn. She's not exactly my favourite person, sure, but not even she is capable of doing something so evil.'

'You'd better believe it.' He gave a mirthless chuckle. 'Melissa the Malicious. She's too ambitious for her own good - for anybody's good.'

'And Aaron Janssen? I can't believe he'd agree to any of this...' Her voice faded away at Finn's sceptical look. 'Really?'

'Racing's nothing more than a marketing tool to him, like I said. I don't know the exact agreement they came to. All I know is Melissa came to me - in fact you saw us.'

Pippa's jaw dropped as the memory flooded back.

'The night at the Turkish restaurant.'

Finn nodded.

'Yes. She showed me the photos - they were something brutal, Pippa. Really bad.' His face contorted in anguish. 'It would have ruined Cara's career just when it was picking up. Melissa told me she'd destroy the pictures if I let Skylark win the Gold Cup.'

'But he *didn't* win the Gold Cup!'

He shrugged and took a sip of his drink.

'I did all I could. Virtuoso was going to win it doin' handstands. When I looked around, the only other horse vaguely in contention was Skylark.

I put him wrong at the fence, scuppered our chances. No one saw Zodiac coming. What more could I do?'

Pippa stared, unable to answer. She swallowed. Fear for her safety was now replaced with fear for Finn.

'Wh-what happens now?' she said. 'You're up against Skylark tomorrow in the National. Are you going to make Peace Offering lose too?'

Finn shook his head with vehemence.

'No,' he frowned. 'I'm not doing it again. I did what Melissa asked. It's not my fault Skylark didn't win the Gold Cup. It's not my fault Janssen won't do this business deal with her now. The photos should have been destroyed already. Cara was just on the phone in a panic because apparently Melissa still has them. Cara thinks I should let Skylark win tomorrow.'

'You can't, Finn!' Pippa cried.

'I know, I know. That's what I was saying to her. The National is anyone's race. Feckin' hell, there's forty horses in it. Any of them could win. I'm not going to put my neck on the line again on the off-chance Janssen gets his name on the big screen.'

Pippa licked her lips. Finn was being so sincere. But he had been sincere in the past and look what had happened. Another terrifying thought occurred to her, making her throat contract.

'What about Jack?' she whispered. 'Does he know?'

'No. Jack is as straight as they come in racing.'

Her shoulders sagged as a sigh of relief washed through her.

'You have to tell him.'

'No!' Finn replied in horror. 'He'd have me hung, drawn and quartered if he ever found out.'

'But how are you going to get Melissa to destroy the photos? She's blackmailing you, Finn! Jack would help, I know he would,' she insisted.

Finn shook his head, a small smile on his face.

'You are too trusting, Pippa, you know. I didn't want to involve you in this, it's an ugly business. Best leave Jack out of it if we possibly can.'

'Leave Jack out of what exactly?' an icy voice from the doorway spoke up.

Finn choked on his drink. Pippa spilt hers all over her lap as Jack appeared through the open door.

'Oh, fuck,' she murmured.

He walked into the room and looked at them expectantly. Finn and Pippa shrunk in their seats like naughty schoolchildren.

'Well?' A muscle jumped in Jack's jaw and he tapped his fingers against his hips, making him seem even broader and more intimidating.

Pippa darted a look at Finn. He was sitting, dumbstruck in his chair, paralysed with fear. If they could keep Jack calm then he was sure to help, she reasoned with herself. Annoying him by keeping him in the dark would just make things worse.

'Finn?' she prompted gently. 'Tell him.'

The Irishman continued to stare at their boss.

Pippa realised he couldn't speak even if he wanted to. She glanced behind her at the door.

'Where's Melissa?' she asked.

Jack looked irritated at the diversion.

'Downstairs waiting for me to fetch you. We were supposed to be meeting for drinks, in case you've forgotten.'

'I - I got side-tracked. Here, you'd better sit down while we explain things.'

'Explain what?' he scowled.

Pippa gave him a meaningful look and he grudgingly sat down. She took a deep breath. She wasn't so sure now how he might take her accusing his girlfriend of blackmail and race-fixing.

'Right - um. Where shall we start?' She gave a nervous laugh and looked at Finn.

Now that Jack was sitting down and looking less imposing, Finn seemed to have regained some composure. He downed the rest of his whisky and soda in three giant gulps.

'I fixed the Gold Cup,' he announced. 'I fell off Virtuoso on purpose.'

Pippa held her breath and watched Jack for his reaction.

The trainer became very still. He stared silently at his jockey. His eyes were black.

'You fixed the Gold Cup?' he repeated.

'Yes.' Finn exhaled as if a burden of consciousness had shifted off his shoulders with his confession.

'You got the ride on the surest favourite in the biggest race of the season and you threw it away?' Jack's voice trembled with rage yet his posture remained still.

Finn nodded.

'After all the hard work everyone put in, you threw it away for corruption?' Jack's voice rose like an imminent volcanic eruption.

'He was being blackmailed though,' Pippa said quickly.

285

Jack transferred his glare to her.

'What for? By whom?'

She exchanged a nervous look with Finn.

'By Melissa,' she said in a quiet voice.

Jack's eyes widened and he sucked in his breath.

'Ridiculous. Absolutely fucking ridiculous! She *owns* Virtuoso, for God's sake!'

'Exactly,' Finn said. 'Which is how it was so easy for her.'

Jack stood up and shook a finger at Finn.

'Be careful what you say, Finn. You are on very shaky ground right now.'

Finn shrugged.

'In for a penny, in for a pound,' he said. 'I was being blackmailed by Melissa to lose on Virtuoso so that Skylark could win.'

Jack stepped backwards, as if he'd been struck and sat down with a thud.

Pippa remembered Melissa's reaction to the Gold Cup result and how she'd misinterpreted it.

'Remember how she was so upset, or distracted I think you said, after the Gold Cup?' she said.

Jack frowned, but nodded.

'It wasn't because Virtuoso had fallen. It was because Skylark got beaten on the line by Zodiac.' Her heart ached seeing the confusion rage in Jack's eyes.

'But why?'

'She'd done a deal with Aaron Janssen to combine their labels if she bought him some publicity.'

Jack blinked at her, trying to process the information then looked at Finn.

'How did you get involved then? What was she – they blackmailing you with?'

Pippa turned to Finn. This part of the story was for him to tell.

'...but now it turns out the photos are still at large,' Finn finished his tale for the second time.

Jack, who had sat wordless throughout, continued to stare at him.

Pippa twisted her hands in her jumper. She so wanted to shield Jack from the hurt, yet at the same time she desperately wanted him to believe Finn. His silence became too unbearable.

'You believe him, don't you?' she said.

Jack looked at her, an intense challenge sparking his eyes.

'Only one way to find out.' He dipped into his pocket and withdrew his phone. He keyed in a number and without taking his eyes off Pippa, waited while it rang.

'Hi Melissa – yes, I know you're still downstairs. Change of plan. Can you come up to Room 288? I'll explain when you get here... Just come up, will you? Thank you. Okay, see you in a minute.' He snapped his phone closed and looked at them both, like a courtroom judge awaiting the final witness to testify on their case.

Pippa gulped. She felt like an amateur swimmer who'd just survived one tidal wave, only to see another approaching. Above the deathly silence in which they sat awaiting Melissa's arrival, she could hear Jack grinding his teeth. She hazarded a look. He was watching her in a curious yet distracted way. His outward composure was surprisingly calm, only the movement of his jaw betrayed his tension. She bit her lip, wanting to apologise to him. She knew she had nothing to be sorry for – hell, all she had done was come round to raid the minibar. But the need to protect Jack was almost overwhelming.

Ridiculous! She mocked herself that he should need her protection. He was the most strong-minded, strong-willed man she knew, who could withstand the hardest knocks yet for some reason...

'Jack, are you in here?' Melissa called from the doorway.

His eyes flickered away from Pippa and he spoke over his shoulder.

'Yes. Come through, will you?'

Melissa, dressed in a blue and grey satin dress which wrapped itself seductively around her figure, stopped when she saw Pippa and Finn sitting with Jack.

'What's going on?' she said suspiciously.

'Just a small problem, which I'm hoping you might be able to clear up for me,' Jack said airily. 'Come sit down.'

Her eyes narrowed at Finn.

'No. I'll stand, thank you. We've got a dinner reservation to keep.'

'Suit yourself,' Jack replied. 'What do you know about a set of glamour photos of Cara Connolly?'

Melissa's chin lifted ever so slightly in defiance.

'Who?' she replied.

Jack shook his head and sighed.

Pippa noticed a trace of sadness filter through his posture.

'You're lying, Melissa,' he said.

'What? No, I'm not. I don't know what you're talking about.'

'There, you're doing it again. Every time you lie, you tilt your nose up. Yes, you do know.'

'That's just stupid, Jack,' Melissa chortled. 'What is going on? What lies have these two been feeding you?'

Pippa felt like a lab chimpanzee under Melissa's scrutiny.

'Agh, for feck's sake! You fixed the Gold Cup so Aaron Janssen would go into business with ye. Admit it!' Finn said, flicking a dismissive hand at her.

Melissa deigned an offended expression and took a backward step. She looked at Jack, her eyes wide.

'Jack, you don't believe that, do you? You don't think I had anything to do with Virtuoso falling, do you?'

A grim smirk tugged at the corner of Jack's mouth.

'Nobody said anything about Virtuoso, Mel.'

She gaped.

For the briefest of seconds, Pippa felt sorry for her, standing there alone with the three of them accusing her of blackmail.

'What I can't get my head round is why you would go to such extremes,' he continued. 'You let your father down, you let Virtuoso down... you let *me* down.'

Pippa looked at him in anguish, feeling his hurt, his betrayal. Glancing back at Melissa, she found the woman glaring at her. Her laser-beam of spite turned on Jack.

'Let *you* down? While you carry on with Little Miss Sunshine here? At least I can trust my business! It doesn't cheat on me!'

'What? I've never cheated on you!' Jack retorted.

'No? Maybe not sexually, you haven't. But you are so wrapped up in those fucking horses and your fucking secretary, who can do no fucking wrong in your eyes – how do you think that makes me feel?' Melissa shouted. 'So don't sit there on your high horse and tell me I've let *you* down! All I was doing was looking after my own –'

'Yes, but with no feckin' concern for anybody else!' Finn interrupted her. 'You can ruin Cara's career with those photos! I don't know if this has been one big bluff just so you can get what you want from Aaron Janssen, but are you such an evil bitch that you'd bring everybody else down with you when you fail?'

'If Cara hadn't been so stupid in the first place, I wouldn't be able to do this at all! She made her bed, she's got to lie –'

'She was seventeen!' Finn roared. 'She was a child! She's *still* a child! And you know it because you took full advantage of her innocence!' Trembling, he leapt to his feet. Melissa backed away. 'Now, where are those photographs? Give them to me!'

Jack got up and gently pushed Finn down again.

'I don't have them with me,' Melissa replied stubbornly.

Jack sighed and rested his hands on his hips.

'Where are they?'

Melissa sneered at him.

'Why should I tell you anything? Call yourself a boyfriend? Partners defend each other; they don't attack each other.'

'Melissa,' Jack said, his tone grave. 'You know blackmail is a criminal offence.'

Melissa gave a jeering laugh and threw a look at Finn.

'You wouldn't take me to court. All that expense, plus the publicity. The photos would be in the press before the case went to trial.'

Finn glared at her. Pippa knew as well as he did that she was right.

'Finn mightn't,' Jack said. 'But I might. Race-fixing is also an offence. You disrupted my business by making one of my horses lose. You lost me a huge amount of money in the process.'

'Oh, bullshit,' she spat. 'Firstly, the money in jump racing is piss-poor. Secondly, I don't think you'd do something like that. You're so intent on being the good boss...' She laughed mirthlessly in Pippa's direction. 'You wouldn't do that to Finn.'

Jack shook his head and took another step forward.

'Maybe you're right. I wouldn't want Finn to be exposed to publicity when both his and Cara's careers would be in jeopardy.' He paused and a smile creased his eyes. 'However, there is one person who would be mighty interested to hear what I have to say. He trusts me implicitly. I think you can vouch for his loyalty, can't you, since he's your father?'

Melissa's eyes widened and her lips parted in shock.

'You wouldn't,' she whispered.

Jack nodded.

'Yes, I would.'

Her spiteful eyes now filled with tears and she lifted a trembling hand to her chest.

'You can't,' she breathed. 'He'd disown me.'

Jack nodded in agreement, his expression of ironic resignation.

'You bet he would. The Mardling millions would go elsewhere and you know as well as I do, he wouldn't think twice about it once he was certain. Daughter or no daughter.'

'He couldn't. That's my inheritance. And my house, my car...'

'Your father doesn't associate with crooks. He wouldn't want to know you.' He paused. 'Where are the photos, Mel?' he said gently.

A lonely tear slid down her cheek.

'They're in my briefcase. In our room.'

'I think you should go get them so we can be done with this once and for all.'

Melissa nodded, hopelessness rounding her shoulders. She turned to exit the room.

'Oh, and while you're at it,' Jack called after her. 'Get your things packed. You'll need to speak to Reception, see if they've got any spare rooms available.'

Pippa watched her pause by the door then carry on into the hallway without answering. She couldn't help but feel pity for Melissa. What she had done was inexcusable, but the desperation on her face, in her words, her sad reliance on a material world (quite literally) – it was upsetting to witness. She looked at Jack to gauge how he was taking things.

His mouth was set in a grim line.

'I guess that's it then,' he concluded.

He walked over to the whisky bottle Finn had left out earlier and poured himself a couple of neat fingers. He threw it down his throat with a grunt.

'Just about,' Finn muttered. 'She's still got those photos.'

'She'll be back,' Jack assured her. 'The Mardling millions mean more to her than blackmailing you and your sister.'

Five minutes later, sure enough, Melissa walked back into the room. She held up a big manila envelope and tossed it onto the table.

'There you are,' she said, her pose dignified, like a proud Roman emperor surrendering his rule. 'That's all of them. I'm leaving now. I presume we won't hear any more about this?' She raised an eyebrow at Jack.

He shook his head.

'This is the end of it.'

'Good.'

She turned on her heel and strode out of the room. As the door clicked shut, marking Melissa's departure, their attention turned to the ominous yet inoffensive-looking envelope. Finn picked it up and peeked inside. He cringed away from the images, confirming they were the right ones. Getting up, he walked over to the fireplace and using a gas lighter, lit the corner and threw the envelope into the grate.

They watched in silence as the photographs curled up away from the bright flames until all that was left was a few charred frills.

'I should call Cara,' Finn said, looking up. 'To set her mind at rest.'

Jack nodded.

'Good idea.' He turned to Pippa. 'We've missed our dinner reservation and to be honest, I don't have much of an appetite. Do you mind if I cancel on you?'

Realising he probably wanted to be on his own, to straighten things out in his mind, she shook her head.

'Not at all. I think it's probably for the best anyhow. I'm going to head back to my room.'

'Me too. We'll leave you in peace, Finn. We've got a big day ahead of us tomorrow. Hey, cheer up. It's all over now. We won't mention it again, okay?'

The Irishman nodded and attempted a smile, but a sadness still remained in his eyes.

Pippa noticed they were focused on her as she got up to leave with Jack.

# Chapter Forty

Bursts of gusty rain spattered the hotel dining room windows the next morning. Pippa gazed sullenly at the heavy grey outlook, ignoring the full English breakfast in front of her.

'Not hungry?' Jack prompted between mouthfuls.

Pippa shook her head. She'd never felt less like eating. Excitement and fear churned its own recipe in her stomach.

'Have some toast at least,' he said, pushing the silver toast rack towards her. 'You'll need to eat something. It's going to be a long day.'

With a reluctant hand, she selected a slice and spread some butter and blackcurrant jam on it. She watched Jack swab a hash brown in egg yolk and pop the last forkful of food into his mouth.

'How can you eat? Aren't you nervous?'

Jack shrugged and patted his mouth with his napkin.

'So-so. I'll be more nervous come four o'clock.'

Pippa groaned.

'God. Seven more hours. I don't know why I'm doing this, Jack. This is killing me.'

'Don't you remember?' he smiled. 'Dave Taylor is why you're doing this.'

'Bloody Uncle Dave,' she said, shaking her head. 'I wish I'd never found that piece of paper.'

He patted her hand.

'Think of it this way: in seven and a quarter hours it'll all be over.'

'What do I do until then? I couldn't sleep last night so I've finished my book. Oh, I wish I had Tash here.'

'Where is she? I thought she was coming.'

Pippa shook her head.

'She texted me last night to say her boss is making them work all weekend.'

'Bosses, eh? Who needs 'em?'

She managed a smile at Jack's encouragement.

'Yeah. Nothing but trouble, they are.'

He lifted an eyebrow.

'Watch it. You won't get your summer bonus if you slag off this boss.'

292

'Doesn't look much like summer out there,' she said, nodding her head towards the window.

'No, but it's all good. The heavier the ground, the better for us. They say the storm is moving south so it should be clear by lunchtime. How are you getting home if Tash isn't coming? You were both going to drive back to Helensvale, weren't you?'

'The same way I came, I guess. Catch the train.'

'Rubbish. I'll take you home.' His eyes twinkled. 'It's on my way.'

Pippa weighed up his offer for a moment. Five hours on the train with three or four stops along the route compared with three hours in a warm car with Jack? No contest.

'You sure?'

'Of course. Although,' he said with a grave expression, 'if we win, I'll probably be over the limit. In which case, we're going to have to book in here for another night.'

Pippa sighed.

'If we win? God, it seems impossible now. The National was so much easier to win six months ago.'

Jack chuckled.

'We're not without a shout. But if we're to have any chance then I'd better get going. Finn and I have to get over to Aintree to walk the course.'

The prospect of doing something - anything - made Pippa perk up.

'Can I come along?'

Jack hesitated.

'Probably best you don't.'

'Why?'

'Well, it's wet out there and -' He frowned. 'And it's a long way to walk. The course is over two miles long.'

True, Pippa admitted silently, it didn't sound particularly attractive yet the thought of seven hours of doing virtually nothing was even less becoming.

'I don't mind.'

'No, really. Just take your time getting ready. There's a whole card of races before the National to take your mind off things. I'll call you and pick you up before lunch.'

Her shoulders sagged. Great, now even Jack didn't want her around. Fear, anxiety, despondency - everything that comes up on a manic depressive's checklist, stirred inside her.

Jack reached over and tilted her chin so she was looking at him. His blue eyes implored hers.

'Pippa, it's going to be okay. Trust me.'

His concern acted like a comforter on a cold night. For a frightening moment, she thought she was going to cry. His hand slid along her jaw and he cupped her cheek. If his gaze hadn't been so intense, she'd have been tempted to close her eyes against the warmth of his fingers.

'Do you trust me?' he asked, his voice low.

She gave him a faint nod.

'I do.'

A smile, almost bashful, tugged at Jack's lips.

'Then trust me now. Stop worrying. No matter how adamant you might have been about entering Peace Offering in the National, we still wouldn't be here if I didn't think he was capable of running a good race.'

Pippa nodded again and managed a brave smile.

'You trying to take the credit if he wins now?'

'There now, that's more like the Pippa we all know and love –' Jack halted abruptly. His Adam's Apple rose uneasily as he swallowed. His hand fell away and he wrung his fingers together. 'Time I got going.' He rose from his seat, jogging the table in his haste and dropping his napkin. 'I'll call you later.'

'Okay,' she croaked in reply. With a self-conscious frown, she cleared her throat, trying to quell her swirling hormones at the same time.

She watched him stride away, bumping into another table as he left the room.

With his exit, the temperature seemed to Pippa to drop ten degrees. She hugged her arms around her, wanting more than anything for lunchtime to arrive so she could find comfort in his broad-shouldered support once more.

She turned her attention to the plasma television hanging on the wall. A news team was previewing the big race of the afternoon.

'May I take your plates?' a waiter interrupted her.

'Yes. Thank you. It was very nice. I just don't have much of an appetite today.'

The waiter began stacking the dishes and coffee cups into a pile.

'Are you racing later?' he asked and nodded towards the television.

'Yes. My horse is running in the National.'

He looked impressed.

'Really? Which one?'

'Peace Offering.'

'Oh.' He resumed his stacking.

Pippa's heart drooped. The waiter didn't appear so impressed now. She turned back to the screen. A damp-looking presenter stood in front of a huge steeplechase fence.

'This jump is the infamous Becher's Brook. From this angle, it looks simple enough at a height of four feet ten inches. But if we go round to the landing side, past the brook, we find an angled drop of a further ten inches on the other side of the fence and we can see why this fence has claimed so many victims over the years. Most jockeys try go wide as the drop is less severe the further out you are.'

Pippa's mouth went dry as she absorbed the suicidal obstacle.

'To make it even more difficult, horses and riders must jump it *twice* during the race. To raise safety and welfare this jump has already been modified as have some of the other jumps so that the drop is smaller than in previous years. But the risk is now that horses will subsequently jump it faster and be in more danger of falling. Over to you, Bryan.'

The camera cut to another reporter standing in front of a different fence.

'Thanks, Sarah. I'm now in front of the Chair, the tallest and broadest of all the fences in the National,' Bryan announced. He stepped down into the ditch on the take-off side and was dwarfed by the wall of spruce branches. 'The actual fence is daunting enough at five feet three inches high and three feet wide. But this ditch which I'm standing in is *another* six feet wide. I guess the good news is that this jump only needs to be navigated once.'

'Oh, God,' uttered Pippa in a trembling whisper. 'No wonder Jack didn't want me to walk the course.'

'What's that?' the waiter said.

Pippa's fearful eyes met his.

'That – that *Chair* and that *Brook* are enormous. How can any horse be expected to jump those?'

The waiter shrugged and picked up the plates.

'All I know is that the Grand National has been run since the mid-eighteen hundreds and there's always been a winner. Good luck.'

'Thanks,' Pippa murmured to his departing figure.

She swallowed and said a small prayer for Peace Offering and Finn.

\*

'You look very pale. You sure you're okay?' Jack asked again.

He and Pippa stood with a clear view of Aintree Racecourse from the Owners and Trainers roof terrace. Pippa tore her eyes from the horses circling before the Start and smiled.

'Just nervous.'

'You placed your bets?' he asked.

'Twenty pounds to win,' she replied, crossing her fingers. 'Will get a thirteen hundred return on that at sixty-six-to-one.'

Jack snorted and shook his head.

'You'll get a much bigger payout than that if he wins. Think something in the region of half a million pounds and you'll be closer to the mark.'

Pippa gulped and her stomach disappeared.

'You think we can do it?' she croaked.

'We've only got thirty jumps and thirty-nine other horses to contend with.' He flashed a smile at Pippa's saucer-eyes. 'If you removed those from the equation, I'd say we'd be in with a shout.'

'Oh, God,' she said, turning her attention back to the imminent race.

Peace Offering was being jogged in a circle by Finn with some other horses to warm up.

As she watched, the sprawling course, which had lain in murky shadow since the morning's storm had passed on, suddenly became bathed in light as the sun broke through the cloud. Pippa had never been a particularly spiritual person, even in the most desperate of situations, but as the sun glinted off the wet turf, she felt her anxiety subside. Dave Taylor's presence enveloped her, filling her with a new comforting confidence.

The starter climbed his rostrum and the forty horses formed a semi-organised wall, jogging towards the tape.

'We can do it,' Pippa whispered. 'Peace Offering can do it.'

She felt Jack's fingers thread through her own and give her hand a gentle squeeze.

'That's more like it. We *can* do it... if Finn keeps his mind on the job.'

Jack's last words were drowned out by the roar of the crowd as the starter let the horses go. Pippa wasn't sure if she'd heard him correctly. She didn't have time to ponder it though. Her pulse quickened as the stampeding horses charged towards the first fence. Her green and red-striped racing colours could be spotted towards the rear of the field, two off the rail. With caution thrown well and truly to the wind, the horses tackled the first obstacle.

'Firedrake leads them over the first, alongside Faustian and Alpine Pass on the far outside,' the commentator droned. 'We've lost a couple in midfield –'

Pippa's heart thundered in her ears as she tried to pick out Finn among the kaleidoscope of racing colours.

'Shadow Captain and Gunsmoke are fallers as they now go on to Fence Two!' the commentator continued.

The mass of horses obliterated Pippa's view of the next fence as they soared over it like a Mexican wave.

'How are we doing?' she squeaked, unable to tear her eyes away from the race.

'Not bad, not bad,' Jack muttered. 'I wanted him wider out than this early on, but fingers crossed he won't get interfered with by any fallers.'

She swallowed a moan as the spread of Fence Three claimed three more victims.

'Which one's Becher's Brook?'

'Fence Six and Twenty-Two.'

'Oh, God.' She clenched Jack's hand in hers.

The depleted field thundered over the next two fences, inducing a small sigh of relief from Pippa after each as Peace Offering cleared them both. The remaining runners, spread across the course, now edged towards the inside rail as Becher's Brook and the sharp turn immediately afterwards faced them. She winced as Peace Offering was crowded.

'Give him space,' growled Jack. 'He can't see the fence!'

Pippa bit down hard on her lip as Peace Offering hurtled towards Becher's Brook without a clear view.

'Oh!' she moaned as, at the last second, a gap appeared.

Peace Offering gathered himself for the leap and took off. Finn let the reins slip through his fingers as he leant back to counter-balance the steep drop on landing. Pippa clutched Jack's arm as the horse in front of their team over-balanced and somersaulted over. Finn pulled his mount wide. He ricocheted off another runner, but avoided the faller.

'They're over Becher's,' the commentator burbled, 'and we've lost Ciel de Nuit, Bigger Bang, Warrior's Gate and Picture This is also down. On to the Fence Seven, the Foinavon Fence, and Firedrake still leads to Faustian in second. Skylark is kept handy on the inside in third...'

By comparison, the Foinavon Fence looked a doddle after the intimidation of Becher's Brook yet two horses still managed to unseat their jockeys. Pippa leaned into Jack as the runners veered towards the inside rail.

'What are they doing?' she cried as she saw Finn direct Peace Offering at the next jump at a forty-five degree angle.

'It's the Canal Turn,' Jack replied. 'You have to take it at an angle otherwise you lose too much ground on landing.'

'They might not land at all if they take those angles!' She exhaled as her horse rose over the fence and skidded round the turn.

'Good, Finn!' Jack muttered, squeezing Pippa's hand.

Taking comfort from his confidence, she scrutinised the remaining runners before they tackled the next. Peace Offering, by doing nothing but jump accurately, was now running in eighth place, his long neck stretched out as his reaching stride ate up the ground. He pricked his ears and lifted his head as they neared Fence Nine. He took off well away from the fence.

Pippa's knees weakened as she watched him twist over the brook on landing. Her chest tightened as she continually sucked in her breath. Her attention was focused unwaveringly on her horse scrambling to stay upright.

She exhaled. Two or three horses rushed past Peace Offering as his awkward jump slowed him to barely a canter, but she didn't care. He hadn't fallen. He was still in the race.

Five jumps later, they were even more so in the race. The one-time leader, Firedrake, had been pulled up shortly followed by two other front-running contenders who put themselves out of the prize. The crowd's cheering quadrupled as the remaining rivals galloped past the stands for the first time.

'Oh, God, it's the Chair next, isn't it?' Pippa quailed. She darted a quick glance at Jack to see if he was as concerned as she.

His mouth was curved into an unconscious smile and his eyes danced with excitement as he lived the race.

'He's jumping well. He's loving those Aintree fences,' he said.

With Faustian now at the helm, followed by Skylark, the horses streamed down the track towards the formidable Chair. The fifth-placed Corazon crumpled on landing and Pippa groaned. Peace Offering was heading right into their stricken path.

'Look out, Finn!' she cried through gritted teeth.

Horse and jockey took off, the image of united co-ordination. Peace Offering stretched higher and wider to clear the yawning ditch and wall of spruce. Pippa could almost see the surprise register in Finn's body language when he caught sight of the fallen horse on the landing side.

'Please God, help them.'

They touched down a stride away from Corazon. Peace Offering took half a stride and took off again, hurdling the half-risen faller.

'Thank you, thank you, thank you,' Pippa babbled. She wondered how many other repented sins God would allow her. Another fifteen fences' worth?

Once more, the horses passed the point of departure and across the Melling Road, a much depleted and wearier-looking field though. Pippa's already hammering heart stepped up the pace as she saw Finn begin to coax Peace Offering faster.

In a steady rhythm, they moved forward, closing the gap on the five horses in front. The only one she knew was Skylark. She listened keenly to the commentator listing them over the twentieth obstacle.

'Faustian leads by half a length to Skylark on the inside. It's five lengths back to Tarock in third, in company with Saint Blaise. Then another three lengths to Rossroe Boy in fifth. Peace Offering races in sixth with the favourite, Okay Oklahoma, running just behind...'

'Who?' Pippa cried. 'Isn't Skylark the favourite? I thought he was the horse we had to beat?'

'At sixty-six-to-one, there are quite a few horses we have to beat,' Jack murmured. 'This'll test them though – here comes Becher's again.'

Six minutes in and Pippa felt drained. She could only imagine what Finn and Peace Offering were feeling. How could those weary legs withstand the six foot descent being asked of them? She dared not blink. Peace Offering gathered himself for the leap, looking anything but tired.

'Too big! Too big!' hissed Jack.

Finn threw his weight back as if his life depended on it. He lay almost perpendicular to Peace Offering's back, trying to correct his horse's over-exertion. The jarring ground came up to meet them. Overbalanced, Peace Offering stumbled forward with his nose scraping along the churned turf, his hooves desperate to find a footing.

'Please God, I promise never to sneak any more cigarettes and I'll admit to Tash all the ones I've had,' Pippa whispered in desperation.

God approved.

Peace Offering regained his stride and beneath Finn's urgings set off to recapture their lost ground. The pair brushed through the next jump and with expert judgement, tackled the Canal Turn. Finding a second wind, Peace Offering closed the gap between him and the front five. Rossroe Boy's bid in fifth place petered out as he was passed in midair over Valentine's Brook, six from home.

Pippa clutched Jack's arm to her like a life-ring.

'Faustian relinquishes his long time lead five out!' the commentator cried, his voice rising an octave as the race neared its conclusion. 'Skylark takes it up! Saint Blaise and Tarock are in a scrap for third. Peace Offering has made good ground and races three lengths behind. Here comes Okay Oklahoma!'

'Oh-god-oh-god-oh-god-oh-god,' Pippa squealed as the horses raced down the side of the course towards the grandstands.

On the big screen, the camera was focused on the favourite, ranging upsides of Peace Offering. Finn glanced across at his rival and lowered his posture. Peace Offering's limitless stamina reserves kicked in and he pulled clear again. Okay Oklahoma's jockey pushed his mount along, his whip fanning alongside. But the favourite couldn't rise to the Aspen Valley duo's challenge.

Three from the finish, the ditch caught out Tarock. His jockey was pitched over his shoulder into the turf. Behind them, Peace Offering fair hurdled the obstacle. Within a couple of strides, he drew up alongside Saint Blaise.

'Go on, Peace Offering!' Pippa yelled, her nervous excitement bursting out in an adrenalin-filled roar. She watched Finn scrub his hands up and down his horse's neck. 'Go on, Finn!'

In front, Skylark scrambled over the second last.

'He's on empty, look!' Jack said. 'That's just about the smallest fence in the whole race. COME ON, PEACE OFFERING!' he bellowed.

With Tarock, the loose horse keeping him company, Finn steered his mount towards the second last. Faustian jumped slowly, surrendering second place as Peace Offering slogged over the jump.

'Oh, my God. I don't believe this.' Jack raked a hand through his hair. 'He's bloody going to do it. Look, Pippa!'

'I know! I know! I'm looking!' she cried, jumping up and down.

Skylark wobbled and ran out of energy like a power cut. Peace Offering's long stride ate up the margin between them and he stole past the huge chestnut.

Pippa screamed in hysterical excitement.

Only one fence left to jump and her horse was pulling clear. Only Tarock, his reins and stirrups flapping wildly, kept pace on their outside.

She held her breath as the Grand National offered its last challenge to them. In the centre of the track, Finn crouched low in his saddle and let Peace Offering gather himself for a final leap.

With her gaze trained on the pair, she didn't notice at first Tarock changing direction. Then she gasped. The loose horse, looking for a way to avoid the jump altered his route and galloped diagonally across Peace Offering's path. Finn pulled his horse to the inside to avoid a collision. The horses' shoulders slammed against each other as Peace Offering was forced to take off.

The air in Pippa's lungs evaporated as she watched a virtual nightmare become a surreal reality.

The impact was too great.

Despite Finn's desperate attempts to counter-balance his mount, Peace Offering's momentum carried his hindquarters over his shoulder.

'Oh!' Pippa gasped. Her eyes pricked with tears as her horse slammed into the ground and flipped over. Finn, curled into a protective ball, rolled away.

'Fuck,' Jack muttered.

With something bordering on relief, Pippa saw Peace Offering quickly stagger to his feet and look around. His ears were pricked to the sound of approaching hoofbeats from the other side of the fence.

'No, no, no! Move, Peace Offering!' Pippa cried, realising Skylark was still in the running to win.

After giving himself a full-body shake, Peace Offering ambled away, looking no more bothered than if he was in his paddock on a Sunday afternoon. The tank-like frame of Skylark appeared on his horizon, rising over the last fence. The two rivals looked just as surprised to see each other. Peace Offering whipped his tail in like a naughty dog and hopped out of his path. Skylark twisted as he descended and landed heavily. His jockey, already unbalanced by the awkward jump, bounced out of the saddle and out of the race. All that was left was for Faustian to navigate the last and canter wearily beneath the post to claim his Grand National victory.

Pippa blinked, shell-shocked. It had been too good to be true, which was why when it had started to happen, it had felt so marvellous. She looked up at Jack. She saw the disappointment on his face. What marvel

301

had been promised to them approaching the last had been mercilessly snatched away. It made it all the worse to bear.

'You win some, you lose some, I guess,' she said.

'Yes. I guess,' Jack replied. He gave her a grim smile and patted her on the shoulder. 'Come on. Let's go see how the fallen heroes are.'

# Chapter Forty-One

'So what sort of summer bonus were you thinking of giving me?' Pippa asked, sauntering over to Jack's desk and sitting on the edge.

Jack leaned back in his chair and folded his arms in contemplation.

'What sort of bonus would satisfy you?' he countered.

Pippa dipped her face and looked at him under flirtatious eyelashes.

'Oh, I could think of various ways you could satisfy me, Jack.'

'Is that so, Miss Taylor?' A sly smile played on his lips. Getting to his feet, he stood before her. He fingered the top button of his shirt. 'Would this do?' he said in a husky voice, popping the button open.

Pippa reached forward and, hooking her fingers through his belt straps, pulled him towards her. She pulled his shirt out of his jeans and began unbuttoning from the bottom. Her fingers met his halfway before sliding beneath to feel the contours of his chest.

'We're nearly home,' Jack said.

'Hmm?' Pippa questioned blissfully massaging his torso.

'Time to wake up. We're nearly home.'

Jack, standing with his chest exposed, shrunk into a vacuum and was replaced by a dark rain-splattered windscreen. Pippa blinked herself awake. She glanced across at Jack in the driver's seat. A fiery heat flooded her face and neck.

'What?'

'Sorry to wake you. We've just driven past Helensvale.'

'Okay,' she squeaked. She turned her face away and looked out the passenger window, trying to hide her blushes.

'Did you have a good nap?'

The image of a half-dressed Jack sprang to mind and her ears began to burn again.

'Yes, thanks,' she managed. 'Was I asleep long?'

'You've been out since we left Liverpool.'

'Wow. Guess I was more tired than I imagined.'

'Probably done you good. Feeling rested?' He looked across at her with a smile.

A horrifying thought occurred to her.

'I wasn't talking in my sleep, was I?'

'No, you looked very peaceful.'

Pippa exhaled with relief, but still couldn't rid herself of the feeling of Jack's chest beneath her fingers. Having a saucy dream about someone was embarrassing enough, but having it *in their presence* was even worse.

She watched in silence as the Land Rover's blurred headlights lit up the tree-lined avenue, leading to Hazyvale House.

'Horrible weather,' she said as they made their slow progress through the murk.

Jack grunted in agreement.

'It's that storm we had earlier on,' he said, raising his voice above the hammering rain on the roof. 'I was hoping we were going to miss it.'

He swung the wheel and the Land Rover bumped down Hazyvale's driveway. The house, shrouded in darkness, welcomed Pippa home as the car triggered the security light outside the front door.

'I'll get your case out for you,' Jack offered, switching off the engine.

Thanking him, Pippa stretched and opened the door. She gave a squeal as the icy rain splattered her. Holding her coat over her head, she scampered through the puddles to the relative shelter of the front door with Jack hard on her heels.

'Ooh, keys, keys, where are you?' she muttered, scrabbling through her bag.

'Bloody hell, Pippa. I'm getting soaked here. Couldn't you have found them when we were in the car?'

Pippa giggled. Brandishing her house keys, she forced open the door and led the way in. She flicked on the hall light. She grinned at Jack, noticing his hair stuck to his head and raindrops rolling off his nose.

Jack smiled.

'You look like a drowned rat,' he said.

'So do you,' she laughed.

Jack put her overnight bag on the floor and rubbed his hands together.

'Well, here we are.' Through the open door, he looked unenthusiastically at the Land Rover, bathed in liquid silver beneath the glare of the security light.

Perhaps it was his bedraggled appearance or the heaviness of his eyelids, but Pippa paused from sending him out into the night again. She remembered the treacherous conditions on the unlit roads from Hazyvale to Aspen Valley when Mother Nature decided to flex her muscles.

'Would you like to - um - wait until the storm passes?' she asked in a shy voice.

A flicker of relief in Jack's eyes was quickly camouflaged as he shook his head.

'No, I'd better get back.'

His hesitation emboldened Pippa.

'You're tired and I bet you haven't eaten anything since breakfast,' she said. 'I've got some spag bol I can heat up – it's not much, but you need to eat. And the storm will hopefully have passed by the time we're finished.'

Jack wavered.

'I'll be home soon enough.'

Pippa wasn't sure whether it was her concern over his well-being on the dangerous country roads or her desire to remain in Jack's presence, but she latched onto his weakening argument.

'In weather like this, it'll take you ages to get home. Come on, have a break. Here, give me your jacket. It's sopping.'

'Okay, thanks,' he replied with a defeated sigh. He let Pippa slip his jacket off his shoulders.

A smile warmed her faced as she draped it over a radiator. She led him through to the lounge then the kitchen, switching on the lights as she went. Jack appraised his surroundings as she delved into the fridge for a bottle of wine and a Tupperware container of spaghetti bolognaise.

'You've certainly put your touch on this place,' he said.

Pippa paused.

'Do you like it?'

'Very nice. It must be nearly done now.'

Pippa popped the food into the microwave and retrieved a couple of glasses from a cupboard. She nodded, a hint of sadness creeping over her.

'Yes. It's pretty much set to go on the market now.'

Jack took the bottle of wine from her and popped the cork.

'The lads did a fantastic job of clearing up the garden,' she went on. 'I was terrified each time Billy picked up the axe or the shears. He was so keen to fix everything up.'

Jack chuckled and poured out the wine. Pippa leant against the kitchen counter and sighed. Maybe she was just tired, but her great country adventure now seemed to be ending. The Grand National had been run. The house was ready to be sold. The racing season was nearly over...

'I'll be sad to leave this place,' she said, staring down at her drink. 'It's very much a home, you know? And I know that when it comes to selling

Hazyvale, it'll more than likely be to city weekenders.' She looked up at Jack. 'It won't be a real *home* to them.'

Jack nodded, his expression sombre. A frown settled on his brow.

'Do you have to sell it to weekenders?'

'Who else will buy it?'

'Someone local? You might have to wait a while for the right buyer, but you don't have to sell it straight away.' His frown deepened. 'Do you?'

His troubled eyes wrenched at Pippa's heart as she tried to sort through the layers of hidden possibilities in his question. The microwave beeped, making her jump. She hastily turned her attention to stirring the tomato paste into the pasta before popping it back into the microwave. When she looked back at Jack, his expression was as readable as a blank page.

'You said Billy was pretty keen to fix everything up,' he said. 'Did he like the place?'

'I think so.'

Jack looked thoughtful.

'It might be a longshot, but if he and Emmie are starting a family, they're going to need their own place. If you want Hazyvale to be someone's home, they'd be just right. If they could afford it, that is.'

Pippa momentarily brightened then sagged at the mention of money.

'Yeah, it all comes down to money in the end. As much as I'd like Billy and Emmie to live here, I can't afford to sell this place below market value really.' She shrugged and went to get some cheese out of the fridge.

Jack yawned and rubbed his eyes, making her smile in sympathy.

'Why don't you go relax in the lounge? I'll bring the food through when it's ready.'

Jack nodded gratefully.

'I might fall asleep on your couch though.'

When Pippa joined him five minutes later, balancing two bowls of pasta and a bottle of wine in her hands, she was surprised to see Jack very much awake. He was standing in front of a picture on the wall. He turned at the sound of her entrance and hurried to clear a space on the coffee table in front of the couch.

Once they were seated and tucking into their dinner, Jack interrupted the silence.

'It's good.'

'Thanks. It's only reheated pasta though,' Pippa replied, concentrating on taming tails of spaghetti around her fork.

'No. I meant the picture,' he said, motioning towards the painting he'd been studying when Pippa had walked in.

Pippa gulped. *Morning Stables* gazed down at them from within its wooden frame. She hadn't reckoned on Jack ever seeing this very private piece of art. She felt his eyes on her as she sifted through her food.

'Thanks,' she mumbled.

'You captured the scene very well,' he went on. 'It's Aspen Valley all over. But you decided to keep it instead of hanging it in the office.'

Pippa glanced up at his enquiring tone and decided to play it cool... if she could. She gave a nonchalant shrug.

'I liked it,' she said. 'I thought it would look good here in the lounge.'

She waited for him to mention the image of himself in the middle of the picture.

'It's – it's a very personal painting,' he said contemplatively. Whatever he saw in Pippa's expression must have affirmed he was on the right track because he nodded. 'Peace Offering, there in the background,' he said, pointing vaguely. 'There's more to this picture than an average racing yard.'

Pippa succumbed beneath his understanding.

'I painted it when I was doubting myself – doubting Peace Offering,' she admitted. 'I was ready to pack it all in.'

'Good thing you didn't,' Jack smiled.

'We didn't win the National though.'

'Maybe not this time, but he's certain to be at the top of the market for next year's race. We know he's capable of winning it.' He gave a chuckle. 'And we wouldn't have known that if it hadn't been for your relentless faith in him.'

'I don't know about relentless,' Pippa said with a sheepish smile. '*Blind* more like it. I didn't know what the hell I was getting myself into when I tore up to Doncaster to pull him out of the sale.'

Jack grinned.

'Aren't you glad you did though?'

Pippa nodded slowly as she tried to decide. The stress and anguish of the past few months was unlike anything she'd ever experienced before, but compared to the drab existence she had been living previously, she wouldn't have had it any other way.

'Yeah, it's been a helluva ride.'

Jack put his empty bowl on the coffee table.

'I needed that,' he sighed, patting his stomach. He glanced at the window where rivulets of rainwater still coursed a passage down the glass. 'Looks like it's beginning to ease up. I should make a move.'

'Okay.' Pippa hid her disappointment by collecting their bowls and glasses into a tidy pile.

At the door she handed him his still damp jacket.

'Drive safely,' she said needlessly.

'I will. And I'll see you bright and early on Monday,' he smiled. He opened the front door, letting in a gust of cool air.

Pippa hugged her arms around her.

'Thanks, Jack,' she said.

He gave her a brusque nod.

'Thank you, Pippa.' At his gruff words, her heart leapt in her chest. 'Today's the closest I've ever come to winning the Grand National.'

Her heart deflated.

'See you Monday then,' she said.

'Until Monday.'

Leaning against the closed front door, Pippa listened to the growl of Jack's Land Rover fade away until just the patter of rain outside filled the void. She heaved a noisy sigh and wandered back into the lounge. She didn't feel at all tired now. Instead a restlessness gripped her. She sat down and switched on the television, but turned it off with an irritable tut after a few seconds. She tapped the arm of the couch as she contemplated what she could do to occupy herself. She couldn't paint when she was this distracted so that was out of the question. She hoisted herself to her feet and went into the kitchen to check her mobile for messages from Tash. She pulled a face when, no matter what angle she directed it towards, no signal lit the screen.

'I'll have a bath,' she muttered. 'That might make me relax.'

She skipped up the stairs to the bathroom and set the pipes groaning as she spun open the taps. The room was soon clouded with steam, laced with a creamy aroma of bath oils. Undressing, she hesitated as the roar of the taps was interrupted by a muffled knocking noise downstairs. She shook her head, ridiculing her imagination. It was just the hot water filling the cold pipes.

A second, more demanding set of knocks sounded. This time she was sure she wasn't imagining things. She switched off the bath taps and pulled on her jeans and top before bounding down the stairs. She opened the front door just as Jack raised his fist to knock again.

'Jack?'

'Hey,' he said, sounding less than thrilled. Rain slithered down his cheeks and webbed his eyelashes together. 'Slight problem. Can I come in?'

Pippa realised, in her surprise, that she was just staring at him standing in the rain.

'Yes, of course. Are you okay?'

Jack stepped over the threshold, dripping rainwater onto the mat.

'The road is flooded. It's too high for even the Land Rover to get through.'

'Oh, God. Here, come into the warm. You look frozen.'

Jack peeled off his jacket and shook his hair, spraying Pippa with droplets.

'Sorry to gatecrash on you like this,' he sighed. 'The storm's moved away, but it might take a while for the water levels to drop. Do you mind if I wait it out here for an hour or so?'

Pippa's pulse raced and she swallowed.

'Course you can. Come through.'

Jack stepped out of his sodden shoes and followed Pippa through to the lounge. Under the glare of the electric lighting, fatigue was etched across his face.

'Would you like a coffee?' she offered.

'Think I'm going to need it,' he answered gratefully.

He followed Pippa through to the kitchen, where she filled the kettle and set it to boil.

'Are the roads really bad?'

Jack nodded.

'This one especially since it's in a valley. Hopefully, it won't get completely washed away.' He gave her a wry smile. 'Otherwise your little car won't even get you into Helensvale.'

'Wow, I've never been stranded before,' Pippa replied. 'I locked myself out of the flat in London once, but I was able to kip at Tash's. Out here, you're really isolated. Should I have been collecting tinned foods in preparation for this?'

Jack shook his head with a smile.

'The joys of country-living.'

Pippa paused as she reached for a coffee mug and bit her lip. Did she have the nerve to say it? The poor man looked exhausted. Waiting out another hour on the off-chance that the roads would become passable would just add to his misery. Dare she suggest the obvious?

With her back turned to Jack, she squeezed her eyes shut.

'Um, you could always stay here if you like,' she mumbled.

With the kettle roaring and the ensuing silence from Jack, she wasn't sure if he'd heard her or not. She looked to him for a reaction. He was staring at her.

'I mean, I have a spare bedroom. I just need to get some bedding out and we won't need to worry...' Her voice petered out as her courage evaporated. She frowned to herself. What a foolish thing to suggest! What on earth had made her say that? Why did she never think things through before opening her big–

'Okay. If you don't mind, of course,' Jack interrupted her mental self-flagellation.

'Really?' she said, unable to keep the surprise out of her voice. 'I mean, okay, I'll go get some sheets out and... stuff.'

'I hope I'm not putting you out,' Jack said, looking awkward. 'You didn't have plans for tonight or anything?'

'No, no. I was just about to get in the bath, that's all. That's why I didn't hear you knocking at first.'

'Don't let me interrupt then. Please. If you show me where the sheets are, I can sort myself out.'

A playful smile tugged at Pippa's mouth as she realised just how ultra-polite they were being with one another.

'Come. I'll show you.'

In the darkness, Pippa lay on her back, staring up at the ceiling. The "soothing and restoring qualities" promised on the bottle of sweet almond oil had failed to deliver during her bath. Her every sense was keenly attuned to Jack's presence in the adjoining room. She threw off her duvet and fanned herself. Maybe she was coming down with a fever. The cool night air seeped through the silken material of her nightshirt, relieving her burning body.

The movements in the neighbouring room had stilled. Jack must already be asleep. She tried to distract herself in the hope she would drift off. Was spontaneous human combustion really possible? It certainly felt that way. Her tongue stuck to her palate as she swallowed, trying to moisten her dry throat. If she was coming down with a fever, she would need to keep hydrated.

Really?

Actually she wasn't sure, but it sounded good. And a glass of cold water was very tempting right now.

Switching on her beside lamp, she eased herself out of bed and tiptoed to the door. Her gaze flickered towards Jack's closed door as she slipped out into the hall. A large shadow blocked the bathroom doorway.

She screamed, her nerves already at breaking point. The shadow jumped back in surprise.

'Jesus Christ!' Jack hissed. 'You want to give me a bloody heart attack?'

'Oh!' Pippa fell back against the hallway wall, placing a soothing hand over her thundering heart. 'I thought you were already asleep.'

From the dim light shed from her bedroom, she noticed he was dressed only in his jeans. She gulped, unable to resist appraising his half-naked body.

'What are you doing?' he asked, raking a hand through his hair.

Pippa's focus snapped back to his shadowed face.

'What?'

'Why are you sneaking around?'

'Oh! I was just getting myself some water. I - I was - er - hot.' She flapped a nonchalant hand at nothing in particular.

Jack shifted uncomfortably and he looked at his bare feet.

'Yeah, me too.'

A sizzling silence fell as they stood opposite each other by the bathroom door. Butterflies began to flit in her stomach.

'Anyway,' Jack said at last. 'Back to bed, I suppose.'

Pippa moved to the side to let him pass, unable to breathe. He stepped forward, the shaft of light from her bedroom lighting his face. She sucked in her breath as her mental colour wheel at last stopped spinning.

'Brandeis blue,' she breathed.

'What?' he frowned.

A feeling of relief, like she'd been wracking her brain for an answer for ages and had finally found it, overcame her awkwardness. She smiled and reached out her hand to his face.

'Your eyes. They're Brandeis blue.'

A muscle jumped in his jaw as he digested her words. Pippa longed to calm it. Her outstretched hand settled on his cheek as if she could smooth out the tension. His stubble tickled her palm sending sparks of energy rushing through her body. Now she knew the colour of his eyes, she wanted to paint him. To paint him, she wanted to discover, to familiarise herself with every contour of his body.

Jack stood stolid and tense, only his broad shoulders rising and falling as he breathed. His ragged breath made the skin on her wrist tingle as she trailed her fingers over the strong line of his jaw.

Her gaze flickered to the stern set to his mouth. She wanted to erase its grimness. Soft beneath her touch, his lips parted as she stroked her fingertips over them. She looked into his eyes again.

They were three shades darker.

He raised his hand to enfold hers against his cheek then entwining his fingers, he removed her hand from his face. The bold flame that coursed through her veins flickered in doubt.

'Jack,' she whispered.

His fingers tightened around hers and a low groan rose from the back of his throat. In one swift movement he bridged the gap between them and kissed Pippa hard. Her senses reeled as she closed her eyes, incapable of even feeling embarrassed by the moan she uttered in response. She threaded her fingers through his hair, pulling him closer, yearning for his body to cover every exposed pore of her own. His day-old stubble rasped against her cheek and the faint tang of cologne teased her nostrils.

Jack's hands slid over her body in tremulous abandon.

Wrapping his arms around her, he crushed her to him, suspending her off her feet. Revelling in his strength, Pippa allowed herself to be lifted, curling her legs round his waist as her nightshirt rode up. The burning heat of their skin against one another sent ripples of pleasure pulsing through her. She let her head fall back as his kisses sought her throat. She trailed her hands over his rigid shoulders and over his chest, its fine hair tickling her fingers.

Jack groaned, his kisses on her collarbone becoming more savage. He gripped her closer to him and carried her towards the light of her bedroom.

Beside the bed, Jack eased her to her feet. She uncurled her legs as her body slipped down his, feeling his hardness through his jeans graze her inner thigh. In the soft lamplight, she admired the broad set to his shoulders, suspended above the taut curve of his collarbone.

His Adam's Apple bobbed as he swallowed, allowing Pippa to trace her fingers down his neck and over the muscular expanse of his chest. Her fingers followed the narrow path of dark hair over his abdomen, feeling his muscles contract in response. With trembling hands, she fumbled with his belt.

Jack gently moved aside her attempts to disrobe him and snapped open the buckle.

Pippa flashed him a grateful smile. He returned her smile, lending her courage. With surer movements, she unbuttoned his jeans and tugged his clothes down over his hips. She felt him suck in his breath as her fingers folded around his hard cock, sweeping her thumb over its head and slipping her grip down its shaft. She smiled up at him, feeling empowered by his arousal.

He cupped her face in his hands and kissed her fleetingly, flittering touches coaxing her. On her lips, her eyes, down her throat, tender nibbling at her earlobes. He ran his hands over her shoulders and down her arms, lifting them above her head as their mouths met once more. Pippa surrendered herself to him as he pulled her nightshirt up and over her head. The renewed intensity in Jack's eyes was softened by an almost wondrous smile that parted his lips.

'You know how long I've waited to do this?' he murmured.

Pippa closed her eyes as he stroked his hands down her sides and over her hips, tugging her knickers down with his thumbs. Lowering his head, he trailed kisses down her collarbone to her breast, teasing the nipple with his flickering tongue and teeth.

She exhaled, release from such excruciating pleasure coming in short gasps. His arms encircled her, pulling her against him so his cock burned her stomach. She arched against him, exultant beneath his capable touch, grasping his shoulder muscles.

'Oh, God, Jack,' she gasped, feeling his hand slide over her bottom and down her inside leg.

He pulled away from her briefly to look into her eyes.

'You sure you want this?' he asked.

Pippa nodded.

'God, yes, I want you.'

'Good,' he said huskily. Hoisting her into his arms, he lowered her down onto the bed.

Pippa watched him looking at her, her inhibitions lost forever. She enjoyed the appreciation in his gaze as it travelled over her naked body lit by the glow of the bedside lamp. Kneeling over her, he continued his trail of kisses over her ribs. His tongue flickered over her belly button.

She pressed her head back into the pillow and moaned, feeling the flex of his back muscles beneath her hands as he lowered himself over her. Nudging her legs apart, he brushed his fingertips against her sensitive skin, eliciting an appreciative moan from Pippa as he stroked her, kissed her, played with her desire.

Her body took on a life of its own, her muscles contracting as each nibble and probe sent shockwaves juddering through her.

'I want you *now*,' she gasped.

Jack loomed over her, steadfast on powerful arms. He raised an eyebrow.

'Now, you say?' he murmured. 'But we've barely got started.'

Rotating his hips, he ground himself against her groin.

Pippa reached up to kiss him, to assuage the wantonness he'd provoked in her. She grazed her nails down his back before following the contours of his hips with the softest of touches. She ran the palm of her hand down his cock, feeling a renewed hardness push against her.

He breathed in a sharp intake of breath as she stroked the tender skin at the base of his erection. His mouth close to her ear, she heard him swallow desperately as his cock leapt forward.

'Jesus Christ, Pippa. Do you know what you do to me?' he groaned as she held him.

She caressed him with firmer strokes, basking in the feel of his very bold maleness. Jack cupped her breast towards his mouth and sucked hard. Pippa arched against him, wrapping her legs around his hips. With a decisive grunt, Jack swiftly moved out of her hand and into her. Pippa cried out at the velocity of his entrance, a fire that roared through her body in delectation. Clutching his back, clawing at the rumpled sheets, she met him with each satisfying thrust.

She opened her eyes to look at him. His eyes were dark with arousal, a raw wildness in the tense set of his jaw. His mouth twitched as he filled her, a tender smile teasing his lips. Pippa lost herself in him, absorbed by a feeling so heavenly she'd never thought sex could be like this.

Gazing into his eyes, she wallowed in the knowledge that it was *Jack*, finally it was *Jack* that she was touching, sharing this intimacy with. She felt her pelvic muscles tighten, building, gathering momentum. Her breath quickened as a raging heat flooded her body. She thrust against Jack, feeling him respond to her urgency until the floodgates opened.

'*Jack*.'

She cried out, clinging to his shoulders, digging in her nails, not caring if they hurt or not, anything to keep her from losing complete control. Jack's efforts became more savage as he too reached his climax. With a moan, he shuddered, his shoulders shaking beneath her caress, riding out his orgasm to its furthest reaches.

Jack half-slumped over her. With effort he raised his head to look at Pippa again. His satisfied smile mirrored her own. He leant forward and kissed her, his lips lingering.

'I have one question for you,' he said gruffly and rolled over onto his back beside her.

Pippa propped herself up onto one elbow and looked at him. His chest was still heaving, his body damp with sweat.

'Which is?'

He looked at her, bewildered.

'Why the *fuck* have we waited this long?'

# Chapter Forty-Two

Pippa awoke with a smile on her lips. The previous evening's events came tumbling back to her and she took a moment before opening her eyes to savour the memory. She breathed a satisfied sigh and huddled closer to the body lying beside her. When all she felt was rumpled bedding, she opened her eyes. Only sunshine filtering through her window warmed the empty space next to her. A sound behind her made her turn over.

Jack was standing beside the bed, zipping up his jeans. He paused when he realised Pippa was awake.

'Sorry. Didn't mean to wake you,' he mumbled.

Pippa sat up, modestly covering herself with the duvet.

'That's okay.' She hesitated, trying to read Jack's expression. 'What time is it?'

'Nearly eight.'

'You're leaving?'

Beneath her searching gaze, Jack looked down at the floor and buckled his belt. In the light of day, Pippa drank in the broad figure in front of her, from his hair-darkened chest, his toned abdomen down to his slim jean-hugged hips.

'I've got to get back. Horses to be worked. You know how it is.'

When he couldn't meet her eye, Pippa felt a pang of uncertainty. She smiled to cover up her hurt and nodded.

'Yeah. I know.'

Jack looked at her, apology etched on his face.

'Sorry.' He shifted awkwardly and gestured to the door. 'I'll just finish getting dressed and leave you to sleep.'

He strode across the room, leaving Pippa with an uneasy feeling in her stomach. This wasn't how she pictured the morning after the night before to be. But this is Jack we're talking about, she argued with herself. Of course things would be a little awkward. She jumped out of bed and wrapped herself in her dressing gown. Stepping into her slippers, she padded out of the room.

She met Jack on the landing. He had donned his shirt and was buttoning it up as he walked. He stopped and stared at Pippa.

She gave him an encouraging smile.

316

'Can I make you some breakfast?'

He shook his head.

'Thanks, but I'd better get back.'

Pippa followed him downstairs. He paused to put his shoes on and unhooked his jacket by the front door. Something resembling panic began to rise in Pippa's throat. Was he just going to walk out? Just like that?

'At least let me make you some coffee,' she offered.

Jack paused, hearing the helplessness in her voice. He turned to her, attempting a small smile. He tucked a tendril of messy auburn curls behind her ear and took her hands.

'I need to check on how our National horse is,' he said.

Pippa let herself be pulled towards him. He kissed her lightly on the lips.

'I'll call you later, give you an update.'

She pasted a smile on her face, aware that it wasn't reaching her eyes.

'Okay. I'll speak to you later.'

Jack dropped her hands. Opening the door, he stepped out into the sunshine and strode over to his Land Rover.

Pippa leaned against the doorframe and watched him go. She raised a hand in farewell as he started up the engine and pulled away. The cool breeze teased her skin and she wrapped her dressing gown tighter around her. She gazed at the empty driveway, her thoughts in turmoil. Foremost was the hurt of her uncertainty over his departure. Yet every few moments she felt overwhelmed with joy by what they had shared the night before. Hefting herself away from the door and pulling it shut, she drifted through the house in a daze. A smile warmed her face as she poured herself some coffee.

'You just slept with Jack,' she murmured to herself. She shook her head in disbelief and blew over her mug. '*Jack.*'

By mid-afternoon, Pippa was beginning to get restless. She frowned at the canvas in front of her and tried to inject some life into the landscape she was painting. The magic just wasn't flowing, not when she was so preoccupied. She dabbed some lime green across the line of trees, but sat up alertly as she heard her mobile phone ringing downstairs.

Throwing the brush into the muddy water jar, she hurtled out of the room and down the stairs. She paused to catch her breath and control her excitement when she reached the kitchen. Jack had certainly taken his time about calling her, but she was determined to act as nonchalant as possible. She pulled a face when she didn't recognise the number on the screen. It might have been his home number.

'Hello?'

'Hello. Am I speaking to Pippa Taylor?' a woman asked.

Pippa's heart sagged. Not Jack then.

'Yes,' she said, trying not to sound too disappointed.

'Ah, wonderful. Hello, Pippa. My name is Deidre Forrester.'

Pippa frowned at the vaguely familiar name.

'I'm with Kings Art Galleries.'

Pippa placed the name as soon as the woman explained. Her eyes widened. King Art Galleries had about half a dozen galleries around the country. Pippa had been a regular window-shopper at their snazzy London branch, but had never had the guts to approach the management with her own art.

'How can I help you?' she choked out at last.

'We have an exhibition coming up in about a month's time and your name was suggested to us by one of our most loyal clients. We thought maybe you might be interested in showing some of your work.'

Pippa's heart stilled then palpitated in what felt like a samba beat.

'An exhibition? Where?'

'Our Piccadilly gallery.'

Her jaw dropped and she steadied herself against the windowsill.

'Really?'

'Would you be interested?' Deidre said with a smile in her voice.

Pippa nodded furiously and tried to pull herself together. She realised Deidre Forrester couldn't see her nodding.

'Absolutely. That would be fantastic.' She paused as another thought struck her. 'How did you – I mean, I've done a few commissions as well as my own stuff, but... how did you hear about me? I'm not exactly Banksy.'

The woman laughed.

'One of your commission clients got in touch with us.'

Pippa glowed. She could forgive Jack's silence if this was what he'd been doing today.

'Who?'

'Aaron Janssen. I've seen a couple of paintings which you did of his horses. Lovely pieces.'

Pippa's sense of elation deflated at the mention of the fashion mogul's name.

'Oh. Thank you.'

'My husband has racehorses too. I'm sure he'd appreciate your work as well. Is equestrian art your forte or do you do other stuff like landscapes and fine art?'

'I – um – I paint landscapes as well.' She flapped an indifferent hand as she tried to regain her concentration.

'Splendid. Would you be able to send me some digital photos of some more of your work? The exhibition is in a month's time and we're asking our artists to provide up to six pieces to go on display. Does that sound like something you could manage?'

'Er – can I get back to you on that one?' Pippa said.

'Of course. No problem. I have your email address here as well, courtesy of Mr Janssen so I'll send you the contract conditions and you just let me know within the next week. Is that okay?'

Pippa swallowed.

'Yes, that's fine. Thank you for – um – this opportunity.'

Pippa sat, limply holding her phone in her lap after Deidre Forrester rung off. She groaned and let her head fall back. She looked at her phone in bewilderment. Had she really received an offer from one of London's most fashionable art galleries and she'd told them she'd have to think about it? But now that she knew about Aaron Janssen's less than attractive marketing exploits, did she really want to accept his help?

She noticed a text message on the screen of her phone which had come through at lunchtime.

*Peace Offering fine after yesterday. See you tomorrow. Jack*

Pippa felt like she'd just been punched in the gut. A text message? After a night like last night, and all she got was a text message? She wanted to cry. She wanted to shout at Jack and slap some sense into him. She wanted to cry even more – what sense would that be exactly? The same sense that had provoked her to sleep with her boss?

She flicked through her numbers and dialled.


'Hey, sweets!' Tash answered. 'Tried to ring you last night, but couldn't get through. You okay?'

'Mm-hmm,' Pippa mumbled.

'Oh, dear, that doesn't sound good. Are Finn and Peace Offering okay after yesterday? Fucking hell, Pip, you were so close. I made the CEO allow us quarter of an hour to watch it. If that bastard horse hadn't run in front of him, you would have won.'

319

'Yeah, I know. They're both fine.' She thought of Jack's text, still smarting in her chest, and sighed.

'Okay than,' Tash said, sounding intrigued. 'Hang on, let me just pop to the loos for some privacy. I'm still at bloody work, can you believe it... Right, here we are. What's eating you?'

Pippa pulled a face.

'Um, well, you're not going to believe this, but –'

'Oh, my God!' yelled Tash. 'No way! You slept with Jack, didn't you?'

Pippa took her phone away from her ear to look at it, Tash's Indian hollers coming through very loud and extremely clear.

'How could you tell?'

'Oh, my God!' Tash squealed. 'Seriously? Well done, Pippa! Tell me what happened!'

Despite herself, Pippa smiled at Tash's enthusiasm.

'He took me home after the National and stayed for dinner. Then he tried to go home, but the road was flooded so he stayed. And... well, you know what comes next.'

'Pippa Taylor, you saucy minx,' Tash goaded. 'You just bedded one of the sexiest men in Britain. Was it worth the wait?'

Pippa forced herself to breathe as she relived last night.

'Yes,' she sighed. 'It was like – like – like *heaven*. But not just physically. It felt so complete. Like we were two halves making a whole. I don't know, it's difficult to explain. I've never had sex like it before.'

Tash was silent for a moment.

'Bloody hell,' she drawled. 'I think the reason you've never had sex like that before, Pip, is because you and Jack weren't having sex. I think you just made love for the first time.'

Tears stung her eyes and she brushed them away with her palm.

'You think?'

'Oh, yeah.'

Pippa sighed.

'Maybe I did. But Jack... I don't know. It's just this morning...' she tailed off.

'What do you mean? What happened this morning?'

'He couldn't get out of here fast enough. Wouldn't even stop for a coffee. He was out of my bed and out of the front door in less than two minutes.'

'Was he late for anything?'

'Just work. But it's Sunday. Everything at the stables slows down on a Sunday. He could've taken ten minutes to have a coffee and not made me feel like a - like a -'

'Oh, Pip. I'm sorry,' Tash said. 'Maybe you need to give him a bit of time to get used to the idea. He is Jack, after all.'

'He said he'd call me later. Now I've just found he sent me a text saying Peace Offering's fine and he'll see me tomorrow.'

'Ouch. Okay, this is definitely Jack we're dealing with here. I mean, let's look at this logically. Can you honestly see him rolling over in the morning and acting like a honeymooner?'

'No, I guess not,' Pippa conceded. 'Would've been nice though if he had.'

'He just needs time.'

'I don't know, Tash. He was always so against relationships in the workplace. Now he's gone and done the exact same thing. He's not going to want anything to do with me while I'm his secretary.'

'You could quit,' Tash suggested.

'I guess so - no, I don't know. I couldn't do that. I need to work.'

'You are working though. You've got about a dozen commissions lined up, haven't you?'

'Oh, God. That's the next thing!' Pippa exclaimed.

'What next thing? Tell me!'

'I got a call from Kings Art Galleries wanting me to take part in an exhibition they've got coming up.'

'I don't who they are, but that's great, Pippa! See? It's all good. What did you tell them?'

'I said I'd think about it and thanked them for the opportunity.'

'Thanked them for the opportunity? Have you been watching *The Apprentice* or something?'

Pippa chuckled.

'No, it's just that I was given the offer compliments of Aaron Janssen.'

'And? That's a good thing surely?'

Pippa gasped.

'Fuck! You don't know, do you?'

'Know what?'

'When was the last time I spoke to you?'

'A couple of days ago, I don't know. Tell me about Aaron Janssen!'

'Wow, how can so much have happened in so short a time?' Pippa marvelled.

'Pippa, you're killing me here!' Tash cried.

'Oh, God, you have to promise not to tell anyone. Okay?'

'Hand on heart. Now spill!'

# Chapter Forty-Three

Pippa didn't know if she'd ever been more nervous stepping into the office the following morning. Excitement, fear and dread whirlpooled around her stomach. Emmie was already sat at her new desk, which had been bought to accommodate her.

'Hey, Pippa,' she smiled. 'Bad luck on Saturday. He came so close.'

'Thanks,' she replied. She dumped her handbag beside her desk and sat down. 'It was one hell of a race.' She drummed her fingers on the desk and glanced at Jack's closed office door. 'Is Jack in?'

'No. He popped out about ten minutes ago. Said that if you came in, entries and decs are on his desk and to help yourself.'

Pippa's heart began to thud at the prospect of seeing Jack again. She thanked Emmie and walked over to Jack's door. Nothing was different on the other side. It looked exactly the same as it had last week, except *altered* by the weekend.

She closed her eyes as she reached the desk and took a deep breath. Leather, wood polish and the lingering tang of Jack's cologne tingled in her nostrils. She picked up the notebook and flicked it open to the last entry. A small smile of anticipation flitted over her mouth as she remembered how Jack had left a private note in there for her before.

*12th April – Entries*
*Haydock 1.20 – Bold Phoenix*
*       "       3.10 – Smoking Ace*
*Declarations*
*Wincanton 4.05 – Spurwing Island (blinkers)*

Pippa's smile drooped. The page was glaringly void of any loving messages. She snorted mirthlessly. What was she expecting – Jack to declare his undying love to her as well as Spurwing Island in the 4.05 at Wincanton?

With a deep breath, she drew back her shoulders. She was not going to let this get to her. She sauntered out of the office with her chin held high and sat down at her desk. She was going to be the epitome of aloofness. When Jack appeared, he'd better be prepared because she was going to show him just how indifferent a girl could be.

The door opened and Jack walked in.

Pippa dropped her pen then hit her head on the desk trying to retrieve it off the floor. Jack's gaze flickered from Pippa to Emmie and back again. He nodded a greeting to her.

'Morning, Pippa.'

She stared at him. Jack Carmichael, boss of Aspen Valley had walked into the office, sporting his usual outfit of jeans and flying jacket. Pippa's face burned. She blinked. She couldn't rid herself of the image of Jack Carmichael, sex god and lover, sporting somewhat less clothing than he had on now.

'He-hello, Jack.'

The muscle in Jack's jaw throbbed as they stared at each other. Jack blinked and looked away.

'I'll be in my office if either of you need me,' he muttered.

Pippa's heart hammered against her chest. Her clammy palm slipped over her computer mouse. She wondered if this was what it felt like before one fainted. She hazarded a quick look at Emmie to see if she'd noticed anything amiss, but the girl looked blissfully unaware of the sexual frisson that had almost singed the office furniture.

Emmie smiled at her.

'Well?' she prompted.

'Well, what?'

'Usually, as soon as Jack walks in, you jump up and make him a drink. Do you want me to go make it?'

Pippa thought fast. She wanted to see Jack, but she didn't want to be faced with the awkwardness. She didn't want Emmie to think anything odd yet asking her to make coffee would immediately raise questions.

She shook her head.

'No, no. I'll go do it. Just slipped my mind. Do you want a cup?'

'I bought some peppermint tea if you wouldn't mind making me some of that?'

'Sure,' Pippa smiled. She got to her feet then braced herself against the chair as her knees offered as much support as a papier-mâché bridge crane.

Aloofness, remember Pippa, she scolded herself. Aloof, aloof, aloof.

Who the hell came up with that stupid word, she thought to herself a couple of minutes later as she knocked on Jack's door. When you said it often enough, it started to sound quite ridiculous.

'Come in.'

Jack's gruff invitation shuddered through her. Pushing open the door, she stepped into the office feeling like she was about to meet her maker.

'Tea,' she announced.

'Thank you. Um, close the door behind you, will you?'

Pippa's pulse stepped up to pneumatic dimensions as she did as she was bid.

'How are you?' Jack ventured.

'Good, thanks,' she nodded vigorously. 'You?'

Jack licked his lips and watched her place his drink down on the desk. The liquid shimmied out of the cup.

'Yes, fine.'

He frowned at his desk as a silence descended. Pippa wrung her hands behind her back and wiggled her toes.

'You got my message yesterday?'

Pippa nodded.

'Yes. Peace Offering's okay, is he?'

'A little stiff, but okay.'

Another deafening silence ensued.

'Well, I'd better get back,' Pippa said, motioning behind her.

'Yes, of course.'

Deflated, Pippa turned to leave.

'Pippa?'

'Yes?' She spun round to face him.

'We need to talk –'

Fear constricted her chest.

'– about Peace Offering.'

She exhaled, not sure whether to be relieved that he was avoiding the most pressing subject on her mind or not.

'Okay,' she said.

'I think after Saturday's run, now would be a good time for him to be turned out. I think we should take him out of training and wait for next season.'

Pippa nodded.

'Okay,' she agreed. She managed a smile. 'Go out on a high note... almost.'

'Yes. The season's nearly over anyway.'

With those words, Pippa's heart sank to a new level. The season ending would also mark the ending of her country life adventure. The office

325

telephone trilled from beyond the door as once more they lapsed into silence.

'I'd better get that.'

Jack nodded, his expression grim.

Pippa tore herself away and hurried out of the office. Emmie had already answered the phone. She sat down again at her desk and tried to quell the emotions battering her body like a storm breaker.

How could things possibly progress with Jack? She dragged her fingers through her hair. Her hopes that his awkwardness might abate died an agonising death. Yet how could she blame him when she wasn't the image of grace and dexterity?

With a sigh, she opened up a new window on her screen and set about inputting that week's entries.

At lunchtime, Pippa escaped to the kitchenette to make her and Emmie hot drinks.

'What are you oohing and aahing about over there?' she said as she placed Emmie's cup down on her desk.

Emmie looked up from her computer and sheepishly turned the screen so Pippa could see.

'House hunting,' she replied. 'There're some lovely places up for sale, but so out of our price range. I think we're going to end up renting.'

Pippa leaned against the desk, contemplatively sipping her coffee.

'Hazyvale is going to be put up on the market pretty soon,' she said.

Emmie's hopeful look faded.

'That'd probably be out of our price range too.'

Pippa shrugged.

'If we do a private sale, it will at least knock off the agents' fees.'

'Hazyvale would be perfect. And Billy loved it when he went round to help with the garden,' mused Emmie. 'How much are you selling it for?'

'I don't know yet. I've got someone coming tomorrow lunchtime to value it.'

Pippa received a surge of nervous excitement every time she thought of what price the agents might consider it to be worth.

'Good luck with that. I know you've worked really hard on the house so I hope you get good valuations, but... on the other hand, if the price is anything like this house here,' she sighed, pointing at the screen, 'then Billy and I will never be able to get a mortgage big enough.'

Pippa nodded. She also hoped the agents would give her good news. What if they pitched up and told her that her idea of renovating a cottage wasn't the same as theirs and she might just as well have saved herself the trouble and sold it as it was?

She shuddered. It didn't bear thinking about.

'If you sell then where are you going to live?' Emmie asked.

Pippa dropped her gaze and straightened up to return to her own desk. 'I'll probably go back to London,' she said, offhand.

Emmie looked horrified.

'London? What about everything here at Aspen Valley?'

Pippa fiddled with her pen and shrugged.

'This was never a long-term job. I was always going to leave at the end of the season.'

'But what about Jack?'

Pippa looked up sharply.

'What about Jack?'

'How's he going to cope without you? I mean, I'm still really slow with all this paperwork. And there's just so *much* of it. I'll do his head in.'

'You'll be fine. Everything's starting to quieten down now.' She paused, to ensure her regrets about Jack were well and truly camouflaged. 'Jack will cope just fine without me.'

The clock on the reception wall struck five o'clock the following afternoon and Pippa watched Emmie pack up for the day. The girl paused when she saw Pippa not moving from her desk.

'Are you staying late?'

Pippa nodded.

'Yeah,' she said, pulling a face. 'That agent that came round at lunch took ages looking round. I didn't think they would ask so many questions just because the cottage is old.'

Emmie grinned.

'You must have answered them right. Even though I'm sorry we won't be able to afford it, I'm glad your hard work has paid off.'

'Thanks, Emmie. Me too. I'd have much preferred you and Billy to live there. See you tomorrow.' She smiled and waved goodbye to Emmie.

With the door closed behind her, Pippa leant back in her chair and sighed. Only the purr of her computer's fan punctuated the eerie quiet which descended over the office. Relief that the estate agent today had valued Hazyvale at a pleasing amount was tinged with regret that she would be leaving it soon. She hadn't realised she'd grown so attached to the cottage.

She glanced towards Jack's office, closed while its usual occupier was off racing at Wincanton. She hadn't meant to become so attached to him either.

Pippa chewed her lip. It wasn't a matter of leaving the area that was going to keep them apart. It seemed the crack in their relationship, which she'd first noticed on Sunday morning, had widened into a canyon. An unbridgeable one.

Shaking her head, she stood up. She retrieved the Entries and Declarations notebook from Emmie's desk to take through to Jack's office, ready for the following morning. Emmie had input that day's lists to practice.

Flicking idly through the pages as she walked, she paused before putting it on Jack's desk. She frowned at that day's entries. Realisation crept over and her fingers trembled.

The banging of the reception door made her swing round. Jack appeared in the doorway. He stopped when he saw Pippa in his office.

'Pippa, what are you doing here?'

She looked at him, balling her fists to curb her shaking. She lifted the notebook for him to see.

'I was just putting this back on your desk for tomorrow.' She swallowed and took a ragged breath. 'Emmie did them today. She didn't mention that Finn isn't riding any of the horses though. You've got Mick Farrelly as first string.'

Jack sighed and carried on into the office. He shrugged off his jacket and hung it on the back of his chair. Pippa watched him, her anger simmering and waited for his excuse.

'Finn and Aspen Valley have called it quits,' he said at last.

Pippa gasped.

'You *fired* him?'

'No –'

'Jack! How could you?' she cried. 'He was being blackmailed! By your girlfriend!'

'Pippa –'

The frustrations of her pent up emotions exploded in indignation.

'When did you decide to fire him? Did you decide right then in the hotel room and just waited for a time most convenient to you –'

'PIPPA!' Jack exclaimed. 'Will you listen for a moment?'

328

Like an escalating bush fire that needed only a spark to start it, Pippa glared at him.

'Why should I?' she said. 'Why, when it suits you, should I stand here and listen? After being completely ignored since Sunday? You just *left* me! How do you think that makes me feel, huh, Jack? Cheap and used, that's what! And now, having to stand here and tell you this, it makes me look desperate and pathetic! Cheap, used, desperate and pathetic. They're not exactly qualities to be proud of.'

'I don't think you're cheap –'

'No, but what you can't stop thinking of is that I'm your secretary, can you?' she challenged him.

She tried to control her breathing as she waited for his reply. Her chest heaved at the strain.

Jack stared at her, his jaw set, his eyes indigo.

'Would that be so inaccurate?' he replied, his tone menacing. Pippa felt like she'd been stabbed. 'What happened over the weekend –'

'It was a mistake, Jack!' she shouted. 'You're right, what we did was a mistake!'

The muscle in Jack's jaw leapt. He swallowed.

'I was going to say,' he continued in a quiet voice, 'what happened over the weekend – what happened on *Friday* night has nothing to do with Finn not riding for Aspen Valley anymore.'

Pippa took a step backwards.

Jack glared at her.

'But now that you mention it, perhaps you're right. What happened on *Saturday* night probably was a mistake.'

Pippa' lower lip quivered and she bit it hard. What had she done?

'What?' she whispered.

'Finn's leaving because the damn fool thinks he's in love with you. You see what I mean about relationships in the workplace? This is what happens. It never works!'

'Finn's in love with me?' Pippa shook her head. 'But he and I aren't having a relationship. We were just friends!' Anger flooded her stomach again as tears pricked her eyes. 'And a damn fool? Is that the only type of person you think could love me? And relationships *can* work in the workplace! Look at Emmie and Billy! All it takes is for both parties to want to make it work! I might not have wanted to make things work with Finn, but –' Her voice quavered and she gulped down a wave of tears. 'But I *did* want to make it work with you.'

Jack's expression was pained. He looked away and stared sullenly at his desk.

Pippa stepped back again. She was fighting a losing battle against the tears.

'I can't do this,' she whispered as she retreated.

Jack looked up sharply and opened his mouth to say something.

Pippa didn't think her emotions could take any more abuse. She interrupted him.

'I have to go. It's time I went anyway.'

'What? Wait! What do you mean?'

She paused by the door. Jack looked at her in horror.

'I quit, Jack.'

# Chapter Forty-Four

The 11pm news broadcast was rounding off its headlines as Pippa pulled into a parking space down the street from Tash's flat.

'And Pippa Taylor quits her job as secretary to National Hunt trainer, Jack Carmichael, and forfeits all chances of a future relationship or happiness,' she added to the newsreader's stories as she killed the ignition. With a despondent sigh, she hauled herself out of the car to unload her two lumpy suitcases.

After beeping her into the building, Tash met her halfway down the stairs. Pippa closed her eyes as her friend hugged her tight and rocked her, finding comfort at last.

'My poor Pip. Come on, let me have one of those. They look like they weigh a ton. Then come upstairs and tell Auntie Tashie everything.'

With a grateful smile, Pippa handed over one of her cases.

'Thanks, Tash,' she said, following her up the narrow stairwell to the second floor flat. 'I'm sorry to barge in on you like this. I just couldn't face being alone at Hazyvale, so close to – to him.'

'Pah! It's nothing. It'll be good to have some company. I've been lonely since you left London, you know.'

They dropped the suitcases in the front room and Pippa looked to Tash for reassurance.

'Really?'

'Of course I have, you muppet.' Tash shook her head and gave her another hug.

'I probably won't be very good company.'

'No sweat. As long as you appear to be listening when I babble on, then you're company enough for me. Now, come on, let's have a smile, eh?' Tash gave her a reproachful look. 'You look shattered. How about some hot chocolate? No better cure for a broken heart, regardless of how often Smirnoff might tell you otherwise. Then we can sit on my bed and chat in comfort.'

Settled cross-legged on Tash's king-size bed, wrapped in a fluffy blanket and sipping hot chocolate, Pippa gave a small giggle.

'You're right. I'm feeling a bit better already.'

'That'a girl. So, go on, I get a tiny-voiced Pippa on the phone to me saying "can I come stay with you for a while" with no further explanation. I haven't been on such tenterhooks since Dirty Den came back to *EastEnders* after fifteen-odd years and said "'Ello, Princess" to Sharon.'

Pippa looked down at the Eeyore-print blanket and picked at the fluff.

'I quit.'

'Oh, sweets.'

'Jack and I had a fight. I said sleeping with him had been a mistake.' Pippa looked up, her bottom lip trembling. 'But I didn't mean it, not really. You know how when you panic you say things – things which you think will protect you, but which – which don't in the end...'

'What did Jack say?' Tash probed gently.

'He agreed. Told me the same old story about relationships in the workplace.'

'It's a bit late for him to use that excuse. He should have thought about that before seducing you.'

Pippa smiled.

'It might have been the other way round. Technically, you might say I seduced him.'

'Sweets, he's been seducing you since you first walked into his yard. It's just that neither of you recognised it at the time.'

Pippa shrugged.

'Well, anyway, maybe he's right. The past couple of days have been torture in the office. He didn't know how to act around me and I wasn't much better. I didn't have a clue how to be around him.'

'Sure, it can be tricky. But he's your boss. He had a responsibility towards you and directing where you'd both go after your Big Night.'

'Maybe he *was* being responsible then. Maybe the way he's been acting these past couple of days is his way of directing our relationship. Directing it towards This-Won't-Happen-Again Street.'

'Come on. Jack having one-night-stands? That doesn't sound like his style, Pip, I have to say. He wouldn't have slept with you unless he cared a helluva lot for you.'

Pippa shook her head and slurped her drink. The liquid scalded her tongue.

'Couldn't have cared that much. Why didn't he stop me when I left?'

Tash leaned forward and rubbed her shoulder in a consoling gesture.

'Maybe he was also feeling a little hurt? A little scared maybe?' she suggested.

Pippa's tears, which she'd managed to keep dammed up for the past few hours, welled in her eyes. The thought of hurting Jack was almost as upsetting as the other way round.

'You think? I don't want him to hurt, Tash,' she whispered.

'Agh, stop. You're going to make me cry and I'm not kidding.'

'Sorry,' Pippa said and brushed away an escapee tear making a getaway dash down her cheek.

Tash sighed and looked at her imploringly.

'You love him, don't you?'

Pippa looked down at Eeyore's woeful expression again. Another tear splashed onto the donkey's nose. She nodded then gave a mirthless snort.

'I think I'm only realising that now though. Same old story, isn't it? You don't know what you've got 'til it's gone.'

'Maybe he'll realise the same thing then.'

Pippa gave her a searching look.

'That he might be in love with me? But what if he realises he's not? I can't go back to find out. It'd kill me if I knew for sure that he's not. I'd rather stay here not knowing than face the truth.'

'Oh, Pip.'

'I know you're thinking I'm a coward, but –'

'I don't think you're a coward at all,' Tash interrupted. 'Hell, you're one the bravest people I know. And you don't have to go anywhere until you feel ready. You're staying right here with me. Okay?'

Pippa gave her a wobbly smile.

'Thanks, Tash. You're a mate.'

'What are best friends for, eh?' She reached out and squeezed Pippa's knee.

Tash perhaps didn't reckon on just how long it would take Pippa to feel ready. A week later, Pippa was still holed up in the spare bedroom. She sat hunched on a stool in front of her easel in the corner of the cramped room. Beneath the tip of her brush, Bristol Harbour in the spring glittered in acrylic sunshine. She couldn't bring herself to paint the landscapes which had surrounded her for the past five months, but when she'd spoken to Deidre Forrester the other day, agreeing to take part in the Kings Gallery art exhibition, she'd been asked to produce a variety of work and not just equestrian art.

Her mobile vibrated on her bedside table, making her paintbrush jump across the canvas. Tutting, Pippa went to retrieve it. Her hand paused over it when she saw the caller ID.

*Aspen Valley*

She hadn't heard from Jack since she'd walked out a week ago. Why now? To have him pick up the phone and consciously dial her number must have warranted a very good reason.

She hesitated. Was it a reason she wanted to know or didn't already know for that matter?

With a trembling touch, she accepted the call.

'Hello?' she answered in a small voice.

'Hi Pippa, it's Emmie.'

Pippa exhaled and sat down on the bed with a bounce. Her heart, having stopped just a moment ago, now palpitated in her chest.

'Hi, Emmie. You all right?'

'Yeah, not bad, thanks. I mean great in some respects, but not so great in others.'

Pippa's throat contracted.

'Is the baby okay?'

'Oh, yes!' Emmie giggled. 'The baby's fine, don't panic. I felt it kick for the first time yesterday. I think it was taking exception to the noise in the office.'

Pippa frowned, her imagination flitting from wild celebration parties being held in her absence to Jack attacking her desk with a sledgehammer.

'What's been so noisy in the office?'

'Just Jack.' Emmie lowered her voice conspiratorially. 'He's been a right grouch since you left. I don't think I've ever seen him so angry as he was yesterday.'

Pippa tried to control her breathing.

'Why was he angry?' she asked, trying to sound as uninterested as she could.

'It was over nothing really. Some horses were turned out in a paddock which is meant to be rested and he got really angry about that. So I made him a cup of that chamomile tea to see if it would calm him down and he completely lost it. Refused to drink it. Told me to throw the box in the kitchen away. Said he didn't want to see it again. He slammed the door so hard, your lovely painting on the wall here fell off. And all over a cup of tea!'

Pippa's pulse quickened. She didn't want Jack to be angry or miserable, but maybe it was what had to happen before he realised he needed her in his life?

'Why did you leave, if you don't mind me asking?' Emmie asked. 'Jack said you had some personal problems which you had to sort out. Is everything okay? Billy and I stopped by Hazyvale a couple of times on the way home from work and there haven't been any lights on. Are you not at home?'

'No, I'm in London. Just... like Jack said, just sorting out some personal problems.' Pippa smiled wryly. Emmie would have had no idea that the personal problem Jack had given as an excuse was himself.

'Are you coming back?'

She pulled a face and looked down at the carpet. How she wished she could give an affirmative answer.

'No, I don't think so. My job was coming to an end soon anyway.'

'Oh, that's too bad. We miss you, you know.' Emmie giggled. 'Maybe that's why Jack's been such a tyrant lately. Maybe he misses you too.'

Pippa forced a laugh which dried very quickly in her throat and turned into a cough.

'Anyway, the reason I'm calling, Pippa, is that I've got great news. You know I told you Billy and I couldn't afford Hazyvale by ourselves?'

'Yes?' Despite herself, Pippa felt her breath quicken.

'Well, our parents have announced that they're going to chip in and help us pay for it! Isn't that fantastic?' Emmie squeaked.

'Oh!' Pippa felt tears prick her eyes. An ocean wave of gratitude that the cottage might become the couple's home crashed against a stony beach of regret that Hazyvale would no longer be hers.

'It is still for sale, isn't it? You haven't sold it to some city weekenders, have you?'

'No, no!' Pippa gave a teary laugh. 'It's yours, most definitely. That's wonderful!'

'Oh, Pippa, this is so exciting! Once we get over all the boring bank loans and mortgages, then we can sort it all out. Billy's dad is a solicitor in Bath so I'm sure we could cut a few costs using him. Isn't this great? Oh! The only downside is that you're not going to be living here anymore. You could buy another place round here, couldn't you?'

Pippa grinned at her enthusiasm.

'I don't know, Emmie. I've got an art exhibtion here in London in a few weeks' time and...' Her voice trailed off as she heard another voice in the background. She gulped as she recognised the speaker's deep tone.

'Ooh, hang on. Jack's just walked in,' Emmie said.

Pippa strained to hear Jack's muted voice.

'Who's that?' she heard him ask Emmie.

'It's Pippa. Do you want to talk to her?'

Pippa's heart crashed against her ribs. Breathing suddenly became more difficult and painful than learning to knife juggle. She waited for his response.

'No. I've got things to do,' Jack replied.

One of Pippa's juggling knives pierced her chest.

'Okay. I'll tell her you say hi.' Emmie's muffled voice became clearer as she removed her hand from the receiver. 'Jack says hi.'

'Right. Well, hi, Jack,' Pippa said with an attempted laugh. She failed. This was too hard. 'Listen, Emmie. I've got to go. Thanks so much for calling. It's great news that you'll be taking Hazyvale. I couldn't be more pleased.'

'Me too! You'll be guest of honour at our house warming party,' Emmie enthused.

Pippa's first thought was to wonder if Jack would be there too.

'Thanks,' she said. 'Anyway, I've got to go. I'll speak to you soon.'

'Okay. Bye, Pippa!' trilled Emmie.

'Bye.' Pippa's reply came out like a drying up stream. She let the phone slip through her fingers and bounce onto the bed. She flopped back and stared up at the ceiling. A nasty brown mark from the upstairs flat's bathroom stained the corner.

That was that then, she concluded. Jack didn't want to talk to her. He was handed the opportunity on a plate by Emmie and he'd walked away. He'd had time to think about it and he still wasn't going to make the effort.

'Who am I kidding?' she muttered. 'Jack isn't some stupid romantic hero. Those things just don't happen in real life.' She threw a pillow across the room, knocking *Bristol Harbour* off its easel. She didn't care. She slammed her head back against the mattress again. 'Stupid, fucking two-dimensional romance crap. They never bloody take into account the consequences.' She snatched up her phone and whirred through her address book. 'Why am I trying to fool myself? Did I really expect Jack to declare his undying love to me in front of Emmie?' Her thumb stilled as

336

she got halfway through her list of numbers. 'It's all bullshit.' She read out the highlighted name on the screen, 'Jack Carmichael,' and pressed *Delete Contact*.

# Chapter Forty-Five

'Knock, knock. Anyone home?' Tash said, appearing in the doorway to the spare room.

Pippa looked up from her book.

'Physically, yes,' she smiled. 'Mentally – well, that's open to debate.'

Tash grinned and stepped into the room. She raised her hand, dangling a pair of shoes by their straps. Pippa looked at her questioningly.

'I come bearing gifts. Your dancing shoes. You've locked yourself away for three weeks now. It's time to stop moping.'

Pippa pulled a face.

'I haven't really been moping. I've been working,' she said, gesturing to the canvases stacked up against the wall.

'Well, then it's time to take a break. You and I are going out.'

Just the thought of stepping outside of the flat made Pippa feel exhausted.

'I don't know, Tash –'

'Come on, it's Saturday! And these are for you.' Tash swung the shoes in front of her.

'But they're your favourite. They're your Jimmy Choos.'

Tash nodded.

'Technically, they're yours. As is the psychiatric consult I promised you if you hadn't bedded Jack by the Grand National.'

'But –'

'You got your act together *after* the National. Albeit only a few hours after, but after, nonetheless.' She looked at Pippa's pained expression sheepishly. 'In retrospect, I feel bad for encouraging you. I didn't take it seriously enough.'

'Tash, it's not your fault,' Pippa protested. 'What Jack and I did – well, we did of our own accord.'

'Regardless, I feel it is my duty,' she said, holding a hand up to her chest, 'as your bad influencing, misguiding best friend to make amends.' She winked. 'I'm taking you out tonight just to show you there is life after Jack Carmichael.'

\*

The tapas bar which Tash took her to was humming with trendy youth when they arrived. In the lowered lighting, they settled themselves at a high table with an ice-bucket and bottle of champagne.

'Have you been here before?' Pippa asked, raising her voice above the noise.

'A couple of times. Can't afford to make it a habit, but it's the new place to be.'

Pippa looked around at the clientele, all fashionably modern and utterly different from the homeliness of The Plough. There wasn't a flat cap or tweed jacket in sight.

Tash poured their champagne into two glasses and held hers aloft.

'To the future and its endless possibilities,' she toasted.

'To the future.' Pippa clinked her glass against her friend's and took a long swallow. The chilled alcohol tickled her taste buds and she grinned. 'Good stuff, this.'

'I'll drink to that. Come on, let's get sloshed.'

The night passed in a haze of champagne bubbles and constant chatter. Pippa squinted at Tash and tried to blink away her double vision.

'And then he looks at his watch and says "My magic watch says you're not wearing any knickers",' Tash recounted. 'So stupid me says "Yes, I am" and you know what he said Pip? You know what that slimy creep said?' She leaned forward across the table, brandishing her drink. 'He shakes his watch and says "Damn! This must be fifteen minutes fast".'

Pippa giggled. Tash looked affronted beneath her grin.

'I mean, the audacity! Can you imagine? Did he really think a classy girl like me would fall for a line like – oh, hello.'

Pippa followed Tash's gaze as her friend sat up straight, her attention focused on the entrance. She laughed and shook her head as a couple of young good looking suits walked in. Her phone vibrated in her pocket and she squirmed in her seat to pull it out.

'Hello?' she answered, still giggling at the smouldering looks her 'classy' friend was throwing to the new arrivals. She frowned when she couldn't hear a reply and plugged her other ear with a finger. 'Hello-o-o,' she drawled.

In the muffled background, she heard a voice.

'Vous voulez autre chose à boise?'

Pippa frowned and looked at her phone. She didn't recognise the number. 'Hello?' she tried again.

'Oh, God. Look who's here,' Tash interrupted.

'Ollie!' Pippa gasped. The three-tone cut-off beep pierced her ear as the caller hung up. She shook her head at the call's minor disruption to her evening and focused on the much more interesting arrival of her ex. On his arm was a slim brunette girl.

'Wonder who she is,' she murmured.

Tash shrugged and took a slug of her drink.

'Dunno. An actress perhaps? Those boobs are definitely not real. She looks partially animated by Pixar.'

Pippa snorted. Unaware of their presence, Ollie and the girl threaded through the crowd to the bar. Tash raised an eyebrow at Pippa.

'Feeling okay?'

'Yes, fine,' Pippa replied. She gave her a genuine smile. 'Seriously, I don't feel anything for Ollie. I just wish that girl luck.'

'Good, that's just what I wanted to hear. Who was that calling you?'

'Don't know. Some heavy breather. Think they were in a French restaurant or something. I could hear them being offered a drink. Then they just hung up. Maybe it was a wrong number.'

'Well, if you're in the mood to be handing out your number, I could point out one person whom I think might like it.' She winked at Pippa in a conspiratorial fashion. 'Because one of those two dishes who walked in a moment ago hasn't taken his eyes off you since they arrived.'

Pippa looked over. A young, brown-haired man, propping up the bar, nodded towards her and smiled.

'Time you got us another bottle,' Tash announced, unceremoniously nudging Pippa off her barstool.

He's not bad, Pippa appraised him as she approached the bar. Young maybe, younger than Jack – no, stop thinking about Jack! She gave herself an internal shake and smiled at the man.

'What are you ladies drinking over there?' he asked as she reached the counter.

'Champagne, but please don't –'

'No, I insist,' he said, taking out his wallet from his back pocket. He flapped it in front of him. 'On one condition.'

'Which is?'

'You tell me your name. I don't like to buy drinks for strangers.'

'Pippa. My name's Pippa.' She gulped. Had she really forgotten how to flirt? Had she ever flirted with Jack? How had she managed to fall in love with him without ever flirting – no, stop thinking about Jack!

He smiled.

'Ah, Pippa. Means lover of horses, doesn't it?'

'Or horse trainers,' Pippa said beneath her breath.

'Pardon?'

'Yes,' she smiled brightly. 'It means lover of horses.'

'Well, it's my pleasure to meet you, Pippa. I'm Bryce. This is Jared,' he said, gesturing to his friend.

'Hi,' she smiled awkwardly. She attempted a flirtatious line. 'Does Bryce have any special meaning?'

'Yes. It means speckled.'

Pippa blinked. He didn't have any freckles that she could see. She wondered what had prompted his parents to call him that. Where exactly was he speckled?

'Oh.'

Bryce grinned.

'Mind if we join you? This place is a little short on seating.'

Pippa kept the smile pinned to her face. She could do this. This was the first step towards healing a broken heart, she told herself. And it had to be done.

'No, not at all,' she replied. 'We'd love you to join us.'

Out of the corner of her eye, she saw Ollie staring at her over a sea of heads. She raised her chin and smiled at him. His jaw dropped. She fluttered a wave in his direction.

'Shall we?' Bryce said, now supplemented with a fat bottle of champagne.

'Yes, let's.'


The following week, Pippa and Tash walked away from the long nylon-cloaked drinks table at Kings Art Gallery with two glasses of wine.

'Two glasses and no more,' Pippa warned.

'For you or for me?'

'Both. I haven't touched a drop since last Saturday and my body still hasn't recovered.'

Tash looked sheepish as they wandered around the gallery, their heels clicking on the laminate wood floors.

'Yeah, sorry about that. It seemed a good idea at the time.'

Pippa tried to look stern, but ended up grinning.

'Do you realise how embarrassed I was when I woke up the next morning on that guy Bryce's couch?' She giggled. 'Poor dude. Thought

341

he'd got lucky and all he really got was me going on about Jack then passing out before he could make a proper pass at me.'

'Maybe you just need more time. Do you feel any less in love with Jack now? It's been a month now.'

Pippa bit her lip.

'Would you be exasperated if I said no? It's not something I can just switch off. I just wish...'

She stopped herself. No matter how many times she told herself Jack was not going to come after her, she couldn't help but hope that might change tonight. He might not have known where she was before, but there was a chance, just a tiny chance, that Emmie might have told him that her exhibition was on tonight. He would know where to find her then. If he was going to emulate Richard Gere in *Pretty Woman* and *An Officer and a Gentleman*, tonight would be his perfect opportunity.

She gazed at the glass doors. All she could see was her reflection standing forlornly in the distance.

A willowy figure passed in front of her and she gasped.

'Tash, look!' she hissed.

'What? Oh, crikey!'

'That's Cara Connolly.' Pippa darted a quick look around. She didn't see Finn anywhere. However, she did become aware of a couple standing nearby looking at her. They looked vaguely familiar.

'See, Julien. I told you it's her,' the young woman said in a hushed voice. Seeing Pippa look their way, she smiled and walked towards her and Tash.

'Mm-hmm,' Tash murmured in appreciation, giving the man a once over.

Pippa elbowed her discreetly.

'It's Pippa, isn't it?'

'Yes.' Pippa rummaged through her memory to place the couple.

'Good evening, *ma'amoiselle*,' the man said. 'You perhaps do not remember us. My good friend, Jack Carmichael let us winter our horse at Aspen Valley. I am Julien Larocque –'

'Of course!' Pippa exclaimed, half in relief that she genuinely did recognise them. How could she have forgotten that French accent and those beautifully moulded features? 'And Ginny Kennedy, right? Caspian's the horse, I remember. Still favourite for the Derby?'

Ginny glanced at Julien anxiously.

'Joint favourites now,' she said. 'He got beat in the 2,000 Guineas last weekend. Some new competition has suddenly popped up this season.'

'Well, good luck with that.'

'Thanks,' Ginny smiled. 'How is Jack? We haven't seen him since Caspian came back into training a couple of months ago.'

'Okay, as far as I know.' Pippa tried to keep her tone light. 'I left Aspen Valley about a month ago. Painting full time now.'

'Something which we are very grateful for,' a voice interrupted. A woman appeared by Pippa's side and squeezed her shoulder. Pippa gave her a grateful smile. Deidre Forrester beamed at the party, her gaze lingering on Julien Larocque for a moment too long. Pippa noticed Ginny's jaw tense. 'Pippa does equestrian art, has she told you?' Oblivious to the frosty look from Ginny, she turned to Pippa. 'Julien trains a few horses for my husband, Basil. He's especially fond of the colt. Shanghai Dancer, isn't it, Julien? Yes. I'm sure he'd love a portrait of him done for his birthday.'

'He'll have a bit of a wait,' Ginny said. 'All thoroughbreds celebrate their birthday on the first of January.'

Deidre gave her a patient smile.

'Basil's birthday, darling. Not the horse's.'

Pippa grinned.

'I'd be happy to,' she said.

'Maybe Pippa can do us a painting of Caspian if she's not too busy?' Ginny said, holding Julien's arm and looking at him imploringly.

Julien closed his hand over hers and smiled. Pippa had to stop herself from heaving a sigh. The Frenchman was so obviously in love.

'Of course, *ma cherie*. Perhaps your father would also like a picture for his mantelpiece, *non?*'

By nine o'clock, Pippa couldn't decide whether she was enjoying her evening or not. Four of her six paintings had SOLD stickers on them and she had three definite commissions lined up. She wished she'd had the foresight to print out some business cards for herself as she'd instead had to resort to writing her contact details on paper napkins for the few other people who were interested in using her services. At the same time, she was very much aware that the evening would soon be coming to a close.

Pippa was beginning to think it more likely that Richard Gere would turn up than Jack. She handed over a napkin business card and smiled as a potential customer departed. Before the door could swing closed though, it was thrust open again. Pippa choked on her mineral water.

'Finn!'

'A *thaisce*!' Finn hurried over to her and bundled Pippa into his arms.

'It's so good to see you. I've missed you,' she said, surprised by how much she meant it.

'Aye. Your company has been missed as well,' he replied. 'I wondered if I was going to bump into you here. I'da come earlier, but for riding at Ascot. I've come to pick up Cara though.'

Pippa fidgeted in her shoes and swirled her drink around the glass. She remembered why exactly they hadn't seen each other for so long.

'I heard you quit Aspen Valley,' he said.

'Yeah, I had to, really. You know how it is.'

'Yes. It's tough workin' with a broken heart, is it not?'

'Finn, I'm sorry –'

'Agh, don't be feeling bad for me, Pippa.' Finn shooed her away with his hand. 'I brought it upon myself, so. You've nothin' to feel ashamed of.' He grinned at her. 'What did Jack tell you?'

Pippa frowned, embarrassed.

'Um, well, he said that you thought you were in love with me.'

Finn chuckled.

'No wonder you're lookin' like you've drowned a litter of puppies by mistake then.' He wrapped an arm around her shoulders and spoke confidently. 'Now, I don't want you to take this the wrong way, *a thaisce*, but your man Jack might have been leanin' on exaggeration a bit.'

'Oh!' Pippa looked at him, her eyes wide with relief and confusion. 'But why?'

'Why aren't I in love with you or why would he be leanin' on exaggeration?'

Pippa giggled.

'Why would Jack exaggerate?'

'I said I was fond of you. I am, but I'm also smart enough to see when the road I'm travellin' leads to a dead end. Rhys Bradford is back now, riding number one. It would have felt like getting kicked in the teeth twice, if you see what I mean.'

'I thought he'd fired you when I found out,' Pippa confessed.

'No. He did try make me stay, you know.' He shrugged. 'He was already upset and now, seein' you here and not in the sticks, I think I understand why.'

Pippa looked down at her hands.

'I couldn't stay, Finn. I couldn't be his secretary and – well, you know.'

Finn nodded, his expression sombre.

'Aye, I know. I knew it the day before the National that it was comin' soon. You and Jack, like.'

Pippa snorted mirthlessly and watched one of the gallery's staff members turn the Open sign on the door to Closed.

'There's no "me and Jack" now. I haven't heard from him since I left.'

'Well, now that's probably because Jack can be a stubborn fecker. The word on the ground is he's been a horror to work for lately. A couple of lads threatened to leave so yer head lad told Jack to take a break. Last I heard a couple of weeks ago, he was in France, hagglin' over some horses for old man Mardling.'

Pippa looked at him sharply.

'He's in France?'

'Aye. Been there for a fortnight, I believe.'

Pippa laughed, half in disbelief, half in relief that at last Jack had a plausible reason for not getting in contact.

'But he doesn't know how to speak French. How will he cope?'

Finn grinned and tweaked her chin in a tender gesture.

'It's really quite endearing just how much you want to look after Jack, you know. Just how much you –' He cleared his throat. 'Jack doesn't know what he's missing.'

'My, my, my,' drawled Tash, sauntering over to them. 'If it isn't my favourite scoundrel, Finn O'Donaghue.'

He grinned.

'A'right there, Tash?'

'Hello, Finn. Long time no see.'

'To be sure. Too long if I may say so.'

'You may say so all you want.'

Pippa smiled at Tash, hearing just how flattered she was by the Irishman.

'What have I done to deserve such friendliness?' he carried on, looping an arm around each girl. 'A useless waste of space that I am.'

Tash shook a finger at him like a schoolmarm.

'Now we're not going down that road again. You're not useless. Remember, you were once the fastest and most victorious sperm out of millions.'

345

Finn laughed, more in surprise than anything else. He nodded to the drinks table.

'I know I'm late for the show, but do you think they're still serving?' he asked.

'Let's go see if we can get you something,' Tash said, taking his arm and leading him away.

Pippa hesitated as she went to follow. A hazy memory stirred.

*Vous voulez autre chose à boise* – the voice in the background when she and Tash had gone to get sloshed.

'Jack's in France,' she whispered.

# Chapter Forty-Six

Pippa tunelessly accompanied Avril Lavigne to the desperate sound of *Wish You Were Here*. She stared forlornly at the opposite wall where *Morning Stables* was precariously balanced on a tatty armchair. '*Damn, da-*'

'PIPPA!'

She stopped at Tash's exacerbated cry from outside the room.

'Yes?'

Tash opened the door, her face a mixture of exasperation and pity.

'Pippa, sweets, I am sick to death of that song. Can we listen to something other than Avril Lavigne wailing over her lost love? *Please?*'

Pippa's look of gloom corroded even further at the thought of upsetting Tash.

'Sorry,' she mumbled. She leaned over and turned down the volume on her CD player.

Tash gave her a sympathetic smile and sat down on the bed next to her.

'You must have played that song about a hundred times these past few days.'

'Sums up how I feel though - desperate.' She looked down at her lap and listlessly pulled at a loose thread on her pyjama hem.

'Listen, Pip. There's something I need to ask you.'

Pippa saw anxiety cloud Tash's usually twinkling eyes and she nodded understandingly.

'You want me to move out? I know, I'm sorry. I was just going to wait for Hazyvale's sale to go through before -'

'Move out? No! Christ Almighty! I'm not going to kick you out!' Tash laughed and squeezed Pippa's hand.

Pippa gave a relieved smile.

'Okay then. What's the matter, Tash? You look really worried.'

Tash chewed her lip.

'I got a call. From Finn.'

'Finn?'

Tash shifted uneasily on the mattress.

'Yeah. Well, you know how he arrived at your art exhibition the other day and the time before when he got shit-faced after the Gold Cup?'

Pippa nodded.

'The thing is, see, I got to liking Finn. A bit.' Tash looked fearfully at Pippa. 'All right, quite a bit, but I knew he only had eyes for you.'

'Tash!' Pippa giggled. 'I knew you thought he was a dish. I didn't think you *like*-liked him though.'

Tash shrugged, looking abashed.

'But then at the art exhibition, while you were there thinking about Jack, I got chatting to Finn and well, you know, we got on. He makes me laugh.' Tash smiled sheepishly. 'And he just called and asked me out.'

Pippa gasped.

'Finn asked you out?' She laughed, part in disbelief, part excitement. 'That's wonderful, Tash!'

'Really? You're not mad, or upset, or – or anything?'

'No, of course not,' Pippa grinned. 'Why would I be?'

'Well, with everything gone pear-shaped with Jack, Finn was yours for the taking and...'

Pippa shook her head.

'Absolutely not. I don't like Finn like that, I don't think I ever have. And besides, Finn would never have been mine *for the taking* when he knows how I feel about Jack.' She sighed. 'How I feel about Jack, well, that shouldn't have any influence on you and Finn.'

Tash grinned.

'Thanks, Pip.' Her smile faded though when Pippa's expression deflated at the thought of Jack. 'You still think it was him that rang that night?'

'Who else could it have been? I mean, I just presumed it was someone in a French restaurant here in UK, but are there really any restaurants here that authentic where the waiters actually speak French to the customers? It had to be in France. But no one else I know of would call me from France. It has to be more than a coincidence that Jack was there at the same time.'

'You know what you've got to do then, don't you?'

'What?'

Tash settled herself more comfortably on the bed so she was facing Pippa.

'Think about it – it's gone past midnight, he's in a country where he can't speak the language, he's got someone plying him with alcohol – *he's missing you.*'

'And I answer the phone sounding like I'm having a whale of a time and blurt out Ollie's name,' Pippa said with regret.

'Exactly. Now, put yourself in his shoes. Would you come after you if you had just heard all that?'

Pippa shook her head.

'No, I guess not.'

'Which means you've got to go after him!'

Pippa's eyes widened as Tash's words hit home.

'I do, don't I?'

'Yes! Go set the record straight.'

Pippa scrambled off the bed.

'Otherwise he'll never know the truth.'

'Precisely! Go get your man, Pippa!'

Standing alert in her creased pyjamas, trying to decide whether she should put some clothes on first, Pippa's shoulders drooped as doubt once again sparked inside her.

'But what do I do? What would I say? Do I just knock on his front door and declare my love for him?'

Tash blinked, not seeing her dilemma.

'Yes.'

Pippa flopped back onto the bed again.

'I can't do that. It's just not *me*. I wouldn't know what to say.'

Tash glanced at the CD player from where Avril Lavigne was still baring her soul.

'Why not quote Avril? You said it's how you feel.'

Pippa raised a small smile and shook her head.

'I couldn't. It would make him feel awkward too. And it would put him on the spot.'

'Well, call him then! Give him some sort of forewarning so he can prepare himself.'

'I don't have his number,' she said, shaking her head sadly. 'I deleted it.'

'Oh, you muppet.' Tash looked at her impatiently and stood up. 'Pippa, you're going to have to make the first move here. He's not coming after you – he shouldn't *have* to come after you. You left him, remember?'

'I know.'

A black cloud of gloom enveloped her, seeping damp into her bones. 'I'm just not as brave as that. Not just yet, anyhow.'

Tash tutted and walked away. She stopped by the doorway.

'Don't leave it too long, Pippa.'

Pippa sighed and fell backwards to stare at the ceiling. She let the tears trickle out of the corners of her eyes. Why was she being such a coward? Why couldn't she take a leaf out of *Bridget Jones' Diary* and run into the snow in her underwear and nab her Mr Darcy?

She rolled over and buried her face in her pillow. Because it's all a fantasy, she told herself severely, and fantasies are so easy to be brave in when you're assured a happy-ending. Reality really does bite.

The following day, Pippa tried another form of counsel. From Tash's thirty-two-inch plasma screen in the lounge, Billy Crystal look imploringly at Meg Ryan and listed all the reasons why he loved her. Pippa wanted to cry. This wasn't the desired effect she was after. Why couldn't Jack love her for the way she ordered a sandwich? Why couldn't –

The front door slammed, interrupting *When Harry Met Sally*.

Pulling herself up on the couch and shaking herself from her failed therapy session, Pippa peeked over the backrest towards the front hall. Tash appeared in the doorway.

'Don't you answer your phone?' she exclaimed, her arms flailing.

'It's charging in my room,' Pippa replied, taken aback. 'Why? What's wrong?'

'I've been trying to get hold of you. *Finn* has been trying to get hold of you.'

'Finn?' Pippa sat up, alert as a meerkat. 'Why's he trying to call me?'

Tash ignored her and marched through to the spare room. Pippa clambered to her feet and hurried after her. They bumped into each other in the bedroom doorway. Tash held out Pippa's phone.

'There. About five missed calls. He ended up having to call me.'

'Tash! What's happened? What's wrong?' Pippa cried, starting to panic.

'Peace Offering's ill! Finn said it was serious. Something about colic and they didn't know whether you could afford the cost of surgery.'

'WHAT?'

Tash thrust a pair of shoes and a coat towards Pippa.

'Nobody can get hold of you. Peace Offering might not make it! You have to go!'

Pippa gulped and stood rooted to the spot with fear.

'He's going to die?' she whispered.

'I don't know!' Tash said, pushing her towards the front door. 'Get down there and find out!'

'He can't die! Oh, God!' She hopped on one foot to pull on her shoes.

'Hurry, Pip!' Tash tossed her her handbag and car keys. 'Let me know as soon as you hear anything.'

'Okay!'

Pippa practically slid down the two flights of stairs and out into the late Sunday afternoon sunshine. Everything looked so serene and so relaxed, basking in the warm spring weather. It seemed impossible to imagine Peace Offering fighting for his life at Aspen Valley at that precise moment.

Fear leant her strength and she raced down the uneven pavement towards her car.

As the M25 fed into the M4, Pippa put her foot down. The Beetle rattled in protest and the speedometer quivered in indignation as it rose above seventy. Pippa clenched the wheel in whitened fists to control the shuddering. The lane ahead was thankfully free-flowing and soon exits for Slough then Reading were flashing past in her rear-view mirror.

The descending sun blinded her and she flicked the visor down. Images of Peace Offering filled her mind. Peace Offering lying on his side, heaving and sweating, gasping his final breaths.

Pippa wasn't sure what colic involved exactly, but she knew it was dangerous to horses. She imagined Jack and the vet, Alan Warnock, standing over her horse, shaking their heads. Of Jack saying,

'We can't get hold of her. Best let's put him out of his misery.'

The speedometer crept higher.

Pippa reached into her bag on the passenger seat and retrieved her phone. She tried Finn's number. The moisture in her throat evaporated as each unanswered ring peeled in her ear.

'Oh, come on, Finn!' she pleaded. Finally, his voicemail cut in. 'Finn, it's Pippa! Please call me back! Don't let them kill Peace Offering! Please! If he needs surgery, I'll pay – I promise!'

Saying the words out loud brought home the situation for her and a renewed flood of panic swept through her body as she hung up.

Such a darling horse as Peace Offering couldn't die.

Gritting her teeth, she picked up her mobile again and scrolled through to Aspen Valley's number. Her heart hammered in her chest as she pressed *Connect* and held it up to her ear. The pumping adrenalin gradually calmed as the office phone remained unanswered. She pictured the deserted office, the desperate ringing unheard by the sombre crowd gathered outside Peace Offering's stable.

She cut the call and scrolled again through her numbers. *Kent Garage, Kurt Morrison, Jade Chinese Takeaway, Jayne Gurney.*

'Dammit!' she cried, throwing her phone down on the passenger seat. 'Why did I bloody delete his number? Don't you dare let him die, Jack! Please save him!'

The birds singing their last chorus in the oak tree at Aspen Valley's entrance rose squawking into the air as Pippa's Beetle tore into the long driveway. The dust cloud in its wake infused with the gold rays of the setting sun. She skidded to a halt in the car park and hurtled out, nearly falling flat on her face as her heel caught in the gravel. The office was closed, no light shining from its windows. The whole yard was deserted of human life.

'Hello? Anyone?' she called.

Inquisitive equine heads appeared over their stable doors, but no humans emerged. She ran over to Peace Offering's box. The sharp ringing of her heels on the concrete brought more horses to their doors, but as she approached and Peace Offering's door remained void, her heart quickened. She was too late. She clung to the top of the half door, her eyes misting over when it creaked open. Inside, the floor was swept clear of habitation.

Was this the end? No more Peace Offering? Had she lost him as well as Jack?

She shook her head. She wouldn't believe it. Not until somebody was able to convince her.

'Anybody?' her desperate plea resounded about the block.

Only a snort from the next door stable replied. Pippa shielded her eyes and looked at the neighbouring hillside where Jack's house lay just out of sight. Taking a deep breath, she turned and ran back to her car.

Her heart seemed to adopt a salsa rhythm on speed when she drove over the rise and Jack's barn conversion came into view. The sun reflected off the silver paintwork of his Land Rover parked by his front door. She took a moment as she got out to steady herself, feeling her legs quake. Then, pulling herself together, she scuttled up to his front door and leant on the doorbell.

She heard Berkeley bark from within, but no approaching footsteps. Maybe he was at the vets signing Peace Offering's death certificate? Did horses get death certificates? Panic fluttered through her and she banged on the door, bruising her knuckles in her urgency.

'All right! I'm coming! Just –' The door was wrenched open and Jack choked on his the angry greeting when he saw Pippa.

'Oh, thank God you're here,' she gasped, closing her eyes. 'I thought you were at the vets signing his death certificate!'

Jack looked at her as if she'd dyed her hair green and suggested they both go chase butterflies.

'Pippa? Wh-what?'

She looked up at him with wide desperate eyes.

'Am I too late? Is he dead? Did you save him?'

'Who? What are you talking about? What are you doing here?'

'Peace Offering, of course! Finn said Peace Offering was dying. Is he okay? Please tell me he's okay!'

Jack stared at her and steadied himself against the doorframe.

'Yes, he's okay. Well, he was the last time I checked about an hour ago. He's in the paddock on the other side of the drive there.'

Pippa gaped.

'He's not dying?'

'No, he's not dying. What on earth are you talking about?'

Pippa chewed her lip and squirmed in her shoes. She gave Jack a suspicious look. He looked puzzled and ever so slightly irritated. He didn't look like he was lying.

'But Finn said...'

'What the hell does Finn know? He doesn't even work here anymore!' Jack said, looking exasperated. 'What is going on, Pippa?'

Relief that Peace Offering was alive and kicking was very quickly replaced by the realisation of her friends' deception.

Jack glared at her, his arms folded across his chest.

'A misunderstanding, I think,' she said quietly. 'I think Tash and Finn tricked me into coming here.'

Jack swallowed. He stood silently defensive.

'You needed tricking?'

'No,' Pippa was quick to contradict him. 'Well, maybe, but not how you think...' Her voice trailed away when she saw Jack's eyes darken. 'Jack, I –' Why was it so hard, so terrifying to tell him how she felt? Her mind turned back to the conversation she'd had with Tash the day before. She took a deep breath and hoped it had worked for Avril. 'I thought I could be tough. And strong,' she said falteringly. 'But with you I've found that I'm not. I – I can't stop thinking about things you've said and times we've shared. You've always been you and well, I miss that.' She tried to read the set expression on his face.

'Sounds like you've been rehearsing that,' he said bluntly.

Pippa's courage wavered. You have no idea, she replied silently.

They faced each other in silence, the birds' singing in nearby trees and Berkeley's whining from behind Jack muted to their ears. She searched his face for some sort of softening, anything that would remove the invisible barricade that stood between them.

'I miss you,' she whispered.

'What am I supposed to say to that?' he asked, his brow creasing in frustration.

'That you miss me too?'

He raked a hand through his hair.

'Pippa, you drive me crazy when you're around. And you drive me crazy when you're not. I don't know how to deal with that. I *can't*.'

Pippa felt like he'd wrenched her heart out with his bare hands. She wasn't going to beg and she'd be damned if she let him see her cry. She swallowed a sigh and gave him an apologetic smile.

'Then I'm sorry for disturbing your evening,' she said.

Jack didn't reply. Only the muscle in his jaw throbbed in response.

Her shoes scratched the gravelled ground as she trudged back to her car. Her senses were keenly attuned to Jack watching her leave, but not stopping her.

As she pulled out of the driveway, she looked back in the rear-view mirror to see him turning back inside.

Pippa sighed with exaggerated effort as her car trundled over the crest of the Gallops. Who's the fool now, she thought wryly? A mirthless breath escaped her when she recognised a small herd of horses grazing in the adjoining paddock. She hadn't even noticed them when she'd hurtled past a couple of minutes earlier.

Peace Offering raised his head as she rumbled towards them.

Pippa thought of the endless drive she'd have back to Tash's now. Exhaustion flopped over her. Maybe she could spend the night at Hazyvale? Emmie and Billy hadn't moved in yet, and no money had exchanged hands yet so technically the cottage was still hers.

She pulled up next to the four horses. Her mobile gave a plaintive beep from the footwell where it had fallen and she bent to retrieve it. There was a text message from Tash.

*Sorry to make you panic, sweets. We had to do it. Hope you understand and all is well. T xxx*

'No, Tash. All is not well.' Pippa tossed the phone down again and got out.

Peace Offering sauntered over to the fence, the blaze down his face tinted pink by the setting sun. She stepped carefully across the verge and went to greet him. In the distance she could hear a tractor's growl.

'What now, Peace Offering? I have no idea what to do now,' she murmured, stroking his long bony nose. She smiled when she noticed a small wild flower among the grass shoots hanging from the side of his mouth. He looked like a typical country lad.

'May I have that?' she asked.

She threaded it out of his mouth, smiling as he tried to lip it back.

'He loves me, he loves me not,' she began. One by one, the white petals floated down to her feet.

'...he loves me not,' she concluded. She looked at the bald flower still in her fingers and ruefully threw it away.

Brushing the pollen dust from her hands onto her jeans, she looked up at Peace Offering who was regarding her with a quizzical air. She turned her gaze to the valley below, drinking in the peace and solitude and the exquisite masterpiece the sky was being painted. Wispy apricot clouds trailed across the deep amber horizon and the white-washed walls of the stables shone pink in the distance. Pippa sighed, knowing she'd never seen skies like this anywhere else in her life. And now she was going to leave it?

'Okay, best out of three. What do you reckon?' she consulted her horse.

She bent down and picked another flower from the tuft growing by the fence post. If this came out right, then it was meant to be. It would be fate, beyond her control.

'He loves me, he loves me not,' she whispered.

If he loved her by confirmation of this flower, she would march back to his door and tell him so. She could be brave.

'He loves me, he loves me not.'

If he didn't love her by confirmation of this flower, she would leave and that would be the end of it. She could live life without him.

'He loves me, he loves me not.' Her voice wavered a little louder. 'He loves me, he loves me not. He loves me –' Pippa's fingers trembled over the last remaining petal. She bit her lip, unwilling to cast this final sentence and seal her fate.

She started as a hand reached out and enfolded hers and the flower. She spun round to face Jack. The softness she had searched for earlier now lit his eyes. She opened her mouth to speak, but only her escaping gasp filled the space between them.

Jack's eyes twinkled. He slipped the flower from her hand. He held it between them for a moment, twirling it between his fingers by its stem. A smile twitched the sides of his mouth and he tossed the flower nonchalantly over his shoulder.

'He loves you,' he said gruffly.

Stepping forward, he gathered her into his arms. Warmth flooded through Pippa as she met his long slow kiss, feeling the solidity of his body against hers, tasted the sweetness of his mouth, the tenderness of his touch. Her heart thudded in her chest, restored and jubilant. Was this fantasy or reality? Could it be both? She had to be sure. She drew back from Jack to look at him, to make sure he was real.

'He does?' she said.

Jack nodded, his smile deepening.

'I've been a fool. We've both been fools. You only drive me crazy when I can't have you.'

'But you can have me,' Pippa replied.

He threaded a lock of auburn hair behind her ear, away from her face.

'I know that now. But love distorts things until you don't know what to believe or which way is the right way up. I'd shut you out before because what I felt scared the hell out of me. Then I convinced myself you had gone back to that Ollie guy –'

'No!' Pippa interrupted him, desperate to set the record straight. 'Not at all. Was it you that called that night?'

'I was in France,' Jack said, nodding sagely. 'Sitting in a bistro with just about everyone around me looking like they were happily in love. It made me miss you even more. So I tried to call... I've learnt never to go to Paris if you're suffering a broken heart.'

Pippa wrapped her arms around his neck, pulling him closer.

'I'm sorry. Tash had taken me out to cheer me up. Then Ollie walked through the door. I promise I didn't even speak to him. I didn't want to.'

'Really?' Jack looked relieved.

'In fact it made me realise just how little I cared for him compared to you. I don't want you to have a broken heart.'

He unwound her hand from his neck and placed it on his chest.

'All better now.'

Pippa grinned, feeling the rapid thud against her palm.

'I love you, Jack Carmichael,' she whispered.

'And I love you, Miss Pippa Taylor,' he replied, humour glinting in his blue eyes. 'Will you come home with me? Promise never to go away again?'

'Hand on heart.'

Jack laughed.

'My heart.'

Drawing her close again, he sealed the promise with a slow kiss.

Pippa closed her eyes, seeing the swirling colours of everything around her in her mind's eye. The greens of the paddocks, the pinks of the stables in the sun's reflection, the oranges, the golds, the silvers, the blues... the Brandeis blue.

## THE END

Lightning Source UK Ltd.
Milton Keynes UK
UKOW04f1142170515

251693UK00001B/150/P